Muse of Fire

Howard Linskey is a former journalist, whose works include crime series and standalones set in the north-east, including the DC Ian Bradshaw series published by Penguin, and two espionage novels. He also writes historical fiction and non-fiction. His books have been published in nine countries. Originally from County Durham, he lives in Herts with his wife and daughter.

Also by Howard Linskey

The Drop
The Damage
The Dead
No Name Lane
Behind Dead Eyes
The Search
The Chosen Ones
Don't Let Him In
Alice Teale Is Missing
The Inheritance
Ungentlemanly Warfare
Hunting The Hangman

William Shakespeare Mysteries

Players of Death
Muse of Fire

Muse of Fire

HOWARD LINSKEY

CANELO

First published in the United Kingdom in 2026 by

Canelo, an imprint of
Canelo Digital Publishing Limited,
20 Vauxhall Bridge Road,
London SW1V 2SA
United Kingdom

A Penguin Random House Company
The authorised representative in the EEA is Dorling Kindersley Verlag GmbH. Arnulfstr. 124, 80636 Munich, Germany

Copyright © Howard Linskey 2026

The moral right of Howard Linskey to be identified as the creator of this work has been asserted in accordance with the Copyright, Designs and Patents Act, 1988.

All rights reserved. No part of this publication may be reproduced or transmitted in any form or by any means, electronic or mechanical, including photocopy, recording, or any information storage and retrieval system, without permission in writing from the publisher.

No part of this book may be used or reproduced in any manner for the purpose of training artificial intelligence technologies or systems. In accordance with Article 4(3) of the DSM Directive 2019/790, Canelo expressly reserves this work from the text and data mining exception.

A CIP catalogue record for this book is available from the British Library.

Print ISBN 978 1 80436 878 7
Ebook ISBN 978 1 80436 886 2

This book is a work of fiction. Names, characters, businesses, organizations, places and events are either the product of the author's imagination or are used fictitiously. Any resemblance to actual persons, living or dead, events or locales is entirely coincidental.

Cover design by Head Design

Cover images © Alamy; Shutterstock

Printed and bound in Great Britain by Clays Ltd, Elcograf S.p.A.

Look for more great books at
www.canelo.co | www.dk.com

For Emily and Abby Chennells

1598

Chapter One

*'Tis a vile thing to die, my gracious lord,
When men are unprepared and look not for it.'*

—*Richard III*

The Lady Anne was frightened. The light she carried was barely adequate to find her way in this dark and quiet corner of the palace, and she was glad of the reassuring presence of her prayer book in her other hand. She needed its comfort now, for it was long after midnight, and her progress had been slower than she would have liked, because of the necessity of avoiding the guards tasked with ensuring no intruder could enter Her Majesty's palace.

But Anne was not an intruder. She lived in Whitehall and, though barely seventeen, was already a trusted lady-in-waiting to old Queen Elizabeth, stemming from a good, noble family. She would hardly be suspected of capital crimes against the monarch. No, it was the destruction of her reputation Anne feared most. If she was found to be lurking in these corridors after dark, it would be assumed she was on her way to a liaison. There was some truth in this, of course, but she could hardly confess the real reason for her being there, which would be even more damning.

The idea of making her way to the top of the stone staircase by the small hall had seemed a simple one when it was communicated to her in daylight, but now she worried what would happen if her candle went out, or if someone smelt the tallow and learned of her presence here. And what if he did not come? How long should she wait before returning to her bedchamber? What if the stories the ladies-in-waiting told, about this wing of the palace, were true? There were wraiths here, they said; the tormented spirits of those who had died unnaturally or before their time, victims of murder, who had been stabbed in their bed, or strangled by rivals. They were ghosts now, who waited till the dark hours, when they haunted the corridors of the castle, hopelessly seeking vengeance on those who had so violently robbed them of life, not realising that they themselves were trapped, in spirit form, and those that had wronged them were long dead.

Anne had dismissed these tales as stories the older women dreamed up to frighten the younger ones, who had to walk further at night to get to their own beds. Now though, as she walked down the pitch-black corridors, her way illuminated only partially by that single candle she held, Anne was less sure. What would she do if she met a spirit? What if it mistook her for someone that had wronged that wraith in life? What then?

It was cold here too. They were in the depths of winter, but, in Anne's haste to quit the chamber that night, she had failed to wear more than she had done during the day. At least then the palace rooms had well-tended fires to keep out the chill. Not so these dark corridors, which seemed to welcome the cold, and she cursed herself for not wearing a cloak.

A harsh sound interrupted her thoughts and Anne froze. It was loud but came from some distance, as if someone had dropped something heavy, possibly made of metal, onto the stone floor and the sound had echoed down the corridors. Anne didn't dare move for a full minute while she waited to hear what would happen next. Would the guard be called out in response? Would others leave their beds and demand to know who was there?

There was no immediate reaction to the sound though, and none further came in reply. Had a guard fallen asleep and dropped a pike or knocked something over? Whatever it was, the palace slept on, and so, tentatively, Anne continued on her way.

If it *had* been a guard who made that sound, she had eluded him so far and must continue to do so, lest she be suspected of a carnal encounter. It frightened Anne to think of the queen's wrath. Her Majesty took a very dim view of her ladies-in-waiting enjoying passionate liaisons, when she herself was denied them. The 'Virgin Queen' may have been in her sixties, having ruled over them all for forty years, but she was still apparently *virgo intacta*, or maintained she was. The ladies of the court wondered if that could possibly be true but rarely voiced their doubts aloud, and never in the queen's company. To question her at all was to risk releasing that famous temper. To contradict her on such a personal matter would be foolish in the extreme.

Still, she did spend an awful lot of time with her favourite, the Earl of Essex, who, on occasion, passed the whole night in her chambers. Supposedly they were playing cards, but what else did they get up to? If not everything, then perhaps something? The Lady Anne, who was genuinely innocent of such matters, and had not yet been touched in that way by a man, could only wonder at such things when they were whispered about by more experienced ladies of the court. They sometimes speculated whether the queen had, in the past, pleased her favourites in 'the French style', or whether she had ever allowed male hands to caress her intimately, while preventing a full-frontal assault upon her famous virginity.

Those same women often took lovers themselves. That had shocked Anne when she had first arrived at court. She had sworn to remain pure until her wedding night, saving her virtue for her future husband, whoever that might be. That was for her father to arrange, of course, but she understood enough of these matters to know that if she was considered to be used goods, her new husband might send her home in disgrace. This was why the behaviour of the other ladies had surprised her. There were unmarried women at court who seemed to imagine they could fool a man into thinking they were still virgins on their wedding night. Others held the view that some men didn't give a damn about their honour anyway, as long as they came to the marriage with a generous dowery and enough land. Some were married already, before God, and yet seemed to think little of breaking the seventh commandment, even though they would surely have to account for this at the end of their lives, when they went before Him.

The high prize of virtue and virginity at court never stopped the men there from trying to bed the queen's ladies-in-waiting at every opportunity. They were all undoubtedly fair, chosen as much for their pleasing countenance as their accomplishments. The queen valued skill on horseback, the ability to play a musical instrument, to fashion something delicate with a needle, to converse with her in Latin, French or Spanish and to dance a volta or a galliard with grace. Some of this Anne could do, to the satisfaction of Her Majesty. It helped that she was small and light, and she had to admit it was exciting to be lifted high in the air like that during a volta, especially when one man in particular had done it during the recent masked ball to mark the queen's Ascension Day. He had been both strong and fair and Anne's heart had raced from the proximity of his body to hers, a feeling she was unused to. She had at least denied his request to see him again later in private, though he had insisted on bestowing a favour upon her and she had kept it. Sometimes she thought idly about what might have happened if she had said yes to meeting him, to her lasting shame.

She may have secretly longed for an intimate encounter, and more than a few of the loftier men at court had hinted they desired one with her, but Anne's father would not have been appeased if she was disgraced. Baron Percy, younger brother to the Earl of Northumberland, had given the queen four hundred pounds for the honour of making his daughter one of her ladies at court. The queen had readily taken that immense sum from one of her northern nobles, not realising the true reason for his generosity, and exactly what he expected to receive for it in return. A good marriage was *supposed* to be the outcome for any girl who managed a few years in the queen's inner or outer chambers without causing a scandal, but his ambitions involving Anne were far greater.

Subsequently, it was scandal, and its accompanying shame and disgrace, that Anne feared now, as she made her way carefully and hesitantly along the corridor, trying not to stumble in the semi-darkness. No one must see her coming this way at such a late hour for there could be no satisfactory explanation for her presence. Her Majesty would simply brand her a whore, and she would be exiled or worse. The queen had even imprisoned those who broke her strict rules against liaisons or dared to marry their lovers without the monarch's permission, but the man Anne would meet tonight was less interested in her body than in what she carried about her person.

On his instructions, Anne had forced herself to be patient, delaying her departure until she was certain the queen's other ladies-in-waiting were all abed and sleeping – something she had made sure of, in fact. Not an easy task, when she had to share her accommodation with the other younger ladies who served Her Majesty in the privy chamber. At seventeen, Anne was not yet old enough to wait on Queen Elizabeth in her bedchamber. That would come one day she hoped, but only if she could avoid being seen by anyone tonight.

Moments later, and without encountering an evil spirit or palace guard along the way, Anne finally reached the top of the staircase and glanced about her to ensure she was at the right place. An enormous tapestry, depicting a hunting party pursuing a stag, hung on a wall to one side. That scene was surrounded by allegorical religious images in separate panels at its borders. Here was a unicorn depicting Christ's presence at the hunt and next to it, a pelican, showing motherly love, presumably associated with the queen. She was further represented by the presence of a lion, signifying courage and nobility. Finally, the devil was represented as a monstrous figure with red skin, a horned head, spiked tail and huge wings. He lurked on the edge of the scene, hoping to tempt people into evil. Perhaps this was not the best place to meet after midnight, with the devil himself so clearly in view.

But where was the man who had urged this meeting upon her? She was perhaps a little late, but this errand was so important, surely he would have waited in the shadows for a while? With a heavy heart, she realised he was nowhere to be seen. Had he been and gone already? Surely not, when she was carrying such a prize. He would have waited, she was certain of it, so he had to have been delayed for some reason. Perhaps he too had been forced to take extra care to avoid the palace guards and that explained his delay. Unless...

She did not want to think about *unless*. That would mean he had been taken. What if he had already been arrested? What would it mean for her if he confessed under torture, as surely all men did, and she was implicated too? Was this a capital crime? If it was, would she be executed using the axe? Or even burned at the stake? Would a mercy of sorts be granted with a sentence of merely life imprisonment? She had heard of such things, but Anne knew she would be driven mad if she was locked up for the rest of her days. All of this could happen, even to a well-born maid like her, if she was discovered.

Anne felt a great wave of fear come over her then. She was too young for this and too unschooled in the ways of the secret world, but then she remembered why she was here. Was it not for the realm, and her father too? Anne told herself to put a stopper in her fear and harden her resolve. What she was about to do could well turn out to be the single most important act of her life, even if she lived to be as old as the queen.

She would stay here awhile then, though every bone in her body was screaming at her to flee and return to the relative safety of her bed. Anne would see this through till the end, despite the danger she was in. She hoped the guards would not be back here for a while. Once *he* arrived, and arrive he surely must, for he had sworn it to Anne, then all would be well. All she could do was wait, but where in God's name was he?

Anne did not hear anyone come up behind her. He moved so quietly, and when he grabbed her, there was no time even to scream. One strong, burly arm went around her torso, in the same instant a hand was clamped over her mouth and nostrils, making it impossible for her to cry out, and her candle fell to the floor. She struggled helplessly, as she tried to wriggle from the unseen man's grip, but he was far too strong for her and she was terrified now.

Had she been grabbed by a guard? Surely this could not be the man she had promised to meet, but who was it? An assassin, a wraith, a demon from hell? Anne wanted to scream, but the sounds she made were instantly muffled beneath his gloved hand and she found that she could not breathe. Was he going to kill her?

In her terror, Anne managed to kick out in the hope of unbalancing her attacker, but her feet swung impotently ahead of her, as he lifted her off the ground and moved forwards with a sudden, deadly haste towards the staircase. God, he was going to throw her down the stone steps. She had only moments to think on what was about to happen to her, while she also struggled to understand why it was happening at all? Had she not done all that was asked of her? Who even was this man who had so easily overpowered her? Was it the one she had agreed to meet or another who had taken his place and now seemed intent on killing her? It scarcely mattered now. Not when he was already bearing down on the stone staircase? Of far more importance was her inability to cry out for help or plead with her assailant for mercy. She had to fight for her very life and she struggled even harder, but Anne was already weakening from lack of breath and knew she might never break free from such an unrelenting grip. Anne kicked and struggled, fighting the man with all of her strength, clenching her fists and jabbing back at him hard with her elbow, but he didn't even flinch. It was as if he was made of stone.

Just as they had almost reached the steps, he veered off to one side and, to her intense relief, Anne realised he was not about to throw her down the staircase. Instead, her attacker pulled her to the right. She assumed he was about to drag her along the landing, but what would he do then? If he was not the man she had arranged to meet, what were his intentions? Would she be taken into a room and raped, despoiled forever in the eyes of future husbands and the queen? Her Majesty would surely blame Anne, for allowing herself to be violated in the middle of the night. Her father would never forgive her; not after paying those four hundred pounds.

Anne did not have to worry long about her father and his money. Her attacker didn't drag her far and there was no room nearby. Instead, he released his grip from around her waist and pushed Anne hard in the back, until she was thrown forwards and pressed against the parapet, which was the only thing preventing her from falling to the ground some twenty feet or more below. Was he trying to take her here in the open? She would bitterly resist the assault, but how? There was no time to think on that further because her attacker bent lower and grabbed her by the legs, crushing them together. Then he hoisted her up and, to her terror, pushed Anne forwards until she was hanging perilously over the edge, the lower part of her body catching against the stone parapet, the upper half free of it already. Oh Sweet Jesus, now she understood, and a great wave of fear passed through her. He was going to throw her over, down onto the hard, stone floor below.

The Lady Anne had just enough time to let out a little scream then, before he pitched her headfirst into the darkness.

Chapter Two

'What's done cannot be undone.'

—*Macbeth*

Sir Robert Cecil stood by the body for a full minute, staring down at the lifeless figure of Lady Anne Percy. She had been brought into the physician's room, though he had not yet been notified of her presence, for she was long past help. The queen's spymaster was alone with her, aside from one of his most trusted men, William Wade, who stood silently waiting for his master to pronounce upon the matter. Finally, Cecil spoke.

'Who found her?'

'A sergeant of the watch.'

'He came to you?'

'He did.' Wade confirmed.

Cecil's great power at court came partly from his ability to know who to enlist to do his bidding, and how to amply reward such men. Their loyalty was only partially to the crown but always to him, which was why the sergeant sought Wade out first, knowing him to be Cecil's man.

'And informed no other?' Cecil asked. 'The queen does not yet know of this?'

'It was not my place to inform the queen, my lord.'

'No, it was not.' Cecil seemed satisfied by that answer, but then he asked, 'Who ordered her body moved?'

It sounded like a rebuke, so Wade was forced to explain himself. 'I had her taken from the stairwell, for her dignity, Lord. All would see her once the ladies began to rise, and I feared they would be distressed.'

Cecil seemed to accept that explanation. 'Describe the position of her body most carefully.'

'She was lying on the ground at the very foot of the staircase. It appeared she fell.'

'Or was pushed?'

'It's possible, my lord, but who would wish such a young maid dead?'

'Who indeed?' He already had his suspicions.

Cecil leaned in closer then and examined the body most intently.

'Her neck is broken,' Wade informed him.

'If this was a fall, then she was most unfortunate. That staircase is not so very steep and there is a balustrade at the bottom, before the final steps curve round. It would likely break her fall before she could end up at the very foot of the stairs, don't you think?'

The question sounded rhetorical to Wade, so he didn't answer, but his master seemed doubtful, as if he was truly pondering whether this could actually have been an accidental act or not?

'Put it out that the Lady Anne's death was a dreadful misfortune, for now. She likely fell in the dark.'

'And if the queen should hear of this?' Wade meant before she was told.

'I shall inform Her Majesty anon.'

'Do you wish enquiries to be made?' Wade asked his master.

Cecil considered this for a moment. 'Not by you. Not this time. This requires delicacy.'

'As you wish, my lord.'

'I know the creature I need.' He seemed to be saying this softly to himself rather than Wade. 'Go now.' He dismissed his man with a wave of the hand.

Wade made for the door and as he turned back to close it behind him, he could not help but overhear Sir Robert, though his voice was quite low. At first, it seemed he was talking to himself, but then it became clear his words were meant for the ear of the dead girl he stood over, though he could not hope to receive a reply.

'Oh, dear sweet Lady Anne, whatever did you do?'

Chapter Three

'Trifles light as air are to the jealous confirmations strong as proofs of holy writ.'

—*Othello*

Will had been in a state of great excitement for much of the day. He had tried to write, several times in fact, but his mind kept wandering from his work to other thoughts, most of them carnal, and all of them about his dark lady. She should be here with him by now. He paced the upstairs room of the inn restlessly, pausing once again to glance out of the window, while hoping to witness her approach and having those hopes dashed once more. The best he could hope for now was that she would be quite late, if she was coming at all.

What had gone wrong? Was his raven-haired beauty delayed at court? Worse, had she been detained by her husband? What if he had discovered their trysts and was even now threatening her life or reputation, perhaps both? Will tried to banish that thought. He didn't like to consider her husband at any time, lest guilt reignited the last residue of shame he felt over their union. Will knew his Matthew; *What God has put together, let no man put asunder.* This dance with Avisa was wrong. Very wrong indeed. And that was to consider only *her* marriage vows, let alone his own to Anne, taken sixteen years ago before God. Will sometimes wondered what form of hell might await him in the next life for being unable to contain his earthly desires in this one? But he could not help himself and neither could she. How could he worry about a future debt now, to be settled before God in the afterlife, when he was about to see the woman who had made these past months bearable in this one? She was the only one who had been able to ease the pain in his wounded heart, and allow him to, if not forget his grief, put it aside, for a time at least?

Yet still Avisa was not here. She had never been more than a few minutes late before. Her husband has found out, Will felt sure of it now. The last time he had seen her was at court and Avisa had said she would most surely come to him here at the allotted time or, if not, allow herself to be proclaimed a liar in the street. With that, he had kissed her, sheltered by the arras he had quickly pulled her behind, before she broke free and told him, 'Patience, my love.' The first word had been a disappointment, but the last two had kept him thinking on her for days since. *My love?* Was he really her love, or had she used the word more lightly than he would? *She* was most definitely *his* love. That much was true. He waited for her now ardently, and without any real or lasting shame, for how could God deny them both? Though admittedly wanton, this love of theirs also had a purity which brought them both so much truth and meaning.

And here she was!

Will bent closer to the window and saw Avisa coming towards him now, walking swiftly, as if she knew she had kept him waiting and wanted to be in his arms the sooner. God, but she was beautiful. He tried to compose himself. He didn't want to look like a fool. He wasn't one of those lovelorn young boys who would swoon over a maid, then write terrible verse for the object of their affections, which would be received with amusement but little love and still less respect. No, he would act the part of the preoccupied writer of plays, he hoped she would take him for. He quickly sat by his table, took up his pen, dipped it into the ink and was poised to write something, even as he knew she must be through the inn door now. Moments later, he heard light footsteps on the wooden stairs, then on the landing outside his room, delicate still but hasty, as if the longing in her was equal to his. Will could not help himself now and he rose, still clutching his quill pen.

The door opened and she stood there framed by the doorway.

'Forgive me, I could not easily quit the palace. The court is in uproar. A girl has been—'

But before she could continue, he was on her, stopping Avisa's words with a long kiss. Whatever she was about to say about a girl at court was forgotten now.

When they finally broke from the kiss, she smiled, noticed he was still holding the quill and said, 'You have been writing, my love.'

He abandoned all pretence then and told her, 'Not a word.'

Will let the quill fall to the floor and took her in his arms.

–

Their embraces were just reaching a most interesting point, when Will realised it might be prudent to lock the door. Before he could do this, however, there came an urgent and persistent rapping upon it.

'Master Shakespeare!' called a voice, which had not waited long for him to answer that knocking.

'Confound it,' Will whispered in Avisa's ear, and he let go of his dark lady then, in case the owner of that voice decided to burst in on them. They would then be caught in a scandalous position her husband would likely hear about.

'Who is there?' called Will, not really expecting that the door would immediately be pushed open. He was confronted by a serious-looking young man he had never seen before, dressed like a legal clerk or perhaps a steward of matters domestical, who was impatient to deliver his message. He ignored Will's companion, or at least chose to be discreet about her. Instead, he entreated Will.

'Good sir, I come to you upon this day and at this hour with a most urgent message from your friend, Cuthbert Burbage.'

'Whatever that message be, if it is from Cuthbert, it cannot be as urgent as the business I must soon conclude with this fair lady. Tell Master Burbage, if he wants me, I shall come anon.' A glance at his lady's alluring smile made him reconsider. 'I shall come tomorrow in fact.'

'No, sir!'

'*No, sir?*' He was shocked by the man's impertinence.

'I entreat thee, it cannot be tomorrow. He bade me tell you forcefully that if you do not come most urgently, eagerly, hastily and vigorously, then there shall be murder.'

'He threatens to kill me?' This seemed highly unlikely.

'Not you, sir, and not he, sir. His brother, Richard Burbage.'

'His brother threatens to kill me?' This seemed even less likely, since Richard Burbage was not only the leading actor in all of Will's plays, but also his firmest friend.

'No, sir. Richard Burbage threatens murder against another, and will do it too, unless your presence prevents it, so swears his brother

Cuthbert, who bids me remind you that you are the only man who can calm Richard when his blood is up.'

'He said all that?'

'He did and more. "Fetch Master Shakespeare, drag him here if you must," so says he to me, "for if he does not come then Richard shall kill a man this very day and will likely swing for it in the morning."'

'Who is this man Richard threatens to murder?'

'One Giles Allen, owner of the lease on the land upon which your theatre stands.'

'I know who he is,' said Will calmly, 'and do recall that Richard has threatened to end his life before, on numerous occasions.' The wrangling, over the cost of a new lease for The Theatre, the first of its kind in London with no need to have another name attached to it, like its successors the Curtain Theatre and the Rose Theatre, had gone on long enough for Richard's threats to have become a regular occurrence. 'Go, and remind Cuthbert of this.'

'He did anticipate you might say this in reply, and does reply to that reply thus; Richard has never gone so far as to reach for his sword, buckle it and march down to the Theatre to await Giles Allen's arrival.'

'Giles Allen is coming to the Theatre this very day?' What could have prompted this?

'He is. Invited to the tavern opposite, by the aforementioned Richard Burbage, to agree the handing over of the lease of the land to your theatrical company, in exchange for a fair sum of coin.'

'But Allen has never wavered on his demands for an excessive amount in return for that lease, a sum we are unable to provide, hence we are these past many months locked out of our theatre, since we will not pay it.'

'Indeed.' He said earnestly.

'Then why comes he to the Theatre now?'

'Because Richard Burbage has given him hope of a rapprochement.'

'Richard would not reconsider the terms of the lease without involving myself and his other partners,' explained Will.

'And yet he has said as much, so that he can meet with Allen and persuade him to moderate his demands, possibly at the point of a rapier.'

'That is unlikely to bear fruit.'

'And this is why Richard, on his own admission, is more likely to kill the man, then, says he, "to burn down the Theatre around his rotten corpse", rather than see the building go to another use.'

Will felt entirely helpless then. Although he wished for nothing more than an hour or so in his dark lady's company, for which he had waited so long, he could readily imagine Richard Burbage not only threatening such a thing but actually doing it too, then swinging from the Tyburn Tree gallows the very next day.

He glanced at his mistress helplessly.

'Go,' Avisa told him. 'Our business, important though it is, can wait awhile.'

'I shall return so that it may be concluded this very afternoon,' he said significantly, but her face told him she very much doubted this.

'I can wait,' she told Will, 'for a time.' But the firm look accompanying her words made him realise that this time would not be long.

Chapter Four

'Since all is well, keep it so: wake not a sleeping wolf.'

—*Henry IV Part II*

Will arrived in Shoreditch with the messenger and met Cuthbert Burbage at the corner of Curtain Road. An agitated Cuthbert urged Will to go straight to his brother with him to prevent a murder. 'We have quarrelled over this.' Cuthbert explained his reason for not accompanying Will there. 'And I am out of words. Richard wishes to hear no more from me in any case. You are my last hope, Will. Save my brother from himself!'

Will walked hurriedly down the street and found Richard waiting in the tavern directly opposite the Theatre, which had been closed to all for the past two years, while they wrangled with their landlord over the terms of a new lease. How many meetings had they endured with Giles Allen without coming to any agreement? Too many to keep track of. Many times, he had told them the terms of the old lease were too unfavourable to him for it ever to be renewed. Then he would once again point out that, although they owned the Theatre, which was built by Richard's father, James, the building was of little use to them with no lease, for they were not permitted to come onto the land without his permission.

For nigh on two years, their company, the Lord Chamberlain's Men, had been forced to give up the main source of their income, while scratching a living touring outside London and becoming increasingly desperate to regain their theatre. Eventually, they were forced to come to a not particularly beneficial agreement with Henry Lanman at the nearby Curtain instead. Playing at his theatre enabled them to make a living of sorts, but since all their profits had to be shared with Lanman, their own income was greatly reduced and they knew they could not go on like this forever. The company would run out of money before long and they would be forced to disband it. Then they would all run the risk of being thrown into penury.

Actors had been known to starve before now, and it was all so unnecessary. Before the expiration of the old lease, the Theatre had been providing all of them, including their landlord, with a good living. They knew they couldn't go on like this indefinitely, but every time they tried to get Giles Allen to see sense and lower his ruinous demands for higher rents, he smiled or shrugged his indifference, and on more than one occasion had even laughed in their faces. Allen told them they had no choice but to agree to his terms or they would never perform in their theatre again. For months now they had hoped his unbending stance was only a bluff. Surely at some point he would have to moderate his unreasonable demands to finally reach an accommodation with them, but the passing of two years told them this was less and less likely. Allen reasoned he had them, and they would be left with no choice but to yield to his terms eventually, for he had other income and could go on like this for far longer than they could.

Now it seemed Richard Burbage had finally had enough of the impasse and wished to end it, by murdering the man in a tavern. Even for a hothead like Richard, this barely constituted a plan, and Will could scarcely believe he was seriously thinking of going ahead with it. Richard, who was sitting at a table, fists balled in anger as if he might strike anyone who tried to prevent him from attacking Allen, assured him he was.

'But you'll hang, Richard. Surely you can see that?'

But all Richard knew now was his anger towards Giles Allen. 'Good then, my problems will finally be over, and I will have done you a service, for you will all be rid of Giles Allen.'

'Then who will act out the main roles in my new plays, if you are gone? Who will be my Brutus in *Julius Caesar*?' This gave Richard pause, for he had been looking forward to that role. 'And with Allen gone, do you think we will get the Theatre back? Not when the lease will go to his heirs. Kill him and they are far less likely to give it back to us. They will tear it down and put up tenements, like they do all over London these days, since the population grows ever larger with each passing year. They say it will reach two hundred and twenty thousand soon, though I can scarce believe a single city could accommodate so many. Kill Allen and you kill us all over time, and yourself by the morning. No, calm your fury Richard and let us try one more time to reason with the man. It has been weeks since we sat down with him. Perhaps he has finally seen the folly of a closed theatre, earning him no rent, sitting on land he cannot use for anything else.'

'You think I should reason with the bastard?' snarled Richard, but at least he was open to the suggestion and less intent on killing Allen, though his blood was still up.

'I think perhaps you should let me try.'

–

Giles Allen himself arrived within the quarter-hour, demanding ale. He was in unusually good spirits and content to reveal the reason why. 'Did you see the hanging?' He beamed at the recollection of the spectacle he'd witnessed, not three streets from there, with an enthusiasm others might have reserved for a good play. 'Eight of them, strung up together at once, for all to see and it has been long overdue. It was a damned good hanging. They quaked before us, and how they kicked!'

According to Richard, Allen had sent word beforehand that he had nothing to say to any of them on the matter of the Theatre's lease, or anything at all, unless they arrived with an improved offer for him. Now, however, enthused by the latest public hanging of thieves and cutpurses, it seemed he might never shut up. Instead, he continued to extol the virtues of an example set by 'the stretching of necks' before a section of the population.

'Is there a better forewarning than that?' he asked. 'To those who would break our laws. The streets are never safe around here. It was high time the queen's men acted to put the vermin back in their place. I've not seen a better display of her power since those apprentices were hanged, drawn and quartered for rioting… back in…' He was struggling to place the moment. '…Five years ago, or was it six? All who saw that still remember their screams.' He laughed at the memory. 'They regretted their lawlessness then, when their punishment came so sharply at the point of a blade. Their executions stopped disorder, and this one will stop it now, mark me.' Then he added, 'For a month or two.'

'There are hangings every week,' Richard reminded him. 'Yet the streets are no safer for it. You think an increase in hangings will prevent hungry men from robbing you? Not if they will starve to death in any case.'

Will did not disagree with his friend but gave him a warning look that told him not to argue with the man who held their fate so tightly in his grip, especially when he was in a more jovial mood than normal, thanks to the hangings.

'How else are we to demonstrate the authority of the state? I would go further and hang the vagrants that litter our streets. Let's string up all the dummerers, whipjacks and kinchin morts too.'

This was too much for Will. Allen wanted to execute anyone who pretended to be unable to speak to gain sympathy from passers-by for a little coin, or to hang those who pretended to have been victims of piracy at sea to improve their chances of begging successfully, which was surely a harmless enough embellishment to their wretched life stories. Kinchin morts were only parentless children after all, and if they didn't beg, they'd starve. 'They cause little harm when you can simply walk past them. No one forces you to give them coin.'

Allen snorted at that. 'No one could. They should at least be forced to work for bread, instead of malingering, and hanged if they refuse. 'Tis simple.'

'That *is* a simple solution,' agreed Will, though neither a fair nor a just one, he reasoned. Allen was showing he had a cruel side as well as a greedy one.

Detecting no contradiction from Will, the landlord of the Theatre retained his good humour, which was so fresh from such an excellent hanging. Will hoped they had chosen the right day to meet with him and he began to appeal to the man's good nature, if indeed he had one.

'Our arrangement dates back over twenty years when the first lease was signed by Richard's father, James…' he began but was cut off by Allen.

'And it was a twenty-year lease, which expired some twenty months ago. If I cared for history, I would come to one of your plays. Now is what matters, and the future. I care naught for the past.'

'But we wish to continue our business together into that future.'

'I have already stated my terms.'

'For the continued use of *our* theatre?' Richard interjected.

'*Your* theatre?' Allen was having none of it.

'Built by my father's hand,' Richard reminded him sharply.

'On land owned by me.'

'Which is why we desire an accommodation from you,' Will pleaded, though this was looking less and less likely, to his great frustration.

'It would seem to me that, now your lease has expired, any accommodation must come from you. Since you cannot enter your theatre without a new lease when it is housed on my land.' He seemed to think that was the end of the matter and was quite content.

'A good point well made,' Will said, through gritted teeth. He was trying to sound reasonable. 'Yet there would be little point in us entering our theatre at all, if it profits us nothing to perform there, when all the coin we earn from our performances goes straight to our landlord.'

'Not *all* your coin. You think I don't know how much you earn from your make-believe? A thousand groundlings pay a penny each to stand in the pit, perhaps another eight hundred arses in the galleries, parting with tuppence to be seated there, more if they want a cushion. You must have been making three pounds a day.'

'That's not so much,' Richard protested, 'when our costs are many and so high. Costumes for the players, payment for all the actors, as well as the musicians who play for the crowds.'

'So, 'tis easy, pay them less.' He considered the solution obvious.

Richard ignored this. 'Then, there is your rent.'

'Which is reasonable.'

'Which *was* reasonable, but now you ask for too much,' Richard told him firmly, his temper barely in check.

'I only ask what is fair.' Allen took exception to any implication of greed.

'*And* you want to own the building.' Will reminded Allen of that particularly unreasonable demand.

'Eventually,' he said airily.

'Within three years.'

'You yourself own a building, Shakespeare. You claim the company has so many expenses and that you can scarcely make a living once you have paid everyone, and yet I know you boast of owning the best house in Stratford.'

'The second best,' Will corrected him but cursed himself for being foolish enough not to hold his tongue, when he had indeed purchased the second finest house in his hometown for his family, so proud had he been of himself that day. 'That was from money earned from performances for the queen and other ventures, not from the Theatre.'

'Then perhaps you should have bought your family a less grand house, then you would still have money left to pay me my due.'

Will once again tried hard not to show his contempt for this bully and his unreasonable demands. 'I implore you once again to reconsider the amount that you regard as your due for the land, and also your request for the right to one day own the building.'

'It is hardly a matter worthy of discussion. Since I own the land the building is on, it is already mine. Whether I own the Theatre in the eyes of the law or not is of no consequence.'

'Not to me,' said Richard who seemed barely able to contain his fury now.

'Because your father built it, yes, yes. Well, your father is dead and gone, and all things must end. There is no room for sentiment in our arrangement.'

Will half expected Richard to strike the man, in an unsentimental manner, for daring to dismiss his father's death and legacy in such a way. To his credit, he contained his anger and instead asked, 'What else could you do with the building, if it were not let to us?'

'I could let it to other players.'

'Who? What company could actually fill a theatre that does not have one already?'

'I'll turn it into an arena for bear baiting or cockfighting then. Perhaps I'll move in a company of whores, instead of a company of actors. Tell me, would anyone really miss you if I did?'

'Come now, Master Allen, can you not see reason nor sense?' Will pleaded desperately. 'The current situation profits no one. Our doors are closed and have been a good while now. You have made your argument and your point, but if you continue to keep them shut and prevent us from renewing our lease, then there will be no money for anyone.'

'There is a difference between us, Master Shakespeare, and you seem to have forgot it. I have other ways to make coin and can outlast this current state, for years more if need be. I can keep the Theatre shut for as long as I wish, for it represents but a small part of my fortune, whereas you make all of your money from a stage that is currently closed to you. How long can your company survive without it? Can you afford to pay the Curtain to house you forever? I'll bet Lanman charges as much as I want.'

'He does not,' said Will, though in truth he did charge too much for the Curtain to be anything more than a temporary solution to their problem.

'It matters little. I'll reopen *your* theatre on my land, but only when you meet my terms. I want twenty pounds a year in rent, plus a share of your profits…'

'This is an outrage!' boomed Richard.

'I am not finished, Master Burbage!' Allen yelled back. 'As an accommodation to you and because of my good will, the ownership of the Theatre will be transferred to me after five years, not three. I will own it outright then and will do with it whate'er I please. That includes tearing it down if I wish.' He added arrogantly.

This was too much for Richard, who stood up to face him. 'A pox on you, you skirvy dog!' He moved to draw his sword then, but Will placed his own hand firmly over Richard's to restrain his friend.

'Let us not fight over this matter. Are we not reasonable men?' he implored.

'*We* are,' Allen chided, then he pointed at Richard. '*He* is not!'

Will tried one last time to reason with Allen. 'We do hear you most clearly regarding your desire to have a fuller and fairer share of the profits of our plays. However, I beg you to consider accepting somewhat less than you demand in rent, otherwise there is little point in us continuing in the enterprise at all, and you will be left with a closed and empty theatre providing no coin to any of us.'

'And I have told you already, I can survive the loss, whereas you cannot.'

'Why must there be a loss at all when we can all prosper? Think on it further and give us an answer in a day or so, when we will all be in better humour and in less rancour.'

'I will think on it,' he told Will. 'But I warn you now, I am in no mood to bend.'

Allen drained his drink then and left.

They watched him leave and Richard said, 'You should have let me kill him.'

'Perhaps.' Will was almost as frustrated by Allen's stance as Richard. 'But if he still lives and breathes, then so do you, and that is at least something. Let me think on it, Richard, and swear to me you will do nothing to harm his person in the meantime.'

'You will think on it? He will also think on it,' Richard reminded him, 'but is in no mood to bend. What good will it do for you to think on it more, when we have thought of little else these past two years. There is no solution. I tell you, Will, I am deep in my despair. My father is dead, and I am about to lose the theatre he built with his own hands. I feel the shame of that most keenly.'

'I know you do, my friend. Be assured I respected James Burbage as much as any man alive. I will do whatever I can to keep his theatre in your hands, which is why I urge you not to give up hope.'

'Then I will stop wishing for Allen's death, at my hand or another's, and will instead pray for a miracle. I will beseech God to give my dear friend William Shakespeare the wisdom others lack to find an answer to our prayers.'

'Thank you, Richard.' His acquiescence was at least something and it had bought Will valuable time.

'For the moment,' Richard warned him, 'but if you are unsuccessful, my thoughts will readily return to slaughter, for I will not permit Giles Allen to keep my father's theatre on his land and prosper from it. I'd rather burn it to the ground, with him in it!'

—

Will made to leave then and return to Avisa, for some small hope remained that his dark lady might still be at the inn. He wondered if her passion for him burned as fiercely as the one he held for her. If it did, then surely she would never dream of leaving.

'Sir?' A voice came to him from the door of the tavern and Will deliberately ignored it, for he certainly did not want to be delayed any longer. 'Sir?' the voice called again, and he realised that, whoever this messenger was, he could only have been there for him. Will resolved to creep out through the rear of the tavern, but as soon as he began to move, the other man's voice seemed to fill the room and everyone looked towards him. 'Master Shakespeare!'

There was no ignoring it this time. The voice was young but carried the kind of authority that was usually invested in it by the court.

'You sir, Master Shakespeare, you are sent for!'

Will turned to face his tormentor then, exasperation making his voice louder than it needed to be, as he demanded, 'Again?'

Chapter Five

'Confusion now hath made his masterpiece!
Most sacrilegious murder hath broke ope'
the Lord's anointed temple,
and stole thence the life o' the building.'

—Macbeth

Whitehall was said to be the queen's favourite palace, though she had a dozen others to choose from and her court moved regularly and often, staying put only for as long as the drains could cope with so many courtiers, before shifting to another location. There was Greenwich, where she had been born in 1533, and Hampton Court, whose gardens she still apparently enjoyed, despite being held there under house arrest for a time. The Catholic Mary had still been queen, and was agonising over whether she should execute her heretical half-sister. Hatfield House was where Elizabeth had learned of Mary's death, and her own ascent to the throne. She also had St James' Palace, Richmond and Windsor Castle at her disposal, but today Will had been called to Whitehall. The queen liked its size. It was said to be the largest palace in Europe and was big enough to accommodate all the members of her vast court. She regularly spent Christmases at Whitehall too, and Will had performed here before for Elizabeth and her guests.

The messenger had made his business that day clear. This time, Will was summoned not by royal command, but on the whim of her spymaster, Sir Robert Cecil. Her Secretary of State was a man she trusted almost above all others, barring a few court favourites who competed among themselves to charm and beguile the ageing queen into doing their bidding. Cecil was not one of those who knew how to use honeyed words with the queen, nor could he ever be described as fair. He was a very small man with a crooked back, who stood barely five feet, four inches tall, but what he lacked in looks and grace, he more than made up for with ruthless cunning and a clever mind. Will had feared the man ever since he had first met him, some six years ago now, and was given orders by Cecil to spy on Will's patron, the Earl of Southampton, a Catholic suspected of involvement in plots against Her Majesty. That suspicion of Cecil's had been heightened by his own personal loathing of Southampton.

Will had been placed in an impossible position, since he was unable to refuse Cecil, and his fear of Sir Robert had never gone away. Periodically, Cecil would summon Will to take advantage of his legitimate place at court, as a company member and partner in the Lord Chamberlain's Men, as a ruse to use him for other means. He could look into matters Cecil's own loyal men were too well known for or considered too rough to comprehend. Cecil would use the pretext of planning appropriate, non-heretical entertainment for Her Majesty and her foreign ambassadors to meet with Will openly at court, where they often discussed anything but.

Cecil did still retain an interest in the contents of Will's plays, and would pass critical comment upon them, insisting on omissions. Occasionally, he would steer Will in the direction he wished him to go, but it was a lighter touch than Will might have expected from a man who seemed to control everything and always knew the power of words. Usually, though, Cecil's mind was on weightier matters. Predominantly, he worried about the safety of Her Majesty's person and the protection of her Protestant realm against the many Catholic plots he heard whispers of, usually backed by the enemies of England in France or Spain.

Latterly, though, Will had gained the impression that Cecil's mind had become preoccupied with threats much closer to home, even from within Elizabeth's own court. There were still those who privately wanted to see an end to their queen's reign. Some of them were even more open about their disdain for Robert Cecil. He was a man they considered inferior to them in every way, from his lower birth and smaller stature to his willingness to carry out the dirtier work of Her Majesty's government, particularly when he confounded their own ambitions with his intriguing.

Will always felt he walked an incredibly narrow and dangerous path in his dealings with the man. Offend Sir Robert and you could be imprisoned, tortured, executed for some invented crime, or quietly murdered by one of the many questionable characters he employed to safeguard the realm. Men like Robert Poley, who was waiting to meet Will on his arrival at Whitehall, to usher him to Cecil's quarters. Poley was a rough man and a long-standing associate of Cecil's, who had played a large part in bringing down a queen. His involvement as a double agent in the Babbington plot provided Cecil's father, William, with the evidence he needed to condemn Mary Queen of Scots as a traitor. Even an unwilling Queen Elizabeth had to accept she must die then, reluctantly signing the death warrant of her own cousin, but it was William Cecil who had actually managed her execution.

By the time Will had his first dealings with Poley, the man was already widely known as both a spy and someone never to be crossed. Will certainly knew better than to trust him, since Poley was one of only three others in the room when the great Christopher Marlowe was taken from them and stabbed in the eye during 'a brawl', an explanation Will had never accepted. He knew his friend and fellow playmaker was murdered, to ensure Marlowe's own role, as a spy working for Robert Cecil in the lowlands, was never made public once he had become suspected as both a heretic and traitor.

Who was the more dangerous of the two? Will wondered. Cecil who gave the orders, or Poley, who carried them out? In truth, it mattered little. Cross one and you crossed them both, for their aims were always aligned. What choice did Will have then but to occasionally do their bidding when asked, and hope he would not be chosen too often for dangerous tasks surely better suited to rougher men?

Poley had acknowledged Will's arrival with a grunt, then led him into the palace without speaking further. There they joined a small crowd of people all trying to gain access to the queen's court. Many of them were hoping to present petitions to her, containing grievances or legal claims for lost lands and contested inheritances. Hardly any of them would be granted an audience, much less her favour in the matter they were petitioning. At one point, Cuthbert Burbage had tried to present the matter of their contested lease to her, but he did not even make it through the main door. The queen would likely not have cared about it anyway, since she never had to attend the theatre herself and simply summoned them to the palace when she wished to see a play.

Others were there because they were regularly admitted, as part of a substantial group of followers Her Majesty found interesting or amusing company. Usually, it was a simple matter to separate the two groups, and they could enter while the petitioners were kept back and dealt with separately by court officials, but not today. Something had changed, because this sizeable group all found themselves herded together while the queen's guard examined and questioned each one as to his purpose. This increase in security caused inevitable delays and soon there was some pushing and jostling, as well as shouting from the palace guards who were trying to keep order.

Will recalled Avisa's words then, before he had kissed her. Something about the court being in uproar because of a girl? He did not have to wait overlong to be enlightened further, as news spread from the front of the small crowd to those waiting further back. The usual palace guard had been doubled, the better to examine everyone arriving at court that day. A young woman was dead, and not just a low-born servant but a lady. Someone else said she had been found at the foot of some stairs and there was muttering about whether she had fallen or been pushed.

Still the crowd of courtiers and petitioners was held back while the guards questioned each in turn. Others arrived behind Will and added to the crush in the anteroom. Poley was pushed further ahead, while Will's own progress was stifled. He found himself shepherded quite naturally into the path of Sir Walter Raleigh, just as the whole group ahead of them stopped abruptly in a narrow hallway, while the guards took their time questioning those further up ahead. They were left in the awkward position of two men, quite unequal in stature, one the queen's former court favourite and the other a mere poet, pressed into acknowledging one another. Will knew Raleigh fancied himself a poet too. He had even been present when the adventurer had delivered a quite accomplished riposte to one of Christopher Marlowe's sonnets. 'The Nymph's Reply to the Shepherd' was a humorous destruction of that shepherd's overly romantic entreaties to his love to come with him and live off little more than fresh air. In Raleigh's version, she was having none of it. Since that day, Raleigh had always thought himself something of an expert on verse and plays, never failing to offer Will an opinion on his work.

'What is this?' Raleigh called ahead in frustration, but the crowd failed to part for him, and the guards either did not hear or chose to ignore his complaint. 'It's an indignity!' he called to show his displeasure while pretending to tolerate it, just this time, though he obviously considered the wait beneath him. He sighed dramatically to show that he was an important man kept waiting for no good reason, then he turned his attention to Will. 'This is Cecil's work,' he told Will, who knew that most of the bad things that happened at court were blamed on Cecil. 'Because of that girl.'

'What girl?'

'The one who was kil—' Raleigh corrected himself, '...Died. Anne Percy.'

A flash of recognition then and a young, fair face came easily to Will's mind's eye. He knew the girl, not well, but enough to be shocked by her death and saddened by the loss of this lady.

'She fell down a staircase in the dark,' Raleigh explained and he waved a hand in exasperation. 'So now we must wait.'

But if the lady did indeed die in a fall, why would those arriving at court be subjected to this delay and extra scrutiny? Unless she really was killed, as Raleigh had seemed to let slip. Did he know something others did not but was trying to be discreet – a state that never suited him. Was it the opinion of courtiers that the young woman had been murdered in the palace? Were they even now searching for her killer?

'She was one of the queen's ladies, I believe,' Raleigh continued vaguely, as if he could not really recall her. But Will knew that a man like Raleigh would have been very aware of every young woman close to Her Majesty. He would doubtless have tried to charm the girl into telling him the queen's mind on all manner of things, particularly whether she ever spoke favourably of Walter Raleigh these days. So why would he now claim little knowledge of a girl even Will had noticed from his far less regular visits to court? He seemed to deliberately change the subject then. 'I have heard intelligence about you, Shakespeare.' Raleigh's tone was confiding. 'They say that you are part of a clever plan to fool all of London.'

'They do?'

'Indeed, but you cannot make a fool of Walter Raleigh.'

Will was mightily tempted to answer, '*Because he is one already?*' but he held his tongue. It seemed Raleigh was expecting Will to confess to some cunning subterfuge. 'I fool no one, unless you talk of the normal pretence upon the stage.'

'Well, it is joined to your plays, but it is a performance that continues long after your players have finished.' He seemed to be speaking in riddles.

'I confess I have no idea what you are talking about, Sir Walter.'

'Oh, come now, how many times have I told you that I considered your work to be not quite as fine as Kit Marlowe's?'

'You *have* told me that,' Will admitted, 'many, many times.'

'Well then, you have proven yourself to be all the cleverer, by almost fooling me.' He laughed then. '*Almost.*' And he tapped a finger against his nose to show how he knew better.

Will shook his head in confusion.

'How inspired of you to consort with Kit Marlowe to write plays in your name that were almost his equal but not quite, leaving most of us to never doubt the question of their authorship.'

'You think I conspire with Kit Marlowe?' Will asked Raleigh in disbelief.

'You do.' He insisted.

'But... Kit Marlowe is dead. He has been dead these past five years.'

'Is he?' The smile was a fixed one and Raleigh was looking at Will as if he expected him to suddenly crumble and share a confidence between the two of them. 'Is he *really*?'

'He was stabbed in the eye in Deptford. You know this, all of London knows it. Did you forget?' What in God's name was Raleigh talking about?

'I did not forget and, yes, all of London knows it because that is what was put about, but there were only three witnesses to this supposed stabbing, and all of them were friends of Marlowe.'

'Frizer, Skeres and Poley were once friends of his,' admitted Will, 'but proved themselves to be the most fickle and deadly of companions. They were turned into his mortal enemies on the promise of gold, and the assurance of a pardon for killing him.' Will felt safe saying this aloud because Poley was some way ahead of him now and could not possibly have heard their conversation.

'That sounds like a most incredible plan.' Raleigh scoffed.

'Is it more incredible than your suggestion that he is in fact still alive?'

'And writes your plays.'

'And writes my plays.' Will sighed. 'Where is he then?'

'Hiding somewhere in London, or the Lowlands perhaps.' He was vague, as if that part was of little importance.

'If he was in London, he would have to stay hidden away all of the time, in case anyone saw him,' Will suggested.

'Quite so.'

'You think Kit could survive without taverns? He stays in a house then, and never goes out, which gives him lots of time to write plays, which he then gives to me but takes none of the credit for them? What about the money? Do we share it between us? That's not much of a living.'

'I imagine you come to some arrangement that benefits you both,' Raleigh said airily.

'Who in God's name has told you of this?'

'I… do not recall who first mentioned it to me… but it seemed quite believable since Marlowe is the better writer than you and has to make his living somehow.'

'Being not dead?'

'Exactly. Now look me in the eye, Shakespeare, and tell me it is not so,' Raleigh demanded.

Will did look him in the eye then. 'I will tell you the truth of the matter. When men learn I am Shakespeare the playmaker, they often cannot resist the urge to tell me the story of the play they think I should write next, assuming I will be most grateful for their counsel. Sometimes these men are quite mad and have lost all of their reason. So, the plots of the plays they suggest are absurd, drawn as they are from the well of the madness that afflicts them.'

'What of it?'

'Yet even they have never told me of anything quite so ridiculous as this. Your idea, that Kit is not actually dead but alive, seemingly well but hiding in a room somewhere, with the shutters closed, while writing all my plays for me, and receiving a pittance in return for them, yet none of the acclaim, is quite simply the most deranged piece of nonsense I have ever had the misfortune to bend my ear to.'

Raleigh looked shocked and angry at this, but Will was angry too. Before Raleigh could berate him, he beat the man to it.

'I know you used to be the queen's favourite and are still a powerful man at court, with followers. I realise that you could have me stabbed in the street or in a tavern, like Marlowe, simply for contradicting your vile slander. But I tell you, sir, that I would be doing you a grave disservice if I did not dissuade you from believing in this ridiculous notion, lest other great men at court hear you say it more widely and roundly mock you for your foolishness.'

When he was done, Will braced himself for the volley of angry threats and abuse he would doubtless receive, from a man who had grown far more grand than he under Her Majesty's patronage. Raleigh's face seemed to betray his emotions; first shock, then fury and finally embarrassment at being called out for his stupidity. Perhaps it was the latter emotion that saved Will.

'I was joking,' said Raleigh, even though he clearly had not been. 'I was jesting to see if I could enrage you, Shakespeare, and I succeeded. Of course, Marlowe is dead! Ha, you should have heard yourself just now, Will! For a writer of comedies, you show little humour. I fear you take yourself rather too seriously.'

'So, it was all a jest?'

'It was,' he protested, 'the bit about Marlowe in any case, but there are still men at court who think you cannot possibly have written all of your plays. You were never a soldier, nor have you crossed the oceans as I have, yet you write of these things as if you know them.' He seemed to think this was proof alone that Will could not possibly have been the author of all his plays.

'I have never been a king either, nor a queen or a great lord. I have not been a faerie nor a sprite, or a general in the Roman army and I do not possess a hunchback,' Will conceded. 'Yet somehow, I am able to think of what it must be like to be those things. Why? Because I possess a mind. We playmakers use it, to imagine things.'

But Raleigh was not really listening. He was lost in his own thoughts now. 'There are even those who have asked me if I wrote your last play. Because my own poetry is so fine, they did think it so.'

'And did you believe that rumour too?' asked Will. 'It is no less fanciful than the one about Kit.'

'Of course I did not believe it. If I had written your plays, I would surely know,' and Will realised what a fool Walter Raleigh could be when he was not talking about sailing or exploring new lands.

'What are you bringing us next?'

'*Julius Caesar.*'

'Good, good.' Raleigh nodded his approval. 'Stick to a historical. You're better at those. But make sure the murderers of a monarch are shown to be punished, unless you wish to write your next play in the Tower.' He chuckled to himself at the notion of Will spending months, perhaps even years, writing about the world from a tiny and uncomfortable corner of it. It should have been easier to like Walter Raleigh. He was a low-born man too, who still had a strong Devon accent, which amused the queen so much she often called him 'Water' because that was how he appeared to pronounce his own name, at least to her ear. He had once been her favourite but had fallen foul of the queen by tupping, then secretly marrying her lady-in-waiting Elizabeth Throckmorton, without Her Majesty's permission. They were both briefly sent to the Tower for that transgression. Good service to the queen during the capture of Cadiz restored some of her favour to him, but, by that time, he had been eclipsed by the stunning rise of the Earl of Essex, whom the queen favoured more than any other these days. Unsurprisingly, the two men hated each other and plotted to entirely ruin their respective enemies, which was an open secret at court.

Raleigh might have learned some humility, thought Will, but his self-love was so strong he still considered himself better than almost all of her other subjects, even the most lofty, which was why he was so widely despised by so many of her other courtiers.

Will realised there was little point in debating matters with Raleigh further. It was far easier to win an argument with someone who was your equal in intelligence, than to try to alter the mind of a fool. He did a small bow then and stepped back slightly from the man just as the crowd finally began to move forwards, so that others soon filled the gap he left.

Raleigh turned his full attention back to the guards who were delaying him. 'It won't bring her back, you know!' he shouted to them, exhibiting a startling lack of compassion for the dead girl he had mentioned to Will.

Poor Lady Anne. Once, she was a rare and admired beauty; now she was dead, it had turned her into little more than an inconvenience for men like Raleigh, who clearly felt they had better things to think about, most notably their position at court, which seemed to mean everything to them.

The palace guards must have taken too long examining everyone attending court that day, so that even their own sergeant eventually grew impatient. 'Move on here! Move on! Go to! Go to!' he cried and the lines of men ahead started to move at last. Perhaps the queen had wondered where all her courtiers were and had ordered him to speed them along, which he did now, hastily, in order to avoid Her Majesty's displeasure. Will was perhaps the only man there who was in no hurry to be admitted, but then he had been summoned to the palace by the queen's inquisitor in chief, Sir Robert Cecil, arguably the most dangerous man in the realm.

Chapter Six

'Grief fills the room up of my absent child,
Lies in his bed, walks up and down with me,
Puts on his pretty looks, repeats his words,
Remembers me of all his gracious parts,
Stuffs out his vacant garments with his form;
Then, have I reason to be fond of grief?
Fare you well: had you such a loss as I,
I could give better comfort than you do.
I will not keep this form upon my head,
When there is such disorder in my wit.
O Lord! my boy, my Arthur, my fair son!
My life, my joy, my food, my all the world!
My widow-comfort, and my sorrows' cure!'

—*King John*

The large doors ahead swung open to admit them and the courtiers all hurried through and went directly to the queen's hall, while the petitioners were held back or diverted away from there. Poley stood aside, letting them go, and he waited for Will to catch up with him. Then, his escort made for a much smaller door off to one side, which promised discretion, since it opened onto a dark staircase that few knew about, leading directly to Sir Robert Cecil's rooms. If Cecil wanted to meet men in private or allow someone to come to him who did not wish to be seen, they could be quietly ushered to him from here.

The stairs arced round tightly, took them up two floors, then opened into a narrow corridor. At the end of this, the way widened and they went past a series of closed doors until they finally reached the room Cecil worked from. Poley knocked, then opened the door, ushered Will through it, then closed the door and waited outside.

The room was spacious but not grand. Apart from some well-made furniture, including a desk from which Cecil liked to conduct much of his business, there was little to speak of here, aside from the many books and official papers that competed for space on every shelf, ledge and corner of the room.

Cecil was standing by a large table, peering down at an impressive number of letters that had been arranged there, face up and side by side, all written in the same neat, formal hand. His crooked back gave him a natural stoop and he was staring at them as if transfixed, lost in his own thoughts, and he did not appear well. It had been four months since they had buried his father, but the mighty Sir Robert Cecil still looked bereft.

'My lord,' said Will and he awaited instructions, but none came. Instead, Cecil continued to gaze upon the letters with an air of complete preoccupation.

'One hundred or more,' he said eventually. 'All from my father.' He gestured towards the letters. 'Instructing me, as he always found time to do, on how to complete every task he could imagine that might be needed to safeguard this realm, protect Her Majesty against her many enemies, and maintain her presence on the throne. Now I must somehow find the strength to carry on without his hand to guide me.'

This was a highly uncharacteristic display of emotion and self-doubt from Cecil, who would previously have considered a public declaration of this kind from anyone else to be a sign of weakness, but Will knew how affected he had been by his father's death. They were not simply close. William Cecil had been the queen's dearest and most trusted advisor for the entirety of her reign. He had been with her for forty years. He was also his son's guiding hand and had trained him, almost from birth, to take his father's place by the side of their monarch.

'The loss of a father hits a man hard,' said Will, while telling himself that it could in no way be as dreadful as the loss of a son. Will's own father, John, still lived, though he was sixty-seven now, and Will knew that one day his loss would be a difficult one to bear. But that would be in the natural order of things and as nothing compared to the grief Will had felt upon the death of his only son, Hamnet, at the age of just eleven. Two years had passed since then, but not a day had gone by when he had not thought of his boy and mourned the loss of him most keenly. Will found he rarely smiled these days, as if even to have a happy thought would be a betrayal of Hamnet's memory. Instead, he worked, writing for much longer each day than he ever had before his son's death, deliberately exhausting himself, so that he fell into sleep almost as soon as his head touched the pillow, the better to keep dark thoughts from spiralling in his grief. He banished Hamnet's memory from his mind now. 'But there is a time for every son to emerge from the shadow of his father,' he told Cecil, 'and become the man he was destined to be.'

Robert Cecil looked at him in wonder then, and Will feared he might be punished for such an impudent suggestion. *Let him do it then. I deserve it, for my sins. I must do*, he reasoned, *or God would not have taken my only son from me*. 'Perhaps you are right,' said Cecil, 'though no one has ever put the point to me quite like that before.' He frowned in thought. 'Some at court say you understand everything, Will Shakespeare. Is that true?'

'It is not,' Will assured him, 'but I know loss and grief.'

'Your boy,' Cecil recalled. 'The bearer of your name.' His solemnity indicated he understood just how big a loss that had been for Will, though it did not take him long to move on to the business he had summoned him for. 'There is another who grieves here now. The father of Anne Percy, one of the queen's ladies-in-waiting, found dead within these walls.'

'I had heard of this.' It would likely be all the court would talk about for a day or two. Deaths in the palace were uncommon enough and almost always due to illness of one kind or another. It was rare for one of the queen's ladies to succumb.

'What know you of the Lady Anne?'

'Only that she was a most unfortunate maid who fell down a staircase?' Will did not want to admit any more knowledge than this or that he had entertained the notion that her death might have been in any way suspicious, judging by the activity of the palace guards as he was entering it.

'She was a young lady in the queen's service, who rose in the night and must have walked too close to the staircase in the dark. She stumbled and fell down it to her death. A most tragic occurrence.' Cecil related this in an unemotional manner, before adding, 'That is the story put about.' And Will knew it would have been Cecil himself who had put it about. 'But what do you know of her?' he pressed, as if Will was concealing some hidden knowledge.

'But little, my lord.' And he tried to recall more of the Lady now. Will had been at court on the very day she had first attended it with her father, brother and older sister. 'She was the daughter of a northern lord, kin to the Earl of Northumberland?'

'A cousin to a most treacherous family,' Cecil observed. 'Both the sixth and seventh earls were executed for treason. The eighth likely would have been too, if his death in the tower had not been ruled self-slaughter. As for the ninth and current earl, Henry Percy, only time will afford us the truth of his character. You know they call him the Wizard Earl.' He sneered at this notion. 'Because he practises alchemy and believes in science.' Will could not tell which of these two disciplines Cecil disapproved of most. 'I suspect he is a secret recusant.'

'The Lady Anne's family, though, are Protestant?' Will wasn't wholly sure about this but assumed it would have been a barrier to her advancement at court if they were not.

'Outwardly,' confirmed Cecil. 'Her brother, Edmund, seemingly so, and she has a sister who is married to a Scottish lord, who is an avowed protestant. I suspect her uncle, though. The earl always pleads moderation in our dealings with Catholics. I fear the Lady Anne may have been caught up in some plot or intrigue for which she was too innocent and unschooled to survive.'

'She was young and fair,' Will recalled, 'but modest and the queen seemed to take to her.'

'She did,' he confirmed before adding, 'A young woman of noble birth who has served the queen is most sought after.' Then he said, 'Though there is always a risk of exposing them to the vices of the court. It can be the cause of a naïve girl's undoing.'

So far, Cecil had failed to cast any light on his reasons for telling Will about all this. 'How can I be of assistance in this matter, my lord?' He meant it quite literally. What on earth could a playmaker offer the spymaster this time? He had once been tasked with looking into a suspicious death, but that was years ago and the initial request had come from his patron, the Earl of Southampton. Cecil's involvement only came later when Will was ordered to spy on the earl for him. That death had occurred in the city of London, not here at court, a nest of vipers whose ways Will had not yet come close to understanding, let alone mastering.

'Enquiries will have to be made,' Cecil explained. 'If Lady Anne fell, then that is one thing. If she did not and was killed, then there is a murderer in the palace. Who knows who might become his next victim?'

Did he mean the queen might succumb to this madman? There had been attempts on her life before and the young maid was not very far removed from Her Majesty. Who would dare murder one of her ladies though? A respecter of nothing. Would they then be fearless enough to try and kill the queen herself? Perhaps. That would explain the doubled guard and increased scrutiny of everyone walking in or out of the palace that morning. It was indeed Cecil's doing then.

Will could understand the need for enquiries to be made, and that almost everyone might initially fall under suspicion, but surely others were far more qualified than he to do this work? 'My lord, would this not be a task better suited to rougher men? I am neither a spy nor a soldier.'

'No, you are a writer and an actor, and that is precisely why I have chosen you. I cannot rely on any man linked to me. No one, save for myself, William Wade and Poley, knows that you have done me good service before. You have proven yourself to be discreet, and any interaction you do have with me can be explained by my concern to keep heresy and sedition out of your plays, which are performed in front of thousands.' Then he said, 'It is vital that no one can accuse me of being responsible for any investigation into this death. If my worst suspicions prove correct, it could involve those at the very heart of Her Majesty's court. I must not be seen to be either acting on behalf of the queen, nor proceeding without her authority. I can deny this if I am accused of it, simply by denying you, Shakespeare.'

This was not a comforting thought for Will. He now knew that, if any powerful person at court suspected him of taking an interest in matters he had no right to delve into, he could be arrested, tortured or killed.

'Don't look so pale, Will. You have done this before and know how to fade into the walls. You are a lowly man with no ambition for a place at court and there is little reason for anyone to assume you conspire against them. You are in very small danger.' Will was not convinced of that. 'I, on the other hand, find myself in grave peril these days. Since my father died, I am without allies. They buried him with all honours and told me they would not see his like again, and yet…' His words trailed away.

'And yet, my lord?'

'It was but the matter of a few hours before those lords consigned him to a memory and commenced their plotting; for his position, his power and influence, his place by the queen's side.'

'That is your place now, Sir Robert,' Will reassured him.

'Is it? For how long, I wonder, if they have their way? They are conspiring against me and, now that my father is gone, I must defeat them all on my own, which I shall do.'

'By outwitting them, Lord. By being cleverer than they are.' Will reminded himself that, if in doubt, while standing before a great man, use flattery. It usually worked.

Cecil's tone was defiant now. 'Every one of the queen's favourites and her landed nobles wants to see me sent to the block. My crime? Daring to advise Her Majesty on the best interests of herself and the realm, and they call that treason. They see me as her Cardinal Wolsey or Thomas Cromwell, a man born lowlier than they, who has ascended above them all using his wits alone. Wolsey was a butcher's son, and Cromwell had a blacksmith for a father. Both were brought down by jealous earls. My own father was made a baron, but our family came from the Welsh Marches before gaining favour with the queen's grandfather, so I am still considered low-born and an upstart by these dukes and earls at court.' He sneered at their plotting. 'They resist no opportunity to remind the queen of this. If she were to be poisoned by their words just once, and doubt me for an instant, I could be thrown down, but alas for them all, she needs me. My enemies would drag me to the gates of hell if she let them.'

'Then surely it is wiser to leave such a delicate investigation to men more suited to such matters.' He meant Poley, who was presumably still standing outside the door. The last thing Will wanted was to be set to work by a man everyone else wished to destroy.

'I want fresh eyes on this,' Cecil informed him. 'It is my burden to protect the queen from her enemies, foreign and domestic, and I see plots everywhere. That is both a blessing and a curse. Sometimes I wonder if I imagine intrigue even where there is none? I have a network of informants who rely on me for their patronage, but they do tend to feed me the meat I most hunger for.'

'You think they invent plots?' How ironic, since Will had once been asked to invent one against the Earl of Southampton by Cecil himself. It had taken all of Will's courage back then to refuse.

'Almost certainly. They take coin from my purse and immediately feel obliged to repay me with information about the queen's enemies, some of which they spin like webs into wider conspiracies, to increase their importance in my eyes and gain preferment.'

'You tolerate this?'

'I must, for I need every piece of information they provide. It is my duty to sift through it all and find gems. But, this time, I cannot afford to be misdirected. Time is against her. If there is a killer, we must find him and fast, lest he strikes again. The men of the watch, the palace guards, my usual spies will all watch and listen as ever, but I want you, an ordinary man, to look into this matter for me, without fear or prejudice, and most quietly, mark you. Can you do that, Shakespeare?'

An ordinary man? How many times had he been called that over the years, and almost always by men like Sir Robert Cecil, or the earls who served the queen alongside him in the Privy Council, as well as the other nobles of the court, even some of his fellow actors and writers. And it was true. Will was ordinary. He was not tall, nor particularly fair, nor was he the best actor in his company, or the best singer, dancer or swordsman. He was in all aspects ordinary, apart from being a better than normal user of words.

Will knew Cecil was right. Most of those lords did indeed want to see Cecil fall, especially now that his father was no longer there to protect him. They might have been natural allies. Both were outsiders in a world where being born rich and grand, and looking fair, were all that really mattered. Cecil was looked down upon in a literal sense too, for he was very short, certainly not handsome and had been born with that crooked back, which most assumed was a punishment from God.

'I shall do my best, as always, to please my lord,' Will answered while secretly dreading the thought of serving Robert Cecil again, but knowing he had little choice.

'Seek the truth and report back to me, but do it quickly. Walsingham used to say he could smell an intrigue. I cannot, but there is at least the whiff of one here. That lady likely did not fall, which must mean she was pushed or thrown, unless...' He seemed reluctant to state the only remaining possibility: that she took her own life on that staircase. 'We need to know who killed her and why?'

'My lord.'

That seemed to placate Cecil and he switched his attention to Will's own circumstances. 'I hear it goes well with you, Master Shakespeare. They say you bought the finest property in Stratford.'

'The second finest.'

'Oh, then why not the finest?'

'He wouldn't sell it to me.' Will would have liked to have bought the finest house in his hometown, to show how far he had come in the world, but had to settle for the second best. 'My lord, you are more learned than I and have loyal followers.' Will meant Cecil's network of spies, who seemed to be everywhere. 'What think *you* of Lady Anne's death? Why would someone set out to kill one so young and innocent.'

'Her innocence is assumed, but there are many corrupting influences at court. So-called gentlemen take great sport from undoing ladies-in-waiting and caring not if they fall. They brag of it even. I suspect the Lady Anne was too chaste for them or their like, but it is always possible that a young, unworldly girl might have believed the honeyed words of a dishonourable man, if he talked of love and promised marriage. It has happened before.'

'You think she left her bed that night to meet a lover?' There were always rumours of such things.

'It is one explanation.'

'There are others?'

'That is for you to find out, Shakespeare, but when men kill, outside of battle, they almost always do it for the same reasons: love, lust, money, power, hatred or revenge. This you already know, since you write about all of that in your plays, do you not?'

'But why would anyone hate the Lady Anne or wish to seek revenge against her? Did she have rivals at court?'

'Everyone does,' he said flatly. 'Find out.'

'You mentioned power and money. Would killing a girl lead a man to either?'

Cecil's eyes locked on his for a moment. 'That would depend.'

'On what?'

'On whether the Lady Anne had a secret perhaps, and what value knowledge of it might bring. Use that writer's imagination of yours to picture a scene in which some unknown person might have seized that maiden and thrown her from the balustrade to her death.'

'I will try.'

'Then think more on it and find me the reason why some godless soul would commit such a terrible act against such a blameless lady.'

'Blameless?'

'Whatever caused this, it was not by her doing. She was too innocent to have had willing involvement in anything that could have justified her death.'

'You're sure of that.'

'William Wade searched Lady Anne's belongings but found no letters, cyphers or forbidden books.'

This was the second time Cecil had mentioned William Wade. From what Will had heard at court, Cecil trusted the man to carry out more and more of his orders with the Secretary of State's customary ruthlessness. He was far more of a gentleman than Poley, too, and able to move in more exalted circles, but if you crossed Wade, got in his way, or were suspected of being an agent of a foreign power, the end result would be the same and you likely would not live to rue that day.

'I did know that lady,' Cecil said then. 'It is not just that she was young and fair.' He seemed genuinely affected from recalling the girl now. 'I have known many women in this court. They come, they serve the queen for a time, then they go. All are beautiful, but that is no guarantee of a good or kindly heart. Most are quick to make sport of me, as if I asked God for this condition, or are in some way deserving of it. They call me pygmy, and other names. I have heard them all before, of course, many times and care not. They hurt me when I was young, but now…' He made a dismissive pah sound, as if a man of great power could no longer be wounded by a personal affront, but Will found he did not believe him. 'The Lady Anne never took part in that sport, nor did she act towards me as if I was sent here by the devil. Here was a gentle lady, with a kind and goodly heart who declined to join the other ladies-in-waiting when they called me a crookback and a toad, nor did she think me unworthy of a smile. I will not forget her for that.'

Cecil turned his back on Will then, ostensibly to look out of his window, but Will got the impression he was hiding his emotion. He gave his master a moment, then asked a question, as much to extricate them from the awkward scene as anything else.

'Did anyone see or hear anything that night?'

'Only a serving girl, who claimed to.' Cecil was dismissive.

'May I speak to her.'

'That would do you no good. Wade already questioned her and cursed the time he wasted.'

'What did she see?'

'The devil himself.' Cecil laughed bitterly at this notion. 'She swears she saw him leaving the scene of this terrible crime.'

'She saw the devil?' Will rather doubted that. 'What did he look like?'

He shrugged. 'Pointed horns, a tail and hooves.'

'She said this?'

Cecil sounded impatient. 'I am assuming that if she thought she saw the devil and not some mortal man, that she would have described him thus. We all know what the devil looks like. Still, it matters not what shape he took if he did this or tempted a mortal man to enact his bidding. He is the father of lies, and his presence in this court and elsewhere in the realm is always assumed, so we must all be forever on our guard.'

'And what did Wade say of this servant?' Will wondered why he had been so disdainful of her account, since most at court generally accepted that the devil was often among them.

'He said she was young, no more than fourteen, unworldly and may or may not have seen what she thought she saw. She was most terrified by the spectacle of the figure she encountered as she looked up from her bed, upon hearing what she took to be a scream, presumably from the Lady Anne, for this was at the hour of her death.'

'Did he find her believable?'

'He thought she told the truth as she saw it, but, if it was the devil fleeing the scene, then how will this benefit us? We can hardly follow him into the pits of hell to question him further.'

'I can see the problem. But tell me, what is her name?'

'Her name is Agnes Hogg,' said Cecil.

Agnes thought Will, coming from the Greek word *Hagné*, meaning holy or pure. It was always his habit to recall the origins of a woman's name, usually to charm her, but not this time.

'But I command you not to waste your time on her,' Cecil told him.

'And why not, my lord, since you seek the truth?'

'One: she is a woman; two: she is of low station, and finally: she is very young. So her account of what she saw cannot be trusted on three counts, nor is it of any consequence if all she saw was Satan.'

All three charges Cecil levelled against the witness, of being young, female and of low birth would, of course, count against her when set against the word of a man. But wasn't she the only witness they had? Will would have liked to have at least spoken to the girl, but Wade had already done so and dismissed her. Will doubted that the devil himself had appeared at the palace, to roam its corridors before killing one of the queen's ladies-in-waiting. He was in no position to argue with Sir Robert about it, however, and he let this go.

'I do not know if murder has been committed here, much less have reason to go to the queen for permission to test a man.' By 'test', Cecil meant torture, and it seemed that even he still needed the queen's blessing for such an extreme course of action. 'But this court has become infested by vice.' He announced then: 'It is riddled with recusants, pederasts, sodomites and blasphemers. Some of them seek daily to bring down our queen and replace her with a foreign, papist monarch. I will not allow that. Make your enquiries and, mark me well, look to the supposed great men of the court. There are four in particular who are at the heart of every intrigue. One of them might very well be responsible for the death of this lady.'

He looked into Will's eyes then to ensure he had his attention before he explained who they were.

'The queen's favourite – Robert Devereux, a most sly, cunning and ambitious man.'

Will pictured the Earl of Essex then, since he had seen him often enough, always striding arrogantly through the court as if it was his and not the queen's.

'Then there is your patron, Henry Wriothesley, the Earl of Southampton, and a known recusant.'

And your old enemy, thought Will, who often recalled two of the most powerful men in the kingdom trying to bring each another down, and how he himself had almost been crushed in between them and their feud.

'Next, Sir Walter Raleigh, the *adventurer*.' Cecil almost spat the man's name and sneered the word adventurer. 'He would do anything to regain the queen's favour.'

For what was he without it? thought Will. Would Raleigh kill if it meant he was able to clamber back to the very top of the court? Probably.

'And finally Charles Blount, Baron Mountjoy, a man who all can see is on the rise.'

Will could see it too. Mountjoy even rivalled Essex for the queen's affections, and that meant he was favoured by her, so was surely still an enemy of Essex, even if outwardly they were friends.

'If there is a conspiracy and Lady Anne's death is at its heart, then it will involve at least one of these four.' Cecil thought for a moment. 'Or possibly all of them. I do not trust a single one. They are all disloyal and inconstant. Their love for the queen is entirely conditional on her patronage and they will bend like a branch in the wind should some other power offer them more than she will. Discover if Lady Anne was murdered, Shakespeare. If she was killed because of a plot, I have a sense it will be by someone ordered to it by one of these men. Do not breathe a word about your true purpose, nor mention to anyone it was me who set you to it. You must be subtle and clever. If you are not, I cannot save you from the wrath of these courtiers who hold most of the power in England between them. They are rich, landed and the queen's favourites all.'

Whether Cecil could in fact save Will from these men, if they discovered he had been asking dangerous questions about them, was of little importance. What mattered most was Cecil's desire to avoid damaging his own reputation or to risk his position at court. That meant he was always more likely to deny any association with Will and his investigation. That placed Will in an incredibly dangerous position, as an almost powerless man left entirely alone.

'One final thing, I may have, in the past, inferred to you that I did not care overmuch about the entire truth behind certain treasons, committed by powerful lords. It has been my view that even a hint of treachery is enough proof of where a man's true heart lies. That is often sufficient to lead him to be pressed, until he confesses plots hitherto unknown to those of us who serve the queen. But this is different. I forbid you to give me what you think I want. Only deliver me the truth of what happened to the Lady Anne. Is that understood?'

Will said nothing and Cecil took that silence as agreement.

'If a man is guilty of this great crime, I want proof so I can deliver retribution, without fear of punishing the wrong man and allowing the true villain to walk free.'

'I am at your command, my lord, but this may take some time.' And Will knew he needed to buy it now, while he was still in the room with Cecil. At that moment, he had no idea how to even begin to uncover the truth about Lady's Anne's death.

'Time I cannot grant you. You must find the killer swiftly. Deliver the villain to me. Do that and you are discharged from your duty, but, Shakespeare, if you fail me in this, I will not forget it, nor forgive. Is that understood?' His tone made it clear to Will that it needed to be.

'It is, my lord.' Will had known that much already without having to be told it. If he fell foul of Cecil, he would likely be ruined, or worse.

'You might need this.' Cecil held out something and when Will took it in his hand, he realised it was a fine miniature portrait, painted on vellum and set in a golden frame no larger than three inches across. The painting was of a beautiful young girl. 'It is her likeness.'

Will examined the portrait. It was a fine work, and he had seen its like before. They had become a fashionable item at court, at least for those wealthy enough to be able to commission one of these exquisite portraits from the court painter, Nicholas Hilliard. He was a limner, who could paint miniatures with a tiny, squirrel-hair brush, then place the work inside a little gold frame such as this.

Somehow it was now in Cecil's possession.

'It fell into my hands,' he explained, somewhat self-consciously, as if reading Will's thoughts, and Will wondered how it could have done. Did Anne have it on her person when she died, and Cecil had seized it?

He would have asked, but then another thought struck him. What if Cecil had commissioned this work himself, so he could gaze upon the Lady Anne's face whenever he chose? Christ, he had better not lose this precious object.

'It is so you can show others her likeness, if you need them to recall her,' Cecil explained. 'When this is done, you will return it to me.' He was firm about that, then admitted, 'There is little point in enquiring around the court today, since everyone is so disturbed by her death. My men tell me they speak of little else but foolish notions surrounding the Lady Anne's passing. Some say it was caused by agents of France or Spain, who will kill the queen next, others that the Pope himself commanded it to fill the hearts of all Her Majesty's loyal courtiers with fear. There are other baser ideas that traduce the reputation of Lady Anne based on nothing more than vile gossip, showing no respect for the dead. You will start your enquiries here once the mood is calmer. I will need a day, perhaps two, to convince most of them that we have control of the court and the city of London. Then, when they are calmer and less foolish, you may find the answers we seek. Now, did anyone notice you on your way into court?'

Will was forced to admit that he had indeed been noticed by Walter Raleigh due to the crush outside the anteroom that morning.

Cecil looked as annoyed by that as if Will had contrived it to happen deliberately to foil his plans. 'Does he know I summoned you to court?'

'He does not. He merely wished to discuss my plays with me.'

'Why?'

'I think he perhaps believes himself to be the better writer.'

'Of course he does. Raleigh: the soldier, the sailor, the adventurer and, Lord save us from him, the poet. Why can't men be content to be one thing and stick to it? Must they always attempt to be masters of everything. That only guarantees they will devote little enough of their time and energies to anything.' Then he ordered Will, 'Come, you have been seen, so now we must walk together in the privy gardens.'

Chapter Seven

'Men should be what they seem.'

—*Othello*

Sir Robert Cecil and Will walked openly together now, in full view of courtiers enjoying their leisure, perhaps in the knowledge they might even see the queen, for she was known to enjoy a walk in the privy gardens with her favourites.

'Sir Robert, should we be seen like this, walking through the gardens so publicly?' Even as Will asked of it, he noticed eyes were upon them.

'In case they think you my spy?' He seemed to find this amusing. 'Would I not summon you to some dark and secret place, to make you my creature, instead of us strolling through a garden together? No, they will think the queen's most trusted advisor is instructing her favoured playmaker on what next to write for the queen.'

This seemed an over-elaborate ruse, simply because Walter Raleigh had seen Will enter the Palace of Whitehall, but Cecil had insisted they create a reason for his presence there that day.

He lowered his voice then. 'I will give you a room not far from mine to write in. Then your comings and goings will not be commented on, and your presence here more often will enable you to gain intelligence from the musings of men and women of the court, who would never dare mutter their true thoughts when Poley is within earshot.' Poley had been deliberately dismissed by Cecil once their walk had begun. 'If I need somebody frightened or harmed, then a loyal man like Poley is a useful instrument of the crown, but this requires a sharper mind.'

As the two men rounded a corner in the gardens, their talk deliberately turned back to plays, and most specifically what Will would write for the court next, once *Julius Caesar* was finished, but Will was undecided on that. Their view of the gardens became obscured here by tall hedges to their right, and they accidentally stumbled upon a small gathering at the far end of an area set aside for archery practice. At their end, a target had been set up, so they stopped abruptly and turned to face the opposite end of that long lawn. From there, they could make out half a dozen richly dressed figures watching them.

A moment later, an arrow shot by. It missed the target and, to Will's alarm, landed with a thud against a tree trunk situated between it and themselves. In truth, it was a deal nearer to them than the target. Whoever had loosed that arrow had sent it perilously close, enough to make Cecil start. It could quite easily have struck one of them. This near miss caused a whoop from the young men that was meant to convey shock at Will and Cecil's untimely arrival, but Will wasn't fooled. They had been seen as soon as they turned the corner and had stopped on realising they might be in peril. Only then was the arrow loosed, its aim adjusted to cause them maximum alarm without actual injury.

'Cecil!' cried the Earl of Essex, who was marching towards them now, a look of concern etched unconvincingly upon his face. He appeared shocked that his bitterest rival had almost come to grief, having been foolish enough to walk into their archery practice. Will knew that the queen's favourite was a warrior, a man skilled with the sword, and famed as the English 'Hero of Cadiz'. He was unlikely to be so inept with a bow that he couldn't hit a target from that distance, assuming he was actually aiming at it and not the tree. His real intention had been to scare them both, and in this he had thoroughly succeeded. 'What were you thinking, sir? I could have knocked your hat from your head.' Then he smirked. 'If I'd been aiming a little lower.'

His handful of hangers-on included two of the other men Cecil had warned Will to be mindful of during his enquiries. His occasional patron, Henry Wriothesley, the Earl of Southampton, was known to be the firmest friend and most loyal devotee of Essex, and he could barely hide his glee at the near miss and its effect on Cecil. Will recognised Charles Blount, Baron Mountjoy, next to him, as the coming man at court. They both laughed at the taunt involving Cecil's height and Will wondered how often he was forced to endure these jokes. Daily, he imagined. No wonder Cecil was known to be such a ruthless bastard, when they gave him so much cause.

Cecil bowed to the earl, his teeth firmly gritted. 'I must apologise for ruining your sport. Was it my fault your aim was so far off?' He was making Essex know he understood the arrow's course to be deliberate.

'No matter,' said Essex. 'I was merely making time until the queen sends for me, which she has assured me she will. I hope you weren't hoping for an audience with Her Majesty this afternoon, Cecil, for she has promised herself to me for its entirety. She said as much in her chamber late last night, while we were occupied...' His noble friends smirked and laughed openly at that, and the earl turned and pretended to rebuke them with. '...At cards!' But he was clearly enjoying the implication he had been involved in other pursuits with the queen.

'Oh yes,' hooted Southampton, 'at *cards!*'

And Essex hit him playfully on the arm, as if he himself hadn't encouraged more lascivious notions.

'Who's this?' Essex meant Shakespeare, though he must surely have known who Will was by now. He had seen him act before the court and must have known Will had written those plays. It was equally likely, though, that the earl simply did not think Will worthy of committing his face or name to memory.

'This is Shakespeare,' the Earl of Southampton informed him. 'My poet.' Then he added, 'He writes the queen's plays.'

'Oh yes, Shakespeare.'

Will bowed before him and the earl looked thoughtful.

'I could have use of a man like you. Yes, indeed.' He did not enlighten Will further, nor did he seem to care that he was currently in the company of Cecil or that Southampton was already Will's patron. He correctly surmised that neither man would object, since he was such a favourite with the queen.

'Your Grace.' Will had learned long ago that this, along with 'my lord', was the safest form of response to powerful men who failed to explain their full intentions to him. It was respectful without fully committing him to their service. The last man in the kingdom he wished to be indebted to was the Earl of Essex, however influential he might be. Something told him the man was like Icarus, and one day might fly too close to the sun. Either that or he could end up as the old queen's husband, despite a near thirty-year age gap between them. Was that what he was hoping for? Some said so, quite openly, just as they discussed his many nights 'playing cards' in the queen's bedchamber, often until it grew light again.

'What business do you have with Sir Robert?' The Earl of Southampton asked the question Will was bracing himself for and his tone was sterner than Essex's.

'A new play for the queen.' It was Cecil who answered. 'I need to ensure it contains no blasphemy or heresy, nor any hint of atheism and not a word that might encourage recusants.' He emphasised the last word and it clearly angered Southampton, who had often been branded one. Will knew that both men were intent on trying to destroy the other. It was just a question of who could strike first, and the scale of that success would depend upon the will of the queen. Right now, she needed them both, or felt she did, which was the same thing, so there was an uneasy truce at court between Cecil and Southampton. Essex and Southampton being such close friends meant that Cecil could never sleep easy, knowing how they likely plotted together against him. Now that his father, who had given the queen such good service that she fed him personally on his deathbed, was gone, he was even more vulnerable.

'I smell a plot,' said the Earl of Essex, who evidently didn't believe them. 'What are you planning with Master Shakespeare?' When Sir Robert neglected to reply to him, the earl demanded, 'Tell me.' But this too was met by Cecil with silence.

'No plot, Your Grace,' Will blurted when he could bear it no more. 'Just a play.'

'A play? What play?' and though he asked this of Will, his eyes never left Cecil's, who stared back defiantly.

'The chronicle of Henry V,' answered Cecil.

Essex seemed surprised. 'Really?' and he looked to Will for confirmation.

What choice did Will have but to support his master's statement? 'Yes, my lord.'

Essex frowned. 'Henry V? Agincourt? How ever are you going to place that upon a stage? 'Tis not possible.'

And when Will could find no answer to that, Essex lost patience with him and turned his attention back to Cecil.

'I hear you have been talking to the queen about me. No, don't deny it, but know this. When you speak of me to Her Majesty, it is as if I am in the room with you.' Southampton and the others laughed at the notion of the queen almost immediately betraying Cecil's confidences with her favourite. 'So be careful what you say of me and choose each word prudently, for if I am wronged, if my honour is questioned by anyone, then know that I will make that man pay. Do you hear me?'

Cecil stayed silent and seemed to take the threat from his enemy. Will had never seen him like this before. It was usually Cecil who made them. One of the most ruthless and powerful men in the kingdom had been reduced to the status of a naughty schoolboy being chastised by a master, but Will could not enjoy the spectacle. Essex was taking too much pleasure from Cecil's humiliation. If he did go on to rule them all, using the queen's authority, it would augur well for no one.

'It's strange,' the earl continued, 'how we can never shut you up in the Privy Council, but man to man, you are silent.' When that silence continued, the earl addressed Will once more, while continuing to stare at the object of his derision. 'Do you know why Sir Robert hates me, Master Shakespeare?'

Will felt a deep sense of dread. He could hardly fail to answer the earl, but what he said might damn him in the eyes of one, or possibly both, of the most powerful men in the kingdom. 'I do not, my lord?'

'I think you do. Imagine you are him for a moment. What if you were an actor upon the stage playing Sir Robert Cecil, the crookback pygmy, and I am Richard Burbage playing the most fair Earl of Essex.' His acolytes enjoyed the notion of Will's handsome friend playing the earl. 'Now tell me why he hates me?'

It was obvious that he was not going to allow Will to wriggle free without giving him the answer he desired; that Sir Robert was jealous because he was a small and ugly man, left wanting in fairness next to the tall and handsome Essex. Instead, Will settled on, 'Because you are the queen's favourite, Your Grace?'

'Quite so.' Essex smiled then, seeming to like this answer even more than the one he had been fishing for. 'And he is afraid of me. The great Sir Robert Cecil, the queen's spymaster, knows he cannot touch me, for I am indeed Her Majesty's favourite. All that he has, and all he will ever be, can be taken from him by her in an instant. Sir Robert knows that a whispered word from me is all it would take to destroy him. Power is what he most craves, but, when I am in the room, he has none.' Cecil looked away then, but Essex was not done. He addressed the queen's inquisitor directly now. 'Think on that the next time you speak in the Privy Council to deny me my will.'

By this point, Cecil's humiliation was too much to bear and Will longed for this encounter to draw to a close. The look on the earl's face was one of pure pleasure at the humbling of his rival.

Just then, a messenger, dressed in the queen's livery, arrived in haste and began to walk towards the earl and his friends from the opposite side of the lawn. Noting the livery, Cecil said, 'We shall detain you no longer.'

Cecil set off with Will trailing behind him, so he didn't have to listen to the queen's latest message for Essex. The breathless messenger scurried past them both as they continued. They couldn't hear the words he imparted, but they heard the Earl of Essex.

'Speak up, man! We cannot hear you!' he commanded and the messenger obeyed, booming out his orders from the queen.

'Her Majesty requests that you join her to ride out together this afternoon, if Your Grace so pleases?'

Essex had likely made the man raise his voice because he knew the queen's request would annoy Cecil. His face was in a fury.

'If he so pleases?' asked Cecil through gritted teeth. 'She is the queen and should simply command it.' And when Will had no words in response, he instructed, 'Get you gone, Shakespeare, and complete the task I have set you.'

—

Will did not wait for a second invitation to quit the privy gardens and leave the palace. As he walked back towards Shoreditch, avoiding the street hawkers and ignoring the cries of vendors' apprentices, who called at him from shop doors exhorting him to purchase their wares, he had much to think on. How had he been dragged back into Sir Robert Cecil's orbit again and would he ever be free of the man? Will knew he would have to live once more with the fear of Cecil's merciless wrath hanging over him. If he could not discover the truth about the Lady Anne's death, his own life could be forfeit. People who went against Cecil or disappointed him were quite often never seen again.

Dive thoughts, down to my soul, Will told his fears. Thinking like this would only get him further along the path to madness caused by his terrors. Will knew he had to keep a clear head if he was going to free himself from the perilous position he found himself in.

We need to know who killed her and why?

That was what Cecil had told him, as if this was a simple matter, but how could Will possibly solve the mystery of Anne's fate? He had not witnessed the act, nor knew of anyone else who saw it, barring a young, delusional servant who thought the devil himself was responsible. No one else had come forward. If no one saw it, then who could understand the reason for the act or imagine how it could have occurred? That's what he would have to do, though; imagine the crime, if there was one?

Someone had crept up on Lady Anne in the dead of night possibly, and thrown or pushed her from the balustrade, down onto the hard stone below, breaking her neck in the process. But why? If he could work that out, then he would be closer to identifying the killer, so the first question he should ask himself was why would anyone murder a seventeen-year-old girl, a lady-in-waiting to the queen no less? Who stood to gain from Lady Anne's death or, to put it another way, who might have been harmed if she had continued to live? What did she know and how could this knowledge have been used against someone who felt the need to ensure it was not? Now that he had begun to think like this, Will could not help but feel a certain sense of excitement in pursuit of the truth. Then he reminded himself that whoever killed the Lady Anne, or ordered that killing, would hardly take kindly to someone looking into the matter, on behalf of Robert Cecil, or anyone else. It meant that, from now on, Will's own life would also be in danger.

Once again, Cecil had called upon Will to do him a service, leaving him with little or no choice in the matter but to comply. A lowly man like him was powerless at court and the queen's closest advisors could act with impunity, as long as they did it in her name. Cecil could have him arrested just by stating a case for blasphemy, heresy or treason, requiring little proof to convince the queen or his fellow members of the Privy Council as to Will's guilt.

This was no fantasy but a very real danger. Not long after Will had seen his first play performed, his greatest rivals at that time had all either been tortured, murdered or imprisoned by the authorities, and who was the most powerful authority in England bar the queen? Cecil, of course. Marlowe had been killed in that so-called 'tavern brawl', not long after he was accused of blasphemy and heresy by Thomas Kyd, who had given his friend's name up under terrible torture on the rack, which had hastened his own death a year later. Thomas Nashe had been jailed around then too for publishing a satirical pamphlet.

Will then could never afford to defy those same authorities because he knew what could happen if he did. He would put as much energy as he could into this investigation for Cecil, even though it had come at a bad time. He had planned to spend that afternoon in his chamber at the inn, enjoying the lascivious pleasures of his dark lady, but by now she would be long gone, back to her husband and the court he had just left. Knowing women as he did, a little at least, she was probably cursing Will for wasting her time, perhaps even vowing never to see him again.

How could he contact Avisa to assure her he had done his best to return but had been summoned again? He could not even explain the truth of why he had been sent for. Cecil demanded secrecy in all of his dealings. In any case, Will had no desire for Avisa to know that, on occasion, he was forced to become Cecil's creature, in case that frightened her off. How would he be able to make it up to her then, when even to get a message to his dark lady ran the risk of it being intercepted by her husband or his servants? Even if he could, it would not be easy to meet when much of his time from now on was likely to be taken up with Cecil's investigation. It was all too maddeningly complicated and would have been so much simpler if they were both free. In her case, from a passionless union with her husband, the linguist John Florio. In his, from a marriage that had slowly withered on the vine, thanks largely to his absences in London.

If he was truly honest, he would have to admit to a selfish dissatisfaction at a small life in a tiny town and a marriage he had long ago outgrown. He had seen even less of Anne and the girls since Hamnet's passing. At first, it had been too painful to spend time at their home while the boy's absence haunted him so. He could see and hear Hamnet everywhere; on a chair by the hearth, in the sound made by a creaking footstep upon the stair, and once, thanks to a trick of the light, as a wraith-like figure espied through a window. For a second, it was as if Hamnet himself had been standing there locked outside their home, forlornly waiting to be let back in. Within a year, Will had purchased New Place, a twenty-room home, costing him sixty pounds, that was the largest in Stratford, if not quite the very finest. Even there, he still felt uneasy with his family, as there were four of them in their home now and not five. He could not bear it and had to get away to London once more, but misfortune seemed to follow him everywhere these days.

What he wouldn't give to be able to turn his back on his many troubles and leave forever with Avisa, perhaps for Italy, a place he had read and written about but never actually visited, though Will yearned to go there one day to see if it lived up to the country of his imagination.

Even his writing gave him no comfort of late. Will was trying to pen not just one but several plays and failing spectacularly at finishing any of them. The words would not come and, when they did, they were inadequate. How was it still so hard to write a play, when he had already completed so many? Other craftsmen learned from the toil of their earlier years to make their most recent labours simpler, but not Will. He felt he had learned nothing. It was one of life's mysteries that the writing never got any easier.

And if he did manage to finish one of those plays, where would it be performed when the company had no home? They could not tour forever, nor share the Curtain or the Rose indefinitely with other companies. This brought Will back to the problem of what to do about the Theatre, and how to find a solution that did not involve Richard Burbage killing Giles Allen, then being hanged for the crime. The problem seemed impossible to resolve. They were not allowed to even enter the Theatre now, let alone perform there, even though they owned the building, and all because it was set upon land owned by another. A building was of no use without the land it lay on. If only they could wrap it up in a cloud, float it into the air and transport it across the Thames onto some cheap land on the opposite side of the river. That would require more powerful magic than even John Dee, the queen's trusted astrologer and learned alchemist, could summon. It wasn't possible to make a building rise into the air and float it across a river, much as he might wish it so.

Unless?

Chapter Eight

*'Well hast thou lessoned us,
this shall we do.'*

—*Titus Andronicus*

In his excitement, Will almost ran into the building, causing the Burbage brothers to turn and gaze at him. He was wide-eyed and seemingly bursting with urgent news. Richard was concerned enough to look beyond his closest friend towards the tavern's exit, to ensure he wasn't being pursued by a bear.

'What is it Will?' He couldn't tell if his breathless friend was excited or scared out of his wits.

'Mark me, mark me.' Will held up a palm to halt their concerns and ensure he had their attention, while also attempting to regain his breath. 'I have an idea,' he told them between great gasps, 'and when you hear it, you will marvel at the manner in which we will confound that bastard, Giles Allen!'

—

To their credit, they heard Will out without interruption. He laid out the plan in a few simple stages, for that was as far as he had got with it. No matter. They would surely see the wisdom of his idea, then pronounce it the solution to all their ills.

When he was done, he waited for their reply, but none came. He questioned them with a look, and they stared right back at him. Then Cuthbert turned to Richard and his brother caught his eye. They exchanged no more than a glance, but their wordless communication was enough for Will to understand that, whatever they thought of his plan, they were in agreement. He waited for one of them to speak and finally Cuthbert gave him their verdict.

'Have you gone mad, Will?' he asked softly. 'I ask in earnest, because I feel you must have taken leave of your senses.'

'I have not.'

Cuthbert regarded him seriously. 'You wish to tear down our theatre?' he asked incredulously.

'I do.'

'Put the pieces on carts?' he said this as if it was impossible.

'Yes.'

'Transport those fragments to the river, then ship them to the other side?'

'Correct.'

'And rebuild the entire structure on new land we have not yet acquired?'

'The land can be easily purchased.' Will assured them.

'Oh, well then, if you have looked into the matter and it can be done easily, you have my blessing, most surely.' Cuthbert's words were dripping with scorn. 'Though it might take a moment or two to destroy the work of my father's lifetime, then perhaps an hour or more to put together the many thousands of splinters left over from the wreckage of our theatre. I hope you do not take offence, Will, when I point out that simple flaw in your plan?'

'There will be no splinters,' Will told him assuredly. 'A master carpenter can build things, so he can also take them apart again, carefully and most gently. Nails can be pulled from planks, the planks stacked, and the nails put aside and kept separate to be reused.'

'We are not talking about the destruction of a table or the reassembly of a chair, Will. There are countless nails and hundreds of planks. Taking the building apart would require days. How many carts do you think we would need and how will we float them across the Thames, answer me that?'

'On barges.'

'On barges?' He snorted at that. 'You wish to hire every barge in London for the work, for how else will we complete the task, and who will rebuild our theatre once we are across the river? You? I thought you too busy writing your plays.'

'Peter Street could rebuild it for us.'

'By himself?'

'With other men, obviously.'

'And how will they be paid?'

Will sighed. 'We are already paying a goodly number of men to stand idle every day because we often have no stage to place them on.'

'They are actors, Will, not builders.'

'They are men who can fetch and carry, and they can take instruction from Peter.'

'Can you imagine the kind of building they would put together for us? I can, and it would not last the first spring breeze before toppling over. I ask again, Will, have you gone mad?'

'I have not.'

Cuthbert crossed his arms and sat back in his chair, to indicate that he had said all he was willing to on the matter and was entirely unconvinced by Will's argument.

Will felt himself wilting then, under the weight of Cuthbert's reasoning. It had seemed like such a sound idea when he had only himself to parlay with about it, but now Will began to doubt. If only he possessed Richard's certainty. Will was an actor too, of course, and they were nearly always filled with such confidence in themselves and their own ideas that they used this to overcome all obstacles. But Will knew he was more of a writer by nature, and they always questioned everything, particularly themselves.

All the while he had been speaking, Richard had remained silent, but he appeared to at least be thinking on the matter. Will looked to his friend for support now.

'What say you, Richard? Are you both entirely in accord?'

Richard ignored Will's question. Instead, he told his brother, 'I think Will is right, Cuthbert.'

'You do?' His surprise was obvious.

'Yes.'

'How so?'

'He is clearly not mad.' And he nodded his head slowly as if in agreement with his own argument. 'Drunk quite possibly, stupid perhaps, an idiot most likely, but not mad.'

And that, surely, was the end of the matter.

If Will thought he might be allowed to leave quietly without further embarrassment or interrogation from the Burbage brothers, he was wrong. Cuthbert, however, had no desire to continue discussing an idea which involved the pulling down of their theatre. Instead, he wished to question Will about his latest visit to the palace.

'You were seen,' Cuthbert told him. 'Walking in the gardens.' And he fixed Will with a look that seemed to invite a confession. When one was not forthcoming, he told his brother, 'With Sir Robert Cecil.'

How in God's name had word of this reached Cuthbert Burbage so soon, even before Will himself had made it here? A small diversion to the inn, to make sure of what he knew already in his heart, that Avisa was gone, had been long enough for one of Cuthbert's court contacts to somehow get word of this to him.

'Oh no, Will. Not this again. No, no, no,' Richard protested. 'Whenever that man asks you for service, you put your life in his hands, not to mention all of ours.'

Will now regretted being quite so honest with Richard Burbage and his late father, James. When Robert Cecil had first asked him to become his spy against the Earl of Southampton, he had gone to them for counsel. That was five years or more ago, when Will had been tasked by the earl with solving the suspicious death of his cousin, Lady Celia. The Burbages thought him mad then, for allowing himself to be caught up in Cecil's web. Their fear of Cecil and sense of alarm, whenever he asked Will for more service, had not diminished since. They worried the entire company would be dragged down, if Will ever fell foul of the queen's Secretary of State. Will did feel a sense of guilt about that, because they were right, but what choice did he ever really have?

'Do I, Richard, and there I was thinking it was only my life that hung by a thread, every time that great man summoned me to report back to him, in the name of the queen. I never involve you and have yet to find a way to deny him, without placing myself and our entire company in even greater danger. Unless you can think of one? No?' Richard's silence was a confirmation. 'Then we are in agreement? One does not say no to Robert Cecil.' Then he added, 'But 'tis no matter.'

'It is a very great matter,' said Richard.

'No, for he did not ask me to spy for him. Not this time.'

'Are you taking us for fools, sir,' said Cuthbert. 'You were seen!'

'Come now, Cuthbert, if he was to ask me to become his creature once more, would he not summon me to some dark and secret place, instead of strolling around the garden with me, in front of the entire court?'

He was using Cecil's own reasoning here and Cuthbert thought on this for a moment, then reluctantly conceded. 'I suppose he might.'

'It was merely a conversation between the queen's trusted advisor and her favoured playmaker, on the subject of the next play I shall write for the queen.'

'And which play is that?' asked Richard, who was keen to hear this news.

'*Henry V?*'

'Agincourt? We'll need a thousand archers and hundreds of horses for that! They will hardly fit upon a stage.'

'I was given a choice,' he lied. 'It was either that or a play about our great victory against the Spanish Armada. Then I feared, I would flood your stage and half of London with it.'

A gloom descended on them all then, partly caused by the worry of presenting a play so vast that they would have had difficulty putting it on in a large field, let alone upon a stage. It was increased by their almost unanimous decision to abandon Will's impractical plan to tear down and move the entire theatre, and this brought them all back to a deep resentment towards the architect of all of their troubles, Giles Allen. They decided to drink, then drink some more, but several ales only served to bring Richard's anger bubbling back to the surface. If anything, it had grown since their meeting with the landlord.

'All that we have worked so hard towards, everything we have achieved so far, all of it gone, because he owns the land our theatre stands upon and is determined to rob us. The man is a pirate, and I refuse to let him prosper from the sweat on our backs. I'd rather burn the place down now than give it over to him.'

'I still say I have a better idea,' countered Will.

'Reason with him?' Richard was angry now. 'Is that your better idea, Will?'

'Well, it was…'

'Then it was a poor one. The man cannot be reasoned with. I'd rather we trap him in the street and beat him down with clubs until he breathes no more. I am so angry, I would laugh at the gallows if my vengeance was granted.'

'You are right, Richard.'

'You want to kill him too now?' Richard was surprised. 'Let's do it then and be done with him.'

'You are right that reasoning with the man was a poor idea,' Will clarified. 'I am done with reason but have no wish to swing for his murder. So, I say again, let's take down our theatre piece by piece.'

'Do you know how many pieces there would be?' asked Richard.

'The same number your father summoned to the site when he built it,' said Will defiantly. 'No more, no less than that and he was not daunted.'

'But he put them together; you're suggesting we tear it down?'

'Not tear it down. Remove each piece, one at a time, with great care, then place them onto carts and roll them away.'

'Do you know how many carts you would need, man?'

'No, but it could only be the same number used to bring the pieces here in the first place. Given time, it could be done.'

'And what would we do with all of those pieces?' asked Richard. 'I like the idea of taking down the Theatre, so Giles Allen could never own it, but where would we store it all and for how long?'

'We make a mark on each one so they may be recognised again later. Then place it all in a warehouse by the Thames. We find a patch of land over the river, cheap, unused and beyond the reach of the watch and the city authority.'

'I say it cannot be done,' refuted Cuthbert.

'And I say it can.' Will banged his cup of ale against the table for emphasis. It wasn't just the drink that had given him newfound confidence in his plan. He'd always thought it a good one. It was the Burbages that had scorned it, but Will wasn't going to give up trying to convince them otherwise.

'Since we have no way of proving it?' Cuthbert was dismissive.

'There is a way,' Will told him.

'How?'

'We speak to Peter Street and ask our builder whether it be folly or not?'

Chapter Nine

'My heart suspects more than mine eye can see.'

—*Titus Andronicus*

Will awoke with a sore head and the sudden realisation that he had passed the night in Cuthbert Burbage's rooms, because his own home had seemed too far away after so many ales, particularly in the dark. Will knew that Cuthbert would not mind this, but he would definitely not take kindly to what Will was about to tell him, for he had woken that morning in a quandary.

Will knew he had to find out what had happened to the Lady Anne or fall foul of Sir Robert Cecil, but he lacked something Cuthbert possessed, and he needed to draw on it now. He had, however, blatantly lied to the Burbage brothers, when he'd denied that Cecil had recruited him for some mission or other. It had seemed politic at the time to ease their fears by claiming he and Cecil were merely discussing a play to put on for the queen. Will realised he would have to admit to that lie now in order to enlist Cuthbert's help. He did not relish this prospect but reasoned it was better to embrace a little scorn from Cuthbert now than to invite more of it from Cecil later.

There was little point in delaying matters further. Will made his admission to Cuthbert while they broke their fast together. He explained how Cecil wished to understand the true nature of Lady Anne's demise at court. Cuthbert took the explanation slightly better than Will might have anticipated, in part because it showed him to have been wise in his earlier suspicions and he enjoyed being right, even if he was still unhappy about it.

'Do not involve me in any of this, nor Richard neither,' he warned. 'We want naught to do with Sir Robert Cecil.'

'Of course,' Will promised. 'I will tread most carefully.'

'Mind you do.' Cuthbert must have thought that to be an end to the matter, but Will was unable to let it be.

'Your father had friends at court,' Will reminded him.

'He did.'

'Did you retain them following his passing?'

Cuthbert gave him a disparaging look. Of course he had retained them. No theatrical company could thrive or even survive without knowing exactly what was being discussed about them at court. The Lord Mayor was constantly beseeching the Privy Council to ban all plays, shut down every theatre and force actors onto the street, since he deemed them to be the root of all sin among the populace. The queen herself regularly agreed to close the theatres' doors, whenever the numbers dying from plague rose above a certain level on the parish lists. Those closures could last for weeks, even months, so it had been important for James, and now Cuthbert Burbage, to get early warning of the way the wind was blowing.

Of course, they could never have been on an equal footing with anyone in a raised position at court, nor could they bribe their way into learning the outcome of Privy Council business from its members, but there were other ways. Great men had servants, stewards and clerks and seemed to act around them as if they were all deaf as well as dumb. These were the common men James Burbage had cultivated most successfully with small bribes. A snippet overheard at court might tell him not to concern himself overmuch about the latest rant from the Lord Mayor, for hadn't the queen herself made it clear she wanted another Christmas play? Another might tell him that the spread of plague would cause his theatre to close within a fortnight. That would buy him valuable time to begin arrangements to take his company out into the country on tour. Cuthbert kept up this practice so he could anticipate how the queen's favour and the Privy Council's appetites might affect all their livelihoods.

'Might you send word to one or more of them?' Will asked. 'That they might agree to help me in my work for Sir Robert.'

Cuthbert did not like this idea. 'I pay them coin for information pertaining to our situation, not to assist Robert Cecil in his plotting. I am not involved in intrigue, Will, merely business and I stay out of the feuds at court. We cannot be seen to choose one great master above another. It's too dangerous.'

'This is not a feud. Sir Robert wishes for me to look into the death of a young woman. That is all.'

'You are sure about that?' Cuthbert clearly doubted it. 'I wager he'll likely drag you into something bigger than a girl dying, mark me on this.'

'So, you won't help me?'

'Our friends at court, as you call them, take coin for specific news about our trade and livelihood. They will not want to be dragged into plots, and nor should you be. I refuse.'

'Well then, my way forwards is clear,' said Will firmly.

'How so?'

'I shall go and see Sir Robert this very day, to tell him I cannot help him in this matter, because I am unable to see a way into it, as no one will speak to me. Of course, he will likely have me arrested and tortured, possibly even killed.' And then he said lightly, 'And you will have no one to finish your next play... nor any other play for that matter.'

Cuthbert sighed. 'Must you be so dramatic, Will? Even for an actor?' But he appeared to at least recognise the peril Will would be placed in if he reported no progress to Cecil on the investigation into the girl's death. He thought for a moment before conceding, 'There is perhaps someone at court I can arrange an introduction to, but that is all I can promise. They see much and hear more, while avoiding the suspicions of the queen's inquisitors thanks to their discretion, but they will expect coin from you. They have been useful to us before, but be careful not to trifle with them, Will, nor place them in peril.'

'I shall not.' Then he asked: 'What is this man's name?'

Cuthbert chuckled then. 'I have just described a careful, wise and most discreet presence at court, who learns much without ever boasting of how they manage to acquire that knowledge. What on earth makes you think it is a man?'

—

When Will arrived at court later that morning, he was directed towards a room not far from Robert Cecil's. The queen's spymaster instructed Will to set himself at a desk with writing materials and to leave them there as evidence that he was completing his play about Henry V. He was instructed to actually do that, too, since the court had already learned of it, while also attempting to solve the mystery of Lady Anne Percy's death.

Cecil then told him, 'You can start by interrogating the physician-in-chief, who examined her body. Perhaps you will learn something about the killer from the manner of her death.'

'Have your men not already spoken with him?'

'Wade questioned him about her, but I want you to examine him anew, without being influenced by reports from my men. Perhaps you will see something he did not.'

'What reason would I have to ask the queen's physician about anything, let alone the death of a girl who was no kin of mine?'

'In this case, you can waive the usual need for discretion. The man is loyal to me and owes his position at court in part to my generosity of spirit.' He meant that he owned the physician and could trust him not to be indiscreet. 'He is expecting you to call on him. Go there now.'

Will left his parchments and quill pens in the room, as instructed, then hastened to see the man who had examined Lady Anne's body. Will had never met the queen's physician-in-chief but already assumed him to be a very brave man indeed, and not just because he did not quail at the notion of examining Her Majesty's person, or the prospect of informing her of something she might not want to hear in relation to her health. Will's respect ran deeper than that, thanks to the terrible fate that befell his predecessor: Roderigo Lopes, a man who had endured the worst death imaginable.

Lopes was a Portuguese Jew, who had converted to Christianity and moved to England. His excellent work as a physician and surgeon at St Bartholomew's Hospital had led him to be given his position with the queen in 1581, and to his ultimate downfall. In 1594, Lopes was accused of high treason, by none other than the Earl of Essex, who was busy setting up his own network of spies and informants to rival that of Robert Cecil's. Essex claimed Her Majesty's physician was involved in a plot to murder the queen with poison. Why he had not done this already, in any of the intervening thirteen years, was a question that was conveniently ignored during the investigation, outweighed as it was by distrust of a foreign convert, accused of still secretly practising Judaism.

Few believed the outlandish accusations at first, let alone Cecil, and not even the queen, who scolded her favourite, but Essex arrested other suspected plotters and, under torture, got them to name the doctor as a co-conspirator, sealing the man's fate. Lopes was found guilty of high treason and given a traitor's death. He was to be hanged, drawn and quartered. On the scaffold, just before they cut him open, Lopes swore his innocence and maintained he loved the queen as much as he loved Jesus Christ. This caused much laughter and derision, thanks to his Jewish ancestry, and his gruesome execution was made even worse by the mockery of the crowd. Recalling that incident now, Will resolved to be even more cautious in his dealings with the Earl of Essex.

Will found the physician in his rooms, reading from a copy of *Praxis medicinae universalis, or, A general practise of physicke*. On seeing Will, he put the book down and told him, 'You are expected.' Though he did not seem happy about that.

Here is another man who has been bent to Robert Cecil's will, he thought.

'I have enquiries,' Will said, while deliberately not mentioning Cecil's name, 'about the death of Anne Percy.'

The physician nodded. 'Just so.'

'They brought the Lady Anne to you. You were asked to examine her body?'

'I was,' he agreed. 'Her death was a most curious affair.'

'How so?'

'To begin with, she walked the castle at night with no obvious reason to do so. She was not one of the queen's usual attendants in her bedchamber, nor was she summoned there, and the direction she followed took her away from the queen's quarters.'

'Where did it lead?'

'Nowhere, as far as I could tell. Only a quiet part of the castle with some rooms that no one sleeps in.'

'If the area was quiet, then it might be a desirable place to meet someone, should that meeting need to remain a secret. Would it not?' Will surmised.

'Perhaps,' he conceded, 'but the absence of a bed might prove a hinderance, though there are those at court who would rut like beasts in a field if they could. Not her though.' And when Will questioned this assumption with a look, the physician added, 'She was *intacta*.' Then he hastily added, 'I was asked to examine her completely.'

'Even if she was still a virgin, this could have been a first meeting with a potential lover?' Will offered.

'How unfortunate for him then that she stumbled and fell to her death before he arrived.'

'You think it likely she stumbled and went all the way down the staircase?'

'A body increases in speed when it falls, which might explain how she ended there, and it was very dark.'

'She would have had a candle. Could she not have been pushed down that staircase?' Will pressed. 'Or thrown over the balustrade?'

The physician seemed surprised by that notion. 'Who would do that to a blameless girl?' He seemed to ponder the possibility for the first time then. 'She was not with child.' He perhaps envisaged that condition as the only possible cause for murdering a maid, to avoid being exposed as the father of that child and the cause of her ruin. The queen would likely jail a man if he was the despoiler of one of her own ladies. She had done it before after all. A man who wronged a lady-in-waiting and left her with child would forfeit the queen's favour and that could be ruinous for him, so murder might be their only way out, but the physician was convinced Lady Anne was a virgin when she died. 'It was for that reason I ruled out self-slaughter,' he concluded.

If Lady Anne had been carrying a courtier's bastard child, she might have killed herself instead of facing the wrath of both her father and the queen. The shame and ruination would go hand in hand with her increasingly obvious condition, but why would she do it by throwing herself down a staircase or from a balustrade? A fall like that might result in terrible injuries with no guarantee of death. There were other ways to end one's own life where you could be more assured of the right result. There were other ways to rid yourself of a baby, as well, that were safer than throwing yourself down steps, but the physician had already explained this away.

'You are sure she was a pure maid?' pressed Will.

'I am.'

'Then perhaps she aimed to meet someone for some other reason?' he observed.

'What other reason could there be, in one so young and unworldly?'

In truth, Will could think of none, but he was mindful of Cecil urging him to look for conspiracies involving great lords, as a possible cause of this terrible crime, if it indeed proved to be one?

'So, in the absence of a lover, much less a child, I concluded the whole affair was an unfortunate accident, caused by a steep and unlit staircase, and did advise the queen of this. She seemed satisfied.'

I'd wager she was, thought Will, when the alternative was a scandal, involving her lady and possibly even one of her favourites.

Chapter Ten

*'O God, that I were a man!
I would eat his heart, in the market-place.'*

—Much Ado About Nothing

Will had been ordered to report his earliest findings to Sir Robert Cecil and assumed he would walk into an interrogation. He was expecting to be met by a serious and sober-minded Secretary of State, not the exultant, almost giddy figure he saw before him now.

'The Earl of Essex has gone mad!' Will had never seen Cecil more gleeful. 'You would not believe what he has done, Shakespeare, for even you could not invent it! Once again, we were discussing the rebellion in Ireland in the Privy Council, and it became heated, as it so often does. But this time, his tone and manner towards the queen was so insolent that even she could take no more. In her fury at his impudence, she rose from her seat, advanced upon him and boxed his ears like the unruly child he most surely is.'

Will was taken aback. What on earth could Essex have said to prompt such a strong reaction, from the woman who had indulged him above all others for so long. 'Was he shamed? Did he beg her forgiveness?' Will could imagine no other outcome.

'Oh no.' Cecil was thoroughly enjoying himself now as he recounted the tale. 'The ridiculous man rose from his seat in a fury. He regarded the queen with utter contempt.' He took a deep breath now to prolong the suspense. 'Then he drew his sword on her.'

'He did not!' It was not that Will disbelieved or disrespected the queen's spymaster, simply that he could not comprehend how a man would pass an immediate death sentence upon himself, by trying to run the queen through with his rapier.

'I swear it is true. He only escaped being struck down by her guards or run through by one of the other gentlemen there, because he was grabbed and restrained by others, meaning his sword never left its scabbard. If it had, his life would have been forfeit. He is simply banished by Her Majesty, but that is enough, for now. Even he will never be able to come back to court again, let alone into Her Majesty's favour. Not after this! Before storming from the Privy Council chamber, he said he neither could nor would put up with so great an affront and indignity, neither would he have taken it at the hand of her father, King Henry VIII. He was even heard to describe the queen to his followers as being as crooked in her disposition as in her carcass. That's what he said, Shakespeare, in front of witnesses. He is finished!'

At that exact moment, their came a loud, incessant rapping at the door to Cecil's room.

'What is it? Come in, damn it!'

The door swung inwards to reveal a breathless William Wade. Whatever it was that he had to say to Cecil, he was clearly energised by his news. Only the presence of Will standing by Cecil's desk gave him pause.

'It's all right,' said Cecil, who was still in good humour, despite the interruption, at the thought of his greatest rival's downfall.

'You may wish to attend to the queen, my Lord.'

'Is she unwell?' This alarmed him.

'No, my lord.' But his tone made it sound as if it could be worse than that.

'What then?' Cecil pressed.

'Since she banished the Earl of Essex this morning, she has been unattended, save for the ladies of the Inner Chamber. I am told by... one of them' – he clearly did not wish to reveal the name of his spy in her inner chamber in front of Will – 'that she has gone from anger to regret, thence to a state of distress and even a denial of what all saw in the Privy Council.'

'How so?' Cecil was visibly subdued by this news.

'First, she had a steadfast resolution about her exiling of Essex from court. This did not last o'erlong, my lord, until she began to question aloud whether she had indeed done a just and right thing.'

'How could it not be?' Cecil demanded.

'Thence she came to a place of regret, saying she may have treated him too harshly. Further, she almost immediately began to excuse the worst excesses of his behaviour, by saying that he never meant to draw his sword upon her, nor would he ever. Next, she told all that would listen that the earl did not actually do it at all, since it never left the scabbard. Her Majesty is now said to be in a pitiful state and is raging no longer about Essex but to herself, over how she acted too harshly, in boxing his ears for such a tiny offence, and should never have humiliated him so in public. She has already sent a messenger to Essex, asking him to return to court so they might renew their previous good humour with one another. Now, while she waits for his answer, the queen sobs in her chamber and will not be consoled by anyone. That is the whole of it, my lord, and the reason for my haste in coming to you.'

If, like Will, Wade had assumed the normally resolute Cecil would leap into action and come up with a strategy to combat the queen's flawed reasoning with Essex, they were to be disappointed. Cecil's immediate reaction was to sit down, heavily, with a look of shock painted on his face.

A moment passed and then another, until Wade could no longer bear the silence from his master. 'My lord?' he asked tentatively. 'Will you not come?' Wade had obviously assumed Cecil would want to.

'She has lost all reason,' was all Cecil offered in response.

Will and Wade could not help themselves and they exchanged alarmed looks. Both of them knew how dangerous those words were, but they were even more alarming coming from the one man they could have expected to know better than to utter them in front of witnesses. The look Wade and Will shared then was a pact of sorts, to never reveal Cecil's response to anyone outside of that room, lest his own words be used to bring him down.

'I believed he was done, finished, over with, and that I might never have to see his villainous face again,' Cecil continued, 'unless his head was set on a pike at Traitors' Gate. Now, within the space of a day, the queen looks set to bring Essex back from exile and forgive him!' He shook his head in disbelief. 'Nay, not so long,' he corrected himself, 'it has been but a matter of hours since she boxed his ears and saw him attempt to run her through. He had to be dragged from her, his sword-hand held down firmly, or he would have killed her, and now, scarcely more than an hour or more since he committed that act of high treason, she regards herself as the sinner and he the sinned against? It is not to be believed!' But his anger showed that he did indeed believe it. 'Mere minutes have passed since his downfall. Is he to be elevated again already, within the half-hour?'

Will noticed that, in his raging, Cecil seemed to have lost all track of time now, as if the earl had been dragged away from his sight just moments ago.

'A beast that wants discourse of reason would have raged longer!' and he banged his fist down hard upon the table. 'It is madness,' he concluded. 'And one that afflicts us all.' He meant that no one was immune from the consequences of the queen's folly where Essex was concerned.

Cecil's outburst seemed to rob him of what energy he had left and his body visibly slumped. Wade and Will watched as he tried to compose himself. It took long enough, but eventually he straightened. His eyes had a dead look in them now, as if he had been stripped of all hope. Only a few moments before, Cecil had been exulting in the earnest belief that his greatest foe would soon be a dead man, and his own problems were finally at an end. For how could anyone recover the favour of the queen, or even be granted her mercy, if he had pulled a sword on her?

Nobody could, of course.

No one except the Earl of Essex – a man, it appeared, who would be spoiled and indulged by the queen until the end of time, or at least until her own life was ended.

Cecil stood then and his voice sounded calmer. 'I will come, of course,' he said flatly and Wade followed him from the room, leaving Will to wonder what on earth would happen next.

Chapter Eleven

'Tell truth and shame the devil.'

—*Henry IV*

Will did not have to venture far into the court to find the careful, wise and most discreet woman Cuthbert had described to him. Thanks to her work, Beatrice Shepherd was in much demand, with rooms at the centre of the palace, not far from the queen's and her ladies-in-waiting. Beatrice was that most valued of Elizabeth's courtiers: a silkwoman. She traded in silks and provided women with linen partlets to wear over their shoulders, along with embroidered blackwork collars, as well as their starched sleeves and ruffs. She regularly met with the queen's ladies and sometimes was even summoned to see the queen herself. She was one of those courtiers allowed to make a good living from her work and would have kept all the money she made. It would normally have fallen to a husband, but her trade was exempt from *coverture*, where women had no independent legal rights that were not merged to their husband's. This would not have applied to Beatrice in any case, since she had never married, though she was fair enough to have attracted suitors, preferring to serve the court instead.

Cuthbert had provided Will with a letter of introduction and the assurance that he could be trusted, urging Beatrice to 'treat him as you would treat me'. His carefully worded entreaty was designed for Will to be allowed to pay Beatrice for information. Cuthbert had assured Will that Beatrice Shepherd's proximity to the queen's ladies meant she knew almost as much about the comings and goings of nobles at court as the queen did, perhaps more so in fact, for Her Majesty only heard what she was told. Beatrice, meanwhile, had the knack of wheedling information from others during a fitting, with the innocent guise of a gossip, and everyone apparently liked to talk to her. 'If only she worked for Robert Cecil,' Cuthbert had told Will. 'Then we would have no need of the rack to stretch a prisoner for information. She could talk it out of him instead.'

Beatrice was alone and took only a moment to read Cuthbert's note before nodding to Will and leading him towards the rear of the room, passing the piles of lace, velvet and silk she was working on. Cuthbert had told Will to pay Beatrice in advance and only then tell her what information he was seeking, though Will would have preferred to do it the other way around. What guarantees did he have that Beatrice would know anything at all about the Lady Anne? But she took his coin happily enough and they began to discuss his interest in the dead woman. He showed her the portrait of Anne in miniature then and asked Beatrice if she knew her. Perhaps that was a mistake, or he had not given her enough coin to stifle her natural curiosity about him, which seemed heightened now by his ownership of the expensive likeness of the girl.

Beatrice's eyes narrowed. 'I wonder why a man like yourself should take such an interest in the daughter of a minor lord?' she asked.

Most people in London knew their place, and almost everyone at court did, but not Beatrice, it seemed. She was clearly unimpressed by his insignificant rank. If she was not fearful of a gentleman's displeasure, then perhaps he could make her imagine a greater peril. 'A man like myself has a master,' he revealed.

'You have a master?' She seemed to be mocking this notion, but didn't all men have one? 'I myself do not.'

'You have no husband, you mean?'

'I chose to have no husband for I want no master,' Beatrice confirmed.

'You think yourself free then?'

'As free as anyone in the realm.'

'So, you believe you can do as you please?' Then he added, 'As long as the queen permits it?'

Beatrice considered this, then conceded, 'I do have a mistress, but then we are all her subjects. I am not so lowly that I must sweep Her Majesty's floors, nor so raised by her that I must marry whom she pleases or come and go with her at all hours.' Beatrice seemed to think she had the perfect position at court, being both husbandless and largely ignored as someone who occupied a position between the lowliest and mightiest. As such, she managed to avoid many of the queen's rules and most of her whims. Will could see the appeal of that.

'Well, I do have a master,' he said again for emphasis. 'But I would caution you to never mention that to anyone, nor utter my name to any other who might follow me here later, for I promise that master would hear of it then, and it would not end well for thee.'

That did seem to give her pause and she had the good sense to say, 'Then I will ask no more of it.' And he resolved not to produce that miniature portrait again since it had aroused such curiosity in Beatrice.

'You said her father was a minor lord?' he said to get her back on track.

'He is a younger brother to the Northumbrian earl's late father and has less land than the mightier lords in the north. Which does rather beg the question…' She said that as if he was likely to guess at it, but he had no idea what she was referring to.

'What question?'

'Why would he part with four hundred pounds to get his daughter a place by the queen's side?'

'He paid her that much?' To Will, this was an almost unimaginable amount simply to make his daughter one of the queen's ladies. 'What advantage could it gain him to be worth such a mighty sum?'

'There was much talk of it when Anne first came to the court. I suppose his daughter could go on to marry well,' she offered, as if that daughter were not already dead. 'And his grandson might become a greater lord.'

'For four hundred pounds, he could buy her an earl.'

'Not without the queen's approval,' Beatrice reminded him. 'She must give her blessing for all unions involving the gentry, and is more likely to do so if one of her ladies pleases her with good service first.'

Will thought on this. 'But there would be no guarantee of it. The queen might not take to his daughter and earls might choose other ladies. Then his money would be wasted.'

'To please the queen directly then?' she suggested. 'By making her a gift of his money, she might look upon him favourably.'

'To a minor lord, four hundred pounds would be a fortune, but to the queen? When she has so much already?'

'Then it is a mystery and has been much commented upon.'

'By the ladies who come to you for…' He waved a hand towards the linens and silks around them, and she nodded.

'In truth, I know not why he would pay so much to get his daughter by the queen's side,' she conceded. 'But you can be sure he would not have done it unless it brought him some favour or advantage.'

Will knew she must be right about that, but, if there was advantage to be had, he could not yet see it and neither, it seemed, could she.

They talked some more of the Lady Anne, but it appeared Beatrice knew precious little about the girl or her secrets, or perhaps she was holding something back in anticipation of more coin from him? He hinted that he might be agreeable to gifting her more of it if she were prepared to share the lady's secrets.

'They would hardly be secrets if I knew them, would they?'

'I was told you were skilled at uncovering the secrets of the court.'

'Some of them, but perhaps the Lady Anne had none, except for the one she took to her grave?'

'Which is?'

'Why, who killed her, of course?' she said matter-of-factly.

'You think her killed then? She did not trip and fall?'

'If she did, she is the first maid to die in Whitehall Palace by falling down a staircase in the three hundred years it has stood here.'

'Are you not frightened by the thought of a killer in the palace?'

'I am not important enough to murder,' Beatrice assured him. 'Nor have I ever given any man cause to do it. A killer must have good reason, when he risks killing himself if he is caught and hanged.'

'Then who do you think killed her?'

She made a show of contemplating this for a while, then seemed about to offer him a name. Will waited for it with anticipation, but instead she said, 'A man.'

'A man?' he scoffed.

'It is usually a man when killing is done, though not always.'

'And the palace is full of them.' He meant that her facetious theory was of no help to him.

'Then you will need look no further to find him.'

'Enough of your games. I tire of them.' It was clear she lacked any further insight into what may or may not have been a murder at the court. Worse, she seemed to be enjoying his predicament. 'It seems

Cuthbert Burbage was wrong to send me to you. I can see that now and will waste no more of your time.' He gave a curt nod.

She ignored his words and instead said archly, 'That physician you saw today?' Christ she knew about that too, though he had not seen Beatrice, nor any other woman or man as he entered the physician's rooms. 'You weren't the only one. Her brother came by also. Before you, in fact.'

'Lady Anne's brother?'

'The same.'

'Edmund?'

'Unless she had another brother at court but kept him hidden till now.'

Obviously, it had to have been Edmund, since Anne had no other brothers and Will felt foolish now. 'When was this?'

'The morning after she died.'

'He wished to discover her cause of death?'

'Perhaps,' she said enigmatically.

'But you think there was more to his visit than that?'

'I noticed something about her brother as he went in to see the queen's physician.' There was an air of mischief about her now. 'Something that was gone when he came out again but ten minutes later.'

Beatrice was deliberately talking in riddles. Will knew he was supposed to ask her what had gone upon Edmund's return, but he also understood this to be a test of his cleverness. He was expected to reason this through, and Beatrice would judge him by his answer. Her opinion of him shouldn't have bothered Will at all, but for some reason it did.

He paused for a moment to consider it. What could she have noticed about Anne's brother as he walked into the room that was missing on the way out? Something Edmund wore or carried perhaps, but whatever it was, it had to be significant enough for her to spot it and draw her own conclusion as to what had happened inside. The answer hit him immediately then.

'His purse?' he offered.

'You are a wise one, Master Shakespeare. It looked full on the way in.'

'But was lighter on the way out?'

'It wasn't there at all.'

Anne's brother must have handed it over completely to the physician.

'But why bribe a doctor?' he demanded. 'To get him to change his mind about the reason for the lady's death?'

'Everyone knows what caused Anne's death. She fell from the balustrade, or was pushed, or she jumped, and her neck was broken. Even the queen's physician cannot alter that or say it is not so.'

'What then?' he mused, but Beatrice gave him no help. It seemed he would have to work this out for himself too. What would a lady's brother want a doctor to confirm? It didn't take Will long. 'That she was untouched?'

She mock applauded him then.

'Her brother wanted the world to know his sister died a maid.'

Beatrice nodded slowly in agreement.

'For her reputation's sake?'

She frowned at this, as if that was not the end of it, so he tried again.

'To avoid tarnishing the reputations of great men at court.'

She smiled again, but even though he had deduced it, he wasn't sure why it would matter so much to Anne's family if she was linked to a great man? Surely her death was such a tragedy for them, it would immediately outweigh the pettiness of gossip at court? Unless the status of the man involved with her was so lofty that placing him in jeopardy might lead to their own family's downfall, or the end to whatever great intrigue they were caught up in?

'Do you think she was a maid?' he asked. 'Or has someone at court had her?'

'I really have no idea.' She told him plainly.

'The women at court never speculated upon this?'

'No,' she said, but that did not mean it hadn't happened in secret. 'If you want to know more about this maid than I can tell you,' she offered, 'there's someone you could see who surely held confidences between them.'

'What confidences?'

'That is the question.'

'Who is this person of whom you speak?' He was getting tired of her way of implying without enlightening him, of dropping hints instead of clues, and wanted answers now.

She pursed her lips then, as if their identity was an even bigger and more dangerous secret than the ones she had already revealed.

Will understood and produced another coin, which he pressed into the palm she held out for it.

He did not recognise the name Beatrice gave him but resolved to go to this woman next, until she told him, 'She has not been seen at court since the Lady Anne died, though I am sure that is just a coincidence.' Her wry tone told him she truly thought it was not. 'But give her a day or two and she will be back, for she is needed here.'

Again, she did not elaborate. It was like getting information from an enemy prisoner, thought Will, not a woman bribed to explain the ways of the court to him.

'Why is she needed at court?'

'Some call her a lady, which she used to be, others an apothecary, of sorts, and still more would describe her as something like a midwife or…'

'Or?'

'Be warned, for there are a few who swear she is a witch.'

'Really? Then tell me more about this witch.'

Chapter Twelve

'Ambition should be made of sterner stuff.'

—Julius Caesar

Before Will left her, he gave Beatrice strict instructions to contact him once this apothecary, or witch, returned to court. If she knew secrets about the Lady Anne, he was keen to learn them.

Beatrice might have helped to solve another problem for him, too. Will was not happy with the name he had given the heroine of his new comedy. What about Beatrice, though? The quick-witted, sharp-tongued heroine spent much of the play bickering with Benedick, the man she loathes, until their friends trick them both into believing that each of them secretly loves the other? Beatrice and Benedick did seem to go together well. He would not dare ask her permission for using her name, though, and told himself he wasn't really, for she was not the only Beatrice in the world.

Richard Burbage had been at court that day too, trying, but failing, to enlist the help of influential men to intercede in the dispute between their company and Giles Allen. He had hoped that the Earl of Southampton, who had oft proclaimed Richard to be the finest actor in London, might intervene on their behalf and either get him to moderate his demands or actually pay Allen a sizeable enough sum for him to drop them altogether, but the earl barely heard him out. 'If it's a matter of money, then why not just give it to him, by Gad,' he had told Richard loftily, with the air of a man who little understood the lives of those without inherited fortunes.

Richard had waited for Will to give him the bad news, then they walked along the corridor to exit the court together. Another man was coming towards them but keeping to the middle of the path, as if he expected those in the way to part for him, as the Red Sea once had for Moses. Will moved slightly to one side, expecting the man to notice him and do the same, so they could both continue their progress. Instead, this stranger looked directly at him and haughtily kept to his course, deliberately crashing into Will's shoulder so hard with his own that the impact turned Will around. Now, he angrily faced the man and demanded to know what he was about?

'Who are you to talk to me?' his assailant demanded, as if Will was nothing.

'I am Will Shakespeare. Who are you?'

'Gelly Meyrick, steward to the Earl of Essex.' He seemed inordinately proud of this fact. 'And what do *you* do here, exactly?' The question was asked with derision, as if he knew that Will could not possibly be raised up as high as he was.

'I am a playmaker,' Will answered him.

'And what is that?'

'A maker of plays.'

'I am none the wiser.'

'And that is hardly my fault, sir.'

'Will is the finest writer in England,' Richard interjected. 'All men agree that he understands everything.'

'Does he? And yet he does not understand his position, nor does he see that when the Earl of Essex's man walks by, he should step to one side.'

'I understand my position right enough and would step out of the way if the Earl of Essex himself walked by, but not when it is merely his steward, who should remember his own position, as a servant.'

'That position, sir, gives me the ear of the earl and he listens to all that I tell him, about everything and *everyone*.' That last word was meant to be a threat.

'Then it is no wonder he is currently out of favour,' Will told him. 'When he listens to fools.'

'He is *not* out of favour!'

'The queen boxed his ears, man, then he drew his sword! Who advised him to do that? Was it you?'

'I was not there.' He denied this but was perhaps taken aback by a man as lowly as Will hearing of it. 'And he did not draw his sword.'

'How do you know, if you were not there?' asked Richard.

'Because it is a vile slander conjured up by his loathsome enemy, Robert Cecil, a man who is best avoided, lest when he falls, he brings others crashing down.' Here was another warning. Will realised that Essex's servant must have seen him conversing with Cecil in the privy garden.

'When a great man falls, he falls hard,' Will agreed. 'And he almost always brings his closest men down with him. Perhaps you should be the one to remember this.'

'Oh, I shall,' Meyrick promised him. 'And when my master is completely back in Her Majesty's favour – which I have no doubt he soon will be, since the queen misses him so – I shall remind him of the disrespect shown to him and his servants by certain individuals, then there will be a reckoning.' He jabbed his finger into Will's chest. 'And men will hang.'

Will took a step closer and the steward one back. 'Do that again and I will break the finger that offends me.'

Richard was clearly startled. He had never seen Will so angry. It was usually Will that was forced to step in and calm Richard's rage, not the other way around, but Richard was in no mood to cease this verbal sparring and very much approved of the way Will was standing up for himself.

There was a flicker of doubt and fear in the steward's eyes and Richard knew he would back down then. Meyrick snorted his derision at Will's threat, as if it was an empty one, but not before he had already turned away from the incensed writer and made to quit the argument altogether. 'I would not sully myself.'

When he was gone, Richard said, 'My, my, Will. You don't normally threaten a man with violence.'

Will was still furious. 'I don't normally encounter such a jumped-up boil on the end of a bull's pizzle, made o'erproud by his vaulting ambition and that of his master's. Every man should join a line to beat that fool.'

Richard laughed at this. 'Come on, Will. Think no more on it. Ale awaits us.'

But Will did think more about it. It would be hours before his natural good humour was restored. In the meantime, his mind was preoccupied by the encounter with Essex's loathsome steward, Gelly Meyrick, a man who, like his master, had walked round the court as if he ruled it, and would seek to hang enemies for his own amusement. Is this what would become of England, wondered Will, if Essex was allowed to return to favour with his rule unchecked?

–

Peter Street was staring at the Theatre intently from a little way off, as if only truly seeing it now for the first time. Their builder scratched his chin, frowned, opened his mouth as if ready to speak, paused, closed it again, then scratched his chin once more, while Will grew increasingly impatient.

'Can it be done?' he asked Street, and the builder regarded him as if he was quite mad. This was a look Will was becoming used to.

The Burbage brothers watched on with more than a passing interest as Street considered his notion that an entire theatre could be deconstructed and taken away in a day, as Will had suggested.

'It's three storeys high, Will. There are galleries, a stage and an attiring room and God knows how many beams? Then there is the ironwork, which must weigh…?' Street shook his head to indicate that he had no idea how much all the ironwork would weigh, but it would be a lot.

'Yes, but can it be done?'

'You want to take this theatre down, beam by beam and piece by piece, in a day, load it onto a dozen or more carts and transport the entire building to my warehouse on the Thames, so it can be stored for the winter? Then you want me to put it all back together again in spring, on a piece of land on the other side of that river?'

'Aye,' said Will. 'What say you? Can it be done?'

'No.'

The Burbage brothers let out a sound in tandem. It was part exasperation at Will's plan being so easily foiled and part satisfaction at being proved right to mistrust it.

'Are you certain?' probed Will.

'Yes.'

'Damn it all to hell.' Will was out of ideas now and he made as if to walk away.

'Not in a day,' Street said and Will turned back to him.

'Wait, are you saying it *could* be done… with more time?'

'All can be done if time is of no concern, but I suspect you want it done in a day for a reason. I would wager that reason is likely to be your landlord, who would set men about you if you tarried overlong.'

Will waved that away as if it were of little consequence. 'How long then? How many days would you need to do this just as we said?'

Street frowned at this, thought on the matter, then frowned some more. 'Three days, at least, perhaps four. Yes, four.'

'Four days?' asked Richard. 'We haven't got four days. Giles Allen would be here or hereabouts as soon as word reached him of our plan. He is rarely far from his business in London and then not overlong and he would, as you say, set men about us.'

'That's the end of it then,' pronounced Cuthbert sadly.

But something in Will stubbornly refused to give up on the idea. He thought some more and came up with another suggestion. 'What if we wait until Christmas? It's not long away.'

'What difference would that make?' asked Cuthbert.

'Giles Allen always celebrates Christmas at his family home in Hadleigh. He will be gone to Essex for days. More than four, I'd wager.'

'That's right, he does,' agreed Richard. 'Always. Why should this year be any different?'

'Nothing is certain,' warned Cuthbert. 'What if he changes his plans?'

'Won't he leave men behind to guard his property?' asked Street, and when Richard looked sternly upon him, he amended his words. 'That which he considers to be his property.'

'He will,' said Cuthbert. 'There are men there already, in fact.' And he tilted his head towards the small group standing off to one side outside a tavern not far from them, ready to intervene if they tried to force their way into the Theatre. 'Big men,' he added as if that was not already obvious.

'One or two,' admitted Will. 'Three or four at most. But we are many. An entire company would be more than a match for them.'

'You want to ask a company of players to start a brawl, then tear down a playhouse?' asked Cuthbert. 'They won't stand for that.'

'They will if it is the only way to ensure they have bread in their mouths, and it is,' Will assured him. 'We must unbuild this theatre, then carry it across the water, on our backs if we have to, or all will be lost.'

'They will come,' said Richard. 'Once they know the nature of our plan and there is not a man among them who would not want to be there to see the look on Giles Allen's face when it's done.'

'I confess I would like to see it too,' admitted Cuthbert. 'For he is a most wicked and greedy landlord.' He took in the Theatre's size anew. 'But the building is so very big, and we have naught but a few tools and our bare hands.'

'Tearing down a building is no quick thing by itself, Will,' said Richard. 'And if they resist, which is most likely, there will be a fight. Blood will be spilt and men hurt, perhaps even killed. Are you prepared for that?'

'I have thought of it, and I am.'

'But can we really do this?' Richard pleaded.

'We can and we must,' said Will.

Cuthbert offered no more objections, saying only, 'We should at least try. But might I make a suggestion? If we assemble the company, should they perhaps be armed?'

Richard laughed grimly. 'To the teeth.'

Chapter Thirteen

'That a woman conceived me, I thank her.'

—Hamlet

Witch or no, Will was resolved to see the woman that, according to Beatrice Shepherd, held confidences between the Lady Anne and herself. After explaining that she was also an apothecary of sorts, Beatrice had described witnessing the two of them walking together on more than one occasion of late, sometimes in the morning and even just before it became dark. She had noticed it because of the difference in the women's ages. These were not two equal companions with a shared experience of the world because of the way they were both treated at court. This was, rather, a younger woman being guided by the older, while seeking counsel from her. At least that was the way it had looked to Beatrice, and Will took note of it.

'Who are you to me or I to you, Master Shakespeare?' There seemed to be no sensible reason for his presence here at Lady Dudley's door, but nor did she appear to be angered by it, just puzzled.

'I was told you might be able to help me, Lady Dudley. In return for a consideration.' He was trying to put the matter of money delicately, but she did not seem offended by his offer. It might well have been most welcome, in fact. Beatrice had informed him that Theodosia Harington, better known at court as Lady Dudley, was penniless, since she had been most cruelly abandoned by her husband, who had 'run off with a collier's daughter'. Whatever the truth of that story, Theodosia still had a place at court, albeit a lowlier one now, and she was reduced to making a living of sorts, using her scholarly knowledge of roots and herbs, tinctures and potions, making her a kind of apothecary to ladies who valued her discretion. They sought her help or advice on all manner of things. Perhaps that was why the Lady Anne had walked with her.

'I have of late...' He hesitated then. On the way to her door, he had considered all manner of pretended ailments to confide in her, the better to gain Theodosia's confidence before bringing up the subject of the Lady Anne.

'Go on,' she urged.

'Lost all my mirth,' he said suddenly, for it was the truth, though he had not intended to speak of it to her until now. Ever since Hamnet's death, mirth was something he neither recognised nor welcomed. He realised if there was one thing he might have liked to find a cure for, it was that.

'You have a melancholy disposition?' she said. 'This is a lighter form of madness but should be treated before it becomes a strong contagion of the humours.'

'How would you suggest I combat it?'

'You have lost hope?' she asked him and when he did not immediately reply, she asked, 'You have lost someone?'

He nodded stiffly.

'Then we should look to heal your spirit to prevent erratic behaviour.'

'And how would we do that?'

'By purging. Rhubarb and dandelion root are good for it, as is ginger and elderberry, but for a more complete purge of the bowels take tea made from the senna plant, which is known as purging cassia. I can obtain some for you.'

'This purging of the bowels puts an end to melancholy?' He was doubtful, but she assured him that physicians all over Europe recommended such treatments, and that people suffering from the melancholy would naturally improve once their bowels were empty, so he agreed to buy some of this senna from her to continue the ruse that he was there to be treated by her.

'How did you hear of me?' she asked lightly.

'I was told you had knowledge of many healing roots and herbs,' he replied.

'And who told you of that? I did not think it widely known outside of the inner court.'

He looked her full in the eye then. 'The Lady Anne.'

She did not react at all and there was no flicker of suspicion in her face, but that in itself was telling. Surely his mention of a young lady of her acquaintance, who had so recently and tragically died, was worthy of some comment? Her silence on the matter might come from a fear that she might incriminate herself in some way. Did she perhaps believe she was being interrogated by an agent, of either the crown or a great noble? If she was indeed frightened of that, he decided to press home his advantage.

'I understand you spent time with her?'

'That is no crime.'

'In and of itself, no. It is not.'

She was immediately suspicious. 'What is your meaning?'

'Spending time with the lady is no crime. What was discussed between you might have been.'

'I spoke of nothing more than one lady might say to another.' And when he questioned her further with a look, she revealed, 'Embroidery, the latest fashions from Europe, passages from her prayer book.' She recited with little conviction.

'So, Lady Anne walked with you early in the morning and at nightfall, so you could talk of foreign fashions.' He glanced at her own simple dress to show his scepticism. 'And prayers.'

She bridled at that. 'Prove otherwise.'

'I really don't have to. All I need do is report that I was unconvinced by your explanations. Intrigue will be assumed, perhaps even treason.'

'Treason?' He could tell even the mention of the word frightened her. 'To whom will you report this?'

Since he was expressly forbidden to give Robert Cecil's name to anyone, Will ignored this and instead attempted to give the impression he was deliberately withholding that information to intimidate her. Perhaps it was better for Lady Dudley to know little but imagine the worst.

'You met with the lady repeatedly and have given me no convincing explanation for the time you spent with her. I am an actor by profession. I know bad lying when I see it, but perhaps you will be more truthful during interrogation.'

'It was not treason,' she swiftly protested. 'It was another matter.'

'Say it then.'

'I cannot.'

'Then you must live with the consequences of your silence.' He meant hard questioning, and did not have to explain this to her. She understood right enough.

'Wait. I wish only to protect the lady's reputation, in death as I would in life.'

'A most noble intent, but think of the cost to you, when you could join her in death.'

He let her think on that and watched as she wrestled with her conscience, before deciding the Lady Anne's reputation might not be worth her own life. 'I simply taught her what to do when a woman falls.'

'Falls?'

'I think Master Shakespeare, you know exactly of what I speak.'

'She was with child?' That might explain her brother's hasty visit to the physician, in an attempt to protect Anne's name. Loss of virtue was one thing but the possibility of a child outside of wedlock would be an even greater scandal.

'She *may* have been.'

'Was she or was she not?'

'We never spoke directly of it. Instead, she talked of *a friend* who might have done something foolish and may now be regretting it.'

'Yet you thought she was speaking of herself?'

'That is not uncommon when a woman's honour is at issue. To talk loosely of a "friend" is a delicate way to approach the matter.'

'But why approach *you* with it and not another?'

'Because women of the court know that I have knowledge of such things. I know how to bring down flowers.'

Will did not understand her at first and his confusion must have shown on his face.

'There are certain plants or herbs that can prevent…'

'A birth?'

She mocked that with a look. 'This is long before birth. Before a quickening even. It is not even a child then.'

'And what flowers can prevent a child, or rid a woman of one?'

'Rue is a herb of grace,' she answered.

'What is the meaning of that?'

'It has a bitter taste,' she told him. 'To rue is to regret what one has done, but it is also the name of a herb that can help undo what has been done.'

'These matters are forbidden surely?' But Will knew he was revealing his own lack of knowledge here. Such things were never discussed among men but must have been between women, who had far more to lose from the consequences of a dalliance with men of the court, particularly if it led to a pregnancy. He was surprised, though, that well-born ladies of court all seemed to know of such matters and felt free to discuss them between themselves, especially since the queen was known to be so strict about such matters. Any lady of hers who was found to have transgressed would be publicly disgraced and banished from court at the very least. Perhaps that was precisely why these solutions were talked about by her ladies then, to avoid the queen's wrath.

'There are receipt books in every household that contain knowledge of such medical matters, and they are not just for maidens,' she informed him. 'A married woman who has children risks her life during every birth. When she has had enough, she might say "no more" and act to prevent them.'

Will was aware of the existence of receipt books, of course, but he had always assumed they included only recipes, not ways to end a pregnancy.

'And what of an unmarried woman? Where could one of the queen's ladies meet a man in secret, when eyes are upon her at all times?'

'There is a tiny bedchamber just off from the maidens' chamber. I am told the occupant can sometimes be persuaded to vacate it, for a time, to allow lovers to meet there. There are other secret places too in the palace.'

'Tell me, are all the women of the court expected to be pure?'

'The unmarried ones, yes.'

'And are they?'

'If the queen orders her ladies-in-waiting to stay virgins, then they must be,' she answered opaquely, 'for no one would dare disobey the queen.'

'And risk being punished by her,' he offered. 'Cast out, with disgrace brought down upon her family. So, if a young lady *was* to fall, then she would do almost anything to avoid that fate, perhaps even take her own life.'

'There are other ways.'

'To prevent a child, yes. To prevent gossip, however...'

'There will always be gossip, but there is a way for a young maid to prove her virginity if the queen orders it.'

'How can she publicly prove such a private matter?'

'With an examination by the court physician, who will decide whether a woman is still a maid and inform the queen of the outcome.'

'The queen will take his word on this?'

'She will, and so will the rest of the court, if she pronounces it so.'

'But if the woman is not...?'

'A virgin? Then she will still be examined by that physician, and he might pronounce her so anyway.'

Will considered this. 'Because he wishes to save her reputation and spare her family shame?'

She smiled at his naivety and shook her head.

He tried again. 'For a price?' and he recalled Lady Anne's brother and the purse he carried on his way in to see the physician, and how it was missing on the way out. She did not contradict him. 'You are saying the queen's physician will take bribes to pronounce a woman a maid when she is not one?'

'Sometimes the physician will eschew the examination entirely, if the lady swears she is of good character, though he will of course expect his fee to still be paid.'

'And that fee is as one might expect it to be, when dealing with prosperous ladies of the court.'

She gave him a half-smile in agreement.

Will knew that the queen expected purity in her maids and that, when they did finally marry, a high value was placed on their chastity, which was sold to her future husband along with his new bride. He also knew that anything with such a high value would likely be protected at all costs.

Will did not care whether Lady Anne was a maid or not. Her virginity, if it had been lost, was only important to him because of who might have taken it from her. If she'd had a lover, then what if they had tired of her or were promised to another? Perhaps they were already married or were one of the queen's favourites, which was almost the same as being married to her. The Earl of Essex, for example, was supposed to be pledged to her, in some form of presumably platonic love, though he was already married. Considering the differences in their ages, how would Her Majesty react if she learned that one of her favourites was actually tupping her ladies-in-waiting? Not well, he imagined. The queen's rages were feared, her jealous ones more so. What fate would she afford to someone who deflowered one of her ladies outside the sanctity of marriage, and what might she do to the lady? It was in her power to take everything you had.

'Anne also asked for herbs that could aid sleep,' she told him.

'She could not sleep?' he asked. 'That is a sign of a troubled mind, is it not?' He assumed an unmarried girl who was with child would doubtless struggle to sleep at night.

'I gave her valerian root,' she answered without commenting on the state of Anne's mind. 'A quantity boiled in a broth can bring on a deep sleep.'

It seemed to Will that he was finally beginning to understand the Lady Anne's life. Thanks to his discussions with the physician, then Beatrice and now Theodosia Harington, he was managing to piece it together one bit at a time. The queen's doctor had pronounced her pure, but a bribe from her brother might have secured that assurance. She had spoken to Theodosia about herbs to end a pregnancy and to get a potion that could aid sleep with a troubled mind. She was likely with child then, but was she killed, or did she take her own life? Either way, he had found the most likely reason for her death. For one of the queen's ladies to have a child out of wedlock would have been an enormous scandal and reason enough to end a life, but who was the father? If he could discover that, Will might then be able to name her murderer.

Chapter Fourteen

'Nothing emboldens sin so much as mercy.'

—*Timon of Athens*

Will had wondered if Avisa might help him to better understand the world of women at court but thought not to trouble her with such matters, at least at first. Not until they were lying in each other's arms afterwards did he mention it to her. He was worried she might not have forgiven him, for being dragged away to calm Richard Burbage and then to court, but it was as if that had never happened, and Avisa had been in a playful, saucy mood that day. Her need for him was less urgent than it had been before, but she did not disguise the joy she still took from the act. He wondered how her earnest husband, John, could neglect her so. He always seemed to be so busy with one thing or another. When he was not translating some scholarly work for the Earl of Southampton, or writing poetry for the court to mull over, he was also a teacher. Some even whispered that he had been used by Francis Walsingham as a code breaker to end the Babbington Plot. All this left Will wondering if he had any time left for his wife at all? That might explain her presence in his bed.

'You are often at court with your husband,' he observed.

'I am often at court without my husband,' she corrected him.

'How is that so?'

She explained. 'We are both regularly at Whitehall, but John works on compiling his new dictionary, translating Italian words into their English meaning. It takes many hours of his day. I scarcely see him at all and am left to amuse myself.' Then she added, 'At court and elsewhere.' She tapped his chest with her finger to indicate that he was the amusement she was currently finding elsewhere. It would have been tempting to forget his questions about the court then, and simply lose himself in Avisa's arms once more, but Will resolved to put that thought out of his mind, at least for the moment.

'What is it like at court, for a lady I mean?'

She considered that for a moment. 'The court holds the best and worst of everything. There is an abundance of food and wine, and all the pleasures that can be found in England are there, from music and poetry, to books and your plays.' She was reminding him of how they had first met, when she had sought him out after a performance of *Romeo and Juliet*, and confessed it had made her weep. 'The women there are the best educated, most accomplished and well born. They can sing, play music, ride, stitch and sew works that would rival a painter's. But they are a nest of vipers too. They have too much time and their days are long, so they fill them with gossip. No woman wants to be the subject of that gossip.'

'Idle hands are the devil's workshop.'

'Indeed.'

'Some of those ladies are favoured more than others,' said Will. 'Explain to me the customs of Her Majesty with regard to her ladies-in-waiting.'

She did not question his interest and must have assumed it was a writer's. 'There are two kinds. The ladies of the privy chamber and the ladies of the bedchamber. The ladies of the bedchamber are in the position of highest esteem, since they attend to Her Majesty at the beginning and the end of every day. They are most intimate with her, helping to make up her face, apply her wig and dress her in all her finery in the mornings, then getting her to bed at night. This all takes time. More so now that Her Majesty is no longer such a young maid.'

'It takes longer to paint the portrait required of her?' he mused. 'To be the ever-youthful woman, who never ages nor inspires in her subjects a fear she may one day die and leave them to fend for themselves.'

'Quite so.'

'And the ladies of the privy chamber? What do they do?'

'They are the queen's companions during the day. They help to amuse her when she is not in front of the entire court.'

'It would not be considered seemly for her to have men in that company?'

'Men are sometimes allowed, and it is considered seemly, but only if there are other ladies present.'

'And what happens when men are allowed to be near the queen, yet she dismisses ladies from her presence?'

'Then those ladies talk.'

'And what do they talk about, I wonder?'

'I think you know. They ask themselves what goes on behind the closed doors of her private apartments when the Virgin Queen is in there alone with a man.'

'And what does go on, do you imagine?'

'Oh, I could imagine any number of things taking place,' she teased. 'Conversation, a game of cards, some innocent frivolity perhaps.'

'Is that all?'

'The queen doth say so and I would never doubt Her Majesty.'

'The Virgin Queen?' He gave her a look to indicate he doubted this.

'Perhaps she still is, even now.'

'You believe it so?'

She avoided his question. 'If the unmarried queen of a great country gave up her maidenhood and was left with child, I cannot imagine a bigger scandal, can you?'

'It would be a great risk,' he agreed. 'At least it would have been, if that queen were still young.'

'Now imagine denying yourself the blessing of physical love for years, decades even.' Her tone was coquettish now. 'Wouldn't you long for it?'

'I long for it within days,' he informed her.

She laughed at that. 'I know you do.'

He wondered what exactly she was trying to tell him? That the queen must have been terribly lonely and frustrated with her sexless life, or that she couldn't possibly have lived one for so many years?

'It would be most unnatural for a woman to deny herself contact with a man for her whole life, but to actually take one as her lover would be incredibly dangerous for them both.'

'And so?' he asked.

'There are ways to *be* with a man that do not involve the risk of bearing him a child. All unmarried ladies are aware that they cannot be anything more than a virgin on their wedding night. If there is no blood on the sheets in the morning, they risk being sent away in disgrace by their new husband and branded a whore. But they can kiss and be kissed, touch and be touched and imitate the actions of marriage in other ways. The French are famed for it, are they not? Though why they should be noted for this act above other nations, I cannot tell.'

'You think the queen—'

She interrupted him then, 'Is a virgin? Yes, quite likely. Has she always been entirely maidenly with her favourites over the years? Who knows what caresses they have exchanged once her ladies are sent to the maidens' chamber for the night?'

'You think perhaps that when the Earl of Essex arrives to play cards...'

'They play cards, or so says Her Majesty.'

'I see,' he said. 'And I suppose that when the queen was a young woman, she would know how to please a man and he how to please her, without risking a child.'

'All ladies know of this.'

'Is it really spoken of openly between you?'

'Not openly. No one confesses it. They merely hint in gossip that this lady or that lady has ways to ensure she does not fall.'

'They use the examples of others when they really talk of themselves?'

'They acknowledge what all know and do, by hinting at it through the assumed actions of another. That is how knowledge is passed from one maiden to the next.'

'And what of knowledge of other things, such as when a woman falls?'

'That is another matter and only whispered between friends with the greatest of trust between them, yet all women acquire a knowledge of these things. We learn what herbs might prevent a child or ensure that one never grows inside the belly. These things are passed from woman to woman.'

'Without men knowing of it,' he mused.

'What man wants to know of such things?' She was dismissive. 'It falls to a woman alone to protect herself from ruin.'

Later, Will thought on this some more, and he kept coming back to one thing Avisa had said that might help him the most. *That is another matter and it is only whispered between friends with the greatest of trust between them.*

Why had he not thought of it before? Anne lived in the maidens' chambers with the other young ladies-in-waiting. If she had a very close friend there, would they not perhaps share confidences between them? He already knew that Theodosia was an older woman Anne went to for advice, and that certain things between them were only hinted at, but to a true friend she might have revealed more. She could have told her everything, in fact, including the identity of her lover. With Anne now dead, that friend could be the one person left who might know Anne's secrets. If he could discover who this was, and he was careful how he questioned the girl, she might even reveal them to him.

Chapter Fifteen

'Brevity is the soul of wit.'

—Hamlet

Will Kempe had been on stage at the Curtain for almost twenty minutes, but some groundlings remained to witness the very end of his latest comedic jig. It always closed the show, no matter what came before it, whether history, comedy or tragedy, and the rest of the players in the Lord Chamberlain's Men were used to being less favoured by the groundlings, for they all loved Kempe, usually.

Will and Richard Burbage watched him now from the side of the stage, as he twirled and ducked, danced and pirouetted, mugging at the audience and coaxing laughter from them, with a twist of his face to signify mock shock or faked humiliation at a pretended stumble or misplaced step. They were still laughing, but not as heartily as they had been when he was only five minutes into his jig.

'He has been out there overlong,' said Will.

'That jig gets more prolonged with every performance. Kempe needs the applause more than he ever did.'

'It is as if increase of appetite had grown by what it fed on,' observed Will.

Richard turned to him and said, 'You should use that.' And when his friend did not react. 'You already have, haven't you?'

'Wait and see.'

Richard would have answered him but was cut off by Kempe, who danced right up to them at the side of the stage. He grabbed Richard then and pulled him back onto the stage to repeat the same two-man jig they had performed at the beginning of his act. Richard pretended to be amused at being accosted by Kempe. He even received a few half-hearted cheers for his reappearance, but Will wondered why

Kempe could not see that even the groundlings were beginning to tire of him.

Kempe clasped Richard's hand, and they twirled each other around like two drunks dancing at a wedding. A large false smile was painted across Richard's face until Kempe turned back to what he seemed to believe was *his* audience, leaving Richard free to bounce from the stage, his smile immediately vanishing. 'The man is insufferable,' he told Will. 'Drag him off, for the sake of God and the theatre, for he offends both!'

'Have you noticed the gaps?' asked Will, for more groundlings were leaving but Kempe danced on. 'Does anyone who still remains even remember the play they came to see?'

'He has been dancing so long, I have almost forgotten it.' And this from the leading man of that afternoon's performance of *Much Ado About Nothing*.

'At least it was a comedy,' observed Richard. Anyone who had seen their *King John* or *Henry IV* recently would have had the memory of it tainted by Kempe's bawdy antics.

He finally made one last leap, landing theatrically by the edge of the stage, then took his bow to quite slender applause from the diminished audience.

'I need to explain to Master Kempe that we are a *company* of players,' said Will, 'and that my plays are not about him.'

Kempe was bowing and waving at the groundlings as he exited at the opposite end of the stage to Richard and Will.

'Much ado about nothing, indeed,' said Richard venomously.

—

They were in a foul enough mood already thanks to Kempe, but Cuthbert Burbage brought them more bad news. Will and Richard went to his rooms to take him for supper after the play. His first words on seeing them rocked them both.

'He's going to tear it down.' The look on Cuthbert's face told them everything they needed to know. *He* was Giles Allen and *it* was their theatre.

'Says who?'

'Says Allen, and now so says everyone else. He was in the tavern telling anyone who would listen about the insolence of the Burbages and impudence of Will Shakespeare. Not only will he not back down over the lease, but he has decided there is more coin to be had in other uses of the land. He intends to pull down the building in the new year, sell the materials and start afresh.'

'The bastard.' Richard was appalled by this wanton act of vandalism.

Will's idea to take down the Theatre, piece by piece, and reassemble it elsewhere had seemed a daunting prospect, but it was surely all they had left now. The building was huge and contained heaven knows how many parts, the majority of which were made of wood. They had become toughened over the years from being exposed to the elements, making them less pliable than virgin timbers. The difficulty of removing then storing the materials, until they could find and lease a patch of land large enough to rebuild on, meant that none of them really wanted to take on this Herculean task, but now they knew there was no prospect of Giles Allen ever coming to an accommodation with them.

'He has been foolish to boast to everyone about his plans,' Will said. 'All that has done is harden my resolve. If he plans to tear down our theatre in the new year, then we shall take it apart over Christmas, while his back is turned. We must screw our courage to the sticking place. Think of the look on Allen's face when he finds his land empty with all of the timbers gone.'

Richard considered this. 'I'd settle for that, though I do still reserve the right to kill the villain later.'

Chapter Sixteen

'If you crown him, let me prophesy,
The blood of English shall manure the ground
and future ages groan for this foul act.'

—Richard II

Since Will's last visit to court, Cecil's most dire prediction had come true. Her Majesty had not only forgiven the Earl of Essex for his attempted attack on her, but the rumour was that she had also, in private at least, even apologised to him for boxing his ears in public. It was astonishing to Will that not only had he escaped severe punishment, and even received a quite undeserved apology from Her Majesty, but this was still apparently not enough for Essex. The man seemingly continued to hold onto a grievance about the incident, when surely it was the queen who was the more wronged? Indeed, it had taken many entreaties from intermediaries, including Mountjoy and Southampton, before he had finally agreed to end his childish sulk and return to court. Now that he was back, everyone, including Cecil, was forced to act as if the whole incredible episode had never happened, because that was the way the queen wanted it.

Will was walking towards his writing room at the palace, hoping to avoid Cecil, when the Secretary of State suddenly appeared, marching purposefully towards his own rooms. He beckoned Will to follow him and, once there, Will fully expected to be interrogated about the Lady Anne. It seemed however that the urgency around solving the mystery of her fate had been overtaken by events. 'I have just come from the Privy Council,' Cecil told him. 'Ireland is talked of endlessly there and the queen has decided it must be tamed. Fifteen hundred Englishmen have been massacred by O'Neill's rebels at the Battle of the Yellow Ford.' No wonder Cecil's mind was on Ireland alone. This was a stunning defeat for the queen's army. 'The rebels must be put down. But the question remains, who should lead the queen's force to rout O'Neill's men?'

'Who is likeliest to be her colonel?'

'Every man who serves the queen longs for the chance to prove himself to Her Majesty, by leading her armies into battle,' he said, 'but not in Ireland. It is a most inhospitable place, full of savage people, and it rains constantly. Ireland is cold and wet, there is much mud and fever, with little glory to be had there. The queen will still reward a man who can vanquish the rebels and restore her authority, though it is no Cadiz.'

His mention of the Spanish port recalled the previous exploits of the Earl of Essex, who was commonly known by the populace of London as 'the hero of Cadiz'. Three years earlier, he had inflicted a notable defeat on the Spanish there in a raid. In typical fashion, Essex had gone on to squander most of the treasure and much of the goodwill acquired in that action.

'Will Essex offer to lead? Surely this would be the obvious way to bring himself back fully into the queen's favour?'

'She perhaps wants him to,' Cecil mused, 'but also wishes him to stay by her side and never leave England again. He is like a hound leashed in by her, straining to get away and seek glory in Her Majesty's name, but Ireland has little appeal.'

'Would you want him at the head of an army, my lord?' Will doubted this, but it was always hard to tell Cecil's mind. He saw things differently to other men, but would he prefer Essex to be away from court, so he could not interfere in government, or fear his rival more if he had thousands of soldiers at his command and the queen's authority behind him?

Cecil did not choose to answer that. Instead, he said, 'For the moment, she seems to favour Baron Mountjoy to lead her army.'

Everyone with even the most limited knowledge of affairs at court knew of Charles Blount. He was one of those four great men Cecil told Will he trusted least at court. The 8th Baron Mountjoy was the coming man and another dandy, like the Earls of Essex and Southampton whom the queen favoured, just as she had once favoured Walter Raleigh before them. Handsome enough to have caught Elizabeth's eye at a young age, Blount was cut from the same cloth as other men she admired and engaged with in the art of courtly love. The queen flirted and allowed herself to be flattered and courted, as if she were not decades older than the men who fawned on her and sought her favour in return. Mountjoy was an able horseman, fencer and a soldier, whose presence in court and approval from Her Majesty had initially placed him in direct opposition to the Earl of Essex, who soon became jealous of this new arrival. Things almost inevitably came to a head when they quarrelled so vehemently it led to a duel.

Essex fully expected to defeat his new rival in front of the courtiers, but Mountjoy managed to disarm him and slash his leg in the process. Will would have expected this public humiliation to be the beginning of a lifelong enmity between two bitter rivals, but it proved to be the starting point of an unlikely friendship, forged by a mutual respect in the aftermath of that duel. Their ties were undoubtedly strengthened further by Mountjoy's choice of mistress, Lady Rich, the Earl of Essex's sister, who was now close to both men.

'He is a friend of Essex, is he not?' asked Will.

'And his rival for the queen's affections. Essex does not want to go to Ireland, but nor does he wish to see another man take his place there, to win honour by serving Her Majesty with distinction. If she sends Mountjoy and he distinguishes himself in the field, then perhaps he might become the queen's new favourite. Essex couldn't countenance that. He is already telling the queen that Mountjoy has too little experience of the battlefield, even though he was shot and wounded in the Lowlands.'

'So, Essex will volunteer himself to lead her army?'

'I am beginning to think he has to, but he would be a dreadful choice. Openly, I cannot be seen to doubt him and must back his appointment publicly, but when I am alone with the queen...' He left Will under no illusion that he would be doing everything he could behind the earl's back to prevent Essex from being sent to Ireland to win glory and even greater favour. That was a dangerous game, for had not the earl himself cautioned Cecil against doing just such a thing, reminding him, *When you speak of me to Her Majesty, it is as if I am in the room with you.* And yet Cecil must have thought that the risk of doing nothing was even higher. Then Cecil seemed to remember why he had taken Will back into his service, and he asked, 'Have you found Lady Anne's killer?'

'No, my Lord, not yet but—' He was about to go into some detail on his progress so far for Cecil's benefit but was interrupted.

'Then do not trouble me again until you have. I have no time for it.' And he waved Will away contemptuously.

—

Will's luck was out. No sooner had he left Cecil's rooms and was hoping to quit the palace entirely than he ran into his sometime patron, Henry Wriothesley, the Earl of Southampton, who was walking with the same Baron Mountjoy he had just been discussing with Cecil.

Will bowed low, hoping to be excused to continue on, but the earl had other ideas.

'Shakespeare. A word,' he said and beckoned him to one side so they could have that word discreetly while others passed by. 'I have a mind to commission you to write a sonnet.'

'On what theme, Your Grace?'

'Marriage,' Southampton told him. 'It has been almost a year since I risked everything I had to marry my most earnest love.' This was no exaggeration. The earl had indeed married his pregnant mistress, but he had not sought the permission of the queen. She might very well have refused to grant this, since the woman he had despoiled was no less than her chief lady-in-waiting, Elizabeth Vernon. The queen did not take the unauthorised marriage well and subsequently sent both bride and groom to the Fleet Prison, but only briefly. Will surmised that the Earl of Essex may have been instrumental in securing clemency from Her Majesty for one of his acolytes, but, though free, Southampton was still somewhat out of her favour, and he knew it.

'You wish me to write a sonnet for you about your most virtuous and admirable lady wife?'

'I do.'

Will considered this, then suggested, 'Then might you also commission a second sonnet from me?'

'On what subject?'

'The queen's endless wisdom and most merciful qualities.'

Southampton seemed taken aback at first, but he could not fault Will's suggestion. 'That might be politic under the circumstances,' the earl agreed but almost instantly his attention was diverted. 'We will talk more on this another time,' he announced, because the Earl of Essex was marching in their direction now, and even the great and lofty Earl of Southampton acted like a well-trained hound on a leash whenever the queen's favourite appeared.

It was not that the Earl of Essex had any intention to confide in Will. It was simply that he cared naught whether he was there or not. His comments were aimed at his close friends, Mountjoy and Southampton. 'Sir Robert Cecil seeks to undermine me with the queen,' he announced solemnly, and Will knew then that Cecil's tactics had backfired on him, with the earl instantly learning the truth of them. 'He lets it be known that he thinks I am the best man to lead her campaign against the Irish rebels.'

'Because he wants you away from court, obviously,' countered Mountjoy.

'So it would seem, and that is why I have always resisted the temptation to take this command, until now.'

'You must not take it,' cautioned Mountjoy. 'Bagenal lost fifteen hundred men at Yellow Ford, all slaughtered by that rebel O'Neill's men, Bagenal included.'

'But I am no Bagenal,' Essex reminded Mountjoy, 'and he had but four thousand men in his army, to tame the whole of Ireland. I would take ten times that number.'

Southampton was less concerned about the fear of slaughter. 'Ireland is naught but rain and mud. An army would get bogged down there. There is no honour in it.'

'I thought so too, but then I learned something of most interest to me. Though he pushes my name forward for the governorship of Ireland in the council chamber, privately Cecil tells the queen I cannot be trusted with such a powerful position at the head of an army, and that sending me to Ireland would lead to a calamity for the realm.'

'The impudence of that man!' Southampton sounded outraged.

'But I thought he wanted you gone from court and away from the queen's ear?' asked Mountjoy.

'So did I. But think about it, man, what would he gain from me going there? If I defeated the rebels — which I could surely manage in a week, a month at the outside — I would return covered in glory. The people would love me more, the queen would love me better even than now, and then I could demand whatever I wanted from her.' He let that sink in.

'Cecil's head,' Southampton beamed, 'on a spike?'

'You know my heart, brother.'

'Then you must do it,' urged Southampton. 'Go to Ireland, crush the rebels, then return and rid us of that foul pygmy.'

'I shall.'

Their glee was only stifled when Southampton remembered Will was standing there with them. 'Not a word of this to Sir Robert, Shakespeare,' he snapped.

'Of course not, my lord. I am your man.'

'You had better be,' Southampton told him.

'Yes, you had better be,' Essex agreed. 'Or I will hear of it, and upon my return from Ireland, I shall demand two spikes.'

Chapter Seventeen

'I am one who loved not wisely but too well.'

—*Othello*

The Lady Imogen was young and undeniably fair. She was the kind of maid who, like Anne, would have attracted attention from the men of the court, particularly raffish adventurers like Raleigh, Southampton, Mountjoy and Essex, who turned a pursuit of the queen's ladies-in-waiting into a game. It was Beatrice Shepherd who had put Will on to her. He had gone back to the silkwoman to ask her who out of the queen's ladies Anne Percy had been seen with the most, aside from Theodosia. She had thought for a time, then told him that young Imogen Russell was most often at her side. Being of the same age likely helped them forge a friendship, since they were by some way the youngest of the ladies-in-waiting.

Imogen was reading from a prayer book when he found her. Will respectfully introduced himself by explaining he was a court poet who had been asked to write a sonnet in honour of the Lady Anne. Though she seemed to have no prior knowledge of who he was, she appeared to accept this explanation, but almost as soon as Will had mentioned her friend's name, the tears began. He tried to comfort her by offering sympathy for her loss.

'I have clumsily brought back your most recent grief and do beg forgiveness, my lady. Did you perhaps see her on the very night she died?'

'I did.'

Will left a silence then for her to fill.

'She made a broth for us ladies who sleep in the maidens' chamber. It can be a cold room and the broth was most warming. I commended her on it before setting my head down upon the pillow to sleep...' She realised something then: 'And those were to be the very last words I spoke to her. I did not know it at the time…' The tears flowed freely now.

'How could you have known? No one could,' he consoled her while she wiped those tears away with the back of her hand. 'You must have been a very close friend of the departed lady.'

'There was none closer than I,' she assured him.

'That is why I dared to approach you,' he said in the hushed, respectful tones of a clergyman. 'So I could plead for your indulgence, to help me honour your dear friend in verse.'

She was puzzled. 'How can I be of help to a poet?'

'By explaining her virtues to me and describing the things she loved most.'

She shook her head at this, but he did not take it as a refusal, more a failure to understand how she could go about it.

'I understand she was a most pious lady?' he prompted her.

'Oh yes, I never saw her without her prayer book.'

'She carried it with her at all times?' Will knew that ladies of the court often had prayer books, but they usually left them in their rooms to conduct their devotions privately there or in chapel later.

'She never let it out of her sight.'

'What a godly woman.'

'She was indeed. Anne was never without her prayer book and regularly would retreat into a private space to offer her thanks to God, whenever she had a moment free from the queen's company.'

'And the queen did enjoy her company?' he asked.

'She would often say that Anne was the most gentle, kind and pious of us all, but we were never jealous,' she added quickly, in case he should think it, 'not once. Because she really was, and none would do her ill.'

'I knew it,' he told the girl, as if he was satisfied that she had contradicted someone else's opinion of Anne. 'Those rumours were such foolishness.'

'What rumours?'

'Why, that anyone might have wished to see her dead. Such a foolish notion when it could only have been an accident. Could it not?'

'Oh yes, of course, an accident. A dreadful accident.' But she glanced away then and avoided his eyes.

'She had no enemies, after all?' he said simply.

'None.'

'And that other gossip at court? Well, I simply did not believe any of it.'

'What other gossip?' She was becoming alarmed now. He could tell.

'I could not repeat it in front of a lady,' he protested, but she was staring straight into his eyes now and though he feigned reluctance, he told her. 'Unless you were to wish it so, the better to prepare yourself, should anyone dare repeat such a slander in front of the queen. Then you could refute it, and Her Majesty would rebuke them most severely.'

'I will defend Anne's name until my dying day,' she pledged.

'I am certain there is nothing to defend, but there is a persistent slander against that most virtuous of ladies.' He made a point of looking about him to ensure they were not overheard, then leaned in closer. 'It is said she had the attention of a gentleman at court, and that he was her beau, and may have been even more.' He shook his head then, as if he was shocked that anyone should conjure up such a falsehood against the Lady Anne. 'And it is further said... Forgive me, lady, for even to voice this slander should be a crime, but I do it in full knowledge that you would never believe such an unfounded accusation... that...'

'That what?' Her own voice faltered then.

'She had fallen and was with child when she died?'

'No,' she protested, 'not Anne, no.'

'I knew it,' he assured her. 'I would that I had boxed the ears of the man I heard it from. I can tell it is untrue, for if a girl were to fall in such a way, then surely she would turn to her dearest friend for succour,' he gestured towards the Lady Imogen, 'and counsel on how best to act if a gentleman left her with child.'

'Certainly, she would have,' she asserted, before quickly adding, 'but she did not.'

'And you are aware of no particular gentleman who might have at least tried to tempt the Lady Anne away from the path of purity?'

'We are in the court, sir. There are always men who will try to use honeyed words to tempt us from the path of righteousness.'

'But you remained chaste?' He said it as if he meant both of them, but again her eyes betrayed enough to leave him with some doubt. Did Imogen perhaps believe her closest friend was less innocent than she was usually portrayed at court?

'All the ladies-in-waiting know they must remain so,' she answered.

'The queen is vengeful towards those who transgress,' he stated. 'Rightly, since she must insist on the highest standards of behaviour from her ladies.'

'She does often remind us to reject the pleasures of the flesh and turn to prayer whenever we feel tempted to weaken.'

'That is, of course, not always easy for a young and unworldly girl, who leaves her home and is placed at court away from her mother's guiding hand. The men here are often young, handsome and know how best to speak to a lady to win her heart. There are other men too, who would lure a young woman away from her friends on some pretext and seek to take advantage of her once she was alone.' When she did not deny this, he continued, 'I know of women who have been cruelly undone in this way, taken against their will and left in a wretched state afterwards, unable to tell anyone for shame. If they are particularly unfortunate, they are even left with child. In such circumstances, how could anyone blame a young girl, little more than a child herself after all, who has been cruelly preyed upon by a wicked lord?'

His vivid portrayal of this hypothetical situation had a most profound effect on Lady Imogen. Tears started to form in her eyes again, though she made an effort to stifle them. He decided to press her then.

'Forgive me, for I can see that my unthinking words have placed you in a state of distress. Have I unwittingly uncovered the cause of Lady Anne's travails. Is that perhaps what happened to the poor girl?'

'No, sir.' Her voice was almost a whisper.

'If it did, she would have been left with little choice but to approach a woman of the court with knowledge of how to prevent a most unfortunate event' – he tried to speak as delicately as possible – 'and rid herself of a lasting shame that could only have brought ruin to herself and her family.'

'Sir, I know not of what you speak, but can assure you that Lady Anne was as blameless in her conduct with the gentlemen of the court as she was in all other things.'

'Then why did she visit that lady, I wonder, and ask her how to bring down flowers?'

The shock on Lady Imogen's face was clearly visible, but was she surprised to learn of this meeting or simply astonished to hear that Will knew of it? 'That is a lie, I assure you.'

'And I am sorry, but I too must assure you that it happened. Lady Imogen, I cannot in all conscience and, in front of God, compose a sonnet in tribute to a pious, dead lady if she was not in truth a maiden. The queen would not permit it and nor would God, who would surely punish us all, so tell me true and on your conscience now if there is anything in this tale. You must swear to it, in fact, upon your prayer book.'

It took Lady Imogen a while to compose herself sufficiently to answer him. The young woman was easy to read, and he could almost see the conflicting thoughts dancing through her mind. She wanted to protect the reputation of her friend, but not at the cost of damnation, for swearing an untrue oath with her hand placed on a holy book. When she spoke, her words had conviction, and she kept her hand upon the book.

'I swear that my dear friend, Lady Anne, was chaste and pure, and never had cause to talk to anyone about bringing down flowers for her sake.'

And for the first time since they had begun to speak to one another, Will found he truly believed her.

'Then I thank you, dear lady, for we are done.'

—

Will had hoped for more, something that might have heightened his suspicions and added to his conviction that the Lady Anne had been despoiled by a man of the court and was with child when she died, but her closest friend, Lady Imogen, had been resolute that Anne was still a maid.

She had said something else that came back to Will though, about the night that Anne had died. She had made a broth for the ladies of her chamber to warm them. That seemed like an odd enough thing for a lady-in-waiting to bother with when servants could be commanded to do it instead. It might perhaps have been explained away as a device to keep out the cold, if it had not been for one thing: the last time Will had heard the word broth was when it was spoken by Theodosia, and what had she said about it? Will had an actor's memory for words and could recall hers now. *I gave her valerian root. A quantity boiled in a broth can bring on a deep sleep.*

So, the Lady Anne had taken Theodosia's valerian, but not for herself. She hadn't made a broth with it to aid her own sleep, but to ensure that every other lady in that shared chamber of hers went into a deep slumber. Only then had she crept silently from their chamber unnoticed by any of them, but who was Anne meeting that night and why was she so careful to hide the assignation from them all?

Chapter Eighteen

'Be great in act, as you have been in thought.'

—*King John*

When Christmas finally came, there was great revelry at court, with much feasting and toasting, games, dancing and, of course, plays. Will found he could not enjoy any of it since he knew what was to follow. They had agreed to wait for three days, to allow Giles Allen to rest easy in his family home and be distracted by his own festivities, before marching on the Theatre on the twenty-eighth of December and attempting to take it down, no matter who stood in their way.

It would have been impossible to do it any earlier, since the queen had already commanded they perform at court as part of the festivities. They gave her their new comedy *Much Ado About Nothing*, on the strict understanding that Will Kempe agreed not to do a bawdy jig at the end of it, and even he seemed to agree that was for the best. Robert Cecil had noted the title of the play with amusement before asking Will if it was about the Earl of Essex?

Before taking to the stage, Will met with Richard and Cuthbert in a quiet corner and asked in a low voice, 'What news of our endeavour?'

Cuthbert was equally discreet, making sure none nearby could hear him. 'We found a site near St Saviour's Church, just west of Dead Man's Place. It's six pounds a year cheaper than the rent Giles Allen is demanding.'

This plan met with Will's approval. 'Excellent. We will store the timber in Peter Street's wharf at Bridewell Stairs, then, once the weather turns milder and the ground is soft enough to dig foundations, we can carry it over the river on barges.'

'Good,' said Richard. 'Then all that remains is to muster the company, fight Giles Allen's blackguards into submission and dismantle the whole theatre before he learns of this.'

'Such a simple matter,' Cuthbert told him archly. 'I'm surprised we didn't think of it sooner.'

And with that, they were notified of the queen's impending arrival and went to take their places.

—

On the morning of the twenty-eighth, Will stood by Richard while he addressed the assembled company as if they were about to go into battle, and few among them doubted it. They would march down several streets together until they reached the Theatre. There were men guarding the building and they would surely not let them pass without a fight. Those men would be armed and so were the actors in the company. Some, including Will, carried swords but most had clubs or cudgels, with a dagger worn on their belts. There was the strong possibility of a battle in the streets that morning, which could lead to one or more deaths, and at the very least the watch would likely be called on them before they had even removed one plank from the Theatre. If men died in the struggle, others would be held to account and might hang for it. The company could be closed down by the Master of the Revels and its actors jailed or cast out onto the streets with no livelihood, to face the very real prospect of starvation.

Knowing all this, they remained resolute, for they had watched helplessly for two years while Will, Richard and Cuthbert had tried time and again to resolve their dispute with Giles Allen. Now they were all sick of the man who had blocked them from playing to packed houses at the Theatre, threatening their living, and their patience was at an end. Their blood was up, and they were ready to jab back at Allen for his greed and unwillingness to bend.

'There will be men at the Theatre who have been paid by Allen to make sure we do not break in and put on a play while their master is away,' Richard told them. 'They will be of the roughest kind, who will not hesitate to break limbs or crack your heads.'

'Let them try,' called one of the men defiantly and there were murmurs of agreement at that.

'They shall repent it afterwards,' warned another and Richard smiled. He could tell they were ready for this.

'Good then. I see most of you have armed yourselves. If you have no rapier or dagger, no club or cudgels, then pick up a heavy pan and beat them with it,' he urged, to some laughter. 'We do not go into this fight lightly, but, having committed to it now, let's make sure it is ours and only ours to win.' He drew his sword then and held it high. 'Onwards!'

—

The men guarding the Theatre had advance warning of their approach. The players had to walk the length of the street and because they were all assembled together, the actors became a mob of a dozen or more. The men by the Theatre all stood and made to face them. There were but six of them, and though the actors outnumbered them by around two to one, violence was how they made their living, so they would likely not step aside now, and were apt to take a good number of the actors down with them in any fight.

The smallest man from that group walked up to meet them. He didn't strike Will as someone capable of violence and he surmised this was a clerk, not a man paid to secure the entrance to the building. The five other larger men stayed back for now, but they eyed the players warily, seeing as they had arrived in such numbers and were all clearly armed. They did not leave their stations, though, and Will felt that it would likely take a great effort to shift them. He wondered if it would even be possible.

'What is the meaning of this assembly?' Allen's clerk demanded.

'We mean you no harm,' said Richard. 'As long as you do not attempt to prevent us from going about our business.'

'That depends on the nature of your business?' He was trying to sound authoritative, as if he alone could allow or prevent them from conducting it.

'And you are?' asked Richard.

'I am Reeves, Giles Allen's clerk.'

'Does Allen pay you well?' asked Richard. 'Enough for you to put your life in peril?'

'Richard,' cautioned Will, because he still hoped to avoid violence, if possible.

'You threaten me, sir?' The clerk was outraged.

'I do, sir,' Richard assured him and he placed his hand on the hilt of his sword but left it undrawn for the moment.

'I have men too,' the clerk protested.

'You have five men. I have a dozen.'

'Then I shall call the watch.'

'And tell them what? That men walk the streets of London? We have done nothing.'

'It is what you are about to do that concerns me.'

'What, pray tell, are we about to do? I will be mightily impressed if you can answer me correctly.'

The clerk faltered. 'You are here to stir up trouble, to break into the Theatre perhaps and put on a play, which you are strictly forbidden to do, since your lease has lapsed.'

'You think we will put on a play with no audience?' asked Richard.

'An audience can be summoned once you are inside, but our men will not permit it.' He raised his voice and addressed the men of the company then. 'Turn around and return to your homes,' he commanded but he sounded weak, and his words faltered.

'Or what?' someone called.

It was clear the clerk had not thought that part through. 'My men will prevent you from proceeding,' he said with more confidence than he probably possessed.

Richard placed a hand on his shoulder and pushed him firmly to one side. The whole company then marched closer, stopping only when they reached the five large men who stood before the Theatre's door. Will noticed how they all carried clubs and daggers and did not appear daunted by these actors, even though they were clearly outnumbered. Some of those actors had only really experienced choreographed fights onstage. This would be another matter entirely.

'Don't let them cross the threshold,' ordered the clerk and one of the actors boxed his ears for it. He cried out and stepped to one side, while Richard addressed the largest of the men, who, from his imposing presence, he took to be their leader.

'You are but five and we are more. We are also armed. Giles Allen has paid you to protect his land, but whatever coin he gave you, you cannot spend it if you are dead.'

One of the men looked a little cowed by this threat, but the others stood firm.

'And who will be the man to rob me of it by my death? You?' the largest man asked Burbage defiantly, as if this would not end well for Richard.

'No one shall,' Will interrupted their quarrel before he ran the risk of losing his friend and leading actor. 'For you have done your service and earned your coin. Giles Allen asked you to protect his land and that you have done, for we shall not set foot upon it.'

'You shan't?' This confused the burly man, and the others looked equally baffled.

'No, for we have no need to.' He flourished the lease then. 'By the terms of this lease, your master owns the ground on which our theatre sits. We seek only to remove the beams and take them elsewhere, leaving the land as intact as before, better in fact for he can then use the cleared ground for his own purpose, as we all know he wishes to.'

'Is this true?' The man was doubtful. 'He owns the land but you the building? How so?'

'It is writ here and signed by your master. Take a look.' And he showed them both where Allen had signed the lease, though he doubted if either man could read its terms.

'If it is writ down, then it is true,' the first man told the second and he seemed keen to believe it, but the other once scratched his chin.

'You cannot deny it is so,' Will addressed this remark to Giles Allen's clerk, who was still standing close by and to one side.

Reeves took the lease and read it.

'I do not deny it.'

'Then all is well.'

'Though I am sure my master shall not see it so and will be most aggrieved.' But he no longer sounded sure.

'Why aggrieved when this is what he signed?' When Will received no further dissent from any of the men, he said, 'Good then, for we are all agreed. We will take our theatre but will not take the land.'

The burly man seemed to be coming round to that idea. 'I will have to stay and watch you, to make sure you taketh not any of the land.'

'Gladly, good sir,' Will assured the man. 'Perhaps you would like to fetch a chair then, for we will be a time?'

And the pliable man did just that. While he was gone to look for one, Will gestured to all that agreement had been reached and they could start tearing down the building.

'Wait!' called the clerk. 'There is one thing you must not do, and I bid you swear to it now.'

'And what is that, pray?' In his impatience, Will glanced to Richard, who seemed just as irritated by this further delay and was perhaps ready to strike the man.

'You can take your building, beams and all, but must not tread upon the land, for it is not yours. If you do, you trespass.'

Will glanced at Peter Street to gain his opinion and the carpenter shrugged as if he could see no way around that argument. Will thought on it for a moment. 'We shall not need to tread upon the land beneath the Theatre for when we take down the beams, we will remove the roof and walls first. Our feet will touch only the floorboards, which we own.' And he spread his palms in a show of reasonableness.

'That's well then,' said the clerk, though he seemed displeased to have been outargued. Then he asked, 'What wilt thou do at the end when you take up those floorboards?'

'We will start at the far end,' Will assured him, 'and as we pull up each one, we shall work backwards towards the street, standing upon the next one, then the next. No foot of ours shall tread upon your master's land.'

'You swear it?'

'I do swear.'

'And you?' the clerk asked Richard.

'I swear it too.'

'And the others in your company?'

'God, man there is not time to have a dozen men make an oath to you. You have my word and Will's and that should be sufficient for you to be satisfied.' Richard's anger threatened to spill over again, and the clerk backed down.

'It is, and I am.'

The burly man returned with his chair and set it down facing the Theatre. He sat down then, as if he was about to watch one of their plays. The others with him relaxed too then and simply watched the men of the company with interest. 'You can begin,' he said. 'But be warned and reminded: I'll not let you take an ounce of soil from here, only the timbers and other materials.'

'That is fair,' agreed Will, for he had no interest in the soil beneath the Theatre.

'And make sure no one treads upon the land underneath the building,' the clerk told him, 'for that would be trespass. No man is to remove his foot from the floorboards.'

'I will watch and make sure of it,' said the big man.

–

By the time they were done for the day, all the men were exhausted, with blistered hands and aching limbs, but the building had been reduced in size by almost a third, and there had been no further arguments with the men paid to guard the land. Will had managed to outwit them with his use of the lease to justify the removal of the Theatre's timbers. He also knew that Giles Allen would fly into a rage when he learned of it. Will hoped they could at least remove some more of the Theatre's materials the following day before word reached him of it in Essex and he arrived at the scene, possibly with more men.

'I was thinking of that clerk,' he told Richard while they ate a bowl of stew in the tavern before retiring to bed. They had agreed to rise early again the next morning and continue their work for as long as possible. If they were lucky and Giles Allen did not arrive at all, then it would doubtless be another long day.

'You ran him round in circles. He was like a dog chasing its own tail.' Richard was gleeful.

'But think on the point he made about removing the beams but not letting us touch an inch of soil. Was that not impressive in its own way, even if he was what the French call a *pédant*?'

'He impressed you?'

'By the way he thought upon the matter, yes, even though we won the argument, and Giles Allen might be left with naught but soil. I will wager that clerk will receive a most brutal beating for it, but he helped me find an ending to one of the plays I have been writing.'

'I do not know why you always work on several plays, Will. Is it not easier to concentrate on one?' Richard was perplexed. 'Aren't you supposed to be writing *Henry V*?'

Will was dismissive. 'I feel the need to start one while I am writing another. I find it stimulating. And there are complications with the King Henry play. This is the one about the Jew?'

'The moneylender?'

'The very same.'

'How did that clerk help you?'

'In *The Merchant of Venice*, a man borrows a large sum from an enemy but cannot pay it back. The Jewish moneylender insists on special terms, in the event that the money cannot be repaid. He wants a pound of the man's flesh.'

'Why ever would he desire that?' Richard was appalled.

'Because he has long been derided by the man he loaned it to, who has a dislike of all Jews.'

'Yet still the Jew lends him money?'

'To trap him, yes.'

Richard thought on this. 'But in doing so, does he not also lose his money?'

'He does, but it is of less importance.'

'Losing money is unimportant to a moneylender? That is surely wrong, Will.'

Will grew impatient with Richard now. 'Are you the actor or the writer? Stay your objections awhile. I shall make it believable.'

'Then forgive me and do so. Continue.'

'Up till now, I had thought of a plan wherein the borrower loses the bet and the pound of flesh that comes with it. The law backs him and naught can be done to prevent it.'

'Would not the people prevent it, by appealing to the lender not to cut the man open.'

'They will, but their pleading does not work.'

'Why not?'

'You are doing it again, Richard. Let me tell the tale anon, but for now, I have a man who was about to be removed of a pound of his flesh, but I could think of no way to save him from their contract and the law.'

'And this foolish clerk gave you the idea?'

'Yes, while we were taking down the beams, I could think on the play without thinking on it overmuch, which is my habit. Holding my quill sometimes stops my thoughts. Today, though, I found my resolution.'

'How will you save him?' Richard queried.

'As he is about to plunge his dagger into the man, a lawyer will tell the moneylender he is entitled to a pound of flesh…' Will paused dramatically. 'But not a drop of blood.' Then he said, 'And this on pain of his own death.'

It took a moment for Richard to ponder the implications of this and the quandary the moneylender would be placed in. 'Oh, that's good, Will. That's very good.'

'Thank you, dear friend.'

'But I am still not sure it works. I mean, would the lender really risk losing his money just so he can cut a pound of flesh from his enemy. I doubt the groundlings will believe it.'

'Do I tell you how to act, Richard?' And before his friend could reply, Will told him crossly, 'I do not. So, kindly leave the writing to me.'

Chapter Nineteen

'Her clothes spread wide
And mermaid-like, awhile they bore her up...
...But long it could not be
Till that her garments, heavy with their drink,
Pulled the poor wretch from her melodious lay
To muddy death.'

—Hamlet

It almost came as a relief to be summoned back to court. Will had endured two days of back-breaking work disassembling the Theatre, before he was called for. Surprisingly, Giles Allen had yet to receive word of their actions, so while Will was gone, the rest of the company carried on stripping the timbers and loading them onto carts, without interruption from the men guarding the Theatre, who had grown used to their presence by now. They accepted Will's absence as some unspecified appointment with a court official to gain a licence for their next play, and he was not missed.

He was due to report to Sir Robert Cecil, who would expect to hear of progress in his investigation into the death of the Lady Anne. Last time, he had been dismissed impatiently and told not to come back until he had found the killer, but Cecil had spoken in anger then, caused by the frustration of Her Majesty's weakness towards the Earl of Essex. Will was not rightly sure what he was going to tell the man. Cecil seemed convinced that Lady Anne's death had been a murder prompted by some secret intrigue against the realm, but Will was far less sure of that now. That the girl had been murdered? Yes, this was the most likely possibility, but what if the reasoning behind it was far simpler than the discovery of a treasonous, papist plot to overthrow the queen?

It now seemed far more likely that the Lady Anne had been involved in a dalliance with a man at court, had fallen pregnant and gone to see a learned woman about ways to rid herself of the baby. Perhaps this remedy had not worked, and she had been abandoned by the child's father. Having lost all hope, it was still possible that she may have taken her own life, but Will thought it more likely she was killed by that same man to avoid the wrath of the queen. Cecil might accept Will's explanation, but, if he leaned towards murder as the most likely outcome, then he would still expect him to come up with the name of a culprit, especially when it might actually be one of the same nobles he had suspected from the beginning: Essex, Raleigh, Southampton or Mountjoy. Will had to admit he was no nearer to discovering the truth of that than he had been at the start of his enquiries.

On his way into the palace, Will encountered the usual crowd of lawyers and petitioners, who all seemed preoccupied with their own business, which was why no one else seemed to notice what he saw. Coming towards him now was a well-born man who was heading out of the palace. Will knew the man, for he had seen him many times at court. This was the Lady Anne's cousin, Henry Percy, the Earl of Northumberland, and he seemed to be in some distress. He was walking too quickly, as if in a hurry to quit the place, and he bumped into one of the petitioners hard, sending him bouncing off to one side, where he collided into two other men, who turned on him angrily. The earl did not stop for a moment. If anything, his pace increased, as if he was trying to escape from something. As he went by, Will noticed that Henry Percy's eyes were red and there might even have been tears in them. What news could have caused this, or was it some sudden renewal of his grief for his cousin, and would Cecil be the one to inform Will of this, or would that remain a mystery too?

—

When Will arrived, he was surprised to see the queen's physician standing in the Secretary of State's office. For a moment, he wondered if the man was there to complain about him, but the truth was much darker.

'Anne Percy's friend, the Lady Imogen Russell, has been pulled from the river this very morning,' Cecil told him. 'She is drowned.'

'Drowned?' Will could not believe that the young maid he had seen just days before was now dead.

'We have put it about that she must have slipped in the mud by the riverbank and fallen in. She was then unable to drag herself free from the water, with her dress weighing her down so.'

Will wanted to challenge him then, to ask him what he meant by *we have put it about that she must have slipped*. Did Cecil mean that he did not believe this and, if not, then why? But Will was too much in shock and could not find the words. All he could think of was his most recent appointment with the young and fair Lady Imogen, who he could have imagined would have had a long life ahead of her. Now she was lying dead somewhere in the palace, a cold, lifeless body destined for a grave.

'I have taken the physician fully into my confidence,' Cecil revealed then. 'Two young ladies of the court are dead now, so it was necessary to dispense with some of the usual caution.'

'You examined the girl's body?' Will asked the physician.

'I did.' But he was giving nothing else away.

'She was definitely drowned?' Will wanted to be certain that Imogen had not been hit over the head and thrown into the river, perhaps by the same man who could have murdered the Lady Anne.

'She was.' But there was a tension here, Will could feel it.

'An accident then?' he offered lightly.

'I will tell the queen so,' Cecil informed him.

'Then you will forever be in the debt of the young lady's family,' Will suggested, for it was all becoming clear to him now. 'For discounting the notion of a self-murder.'

The physician could not help himself. 'How did you…?' he asked before he could stop himself, then he looked to Cecil to see if he had been indiscreet in confirming Will's suspicions.

Cecil made a tiny gesture with a hand to indicate it mattered little and he waited for Will to account for this.

'The lady was with child, though considered a maid,' Will told them. 'I know this because her closest companion was the Lady Anne Percy, who sought advice from a woman in the court who knew how to bring down flowers.' Will could tell the physician understood the phrase. 'You swore Lady Anne was a virgin and the woman she went to for advice told me she asked for herbs for a friend. That lady took it to mean that Anne was actually referring to herself, but it is clear to me now that she was not. It was Imogen who was growing a child inside her, though unmarried and barely past sixteen. She faced the wrath of the queen and certain disgrace for herself and family, unless she could persuade the father to marry her, and it must have seemed that was never going to be possible.'

'Perhaps even then,' the physician interjected, because even a hasty marriage might not have saved her from ignominy in the eyes of Her Majesty.

'Indeed, but her fate would have been sealed once the father rejected her.'

'It would,' he conceded.

'That man might not have wished her dead, though. He may even have held her in high regard for her grace and beauty. He might have loved her but been unable to take her as his wife, if he already had one?' He was recalling Henry Percy now, who had quit the palace so hastily that morning, with such red eyes. He could have met the Lady Imogen quite naturally enough, since she was his cousin's closest friend. Did they meet through Lady Anne and fall in love perhaps, even though he was married and almost twenty years her elder? The look on his face when he left the palace indicated he had just learned some terrible news. Will instinctively knew it was Imogen's death that had affected him so. What else could have caused his pallor, his tears and haste in quitting the palace? It seemed more than just a tupping had passed between them. Now he had lost his cousin and his love in quick succession, poor man.

'He might.' The physician's eyes narrowed, and he was watching Will most intently, as if fascinated by what he knew, but also wondering how he could possibly know it.

'Being not a hard-hearted man, when he learned of the lady's death, he may have been unable to stop his tears,' Will explained then.

'If that is something you think you saw, then I would caution you against naming that man,' the physician said and Will realised they both knew who he was referring to, though they were determined to bury that lord's involvement. 'If he is indeed a great lord?' Will also knew that if Cecil managed to successfully hide the girl's relationship with Henry Percy and explain away her death as an accident, he would doubtless expect favours in return from the Earl of Northumberland. Who knows how long he would wait to remind Percy that he was deep in debt to the Secretary of State, then demand repayment in some form or another.

'What good would it do to name him now?' asked Will. 'Lady Imogen is dead, her lover grief-stricken. Why add to the agony of two families by making public that which should stay hidden, for decency's sake?'

The physician seemed content with that answer and so did Cecil.

'It was self-slaughter, was it not?' He could not help but ask the question, even though he was dreading the answer.

It took a while for the physician to admit what Will knew, but then, in a low voice, he said, 'Her dress was weighted with stones, sewn into it.'

'She committed this terrible act against herself,' said Cecil with little sympathy. 'Disgraced by her own lewd conduct. An unwed girl, finding herself with child and realising her downfall was unavoidable. Shame caused this. She killed herself and her unborn child, so that's twice the sin. She will likely go to hell for it as a murderer twice over.'

That terrible image made Will break down. 'This is all my fault.'

The physician immediately drew the wrong conclusion. '*You* wronged the girl?' he demanded. 'This was *your* doing?' It must have seemed to him that Henry Percy might not be the culprit after all.

Will shook his head. 'No I... That's not what...' But he could not find the words to acquit himself from blame, since he felt as responsible for the poor girl's death as the man who had left her in that condition. He recalled now how he had painted a portrait in her mind, of a young girl in disgrace, a desperate creature with child, who had been left with no choice but to kill herself to avoid the ultimate shame she would bring down on herself and her family. Will had been describing a situation he assumed Lady Anne to have found herself in. Now he realised he had all too vividly outlined a scenario that actually applied to Imogen. She must have confided in Anne about her pregnancy, and her dear friend had gone to see Theodosia Harington to ask her how to bring down flowers to rid an unfortunate friend of an unborn child. She was doing this not for herself, as Theodosia and subsequently Will had surmised, but for her closest friend. Now they were both dead. He had succeeded only in making Imogen realise her situation was so hopeless she had no option but to take her own life. Will felt he had as good as killed the girl himself and was now bereft.

'Her Majesty shall hear of this,' the physician was telling him. 'Imogen was one of her favoured ladies-in-waiting and she has taken her death hard, coming so soon after that of Lady Anne's. If you are responsible for her fall, then I pray you think on how to beg mercy from your queen.'

Will was too much in shock to answer him, but he didn't have to.

'Don't be a fool man!' snapped Cecil. 'Shakespeare is not responsible for this girl's fall. He did not father that child. All of us know who did. How could a mere player gain access to the queen's lady-in-waiting at any hour, let alone after dark?'

The physician was so startled by the ferocity of this rebuke that he immediately bowed and started to stammer his apologies. With the physician silenced, Cecil turned his attention to Will.

'Why did you say it was your fault?'

Will confessed then that he had unwittingly been the one to fill the girl's head with notions of her disgrace and impending fall, which likely led to her self-slaughter. He did not expect to receive any sympathy from a man as famously ruthless as Cecil, nor any real understanding of why Will was now in deep shock over the death of a girl he hardly knew, but he was surprised by the reply he did receive.

'This is not your fault,' Cecil told him. 'We are often forced to paint unpleasant pictures of the future for those we interrogate. We cannot control the thoughts they have later, nor the acts resulting from them. She was doomed anyway. If you wish to blame anyone, blame the man who put that child inside her.'

Chapter Twenty

*'You have such a February face,
So full of frost, of storm, and cloudiness.'*

—Much Ado About Nothing

It was two days before Will could force himself to believe that Cecil was right, at least in part. During that time, he wrote little and drank more than he should have, so he could slump into his bed at night and collapse into a troubled sleep, trying not to think of the poor girl drowning herself in the cold waters of the river, blaming herself for that awful act. He realised he would never know if it was his words that had prompted her to do it or if they had been the final straw, when she knew that falling to a married man might have been an unforgivable act in the eyes of the queen. Worse, her lover was married to Lady Dorothy Devereux, sister to the Earl of Essex no less. Imagine her fate once it was known that she had wronged the queen's favourite, by embarrassing his sister and the punishment from Her Majesty that would follow. Maybe she was better off dead, poor girl.

Nevertheless, Will knew he would never forgive himself for his careless talk, when he thought he was describing the Lady Anne's situation to Imogen. He, above all, should have known the power of words and would repent his stupidity for the rest of his days. Now though, he knew he had to drag himself from his bed and go on, just as he had been forced to after a time mourning the loss of his only son. If he could carry on after that devastating blow, then he could continue now, for the benefit of those who relied upon him. He had a play about Henry V to write, and there was the small matter of the Theatre, which he had failed to return to since he had been told of Lady Imogen's demise. He would go there now and hope his absence would be forgiven if he helped them to complete the task.

It had taken them four long, arduous, backbreaking days, but just before nightfall on that final one, the floorboards were lifted and the last remaining timbers from the Theatre removed, leaving a bare plot of land in its place. Just as Will had promised, they had started at the far end and pulled up the boards one by one as they retreated towards the street. They ensured that no member of the company set foot upon the bare ground as those boards were lifted. Giles Allen's clerk had insisted on remaining there for the whole four days, so he could be present for this last act, to guarantee the terms of their bargain were carried out to the letter. When it was done, he pronounced himself satisfied with the conclusion of their work. Now he would write to his master to tell him what had transpired. Will pitied him. When the clerk tried to explain to Allen what a good bargain he had struck, he would surely be dismissed and most likely take a beating too for his trouble, but Will had little time to worry about that now.

He watched as the final cart, containing the floorboards was ridden away to Peter Street's warehouse by the Thames, where they would be stored until the ground softened enough for building. The site they eventually leased across the river would have to be cleared of its existing buildings and drained, huge pillars would need to be sunk into the ground to support the foundations and, when that job was complete, the enormous task of reassembling the Theatre from its thousands of component parts could finally begin.

That night, before finally succumbing to sleep, Will worried and fretted over the next stage of their endeavour. What if the timbers proved too weak to support the structure now that they had been wrenched apart. What if the whole building collapsed on top of them, and they were left with naught but an enormous pile of wood and nowhere to mount a stage? They would be ruined, and Will would be the one to blame for this huge folly. It did not bear thinking on, and he resolved to banish the doubts from his mind before lapsing into a deep, exhausted sleep.

A day later, Will met with Richard and Cuthbert, as planned, for supper. He had hoped they would be satisfied with the progress they had made so far and buoyed by having outwitted Giles Allen, their hated landlord, but instead he found them both in a low mood.

'We are undone by another calamity,' Cuthbert told him gloomily.

'What now? A plague of locusts? What else is there left that could possibly befall us, apart from death itself?' Will felt incredibly weary of it all now.

'The land we hoped to lease.'

'What of it?'

'We can no longer afford it,' Richard chimed in.

'But we can. We know its price.'

'The price has gone up,' Cuthbert told him.

'Since when?'

'Since word got out that the Burbages had dismantled their entire theatre and are in a most desperate hurry to lease the land upon which to build a new one.'

'How much are we short?'

'Too much to simply borrow it. Usury for a sum like this could bankrupt us all.'

'Not having land for our theatre will most definitely bankrupt us,' Will reminded him then. 'How much do we need?'

'To lease the land then have the theatre rebuilt there – ninety pounds,' Cuthbert informed him.

'*Ninety?*' Will could not believe it. 'How can it be so much?'

'We spent all we had in our coffers. It was barely enough to take down the old theatre and keep its timbers stored in Peter's warehouse. The company has no money and no method of making any.'

'We could tour?' suggested Will.

'And make how much in the provinces?' Cuthbert shook his head. 'Once we pay the actors, there'd be barely enough to cover our costs.'

'What then can we do?' Will considered this then asked: 'How much do you have?'

'How much do *you* have?' asked Cuthbert, a trace of resentment in his voice. He clearly believed Will was trying to persuade the Burbages to pay for all of the additional expenses.

Will mused on it. 'If I clawed back the coin from every venture I have been engaged in of late… I could possibly provide ten pounds.'

'Possibly?'

'It shall be ten pounds,' he assured them. 'You have my word.'

'Then I could provide twenty,' Richard was quick to double his friend's offering, and he looked to his brother.

'I could perhaps come up with a similar sum, but I'll be stretched to the limit,' Cuthbert warned his brother. 'No more than twenty, else I'll be ruined and end up on the street.'

'Then we have fifty pounds already,' Will asserted.

'Which is little more than half of what is required,' Richard reminded him.

'We are still short of forty pounds, Will. That is no small sum,' confirmed Cuthbert. 'No patron would gift us that, nor could we ever earn it from touring. And who will lend it to us when we have naught to put up against a loan to secure it? I fear we are undone. We can't even afford to keep the timbers dry in the warehouse overlong. The rent for that alone is draining us of coin.'

'I hate myself for admitting this, Will, after everything we did to take down the Theatre, but I fear it was all for naught,' Richard bemoaned. 'The sooner we accept that this is over, the quicker we rid ourselves of debts and give ourselves some hope of avoiding complete ruin.'

'And do what?' snapped Will. 'Do you have another trade, Richard? I have none. Who will pay you to act or me to write? Do you want to scratch your living at the Rose, begging Philip Henslowe to let you do a play or two?' And if the prospect of that humiliation was not alarming enough for Richard, he added, 'In lesser roles.'

What was left of the colour in Richard's cheeks seemed to drain from them then, for Will had just described his leading man's worst nightmare.

'I'd rather die.'

'Then you shall,' said Cuthbert icily, 'for what else is there for us now, without forty pounds?'

'There must be a way,' Will said in desperation. 'There has to be!'

'There is not,' Cuthbert told him.

Chapter Twenty-One

'He that is truly dedicated to war hath no self-love.'

—*Henry VI Part II*

Will had thought it politic to make his way to court again and work in the room he had been given, ostensibly to write *Henry V*. He had even managed to get some words down onto the parchment, but he lacked inspiration. The Theatre was in pieces and the company lacked the funds to rebuild it. Will was still under great pressure to write this new play to be put on before the queen, but he had the same problem as before. How to put events such as the Battle of Agincourt on to something as tiny as a stage.

There was also the not exactly trivial matter of the death of Lady Anne, the mystery of which Robert Cecil still wanted him to solve. He had wasted time and effort in following a false trail of his own making, because he believed she had been wronged by a man from court and left with child. He had not just been mistaken about this but had inadvertently contributed to the death of another girl. Cecil had been uncharacteristically understanding of that, but his sympathy would not last long. Will would still have to find Anne's killer.

When Cecil looked in on him later that morning, he had news. 'The queen shall send the Earl of Essex to Ireland with five warships,' he confirmed in a neutral voice, as if he was informing Will of the elevation of a stranger and not his nemesis. 'He will ride there at the head of a great army of some sixteen thousand men, two thousand of them seasoned in battle, with thirteen hundred horse. They will be reinforced by a further two thousand men a month. The earl is tasked with bringing the rebel Irish lord, Hugh O'Neill, to heel.'

'That will be a great undertaking,' observed Will.

'Three hundred thousand pounds has been set aside for victuals, muskets, powder and ordinance, and enough left to pay for a year's campaigning. That is a mighty sum and twice the cost of the war in the lowlands. Do you know what this means, Master Shakespeare?' Cecil's tone was unemotional, as he outlined the extent of the forces at Essex's disposal.

Presently, Will ventured, 'That the earl was granted all he asked for from the queen?'

Cecil corrected him. 'That he cannot afford to fail.'

'You think he will fail? With a force that large?' It seemed impossible that a few hundred Irish rebels could not be put down by such a huge and well-resourced army, led by the hero of Cadiz, a man already popular with his troops. Essex may have been many things, few of them admirable, but no one could deny the reputation he had gained from his past military service. He was surely a born general.

'He may, but if he does not, he will have merely gained an expensive victory already expected of him. His esteem in the queen's eyes will not be much elevated.'

Will felt this was too much of an optimistic reading of the situation. An expected victory or not, success in Ireland would be an excuse for Her Majesty to shower her favourite with even more honours. How long before he was powerful enough to call for Cecil's removal, perhaps even his head? Will had overheard him say as much to Mountjoy and Southampton. If Essex tamed Ireland for her, the queen would likely deny him nothing.

But Cecil could not see that. 'And if he fails, he will return much diminished, and she will be angered. You have witnessed the queen's fury? I have and men do quake before it.'

And rightly, but not Essex, Will recalled. He had drawn his sword on her. Essex was the one man who could tame the queen, persuade or cajole her, throw childish tantrums in front of her, publicly show his ingratitude and storm from her chambers, and yet still be summoned back to her. Then he would be greeted with soft, reassuring words and handed even higher honours.

Will could not understand why Cecil seemed so calm and sure of his position. Had he not always opposed the elevation of Essex to commander of the queen's forces in Ireland, at least to Her Majesty? Why the change of heart now? How had he convinced himself this was actually a good thing that might even bring the earl to his knees? He was surely deluded.

There was something else Cecil had failed to take into account. Even if the earl did not achieve the great success he had promised the queen. She had set him at the head of a mighty army of men and placed a fleet of ships at his command. If he did fail in Ireland, would a man as arrogant as Essex accept being recalled and dressed down by his monarch in front of the entire court, or would he instead rebel against her authority? He could just as easily march that army to London as Dublin. Then he might bring down his queen, and Cecil too.

'Now that Her Majesty has decided to send Essex to war, she wants you to hurry and finish her play,' Cecil informed.

Will was glad he was at least making a show of writing it that morning. 'When does she want it by?'

'As soon as it is done, so she will be inspired by King Harry's feats of valour at Agincourt.'

Knowing that he was soon expected to fit Henry V's entire French campaign onto a hastily erected stage at court sent Will into something close to a panic, but there was no time to dwell on this because Poley appeared then, clearly looking for his master. Will assumed they would leave together so that Cecil could involve his creature in some new intrigue. Instead, Cecil asked him, 'Where does your investigation take you next, Master Shakespeare?'

Will had been thinking on this for some time, until he had eventually recalled something that the Lady Imogen had said about Anne. 'I have heard it said that Lady Anne took her prayer book everywhere?'

'They say she was a most godly young woman,' Cecil confirmed.

'Then where is it?' asked Will.

'It was not on or by her bed,' Cecil recalled.

'If she really did carry it with her at all times, why was it not discovered with her body?'

'I do not know, but you are right that it was not found.'

'So it should have been discovered by her side?' Will was intrigued.

'Maybe it was not deemed sufficiently important to be brought to my attention?' answered Cecil, but Will had a different idea altogether about that, and it was one that he wanted to put to the test. 'If she carried it with her always, then why would it be worthy of note?' Cecil asked.

'Perhaps it is not, but its absence now *is* worthy of note. I believe we must find this bible.'

'So, go now and visit the men of the watch who found her.' Then almost as an afterthought, he said, 'Take Poley with you.'

—

Poley told Will to wait outside while he went in to speak to the men of the watch. He strongly inferred that they would be distrustful of a gentleman, even a minor one like Will, and might not tell him the truth. Poley felt he would be more able to speak to men of their rank to obtain what was needed from them. Will disagreed but knew it was pointless to argue with Poley, for he had never seen the man back down. He eventually emerged with another.

'This is Vaux, a sergeant of the watch. He was the first person to find Lady Anne's body.' The man dipped his head into an approximation of a bow.

'You raised the alarm?' Will asked.

'I did, sir.'

'And when you discovered the lady, did you find anything by her body?'

'No, sir.' But he looked down when he said this, and Will could tell it was an evasion.

'You are sure?' he probed, but the man answered him with a silence he obviously hoped would be sufficient to avoid Will questioning him further, which only made him more curious. 'Not say, the book of common prayer she always carried, no matter where she went?' Silence was once again the man's response.

'I have heard it said that Lady Anne never would venture abroad without her prayer book, such was her devotion to God. Now, if she did have that sacred book with her, and a man removed it and kept it for himself, because he deemed it of some value, I suspect the queen would punish that man quite severely.' Then Will added, 'Without mercy. If Lady Anne's father or brother were to discover it was taken, they might save our queen the trouble by ending that man's life.' The man looked terrified now, so Will dangled hope. 'Unless...'

'Unless?'

'Unless that man were to have picked it up for another reason, in order to keep it safe perhaps, then he might merely have forgotten to hand it to her family. This mistake might be overlooked.'

'A man could be forgiven for such an error?' Vaux asked hopefully, dry-mouthed in his terror now.

'He could be.' And when the man did not speak or move thereafter, Will commanded him firmly, 'Go now and return with it.'

And Vaux scurried away.

'Why do you wish to see the lady's prayer book?' Poley asked when Vaux was gone.

'I wish to see everything pertaining to the Lady Anne. You do not object?'

'I do not.'

They waited for a while in silence for the man of the watch to return. Will suspected Poley was not good at the type of talk that allows gentlemen to pass the time together. Will could not think of a single topic he would be comfortable discussing with Poley; not religion, the theatre, hunting, taverns or women and, as he ran through these different pursuits in his head, he felt sure that none of them would likely be of much interest to the single-minded Poley, so he stayed silent.

When Vaux returned, he was breathless and flushed, presumably because he had hurried there and back again in his fear. He handed over the book, which was wrapped in cloth, and Will took it from him. The watchman looked as if he was about to say something then, but Will interjected. 'Now begone.'

Vaux hastened gratefully from the scene.

'Shall we examine it together?' asked Poley.

'Not here.'

Chapter Twenty-Two

'He thinks too much; such men are dangerous.'

—*Julius Caesar*

They took the book away from there and went some distance from that busy part of the palace, until they discovered a quiet corner by a window, where the light helped them survey the item. When Will unwrapped it, he found a simply bound but expertly illustrated prayer book.

'It is not one of the richer devotional books,' Poley said with approval, showing his natural distrust of Catholic idolatry.

Will started to examine it. 'There are fewer illustrations than in some books of hours. These have been woodcut, then coloured by hand. It is still a substantial book, foreign made I'd say and expensive.'

Lady Anne's book of common prayer was light enough to carry but sturdy and unlikely to fall apart from overuse, though as Will surveyed it more closely he noticed something. The inside back cover page of the binding had come loose where it was joined to the end pages of the book. He might easily have missed that, had he not been looking for exactly this type of imperfection, for it went together with his idea that the book itself was important and may contain a secret.

'Note the binding; how it comes away here.'

Poley leaned forwards. 'Torn?'

'Not torn,' Will corrected him. 'Cut.' And he leaned closer to survey the neat incision in the material that had been fixed to the inside of the binding. On closer inspection, he realised something important. 'But only partially. The incision was already there, but it has been widened, you see?' He pointed it out to Poley.

'But what does it mean?'

'This space was used to conceal something, a note or letter perhaps, and the gap has been widened, most likely by whoever it was that sent Lady Anne to her death.'

'Before they retrieved what was concealed there?'

'Exactly. Her attacker must have realised he would have only moments before the watch chanced upon the scene, then he would be done for. He must surely have known in advance that what he wanted was hidden here, but in his haste to retrieve it, he cut the book to make it easier to get at.'

'Why not simply take the prayer book?' Poley asked.

'Because he reasoned its presence would be missed, which means he knew enough about the Lady Anne to understand she carried it with her at all times. It *was* missed, of course, in the end, but only because the watchman stole it.'

'Missed by you, you mean.' Will felt Poley was grudgingly giving him credit for this.

'But if the correspondence is gone, then where is it now and what important information does it contain?' Will asked. 'A love note or an invitation to take part in a plot of some kind?'

'We are unlikely to ever know the answer to that,' Poley observed, reasonably.

'Unless we find the letter,' Will remarked. 'If that is indeed what it is and not a map or a different kind of message.'

'Where would we even begin to look for it?'

'Find Lady Anne's killer and we find the letter,' said Will.

'Or find the letter and we find her killer?' suggested Poley.

'Very like,' Will agreed.

'Unless he burned it.'

'Why go to so much trouble to acquire a letter then be rid of it?' Will mused.

'If it contained damaging intelligence that could destroy that man or his master, he might very well ensure it could never be seen by another.'

'You are right, of course.' Will had to admit the likelihood of this, remembering once again that he was dealing with a man used to intrigue.

'Then, if it is destroyed, it can never be found,' Poley said.

'We must try to find this letter at least,' insisted Will, 'for everything now rests on it.'

Will left Poley then, because he had been told to go back to Cecil immediately and report on any progress they had made with the members of the watch. He took the prayer book to Cecil's rooms. When he was shown the secret compartment in Lady Anne's prayer book, Cecil reacted with interest and not a little surprise. Did he find it galling to have to admit to himself that the feminine ideal she seemed to personify might not actually be borne out by the evidence of Anne's conduct? Or perhaps he would find her an even more enigmatic beauty now that he had discovered she was likely involved in subterfuge or espionage.

'I have another task for you then, Shakespeare,' he said. 'I am told you are acquiring land on Bankside?'

'We are aiming to, my lord.' Will knew that the act of tearing down an entire theatre could not have escaped Cecil's attention, but it seemed he knew everything about their plan, even it currently lacked the funds needed to complete it.

'And you wish to build a new theatre there, amid the bawdy houses and lawless taverns of Southwark?'

'We would prefer to build it on the northern side of the river, but there is little land there and none we can afford.'

'Let us speak plainly, you have chosen to build on the south side of the Thames because the authority of the city of London does not hold beyond its walls. You wish to escape the rules that have always applied to your kind.'

Will bridled at that. 'The city officials have made no secret of the fact that they want to close all of the theatres permanently. That is clear from their many petitions to Her Majesty and the Privy Council. They associate us with sin. What choice do we have then but to cross the river?'

'And join the other sinners? The cutpurses, coney-catchers and whores, not to mention the undeserving poor who litter the streets there and fill the air with the sound of their begging.'

'My lord knows the area better than I.' It was meant to sound like an admission of superior knowledge on Cecil's part, but it came out like an insult, and perhaps that was how Will had meant it, deep down. Why did he occasionally feel the need to poke at a man who could lock him up, torture him or send him to the gallows on some fabricated charge without overtroubling himself? He was damned if he knew the answer to that, except that he could not help himself.

'Watch your tongue, Shakespeare.'

Will backtracked immediately. 'I merely meant, my lord, that your business of state must lead you to the roughest parts of the kingdom, for that is where the spies and informers also ply their trade.'

'That they do, and it is sometimes necessary for a good man to mix with sinners, in order to unmask a greater evil, but I assure you, Shakespeare, I have no need to do that myself.'

'Of course not, my lord.' He bowed his apology.

'There are many men who will do my bidding when I give them an order. You are one such, are you not?'

'I am.'

Cecil did not seem placated by this show of obedience and Will cursed himself for his loose tongue, which had clearly caused offence. Now he waited to see what would happen to him because he couldn't control his own mouth.

'You are going to jail,' Cecil told him.

Chapter Twenty-Three

*'In the night, imagining some fear,
how easy is a bush supposed a bear.'*

—*A Midsummer Night's Dream*

Will immediately went down upon one knee before Cecil and bowed his head low. 'My lord, I most heartily apologise and humbly beseech you to show mercy upon your wretched servant. I meant no insult and, if you but spare me for my unwitting insolence, I shall reward your faith by doing your bidding whenever it is required.'

'I have made my decision. I am sending you to the Clink.'

'Please, lord, no.' Will had heard many tales of the conditions in that foul prison and had even visited it once briefly, years before, to see a woman wrongfully imprisoned there. That had been enough to convince Will he wouldn't last a week in such vile conditions. 'I beg of you.'

Cecil did something wholly unexpected then. He laughed. 'Stop begging, man, and stand yourself up. You are going to the jail.' He laughed again. 'But not as a prisoner. I want you to visit someone who resides there.'

The enormous surge of relief Will felt was only slightly diminished, by the knowledge that Cecil had deliberately misled him into thinking he would be jailed, and the Secretary of State seemed to have taken a good deal of amusement from Will's resulting terror.

'If you are seen across the river, you can put it about that you are looking for land to acquire for your new theatre, but while you are in Southwark, you are to see a man imprisoned in the Clink.'

Even a brief visit to that terrible, foul-smelling, desperate place was a deeply unappealing notion to Will, but it was better than the terrifying prospect of taking up a more permanent residence there.

'William Wade found the man. He is a steward of matters domestical accused of theft and being unable to pay money he is owed, so is imprisoned for his debts. He must stay in the Clink until he settles them. Of course, there is little hope of that, for he cannot earn money while in jail.' Cecil seemed to find this cruel paradox amusing. 'He cannot repay his debts and will likely starve there unless he receives some charity.' Then he said, 'I want you to bring him a little of that charity.'

'Why, my lord?'

'Because I believe he holds secrets. They may be the real reason he has been imprisoned.'

'Then why not simply release the man?'

'And betray my interest in him? No, it does not serve me to have him released.' *Then God help that innocent man*, thought Will. 'I had already ordered Poley to question the steward, but he is known and if I send any of my usual men to press him, it would be noticed, so Poley will now leave this to you. I must send someone the prisoner does not suspect of being my creature. Tell the gaoler the man owes you money and you have come to collect it. He will no doubt find that notion amusing as he will have been bled dry already, if he wishes to have any form of comforts in the Clink. The post of gaoler is not well paid, but he can demand fees from his prisoners for the most basic of needs, so his job is sought after.' Cecil took some coins from his purse and sprinkled them onto the table in front of Will. 'Bribe your way in, then use this money sparingly. Purchase that man's secrets one coin at a time.'

'But who is this servant?'

'A Master Edward Seagrave. He was in the service of Lady Anne's father until recently. He ran errands from that northern noble's home to his son and daughter here at court. If anyone knows what has passed between members of that family, then it is he. I believe that is the very reason he is now imprisoned at the word of his master.'

'To silence him.'

Cecil nodded. 'So, make him talk, Shakespeare. Tell him he might be freed if he does and perhaps we will finally discover why Lady Anne was killed.'

'I shall.'

Will waited for a moment to ensure their business was done, so he could be excused by Cecil, but instead the queen's inquisitor heard something and walked towards the window. He turned back to Will, gave him a look, then gazed out of it again. Will took this as an invitation to join Cecil to witness the spectacle outside for himself.

Will looked down at a merry gathering below. There was laughter from the queen's ladies as they ran about on the lawn, pursuing the gentlemen of the court in some game or other, urged on by the queen, who was standing close by, laughing, clapping encouragement and even shouting about which of the men should be pursued and caught next. Whatever game this was, only the most handsome and favoured men of the court were playing it with them. Will recognised among them the subjects of Cecil's enmity: Southampton, Mountjoy, Raleigh and the newly restored Essex were all at the centre of the merriment, as they always seemed to be.

The latter must have caught Cecil's eye then as he stepped away from one of the advancing ladies. 'They say the Earl of Essex was bitten by a Winchester Goose,' he said wryly.

The Winchester Geese was a name for the women who plied their trade in the brothels on the south bank of the river, not far from the Clink prison Will was about to be sent to. They were so-called because they all wore white aprons with yellow hoods to distinguish them from other women, so men would know they were prostitutes. A percentage of the money earned in their brothels went directly to the Bishop of Winchester in the form of rents. Daily, merchants, lawyers and courtiers would join the throng that crossed the river by boat to enjoy some time with these girls, but it was an undertaking not without risk. If you were 'bitten by a Winchester Goose' it meant you had contracted venereal disease. Even the highest in the land was not immune from infection from the lowest. If the allegation was true, you wouldn't know it from looking at the Earl of Essex now. He appeared utterly carefree, as he seemed to dance away from the outstretched hand of one of the queen's ladies, evading her, to the amusement of the queen.

'That was the real reason the earl wanted rid of Roderigo Lopes, not treason.' Cecil said this lightly. 'I never once thought the queen's former physician was a traitor, but he did treat Robert Devereux for the pox, and was foolishly indiscreet about it, telling the Spanish secretary, Perez, about the earl's affliction. That is what led to the doctor's downfall. I do believe that to be the first and only time a man has been hanged, drawn and quartered for spreading gossip.'

A face appeared at the doorway then and Cecil looked towards him. William Wade appeared agitated, and Cecil allowed him to interrupt them.

'We pressed the priest as you instructed, my lord. He would admit nothing, even under extremis.'

'You see, Shakespeare. Catholics are fanatics who will often refuse to reveal their plans, even at the point of death. I am always astonished when they will not give up their fellow conspirators because they believe that to be a form of treachery, even though they themselves are all traitors to the crown. Sometimes, they expire during interrogation having told us nothing.' This state of affairs clearly irked him. 'Luckily, we have other methods and are not always reliant on pressing a man till he can take no more.' He turned back to Wade and asked him, 'Did you bring his possessions as I asked?'

Wade obediently handed over a sack and Cecil pulled out its contents, which included some clothing and a hunk of stale bread wrapped in paper. Cecil seemed more interested in the paper itself than its contents, which he unwrapped and showed to Will, but it contained no message. He tapped the bread against the desk.

'This bread is too hard to keep and yet it has been stored most carefully with paper wrapped around it. Why?' He stared at the blank paper meticulously, then said, 'I think I know.'

Cecil walked towards a candle and held the paper close to the flame. It took a moment, but, before Will's eyes, the heat from the candle caused a change to occur in the paper. As it grew warmer, letters began to appear. Cecil rotated it so that the heat affected every inch of the paper, revealing a detailed message, which Cecil was now able to read.

'A letter of introduction, written by the priest we apprehended, using the juice from an orange,' Cecil explained. 'The Spanish,' he mused, 'even their fruit is treacherous. The juice is rendered invisible to the eye once it dries, but the words are magically restored upon the application of a little heat.' He read the words carefully. 'This message is written on behalf of three young men who were to be dispatched to the lowlands so they could meet with fellow heretics and offer their services, most likely to a Catholic plot to assassinate our queen. And now, we have their names.' He handed the letter to Wade. 'Arrest them all at the same time, so none can learn of the other's fate and evade you.'

Wade bowed in agreement and left to pursue Cecil's wishes.

'Those men will burn,' Cecil told Will, 'as will the priest who wrote this, but first, we will copy his letter of introduction and send our own men to the lowlands instead. Once they are trusted by the plotters, they will strike them all down, leaving their bodies as a warning to anyone else who might be tempted to try to murder the queen. There are always traitors in our midst,' Cecil told him. 'And I cannot rest until every last one of them is in the ground. Plots abound and you have a part to play in this too, Shakespeare, for I believe we may have uncovered another one.'

In a matter of moments, Will had been given reminders of the high stakes involved in the game he had been ordered to play. He had just learned that the Earl of Essex once had a man hanged, drawn and quartered merely for embarrassing him. Now Cecil had admitted the routine nature of torture to extract information from the queen's enemies, and how they would be burned alive afterwards. Essex and Cecil may have been deadly rivals, but they shared a ruthlessness at dealing with their enemies that Will knew he would do well not to forget. If he was not extremely careful, he might one day become another victim of their cruelty.

Then Cecil asked him, 'Before you leave to do my bidding, tell me, what is this comedy you are involved in?'

'Comedy?' Was Cecil worried he wasn't paying enough attention to *Henry V*? Not now that *Much Ado About Nothing* was finished. 'I write no new comedy?'

'I was talking about the farce you are playing out with Avisa Florio?' Cecil clarified. 'Poley learned of it.'

Will's spirits were lowered even further. It was bad enough that Cecil had discovered the truth about Will and his lover, but even worse if the truth had come from Poley. He didn't want to think about that vile man knowing of his most intimate secrets.

Whatever had made him imagine he could keep his affair from Robert Cecil, when the man had eyes everywhere, and so did Poley? It didn't matter that he had taken great pains to avoid being followed. They could have had Avisa followed instead, or simply paid someone from her household, who had guessed what was going on and reported it back to Poley. Will would never discover exactly how Poley had learned of their dalliance, but Cecil knew of it now, and they were both at his mercy.

'I could end it today,' Cecil told him, 'with a word to the queen, or her husband.'

Will waited for him to continue, but it was soon clear he expected an answer. Should he deny this or admit to it?

'I know, my lord.'

Cecil sniffed then and thought on it more. 'Or I could tell myself that what happens between a man and a lady does not always have a bearing on the security of the realm, which requires all of my energies right now.'

'Thank you, my lord.'

'I have not yet made my decision, Shakespeare, though I have to say that I am shocked that you, a married man, and Avisa, a married *woman*' – he stressed the last word to emphasise how appalled he was by her crime since, being a woman, it clearly exceeded Will's, as she was supposed to be possessed of womanly virtue – 'should have sunk so low before God. It is a serious matter, and I shall think more on it while praying for guidance and *both* of your immortal souls. It seems God does move in mysterious ways indeed, for I find it hard to understand why the Lord would bring such a godly woman as the Lady Anne to his side so early, while leaving others on this earth to rut like beasts in a field.'

Chapter Twenty-Four

'A heavy heart bears not a nimble tongue.'

—*Love's Labour's Lost*

Thanks to Robert Cecil, Will was late for their appointment at the docks. When he finally arrived, he found the Burbage brothers gloomily surveying the damp timber that was sitting in a pile to the front of Peter Street's wharf by the Thames. How long before it was all ruined, they were likely wondering.

'I have been thinking and have come to a resolution,' Will told the brothers.

'You concede this venture of ours must end?' asked Cuthbert. 'For what else can we do?'

'I say we can continue.'

Both brothers scoffed at this notion.

'Do you not trust me?'

'The last time you had an idea, Will Shakespeare, we tore down our theatre and now its timbers sit rotting by the Thames. I trust in God alone,' Cuthbert said, 'though I tell you true, he has abandoned us.'

'We have fifty pounds already,' Will reminded them. 'How did we come about this?'

'You know how,' said Richard. 'By pledging it between the three of us. But it is not near enough.'

'Then what if more were to pledge?'

That gave them both pause and Cuthbert asked, 'What are you proposing?'

'A partnership, not unlike the one we undertook five years ago when we founded the Lord Chamberlain's Men, with each man investing on the promise of a share of future profits.'

'But the Theatre is ours alone, Will. It is our inheritance,' Cuthbert protested. 'My father built it. We let you become an investor since you provide the plays, but not others. Why should we dilute our stake in what is already ours?'

'Because, its timbers *sit rotting by the Thames.*' He used Cuthbert's own words for his argument. 'A part share of something is worth more than a full share in nothing.'

There was silence for a time while Cuthbert reluctantly digested this, but he would not yet concede the argument.

Richard picked up a stone and threw it bad-temperedly into the brown waters of the river. 'He's right,' he told his brother then he turned to Will. 'But who has the coin to do it?'

'I have thought on this too. Kempe prospers and could surely provide ten pounds. Just as I am sure he would miss the stage he jigs on far more than he would miss the coin he hoards.'

'He might,' conceded Richard, who was as aware of Kempe's ego as Will was.

'He is not the only one.'

'Good, for we will still need another thirty pounds,' Richard reminded him, 'even if Kempe agrees.'

'Thomas Pope could likely be relied upon for another ten,' Will proposed.

'First you suggest a fool, then an acrobat. What next?' asked Cuthbert.

'An acrobat who already owns a share in the Curtain Theatre. If he sold that, he could invest with us?'

'If he wants to see his money disappear,' Cuthbert noted.

Will ignored him. 'I think Pope could be persuaded. Augustine Phillips too. He has money and a share in our company already. Would he wish to see it dissolved by us? He would not. Let's ask him to continue to prosper with us in our new venture.'

'We would still be ten pounds short,' Cuthbert reminded him, but Will could tell he was beginning to weaken. It was indeed possible that these men from this small troupe of actors, some with the lowliest of backgrounds, might actually be capable of amassing such a mighty sum between them. Since they had already profited from being shareholders in the Lord Chamberlain's Men, they would not wish to see that investment go the way of the Theatre.

'We need one more,' said Richard, and Will realised he was in favour of the idea.

'John Hemminges then. He must have the coin and once said to me he was such an admirer of my plays that, were he not a member of our company, he would pay to see them every day.' Will smiled. 'I shall remind him of that.'

Richard smiled at that notion too. 'He will have to pay. So shall we all. Perhaps with everything we have, if this venture costs more than we imagine. When has a building ever cost less than was planned or been built quicker than the architect promised? Then we must attract large crowds and make them care enough about your words to cross a river to hear them? There is no guarantee that they will. This could all end very quickly, just as soon as the first performance of the first play fails to fill the theatre we laboured so much to build. It's madness, Will. You know this, surely.'

'I do,' Will admitted. Then he asked, 'So, are you in?'

Richard sighed. 'Of course.'

—

When they were done at the wharf, Cuthbert left but Will and Richard walked the banks of the river together for a time, while contemplating the likelihood of their outlandish plan actually succeeding. In the end, they grew tired of discussing such a gloomy subject and Richard changed it entirely.

'When did you last see your family, Will?'

'I confess it has been a while.'

'Why don't you go back to Stratford and spend some time with them?'

'I should, Richard. I know I should, but my heart always feels so heavy in Stratford.'

'Because of your boy?'

'I see him in every street and alleyway, every field we walked by. I can still feel the weight and warmth of his hand in mine when he was only a little boy.' Will sighed. 'I know it is not fair on my girls that I have been away so long, nor on Anne. I leave them to shoulder the burden of our grief, while I am here in London… but when I see their faces…'

'You see his?'

'Yes.' His voice cracked then.

'They likely understand,' Richard consoled him, 'but perhaps you could go and see them in a while, when your grief has softened a little.'

'It has been more than two years, Richard.'

'Is it so long?'

'I know 'tis unmanly grief and I would have thought by now it might have diminished, but it has not. I can forget Hamnet for a time while I am writing or when a play is on, but every morning when I wake, he is the first thing I think of. Every night before sleep, it is his face I see at the last. I am shamed to admit it.'

'There is no love greater than a father's or mother's,' stated Richard. 'A child dying before their parents, though far from uncommon, is the most cruel thing on God's earth. This city is filled with those who, in their quieter moments, secretly mourn their lost children but say naught of it during the day, for we are taught not to.' Richard thought to lighten the tone then. 'But tell me, how does your family enjoy living in the finest house in Stratford?'

'The second finest.'

'The second finest then. It must please them, no? When I first met you, you had no home of your own. You and your children were lodging with your father and mother. Now you have land and property and your family live well in your hometown. That must make you proud.'

'It did,' Will conceded. 'A little. For a time. I bought it the year after Hamnet's passing, to give us a new place and I hoped a new life, but I find I would almost always rather be here than there.'

'Then you bought it for Anne, Susannah and Judith, so they can live in comfort, which means you are a good father.'

'A good father?' He doubted that. 'I know not if I am, or if I am even a good man.' For some reason, he thought of Avisa then and the sin of adultery they were both knowingly committing. That did bother him on occasion, during the rare times he found that he was not longing for her.

'But you try to be,' Richard reminded him. 'And, really, that is all a man can do.'

Chapter Twenty-Five

'Hell is empty and all the devils are here.'

—*The Tempest*

You could smell the Clink prison before you saw it. The stink of shit and other filth emanating from within was almost unbearable and the odours seeped out into the street. Will hoped his visit would not take overlong. He was brought to the gaoler first, who enquired after his business. He gave the man the name of the inmate he had come to see, claiming to be owed money by Seagrave. The gaoler seemed disinterested in this, aside from the fact that Will was joining a queue of debtors, which included himself, and would not be repaid until he had received his dues first.

'How much does he owe you?' Will asked.

The gaoler gave Will a figure. It seemed high for a man who had not been able to leave the Clink to run up any further debts.

'He owes me for the rent of his cell.'

Will knew of this practice. If you did not want to be cast down into a pit, with all the worst that London had to offer, you had to pay to rent a cell for yourself, though this was nothing more than a stark, windowless room, with a stone floor and walls.

'Then there is bedding,' he added before threatening, 'which I should take back from him, as well as sundry victuals, and he will get no more of those from me unless I am paid.'

Will gave the gaoler coin enough to appease him and ensure access to his prisoner. He assured him of more, should he be allowed to see his charge alone for long enough to conclude their business. With that, he was taken to Seagrave, whose cell door was open, since he could not escape the prison's outer walls. He sat on stained bedding, with his back pressed against the wall, and looked to be in a wretched state. There were ulcers on his legs caused by the tightly fitted, iron manacles, which rubbed too hard against him when he moved. He hadn't even the money to pay for looser-fitting restraints, which was the usual practice.

Will did not give Seagrave his name but instead said he was there to do God's work, the better to dispense charity to him, should he need some. The prisoner looked so undernourished and hopeless, he readily agreed to answer any questions Will might have about his circumstances and never thought to question why he was there to dispense charity.

'Are you a murderer, sir?' asked Will, as if he knew nothing of the manner of his incarceration.

'Not I,' he protested. 'My imprisonment here is most unjust, for I have done no wrong to any man,' he assured Will, sitting up straight now in the eager hope that he could persuade his visitor of his innocence.

They could hear the shouts and groans of other prisoners beyond Seagrave's cell; some pleading for release or food, others quarrelling violently in different corners of the jail, and one screaming, who sounded as if he had been driven quite mad.

'Many here would say the same. But tell me what crimes you are accused of? Did you rob a man, take a horse or steal from a church?'

Seagrave vehemently denied this. 'I would never. I am a God-fearing Christian man.' Before swiftly adding, 'A Protestant and loyal servant to my former lord and Her Majesty.'

'Your *former* lord?'

'Baron Percy. I was in his service many years and was a trusted man. Regularly did he urge me to travel great distances for him, to deliver messages to his son and daughter at court and convey their replies back to him.'

'But you abused that trust and lost it? You must have.'

'And I do beseech you, kind sir, that I know not how, for I never once did sin against my master. But before I could even speak to him or his son, I was conveyed here by others and locked within its walls.'

'The gaoler said you have debts?'

'I do not, outside of the money the gaoler demands to keep me here in no comfort at all, but I have run out of coin. I swear I have no other debts but those.'

'Then perhaps, as your sins are not so great, I might be able to offer you some charity, in exchange for more truths about your current state?'

The man may have been wretched, but he must have still had some of his wits about him, as he finally thought to ask, 'From whence does this charity come?'

'Good men, all pious gentlemen from the city of London, who on occasion will give charity for the relief of the wretched when they have fallen as low as you, since they believe it brings them closer to God. Remember Matthew,' Will told him. 'It is easier for a camel to pass through the eye of a needle than for a rich man to enter the kingdom of God.'

He seemed content with that explanation. 'I know my gospels,' Seagrave assured him.

'You owe the rent for your cell?'

'I do.' This almost brought the man to tears. 'The gaoler threatens to cast me down and house me with the most wretched prisoners if I cannot pay him.'

Will took out a coin and handed it to the man. 'This will keep you away from the worst and house you in your cell for a month or more.'

'God bless you, kind sir!' He took the coin as if it was the means of his salvation.

'Then there are victuals, which you seem most in need of.'

'I haven't eaten in two days. The gaoler charges three times what the same food costs outside the Clink, knowing I have no choice but to pay him.'

'Then the Lord shall provide.' And Will showed him another coin. The tears that flowed from Seagrave then were in gratitude, but Will knew he had to harden his heart if he was to learn anything of use. 'In return for a full account of your most recent life serving your lord. Tell me more about those messages you took to his children?'

If the prisoner suspected his motives then, it did not seem to matter, for he at least pretended not to, so desperate was he for food. 'There were some instructions I was to give them that were written down and some that were not.'

'Because he did not trust letters, in case they were seen by others?'

'I assumed as much.'

'Then what was the nature of these messages?' Will probed.

'I confess I did not always understand them.'

'You must have known the meaning of most, if not all, or how could you deliver them?'

'I did not.' But his eyes betrayed the truth of it, and though he would feel considerable guilt later for his actions, Will immediately rose to his feet and made to leave. 'Wait!' cried the starving man. 'Please! I believe I can remember them now. I am out of my senses for lack of food, but it starts to come back to me as I think on it.'

Will returned to his earlier position. 'Go on.'

'My lord did have me convey that his son should be patient, for all was going well with my master's plans to advance the family.'

'Advance them in the eyes of the queen?'

Seagrave hesitated.

'Come now,' Will urged him, 'your lord has abandoned you.'

He must have thought he had no loyalty left to the Percys. 'Not so, I think.' He looked sheepish then.

'In the eyes of another, perhaps?' offered Will.

'I have no proof of it,' Seagrave countered, 'but did think it likely, yes.'

'So, your lord was in contact with someone who might have had an eye on the English throne, should Her Majesty...?' Will didn't wish to complete the sentence in front of a stranger, for even to contemplate the queen's death aloud was considered treason.

'That was the sum of it, I fear,' he admitted. 'And I would surely have conveyed this to others if I had but proof.'

Will doubted this was true, but Seagrave was assuring Will of his loyalty to the realm now, in fear of even harsher penalties than an indefinite spell in the Clink.

'And what did he say to his daughter?'

'That the Lady Anne should make sure of the queen's favour, until Her Majesty began to think of her as a daughter, and then she would enjoy all of her confidences.'

'And could convey them back to her father?'

The man nodded and Will rewarded him with that other coin.

'For your victuals.'

Anne's father had given four hundred pounds to secure his daughter a place at the queen's side and Will could not immediately see the advantage he might gain from it, nor why he would part with such a huge sum. He believed he could see it now, though: to know the queen's mind on the matter of the succession. Imagine the favour a man might gain from a future king or queen, if he was the first to tell them they had the strongest claim to the throne, because the queen believed it so?

Will reminded Seagrave then of the need for more coin to pay for his bedding, candles and faggots to fuel his fire. This seemed to encourage him further.

'I would bring letters to both Lady Anne and her brother, Edmund. Most often to the brother, but occasionally to my lady.'

'And how would they receive them?'

'With great interest and most seriousness. As soon as word of my presence at court reached them, they would find reason to leave it and come immediately to my side, usually at the stables, so it would seem as if I was preparing their horse to go riding.'

'So, they would come immediately, because the news you brought was of importance to them?'

He nodded.

'And they would read the letters while you were there?'

Seagrave nodded again.

'What then? Did they write a reply?'

'There was hardly ever a written reply, only words passed between us for me to relay to their father upon my return.'

'Hardly ever is not never,' Will suggested.

'Once, my lady did bid me wait awhile so she could return to the palace and write a letter to her father, which she gave to me sealed. I did not know its contents.'

'But it was likely a response to his instructions? A reassurance perhaps that she would do his bidding?'

'It likely was, since she was always an obedient daughter and looked to her father in all things.'

'And what of the letters they received?'

'I was instructed by my lord to always take them back, once they had read them.'

'What did you do with them then?'

'I was to burn his letters.'

'And did you always destroy them?'

He thought on this before answering. 'There was one letter I recall above all others. I gave it to the Lady Anne, but what she did with it was most unusual.' He glanced at Will's hand significantly and Will instinctively felt that this would be information worth having.

He handed Seagrave another coin.

'She kept it,' said Seagrave.

'Yet always handed back the other letters for you to burn?'

'Always. I did remind her of that, and she told me that this letter was different and her father had instructed her to keep it close to her person.'

Will felt sure this was the item she had hidden in her prayer book.

'So there were two letters then? One with his instructions and this other letter?'

Seagrave nodded.

'Was this second letter written in her father's hand?'

'It was not.'

'Whose then?'

'I know not, but I did notice something unusual about the words.'

'Go on.'

'I could not make any of them out. I saw the letter only briefly, while my lady held it and looked at it most intently. Some of the letters had been replaced by symbols I did not recognise.'

'A cypher?'

'Very like.'

'Could Anne understand it?'

'No.'

'How do you know?'

'Because she only glanced at it a moment or two before halting. She could not have read it all so quickly and she said something then.'

'What did she say?'

'She said, *I shall leave this to others, but the end shall be the same.*'

'Meaning that she could not decipher it, but others would be able to?'

'I think so, yes.'

'And what would that end be?'

'I know not, good sir, but...'

'But?'

'It can only have been to the family's advantage. I learned as much from the smile that crossed her lips when she spake it.'

Will had been right to come here. The information he had just purchased had been worth its cost. He made as if to leave then.

'Please sir, I beg of you, since I have been of some help to you, could you use whatever influence you have to put my case to those men you serve. Tell your patrons that I am a wronged man, who is both innocent and honourable. I fear if I am not released soon from this vile place that I will die here in its filth.'

'I will do all that I can,' Will assured him.

—

Will was glad to be leaving behind the smells and squalor of the Clink. He walked along the banks of the river for a while towards London Bridge, the only way to cross over the Thames to its north side without taking a barge. Then he planned to seek out his companions from the company and buy them ale, the better to numb his senses against the experience he'd just had. He wished to dampen some of the guilt he felt for leaving the unfortunate Seagrave languishing there. If it had been within Will's power to release the man, he surely would, but it was not. All he could do was try to persuade Cecil to be merciful.

Will was lost in thoughts on how to procure Seagrave's release, when he was stopped suddenly in his tracks by a big man who stepped out in front of him, exuding menace. 'Hand me your purse,' he demanded.

'My purse?' Will was taken aback by the blatant nature of the command. The street was crowded, people were all around them, it was light and the hour still early. A robbery as blatant and public as this one was rare, even for a notoriously lawless London. 'I have no purse.'

Would the fact that he had just spent all of his coin in Clink prison save him now? He had literally run out of money. Will even reached for that purse and held it up, to show that it was indeed empty.

This seemed to confuse his erstwhile robber, who frowned at the purse and said, 'Die then.'

Which thoroughly confounded Will, who had expected the man to turn on his heel and find another more prosperous victim. Instead, he whipped out a dagger that had been concealed beneath his cloak and lunged for Will. The attack would have been a fatal one if it were not for the fact that his assailant stumbled a little as he delivered the blow and Will saw it coming. He leapt backwards, with the practised ease of a player used to springing free during choreographed fights staged by actors who practically danced round one another to avoid blows from wooden swords.

The knife still struck home, though. It was only a glancing blow, but it drew blood as the other man's knife arm slashed upwards, and the point of the dagger struck the flesh by his ribs. Will let out a great cry of pain and alarm and drew his own dagger to face his attacker. It would have likely turned into a knife fight to the death then, if it were not for the general alarm Will had caused from his cry of pain and distress and the bloodstain forming on his shirt.

Onlookers ceased what they were doing, some shouted in alarm that a robbery was taking place, others shrank back to avoid injury but made a din about it, and then there were some who saw Will was being attacked and sought to corner the man who had slashed him, to bring him down. The other man was forced to wave his dagger to ward them off. It didn't take Will's attacker long to work out that he was in peril and the odds stacked against him. He turned on his heel then and ran, leaving Will standing there in shock with a wound to his torso that he dearly hoped looked worse than it was.

—

Back in his rooms, Will tended to that wound and was relieved that it did not appear too deep, though, maddeningly, it kept on bleeding no matter how hard he pressed a dressing down on it. While he stood there waiting for it to stop, he thought back on his time at the Clink and asked himself what he had learned there that day, which might help him solve the death of Lady Anne. Firstly, that the baron was sending secret letters to his son and daughter, using an intermediary. Both knew this correspondence had to be returned to the messenger as soon as they had finished reading it, and he was to ride off and burn it. This proved the contents were damning and would be of clear interest to Robert Cecil, who would assume them treasonous but would lack proof, the letters having been destroyed. All but one of them at least.

Seagrave had confirmed there was a letter that Lady Anne had kept and that this was written in a new hand and was in some form of code. It seemed likely then that it was not from her father. If someone else had written it, there was only one reason for Anne to keep it. The contents would incriminate someone and perhaps even destroy them. Could Lady Anne's father have taken possession of a letter to a claimant to the throne, from someone at Queen Elizabeth's court, possibly one of her closest favourites, maybe even one of the four men Cecil suspected most: Blount, Raleigh, Southampton or Essex? If Anne possessed something so dangerous, then she could demand a high price for it or she might even have been planning to show it to the queen and bring down a great lord? If she could prove he had conspired against Her Majesty, by encouraging a claimant to take the English throne, it would be enough to see that lord brought to the block.

A man might do almost anything to avoid a fate like that, even kill a young maid.

Chapter Twenty-Six

*'But kings and mightiest potentates must die,
for that's the end of human misery.'*

—*Henry VI Part I*

Cecil was bent over a table examining documents. He either did not hear Will enter or chose to ignore him.

'My lord is busy?' Will hoped to be excused from their latest meeting, but instead Cecil waved him over.

Then he gazed at Will closely and asked, 'You have a wound? How did you come about it?'

Will glanced down and realised that a new bloodstain, from the wound he thought he had finally stopped, had seeped through his shirt and left a small mark on his doublet. It was barely visible, but Cecil had spotted it immediately. He forced Will to explain its origin now, and Will described the attempted street robbery after he had left the prison. Once Cecil was satisfied this had nothing do with the investigation, he seemed to lose interest in it.

'And what did you learn at the Clink?' Cecil demanded.

Will gave the Secretary of State a faithful account of his conversation with Seagrave, omitting nothing.

Cecil listened to him keenly but kept his own counsel until Will was finished, then he beckoned Will towards the papers that were spread out on his desk and asked him, 'What do you see?'

He indicated the papers that were face up on the table. They were each different but looked similar. They contained names, as well as lines connecting those names to others, indicating their marriages and offspring. Some of them went back several generations, showing grandparents and beyond, but they all came down to the present day, detailing names that were familiar to anyone who had spent even a little time at court. Will knew what they were but was reluctant to admit it. 'They chart the progress of great families through the generations to the present time, my lord.'

'To what end?' Cecil asked this lightly, but Will feared a trap.

'To show how far they go back, to establish an ancestral claim on their lands.'

'That is not why these papers were written, nor why they were seized. I suspect a man of your intelligence would know exactly what they represent.' It was obvious from his tone that he wished Will to be honest in his answers.

'They appear to be...' he began falteringly, 'documents that might suggest... a claim to the throne.' Before adding quickly, 'Not a legitimate one, of course, but in the hands of the queen's enemies...'

'They could be used to justify her assassination and the usurpation of the crown,' Cecil concluded for him. 'And that is exactly their purpose. Some of these nobles trace their lineage back to the queen's father and grandfather, others go back as far as John of Gaunt, who was never a king but was father to Henry IV and grandfather to Henry V. His descendants think they have a claim to the throne through an ancestor who died two hundred years ago. This' – he waved his hands at the documents – 'is what we must contend with.' Then he said, 'I think Baron Percy has been in contact with pretenders to the throne or knows of others who have.' That seemed a fair assumption. 'But who might they be, do you think?'

'I know not, my lord,' Will replied. 'But Lady Anne's brother, Edmund, might. Perhaps you could ask him?' He suggested this despite knowing that the asking would likely involve torture.

'He has fled to the north,' Cecil explained. 'And I doubt will return soon.'

To avoid being questioned by you, no doubt, thought Will.

Cecil continued then. 'If you are to look deeper into this mystery for me, you will need to know who might stand to gain from that young woman's death and why? She was close to the queen and most likely planning to meet someone that night. This much we know. Some think her assignation was for a lewd purpose, though I myself believe that Lady Anne would have clung to her virtue. If I am right, she must have had a very different purpose. To pass on or to receive information perhaps, or proof of something nefarious? She could have been a conduit to her brother or father, for another person, as yet unknown. If she had a secret, it might be something that could have been used against a great lord, as you suspect, and they may have felt they had no option but to silence her forever. I believe this may have involved a plot against the queen and is most likely due to the succession, which you need to understand in some detail to recognise the motivations of the conspirators and their allies. Is that clear?'

'I believe so, my lord, yes.'

'The succession is not an easy matter. It is complicated by the fact that few dare talk about it, even among themselves, let alone openly, unless they be accused of the crime of wishing the queen's death, or of attempting to create a treasonous plot to place another upon the throne.'

'But if the queen has no issue, then the crown must eventually be passed to another,' said Will.

'And there are several candidates – none of whom are entirely suitable. Even if the succession could be discussed openly, there is no heir men can agree upon who would unite all of the factions at court. It is a great matter that used to occupy much of my father's time, as it does mine now, but only privately, of course. To even mention it to the queen is to risk being reduced by her, or worse.'

Will could appreciate the problem. All reasonable men could see that Her Majesty was past the age when she could possibly produce a natural heir, even if she were to finally agree to take a husband. It would be better for the realm then if all could agree on the line of succession and for this to be given the queen's blessing, but if she would not even permit the matter to be discussed, then a great uncertainty would continue to hang over the country, which would be a danger to all. Men like Cecil would have to contend with this, while knowing that if the queen were to die suddenly, there might be civil war to resolve the matter. This was no fanciful notion. When Elizabeth's brother, Edward VI, had died young, her elder sister Mary's succession was far from guaranteed. An uprising by the Dukes of Sussex and Northumberland, to ensure the succession of a Protestant heir, resulted in the crowning of the nine-day queen, Lady Jane Grey. Mary had retained the popular support of the people, however, and this rebellion soon fell apart. Poor Jane Grey was just seventeen when she went to the block, a largely innocent pawn in a game her father played and lost.

Will was cautious how he expressed his thoughts on the matter. 'I have heard some men say that the Scottish king is the most likely to rule after Her Majesty.'

'He is Protestant and would unite England and Scotland, ending centuries of strife between our two countries. On the other hand, he is *Scottish*.' Cecil didn't feel the need to add anything to that. Being Scottish was considered a bad thing in and of itself, for a large number of Englishmen. 'His mother, Mary, openly plotted against the queen and was executed by her, though he at least showed no loyalty to his mother growing up.

'The main obstacle to King James acceding to the throne is a legal one. King Henry VIII's will explicitly excludes the children of his older sister, Margaret, from the line of succession, since she was a Catholic, in favour of those of his younger sister, Mary, a devout Protestant. Margaret was James' great-grandmother, so by the terms of that will, he is passed over in favour of Edward Seymour, through his mother Lady Imogen Grey, sister to the unfortunate Jane.

'He was born in the Tower of London, however, where his mother was being held for secretly marrying Seymour's father, against Her Majesty's wishes. This was an inauspicious beginning, and his legitimacy has often been in doubt, since there is no documented proof his parents were actually married when he was born. Again, it is the question of legitimacy that could decide matters here. Incidentally, his grandfather was Lord Protector when King Edward was a boy. He proved so arrogant, he turned all against him and was executed.' Cecil half-chuckled to himself at that, and Will could only assume he was privately comparing the executed earl to his equally arrogant nemesis, Essex, and wishing the same fate on him.

'If Edward is considered illegitimate, then the next claimant is Anne Stanley, eldest daughter of the Earl of Derby, Ferdinando Stanley, a man I am sure you remember well.'

Will did indeed remember him, as patron to the acting company he had belonged to during his early days in London, Lord Strange's Men. Stanley had died relatively young and suddenly. Some suspected witchcraft at the time but others poison, since he himself had a small claim to Elizabeth's throne and had seemingly fallen out of favour because of it. Ironically, his untimely death now led to the possibility of his daughter, Anne, succeeding to the throne.

'Finally, Lady Arbella Stuart also has a claim, through her grandmother Mary, Henry VIII's sister, whose offspring are favoured in that will over his Catholic sister Margaret's. Arbella was a promising claimant once.' He failed to elaborate on why she might no longer be promising, but, whatever she lacked, it must have been something that made her less appealing in Robert Cecil's eyes, so her elevation would not be in his best interests. It was a rare and subtle admission that he had any personal preference in this matter at all. 'Her Majesty will not name a successor,' Cecil explained. 'Yet she is sixty-five years old, and no one lives forever. Not even queens.'

'What will happen to England if she...' Will lowered his voice to a whisper, 'dies without naming an heir?'

'That could happen any day. We cannot assume she will ail, take to her bed and spend days dying while her courtiers take down her final wishes. Her heart could give out like that.' He clicked his fingers.

'And the realm?'

'Would be torn apart. Without a quick and clean transition to a new monarch, it would be civil war. That much is certain.'

'By Jesu.'

'The Spanish would pick a side, so would the French. There would likely be an invasion, masquerading as support for a Catholic contender they would then control. England would be lost.'

'Then why does the queen not put an end to this uncertainty and name a successor?'

'Because she fears that once she does, her life could be forfeit.'

'She fears assassination?'

'Just so. The concern is that a claimant for the throne, once named, would grow impatient to seize what was rightfully theirs, in case it was taken from them by another before they could ascend to the throne. They might strike first to ensure it is not. A claimant like that would be very dangerous and have many allies keen to side with the next monarch.

'The queen should perhaps name an heir, but there has always been the issue of legitimacy during her reign. It has hung over many kings and queens of England before now, but Her Majesty was the daughter of her father's second wife, and some never forgave her for that. His marriage to Anne Boleyn was later declared null and void, and she was executed for high treason, with Elizabeth named a bastard long before she was declared a queen. She has not forgot the lesson she learned from her mother's fall. If a queen does not retain a firm grip on her subjects, she can quickly and easily be undone.

'There will always be claimants. What matters most is not whether they are legitimate or not, only that other men think them or wish them so, to achieve their own ends. To back a successful claimant for the throne before he succeeds to it is to ensure great reward for loyalty, which is why you will likely find that some or all of Elizabeth's favourites are already in correspondence with the Scottish king.'

'But is that not treason?' Will was shocked.

'Undoubtedly it is,' said Cecil simply. 'But proving it is not easy. They communicate in secret, through trusted messengers or by writing to James in code. I know it happens, but I have never been able to intercept any of these letters.' He looked at Will meaningfully. 'If I could get my hands on just one of them, it would be enough to bring down one of those great lords the queen dotes upon.'

He surely meant Essex, thought Will. Then he wondered if he might instead be referring to Southampton, or both of them, and then there was Mountjoy or even Raleigh. The four men Cecil distrusted the most might actually be giving him just cause for those suspicions after all. If they were indeed corresponding with James, offering the Scottish king a warm welcome should he attempt to seize the throne of England upon Elizabeth's death, or even, as Cecil surmised, before it, that would be enough to see them condemned to death.

Cecil went on. 'James has the strongest claim to the throne of England. The problem for the King of Scotland is that, without Elizabeth naming him as heir, there will always be those who would deem him an illegitimate king, which puts his life in danger were he to dare to move south unaided.

'So, you see, there are at least four possible contenders, and the succession can be argued over endlessly, on the grounds of King Henry's will and the legitimacy or otherwise of the claimants. What matters more is who is seeking to gain advantage by supporting or manipulating one, or perhaps all of these claimants, which is a task that endlessly occupies me. If Lady Anne was unwittingly caught up in one of those intrigues, then you must discover who is behind it, for they are likely to be an imminent threat to the queen?'

And to you, thought Will, since Cecil was so closely allied to her and would almost certainly die too, if she did.

Before he left, Will sought to honour his promise to Seagrave. 'My lord, you said he might be released?'

'Who?'

'Seagrave from Clink prison. You said he might be released, if he cooperated.'

Cecil didn't even look up from his papers. 'He is a man of no importance.'

And Will realised that the promise he had made to Seagrave, that he would do all he could to release him, had been a false one and Cecil had turned him into a liar. He wondered how Cecil could simply ignore the terrible plight of another human being like this and feel nothing for him, even if he did consider Seagrave a lower personage. This was the same attitude great nobles from long-established families held towards Cecil, and Will would have to hope that he never found himself starving in a stinking prison cell somewhere, while someone more elevated dismissed him as a man of no importance.

Will steeled himself to argue further on Seagrave's behalf. 'My lord, I promised that man if he helped us, I would do all I could to see him released from the Clink.'

'Seagrave is dead,' Cecil told him without even looking up.

'Dead? But I saw him just yesterday.'

'And last night he was stabbed by a fellow inmate in a quarrel over victuals.'

'Really?' Was this another deadly fight over food? Not unlike the one Kit Marlowe was supposedly involved in, which started over the bill for a meal at Eleanor Bull's rooming house in Deptford. Will had never believed that story and had always considered it murder. Was someone clearing away witnesses to a newer crime now? If they were, they were doing it in a manner not unlike that of the queen's inquisitor himself. Did all great men cover their tracks so, by blaming murder on brawls over insignificant quarrels?

'Yes, really. The culprit has already been hanged alas, so there is no way to press him as to whether some other hand was guiding him in this murderous act.'

How convenient, thought Will, for whoever ordered that attack. Alas then, poor Seagrave, who never did get to see the outside of Clink prison again. He had feared he might die in there, Will remembered, and die he did.

'Now do you understand what we are up against, Master Shakespeare? When even a man under lock and key can be killed, it shows we must be dealing with a powerful enemy indeed. You must find Lady Anne's killer before he uses that power against us.'

Chapter Twenty-Seven

'Love all, trust a few, do wrong to none.'

—*All's Well That Ends Well*

It took Will a while, but he managed to persuade the shareholders in the company to expand their investment by purchasing a further share in the new theatre. In a way, he was glad of the distraction because it prevented him from thinking too long on the tragic fates of Imogen Russell and Edward Seagrave, both of whom he had come to know for a short time before death almost immediately came to take them. At sea, Will would have been called a Jonah, for attracting so much ill luck.

Once they had all pledged to pool their money into the new theatre, everyone was keen to put an end to their rootless existence by purchasing the land they needed and setting to work, before the timbers in Peter Street's wharf began to rot.

But the back and forth between Cuthbert Burbage and the holder of the land they wanted to build their theatre on went on longer than they hoped. Every time Cuthbert thought he had almost agreed a deal, the man found a new way to talk up the price and kept him dangling. There were others interested in the land, he reminded Cuthbert, but it was really that he knew they were desperate for a resolution so they could remove their timber from the warehouse and start building. Then the landholder argued that it would not be looked upon favourably if he allowed a new theatre on his land, since all actors were known to be degenerates and plays the cause of much sin. Though apparently an increase in the cost of the lease would be sufficient to ease his troubled conscience about the eroding of his good name. His reasons kept changing and his price was always tantalisingly out of reach. That prompted Will to start making his own enquiries further along the river until he finally found a solution.

'I have discovered a scrap of land we might actually be able to afford,' Will told the Burbages. 'It can be acquired from one Nicholas Brend, on a thirty-one-year lease and is in a most favourable location.'

'Where is it?' asked Cuthbert.

'South of the river,' he said lightly.

'Where *precisely* is it?' Cuthbert was already suspicious.

'Why don't you come and take a look?' Will suggested.

—

The Burbages were standing either side of Will now, staring at the patch of land he had brought them to. On it lay a handful of tenements, but most of what was in front of them was fields, though there was a large ditch in the way before you reached them.

'Do you see it?' asked Will.

'See what?' asked Cuthbert.

'Our theatre,' he encouraged them, 'in your mind's eye. Situated right here in this very spot, attracting all nearby.'

'I do not,' said Cuthbert. 'All I see is… marsh.'

'That's not marsh,' Will retorted, but it was true that much of the land before them was waterlogged. 'It just floods a little when the tide is in, 'tis all.' He said this as if it was of little consequence, but he could tell they were unhappy about the state of the ground. 'Peter Street tells me we will need to sink some good foundations.' He realised he was sounding too dismissive, for even he could see this would be quite some undertaking, and might even be beyond them, but Will couldn't afford to think that way. Having come this far, there was no room left for doubt.

'What do you think, Richard?' Cuthbert asked his brother.

'We would be near to the Rose Theatre, so there's a competitor and Philip Henslowe will be after our blood if we take his audiences from him. This land is close to the bear baiting, the cockfighting, the taverns, brothels and all the worst kinds of people,' said Richard. 'So that is something.' He meant it was a good thing. They could hope to attract the same crowds as those other well-established attractions, and it was often the worst kind of people who stood before the stage among the groundlings. Get enough of them in at a penny a go and they might just be able to fill a theatre and make it prosper, but the important word here was *might*.

'So, you are willing to bet everything on this scrap of damp land and sink our timbers into it?' Cuthbert demanded.

Richard exhaled then. 'What choice do we have?'

'How long does Peter Street say this will take?' asked Cuthbert.

'He has sworn to complete the entire building in weeks,' Will assured him.

'Then we must assume it will take him a year, for builders always lie,' Cuthbert reasoned. 'Or if they do not, they have an inability to foresee the problems that lay ahead. Has there ever been a building in London that was not delayed for one reason or another, nor cost twice more than it ought?'

Will was about to rebut this but then he admitted, 'You are right. I think he lacks the manpower to put up the whole building in that time.'

'He does,' agreed Cuthbert.

'Then we must provide him with more,' said Will.

'Our company?'

'They helped us to tear the building down, they can help us put it back up again.'

'The tearing down took four days, the rebuilding of it will be much longer,' Cuthbert reminded him. 'You can't expect them to labour that long, Will.'

'If labouring gets the job done quicker, if we tell them that they will tread the stage of the finest theatre in England in front of thousands when it is done, then yes, I think they will work, perhaps not all day, nor every day, but when they can, and they must. We are committed to this venture now, and it cannot fail.'

Chapter Twenty-Eight

'I had rather give his carcass to my hounds'

—*A Midsummer Night's Dream*

'The crowds lined up to cheer him on his way.' While Cecil paced his room restlessly, he did not bother to hide his contempt towards the population of London for falling for the Earl of Essex's dubious charms. 'I am told the people stood along his route, praising him, for four miles! Imagine what that will do to his already immense vanity. When he left, he took Blount and the Earl of Southampton with him, though the queen expressly told him to leave Henry Wriothesley behind. He continues to defy her, and I tell you now that will be his undoing,' affirmed Cecil, before he added the caveat, 'eventually.'

Will was not so sure. The whole of London turning out for him was surely proof of the enduring popularity of the hero of Cadiz. Yet Cecil still seemed to think he could somehow dislodge the man. All men *could* fall, of course, but no one had as many enemies at court or fewer friends than Cecil, and the majority of them were lords with power and influence. If Will had been the kind of man to make a wager, he would have placed his money on the Earl of Essex triumphing over the Irish rebels. Then he would ride back, in a glorious procession at the head of his mighty army, and immediately demand the queen get rid of Cecil. Judging by what had happened to Her Majesty's former physician, some treason or other would likely be invented and Cecil would go to the block. It would be an undignified end for one of the most powerful men in the realm, but it was beginning to seem more and more likely to Will. He would have to give the impression of at least putting some distance between himself and the spymaster, lest he suffer the same fate.

'They are all of them bound by blood!' Cecil raged.

'Who is, my lord?'

'The Earl of Essex, the Duke of Northumberland and Baron Mountjoy. How can we trust a single one?' And when Will did not seem qualified to comment, Cecil explained impatiently, 'The Earl of Essex's sister, Dorothy, married the Duke of Northumberland, though he did not want her. His other sister, Penelope, Lady Rich, is the' – he was trying to choose the right word – 'inamorata of Baron Mountjoy, though she is still married to Baron Rich.' Once again, Cecil showed how shocked and prudish he could be about liaisons outside of marriage. Will always found this strange, since the man had seen or heard of so much of this world, and a great deal of it must surely have been more shocking than an extramarital affair at court. 'How then can I trust or control any of them, when they are all in league with one another?' Then he concluded softly as if to himself, 'And all of them wish to see me fall.'

He took a moment to compose himself and it seemed to Will as if he was simultaneously wrestling with anger, frustration and a deep fear for his future. Presently, he calmed himself enough to ask Will in a normal voice, 'I have been a patron to you, have I not?'

This was not strictly true, at least in the artistic sense. Robert Cecil had never commissioned a play or sonnet from Will, nor had he rewarded him financially for any of the other more secret work he had been forced to do for the queen's spymaster. Cecil had, however, smoothed the way for Will, by protecting him from others at times, or by persuading the queen of his merits. The mayor had tried to persuade her to close the theatres and ban his plays, others had tried to have Will arrested, for sedition and even treason, because he had offended a lord or knight of the realm with ill-chosen words. Cecil had managed to wave all this away. That is what he meant by being a patron to Will.

'You have, my lord.'

'And you are my loyal servant?'

'I am.' Though it pained Will to admit it.

'You do not carry a grievance then?'

'Against whom, my lord?'

'Against me.' Will was too taken aback to answer him, but Cecil was not done yet. 'I know you blame me for your friend's death. I am sure you hold me directly responsible for it, though it was not I who stabbed Marlowe in the eye.'

Should he deny it outright or blame drink for his railing against the world about Kit's tragic and untimely death, as he had done in the past? What excuse could Will give for naming Cecil as the perpetrator? None that would satisfy his master. He was sure of that.

'Do you think I ordered it?' Cecil asked. 'What if I said I did not? Would you believe me? What if I told you I was no more guilty of Kit's death than King Henry II was of Thomas à Becket's?' Then he quoted the long dead king. '"*Who will rid me of this troublesome priest?*" That was what he cried, was it not? Or some such like? Four loyal knights took that to mean the king had as good as ordered murder, so off they went to do their master's bidding, and oh what tragedy. Becket was slain at Canterbury Cathedral and the king repented his unwise words for the rest of his life.'

Was Will really supposed to believe that, like King Henry, Cecil had uttered angry words and his loyal followers, Poley, Skeres and Frizer, saw fit to interpret them as an order to do that they thought was his bidding, by murdering poor Kit? It seemed most unlikely, though Cecil did appear to be in earnest when he claimed this.

'Do you think I did not mourn Kit Marlowe? Of course I did. He was a most uncommon man with a fine mind. His company was of the most interesting kind. I felt his loss and if I was in any way responsible for it, however unintentionally, then I will carry that burden for the rest of my days.' This seemed to fall far short of an admission.

Several conflicting thoughts danced around Will's mind then. The first came from his instinct for self-preservation, and if he was to survive this encounter at all he needed to make Cecil feel he believed his master's explanation. 'I know you knew Kit's worth, my lord, and must have felt his loss keenly, as I did.'

Cecil fixed him with a look. 'You are loyal, then?'

'I am.' And he was. That part was true – though his loyalty to Cecil was partly born out of the fear of retribution directed against him if he was not. He knew one more thing, too. If it looked as if Cecil might fall, he would have to appear to be just as loyal to a new master, whether that was Essex, Southampton or Mountjoy, if he did not wish to be swept away with him.

This seemed to satisfy Cecil, though Will still doubted he was telling him the truth. Was Cecil lying to Will, or to himself, to try to ease the guilt on his own conscience?

It crossed Will's mind that Cecil had acknowledged what a fine intellect Marlowe had and how he had enjoyed his company. Perhaps he had used Kit, as he now seemed to be using Will, as someone who possessed an intellect that was at least close to being his equal? Someone who could understand and perhaps even console Cecil, when he confessed the burdens of a great office of state? That might explain why he confided in Will now. It also gave Will little solace to know that he was just as expendable to Cecil as his old friend.

'There is a rhyme about me, did you know that?' asked Cecil. 'They sing it in taverns.'

Will did know that. In fact, there was more than one rhyme about Cecil that was sung in taverns. He was blamed for everything amiss in London these days, from the high price of bread to the scourge of corruption, and the queen's seeming disregard for the state of her loyal subjects. All of this was laid at Robert Cecil's door. He was the evil at the centre of the court, the pygmy, a deformed schemer who would stop at naught to enrich himself at the expense of others. Will did not wish to admit he knew of the existence of a rhyme in case Cecil made him recite it and it turned out to be a different one.

'My lord, I did not.'

Cecil recited it himself then. 'Little Cecil trips up and down, he rules court and crown.' He shook his head. 'It's a popular ballad with many additional verses. I would be flattered, if powerful men at court did not use such ditties to show the queen I am grown too grand. They ask Her Majesty who is really the ruler here? If she were ever to seriously question that herself, I would be finished, and they know it. Meanwhile, Essex behaves like an emperor, and she dismisses it as boyish zeal. In time, she will learn who is really her most loyal subject, mark my words.'

Will had noticed a change in the way Cecil spoke of late. He would never have dreamed of sharing a confidence with a lesser man like Will before, but now he sounded vulnerable, quite possibly for the first time, as if wounded by events at court and, most damagingly, the queen's failure to see Robert Devereux's faults. There was something else here too. With his father gone, Cecil had lost his only confidant. Who else around him could possibly understand the nuances of the power struggle he was caught up in? His agents were all ruthless and capable men, but Will could not imagine William Wade or a man like

Robert Poley being someone to confide in. Was this why Will was allowed to hear so many of Cecil's private thoughts about the queen, the Earl of Essex and his many other enemies? Perhaps. Every man needed someone to hear him out and offer some sympathy for his plight. Otherwise, he was entirely alone.

'Uncover this nest of vipers for me. Find me the murderer before I am undone by my enemies. You must unmask this killer, Shakespeare.'

Chapter Twenty-Nine

'If thou rememb'rest not the slightest folly that ever love did make thee run into, thou hast not loved.'

—*As You Like It*

Avisa surveyed the necklace with seeming dispassion while Will waited for her reaction. He had spent time choosing it, and not an inconsiderable sum of coin acquiring it, in the hope she might see him in a new, more affectionate light than she had on their previous meetings of late. The last one had been a brief but admittedly urgent coming together, which had taken him slightly aback, since her need for him had seemed so wanton, even more so than his for her, and he would never have imagined that was possible. When it was over, she had seemed sated enough but in no mood to stay with him, excusing herself by explaining her husband was near, though Will happened to know he was not. He had assumed she was angry with him for some reason – his inability to be with her more often, thanks to the demands of the Theatre and Robert Cecil, perhaps? The necklace was meant to serve as recompense, but now it appeared she had no response.

Eventually she said, 'I wonder, Will, how is it that a man who supposedly understands so much, actually comprehends so little?'

It was as if she had been reading his mind, but he had hoped this lack of understanding did not extend to the choice of necklace, which he had felt sure was a good one, but now it seemed it was not. 'You do not like it?'

She sighed. 'It is a fine necklace, but pray tell me, when and where am I supposed to wear it? And, if it is worn, how am I to explain my coming by it? Should I say I found it in the street perhaps, or that an aunt I have never mentioned before died suddenly and left me it in her will? Or should I simply confirm the suspicions of many at court, that it came from my lover, a man who, in cuckolding my husband, seeks to add further humiliation to his name by branding me as his property,' she held up the necklace, 'with his choice of jewellery?'

'That was never my intention.'

'Intentions are rarely as harmful as consequences, Will. The consequence of me wearing this' – she held it loosely in her hand and at arm's length out towards him – 'would be the ruination of myself, my husband and quite possibly my lover, if he were identified by it. Though I suspect that, of the three of us, his disgrace would be the lesser and more temporary. The outward show of disgust at you would be replaced in private by nods and winks, then chuckles between the men at court over your amorous antics. Yes, I'm certain of it. Meanwhile, I would be branded a whore, my husband a feeble cuckold, and you a rake. Respectable men would bemoan you to their wives, while secretly envying your conduct.'

'You speak as if I see myself this way, and I do not.' But he reached out a hand and took the necklace back from her anyway, knowing it would be as foolish to insist she keep it as it had been for him to buy it for her in the first place. What had he been thinking? Of course she could never wear it, except perhaps alone in her bedchamber while admiring it in her looking glass, and what would be the point of that? He had been a fool, again, and hadn't that always been the way of it whenever he was besotted with a lady? It was as if he would forever be unreasoned by them. And to think he wrote of love, while having so little understanding of it himself.

It was the same with the court. He had been attending it for a number of years now, to perform in front of the queen or secretly conduct business for Sir Robert Cecil, and yet in many ways it was still a foreign land to him. Sometimes it felt like a place where he spoke only enough of the language to get by. He knew he would never understand its subtleties and unwritten rules well enough to ever consider himself a true courtier. It worried him that he was unable to navigate its intrigues as well as someone like Avisa. Though not born to this world, she had adapted herself to it quite naturally. That was something Will had never been able to do. What chance would he have of making his way towards the truth about Lady Anne and her killer in a world he could not fully comprehend? The court was like some labyrinthine maze Will was becoming trapped in, and it might very well prove to be his undoing.

Will realised even Avisa could see that now and it gave him little hope for their future. *She thinks I am a child playing an adult's game*, he realised, *and she is right.*

-

Will was right about one thing, though. The men of the company did indeed agree to work on the theatre, for they were as invested in the enterprise as Will and his fellow partners. None could imagine a life beyond the stage and, if the Lord Chamberlain's Men ceased to be because of the absence of one, then they might easily starve.

Everyone did what they could, all being directed by Peter Street, who supervised everything. The warmer weather helped both their spirits and the endeavour. The ground was softer, and the prospect of working outdoors for hours on end a more pleasing one than when they had torn down the old Theatre in the middle of winter. First, they built a bridge across the ditch to grant easier access for the carts. Street had promised them that the theatre would not just be reborn but would emerge as an even grander building than before. He explained how he wanted to add to the existing materials to make a three-storey building with twenty sides that resembled a circle. He would use the English oak timbers from the Theatre, and limestone plaster, with a roof fashioned from water reeds. There were plenty of those close by, thanks to the marshy ground. He assured them that, when it was complete, the new theatre would accommodate an audience of more than three thousand, and it would be their job to fill it, every day.

Next, they drove wooden piles deep down into the soft, marshy earth, to make a foundation and dug trenches filled with limestone to strengthen them. Then they hauled the timber posts for the walls from the wagons and planted them firmly into the ground, which was a backbreaking job. They added oak groundsills that were placed horizontally as base timbers, before they started on the brick walls, then the wattle and daub was added and it was all plastered with lime and sand. It pleased them to watch the building start to take shape. No one more so than Will, who had a perfect view of proceedings. He had been wondering where he should live, since his business would soon be on this side of the river. It had seemed pointless to stay in Shoreditch and cross it several times a day. The land they had leased came with a house large enough for Will's needs, so he had decided to take up residence there right by the theatre. Now it was the first thing he saw each morning, the last view he had before retiring every night, and he took great pleasure in watching the building steadily grow.

With a play about Agincourt to write, a playhouse to rebuild, Avisa quarrelling with him, and the small matter of a dead noblewoman likely involved in treason against the queen, the very last thing Will needed right now was another argument with Will Kempe, but it couldn't be avoided. Not after the company's latest performance at the Curtain. *Henry IV* had been written by Will two years ago. It was meant to be a historical play, with some comedic elements specifically written for the benefit of Kempe, who played the hugely popular character of Sir John Falstaff. The problem was not that he delivered his lines poorly, for they were well received, but that he continually upstaged the other actors, most notably Richard Burbage, playing Prince Hal, the future Henry V, while Kempe was not meant to be speaking but they were delivering their lines.

'Kempe, your constant improvising and bawdy asides are a distraction,' Will told him. 'The groundlings forget what the play is about, when all they do is wait for your next pulled face or lewd comment, none of which are in my play. Stick to the words I write for you, I pray thee.'

'I do not mind reciting *most* of your words,' Kempe replied, 'but your play can be improved with some new ones, particularly from a master of *commedia improvviso*,' he said grandly, his final words spoken in the accent of an Italian nobleman. Kempe always considered himself a serious scholar of their *commedia dell'arte* and liked to regale the rest of the company with stories of its rich history of improvisation and exaggerated characters. To Will, there was nothing more boring than a comedic actor who took their art almost as seriously as themselves. 'You should learn that a writer is not the attraction on a stage, Will.'

'It is not just me, Kempe. You are putting Richard off.'

'Nonsense.'

'You *are* putting me off,' agreed Richard. 'You *do* put me off. I almost forgot my line last night while you were miming a fart.'

'Did I not get a laugh from the groundlings?'

'Any man can get a laugh from the groundlings by miming a fart,' explained Will.

'Could you? I rather doubt that.' Kempe was being quite imperious now. 'And as for you, Richard Burbage, are you not perhaps taking your performance a little too seriously, when you ought to be putting more effort into entertaining the groundlings? They are our patrons after all. I keep them happy, you send them home downcast.'

'We have been performing tragedies and historicals, man!' Richard argued. 'You can't give them farts in a tragedy.'

'I knew you would be on his side,' Kempe deflected, 'whether you agree with him or not. It is because he is your friend.'

'He *is* my friend, and I do agree with him,' Richard replied. 'Both of those are true. But we are not always of one mind about everything. You have witnessed our quarrels.'

'However, on this point, you are in union?' Kempe noted with some scepticism. 'That point being me.'

'On the point of you being an ass, yes?' Richard informed him.

'Then what is your solution?' He folded his arms and stared at Will.

'You know the solution, Kempe. We have discussed it before, endlessly,' Will told him. 'Stop mugging and gurning your face at the crowd while Richard is speaking. Do not wave your arms around so much, nor wail loudly, or interrupt your fellow actors using words that were not put on the page by me but dreamed up by you.' He took a breath. 'And finally, at the end of the play, cut your jigs down to five minutes and not five and twenty.'

William Kempe listened and appeared to hear him out. He made a show of paying attention to every word and of thinking on them all, as if he might be persuaded by Will's reasoning. Then he announced solemnly, 'That I cannot do,' before making to leave.

'Which part?' demanded Richard.

'Any of it!' snapped Kempe. 'So go, do your worst, rid yourselves of me from your company if you like? I shall certainly prosper, whereas you shall not. Who gets most applause when the play is done? Is it the writer?' He screwed up his face and pretended to consider this? 'No! Is it the dramatic actor, Richard Burbage? No! Is it perhaps the comic performer, William Kempe, who is most loved by the groundlings and most talked about in the taverns afterwards? Yes! Yes, I think it is! What are the Lord Chamberlain's Men without William Kempe? I tell you… nothing!' And with that he stormed from the room, making his exit like the practised actor he was.

'God damn that man!' Richard shouted after him, but he was already gone. Richard sighed deeply. 'It's true though, Will. He is too popular for us to be rid of him. We cannot banish him from the company, much as we might want to. If it be known that we had, the groundlings would all take his side and turn against us.'

'You are right,' admitted Will, but he had no intention of dismissing William Kempe from the company. He had just had a far better idea.

Chapter Thirty

*'How poor are they that have not patience.
What wound did ever heal but by degrees?'*

—*Othello*

Cecil was in better spirits that morning than the last time Will had seen him, which was just as well, as he had little new to tell the queen's spymaster about the death of Lady Anne. Distracted by the building of the theatre he may have been, but Will had not ceased his quest to discover the truth about her death, for he knew much rested upon it, including his own wellbeing. It was not for want of effort, but every time Will made a discreet enquiry, into Anne's movements on the night of her death, her friendships at court, her brother, her father or the possibility that she may after all have had a powerful suitor, it all seemed to come to naught. Weeks passed with little for Will to report back to Cecil, other than gossip that could never be proved or wild speculations around conspiracies involving Anne, of the kind that only an eccentric or a mad man could have believed. Still there was no breakthrough, and Will was glad to find the Secretary of State distracted by seemingly endless Catholic plots and the increasingly woeful situation in Ireland. Cecil was still desperate to find the killer of Lady Anne but seemed to accept that, despite Will's best efforts, proof of this remained elusive. That was not to say he would ever forget the task he had set Will, nor forgive him if he failed to complete it. Today though, Cecil was preoccupied with other matters.

'He has made knights,' he told Will. 'Against the express orders of the queen.'

'Who has made knights?' Will asked, for that was surely only the queen's prerogative.

'Essex. He has created thirty-eight new knights during his wasteful campaign, and the queen has finally lost patience with him. She has said he only draws his sword in Ireland to create knights. She paces up and down, rages at his lack of progress and even stabs at the arras with a rusty sword of her own in fury, as if it was the rebel leader himself she was dispatching. She has sent Essex a direct order to engage with O'Neill in battle and finally put paid to him and his rebels. We shall see if he manages that.' Will could tell that Cecil seriously doubted this. 'He has called on her for reinforcements, but they have been denied, because the Spanish are rumoured to be planning an invasion, so we must keep men here.'

Will wondered who might be responsible for those rumours of a Spanish invasion reaching the queen's ear? It might harm Essex's army to go without reinforcements, but it wouldn't hurt Cecil's position if the earl failed in Ireland.

'The queen held a modest garter celebration this year, due to the cost of the war in Ireland,' he went on. 'Then she learned Essex's only act of any note so far during his Irish campaign was to hold an opulent pageant in Dublin at great expense to her. She would have appointed Essex the Mastership of Wards.' This was a valuable and influential position at court that controlled the lands and monies of orphaned heirs below the age of majority. Those wardships could be sold to the highest bidder or given as rewards to followers. 'But since she learned of his profligacy, that honour has instead fallen to me.' No wonder Cecil was in a better humour. He'd been granted an important position and, better still, had snatched it from his bitterest rival. 'I shall make good use of this,' Cecil told him.

But for how long? mused Will. The queen had given this post to Cecil but could just as easily take it back again. Her favourite had been out of favour on countless occasions before now and had always been able to charm his way back into her affections. Surely staging an expensive pageant in Dublin was not a major sin, and if he did win that battle she had urged upon him, Essex would be restored to favour.

Cecil did not see it that way. He even smiled. 'There is more.'

Will expected to hear of a further disaster in Ireland but instead was told of a young woman who had been banned from court. Cecil explained that Her Majesty's ferocious temper and unforgiving nature had found a new victim. Despite, or perhaps because of, the strain caused by her favourite's failings in Ireland, the queen had taken extreme displeasure from the discovery of a letter he had sent to one of her ladies. Her anger rose once she learned that Essex had been privately corresponding with the Lady Miranda since he had gone into Ireland. How could he spare the time to write to another? she raged. How dare she encourage it, being just a slip of a girl? What did the young and fair Lady Miranda have that she did not already possess? Was a queen not enough for him, by Gad? Her jealousy ensured Miranda was instantly banished from court, along with her father, and they were both sent home in disgrace.

Will had expected to be interrogated about his failure to unearth any new information on the death of Lady Anne, but Cecil seemed too preoccupied with the actions of his rival. When he did finally begin to quiz him, it was in relation to Will's writing. 'Now, tell me, how goes that play? The queen grows impatient for it!'

Will had assured Cecil that the play was going well and would soon be complete, but that had been just another fiction of his own devising.

He confessed the truth that evening to Richard over dinner.

'I have burned through a dozen tallow candles writing *Henry V*, but it all comes down to the same thing. I cannot find the words to write about Agincourt and place it within the confines of a stage only forty feet in length and under thirty in depth. How can it house the vasty fields of France and the shadows of over thirty thousand men. It cannot be done. Even if we drape the stage in smoke and have one man hallooing behind him to five hundred imaginary comrades in arms, it will look ridiculous. Every bowman we place there must represent a thousand.'

'Come now, Will, we have done battles before and know how to show them,' Richard told him. 'Just have most of the action take place offstage, apart from a few men who dash across it swinging swords at each other, as if involved in a much larger skirmish. Our company can shout and scream offstage, while banging metal items together, to make it sound as if two huge armies are clashing.'

'That was sufficient when we were placing a battle inside a larger tale, but Henry V *is* Agincourt, and Agincourt *is* Henry. If not that, then what is there? The tale of an errant boy who put aside his friends from the tavern and grew to be a mighty king? But Agincourt was the proof of it and the making of him.'

'I understand the problem, Will, but you must find a solution, for the queen is promised *Henry V*, and she cannot be disappointed. Brighten though, because she does always enjoy your Falstaff?'

'She does and hath proclaimed it so often.'

'Well then.'

'But shall be disappointed, for Falstaff can have no place at Agincourt, nor any at the beginning of the play. How can such an errant knave, a comedic and bawdy figure, full of lust and sack, ever grace the scene of England's finest victory?'

'But won't she be displeased?'

'No, for this play has no need of his form of humour.'

'How will you explain the absence of Prince Hal's former friend then?'

'I have a mind to kill him, but I'll do it offstage. Mistress Quickly can inform the audience of his death and lament it. They will accept this.'

'So, you intend to kill your most popular character? Are you sure about this, Will?'

'I am resolved.'

'And your *real* reason?'

'I have stated my reason.'

'It is just coincidence then,' he asked, 'that Sir John Falstaff is played by William Kempe?'

'Kempe was not foremost in my mind when I decided upon this course,' Will assured him.

'And what part will Kempe play in *Henry V* now?'

'I have not given it much thought.'

'Best think on it then, Will. When Kempe discovers you have killed his character, he will likely try to kill you.'

Chapter Thirty-One

*'Or may we cram within this wooden O,
the very casques that did affright the air at Agincourt?'*

—Henry V

The stage they built at the new theatre was rectangular and set five feet above the ground. Wooden pillars were painted to look as if they were made of marble. The canopy above their heads was painted blue and decorated with stars. They took to calling it the heavens. Images of Mercury and Apollo added ancient grandeur. Behind the stage was a balcony for musicians to play from. They spread a carpet made from layers of crushed hazelnut shells on the muddy floor before the stage, where it was hoped a thousand groundlings would stand to watch them perform.

'This was no simple task,' recalled Peter Street who was surveying their handiwork with a builder's critical eye.

'It is a wonder,' said Will and he meant it.

'What will you call it? The Theatre, again?'

'Not this time. The old one was the first of its kind, but we have the Rose and the Curtain now, and others springing up. It must have a new name, one befitting of its grandeur.'

'I knew it could be done,' mused Street, 'but did not think it would be so hard. We carried those timbers on our backs, like Hercules.'

This was not strictly true, since they had used barges and carts, but Will knew what he meant and could forgive the mild exaggeration, particularly as thinking on Hercules' labours had just inspired him. 'So, let's call it the Globe then.'

The day before the new theatre opened, a sign was erected. Will and the Burbage brothers took a moment to watch as it was hung in place. Most of the rest of the company stepped outside with them and they all sat together on the grass watching as the sign was pulled into place.

'What is that?' asked Cuthbert.

'Something Will and I settled on,' Richard told him. 'To mark the entrance to our theatre.'

Cuthbert read the Latin words painted on the sign aloud. '*Totus mundus agit histrionem?*' Then he translated them uncertainly. 'The whole world is a playhouse?'

'All the world's a stage,' Will said firmly. 'That is the spirit of it anyway.' His own Latin was good, though not perfect, but most of the groundlings would have no idea of its meaning in any case. It was meant to inspire the actors more than the audience.

'All the world's a stage?' Cuthbert repeated, mulling it over.

'And all the men and women merely players,' added Will. Then, when they both regarded him, 'It's something from *As You like It*.' Then almost to himself, he said, 'A play I wrote a long time ago.' And for the first time in a while, he thought of Rosalind, who he had loved once. She had been the inspiration for that play, along with her companion, Celia.

'I remember that,' said Richard. 'It was a marvel.'

'Your father said London was not ready for it,' Will reminded him.

'Because of the plague,' recalled Richard. 'He thought no one would care to laugh at a comedy when fifteen thousand were freshly dead from it.' Then he said, 'But there is no plague currently and we have a new theatre to fill. Might London be ready for it now?'

'You believe so?' asked Will.

'We open with *Julius Caesar* but need another new play to follow it. Your *Henry V* is not yet complete. But Celia and Rosalind *are* ready, and have been waiting by the side of the stage for a while now to take their rightful place upon it.'

'What is this play about?' asked Cuthbert.

'It's a comedy about love, of sorts, and mistaken identity,' explained Richard. 'The plot is wondrous clever. Our company will enjoy it, and so will the groundlings.'

'But will it fill a theatre?' questioned his brother.

Richard looked again at this new and quite magnificent structure before him, while wondering anew if anyone would take the trouble to cross a river to come to it. 'That we shall soon discover.'

Any further discourse on the likelihood of filling a theatre was ended when a voice from some way off boomed at them. 'Shakespeare!' roared Kempe. 'Explain yourself, sir!'

Will had been circulating his almost finished *Henry V* to the actors in the company, but there was no part in it for Kempe.

Richard watched a red-faced Kempe heading their way and told Will, 'I think Kempe just learned of your plan to kill his Falstaff. I'd better stay.' He even placed his hand on the handle of his sword.

'Your sword arm will not be required. I shall deal with Master Kempe,' Will assured him.

As soon as Kempe reached Will, he roared, 'What have you done, damn you?'

'I have written a play. The best part of it at any rate.'

'You have, but there is a character missing. I will not have this! I demand you write Falstaff back into Prince Hal's play.'

'There is no place for the clown Falstaff in Henry's world now that he is king. He has dismissed the man.'

'As you wish to dismiss me?'

'Not at all, Kempe. I simply wish you to play the parts I have created using the words I have written. That is all.'

'If I cannot be allowed to perform my *commedia improvviso*, then I shall not perform at all,' he told them all grandly. 'I would rather quit this company.'

'Let us be clear then that this would be your choice, Kempe, not ours.'

'I did not say I *would* quit the company, but I'd rather leave than stay on your terms.'

Will greeted this with silence and no one else spoke.

'It is clear to me now that one of us must go! I shall not stay in a company run by a playmaker.' His tone was derisive. Then he raised himself up to his full height, pushed out his chest, stabbed a finger towards Will, and proclaimed with some feeling, 'Either he goes, or I go!'

Kempe was expecting a reaction from the assembled actors. Perhaps he hoped for outrage at the suggestion that he might walk out on them?

At the very least, he probably expected them to urge a period of calm while they all tried to smooth things over between himself and Will. There was a silence so complete then that even a man with the vanity of William Kempe must have begun to doubt whether he had misread them.

'Well,' he entreated them, 'what is it to be?'

'How long can you improvise upon the stage, Kempe?' asked Richard. 'A minute? Five… ten perhaps? Or twenty, if it's a jig?' He shook his head at the foolishness of the man in front of him. 'Will's plays last two hours and more.' Then he explained, 'Without Will's writing, there is no play, and if there is no play, there is no Lord Chamberlain's Men. You wish to quit the company if Will stays? That is your decision? So be it. I think you know my mind and every other man's here.'

Kempe scanned the expressionless faces of those other men and almost instantly realised his mistake. Not one of them appeared remotely supportive of his stance, nor said a word in his defence or offered a single plea between them to make him stay. For once in his life, William Kempe was robbed of the power of speech. He stood there looking aghast for a moment, so sure had he been of a different outcome. It was clear from the look on his face that their collective decision was a complete shock to him. He was obviously wondering how they could possibly have chosen a mere wordsmith over their most popular actor? As soon as he realised there was no coming back from this, he tried to rally and turn his surprise and hurt into anger.

'Well then, here's what I say. To hell with the lot of you! And you will pay for this insult a hundred times over. First you will pay me back for my share of the company, and my part of this new theatre that will never be full. Then you will pay again and again, every night, when the stage you act upon is denied my presence. I'll go to one of your rivals. Henslowe will pay me double at the Rose, no, treble what I get from you, or Henry Lanman will at the Curtain. And when your company is dissolved through debt, and you are all on the streets, I will dance a merry jig then, long enough for all of London to witness it!'

He turned on his heel before they could respond, not that anyone would have bothered themselves to. As exits went, it wasn't a bad one, mused Richard later. He just hoped Kempe's prophecy would not hold to be true. If it did, Kempe's jig around London might be the only thing they would all be remembered for.

Chapter Thirty-Two

'Ignorance is the curse of God,
Knowledge the wing wherewith we fly to heaven.'

—Henry VI Part II

The next morning, the Lord Chamberlain's Men assembled again – to be informed by Cuthbert of a new complication. 'I have had to borrow the coin to pay off Kempe.' He clearly deemed this to be an unnecessary expense. 'The ten pounds are owed jointly by us all, but his share in the theatre comes to us too and will be split evenly between the partners.'

They accepted this silently and without argument. Perhaps the sombre mood among them reflected a deeper concern they jointly shared. Later, the Globe Theatre would open for the first time, and it had to succeed or they all faced ruin. The huge risk they had taken, to tear down a theatre, transport it across a river and rebuild it on what had once been little more than marshland, could not be ignored. The enormity of it all hit Will suddenly then and he asked his friend, 'What if no one comes?'

'You think that likely?' asked Richard wryly. 'The building alone is enough of a curiosity. It is all London is talking about!'

'But will they *come*?' he persisted.

'Of course they will,' said Richard with more conviction than he was probably feeling then.

'Even without Kempe?'

'Even without Kempe,' Richard assured him.

'And what if they don't like the play?'

'They will like the play. *Julius Caesar* has treachery, betrayal, a murder, then a hunt for the killers and justice served up at the end. What more could they want? I believe it to be your finest yet.'

'Thank you, Richard,' said Will, 'though you do say that whenever I complete a play.'

'Well, you get better with each one.' Then he slapped his friend upon his back. 'And with a historical you have no peer, nor will you ever.'

'Yet still they might not come.'

'They will come,' Richard told him emphatically. 'We have built this magnificent theatre for them' – he waved his arm expansively to indicate London – 'and they will be unable to stay away from it.'

'I hope you are right Richard,' said Will. 'For if you are not…'

He did not need to complete the sentence. They both knew what would happen to them all if Richard was wrong.

–

Richard was right, of course. Attracted by the grand spectacle of the new Globe Theatre and reeled in by the promise of another dramatic and bloody historical, from the quill of Master William Shakespeare, London's folk turned out in their thousands and filled the Globe for its opening. The sight of them all walking expectantly towards the theatre across the open ground before it was one Will would remember for the rest of his life.

'There must have been three thousand of them out there!' exclaimed Richard after the play was done. He was exultant at the size of the crowd and its reaction to his portrayal of Brutus. The play, and its performance in such magnificent surroundings, had wholly entertained the audience, who scarcely seemed to notice the absence of William Kempe from the stage, nor did they call out for one of his jigs at the end. It seemed they'd got their money's worth already and the applause at its finale had been long and fulsome.

'Three thousand three hundred to be almost exact,' Cuthbert told them as he finished counting the contents of the boxes, which had been filled with pennies by the audience on their way in, before they had been delivered to him in what he liked to call his box office.

'What a magnificent audience it was too.' Richard was still enjoying the moment when the play came to a close, and the audience had roared its approval. 'By God, London knows how to enjoy a good play! And they always will!'

'Then all is well,' said Will.

'*Today*, all is well,' Cuthbert corrected him. 'Tomorrow, we must find another three thousand, then the next day another three, and so it must go on… possibly until the end of the world,' he said dramatically, 'or, should I say, the end of the Globe, for it will be if it does not stay full.' He smiled then. 'But I must say, it was a most pleasing spectacle to see our theatre so full on its opening, so perhaps this was not such a terrible idea after all.' That remark was aimed at Will, whose suggestion it had been to move their theatre.

Will bowed at this tiny compliment. 'Such flattery, Cuthbert.'

Chapter Thirty-Three

'There's daggers in men's smiles.'

—Macbeth

'I cannot stay,' Avisa told Will firmly.

'But I thought.'

She took the hand he had placed on her rump, then pushed it away. 'I know what you thought.' And she walked to the window of their room at the inn and looked out, as if expecting to see someone outside staring up at them.

She was obviously displeased with Will, but he did not understand why. Surely not the gift of the necklace still? This had happened before, and he had been left trying to guess at how he could have offended her. Will expected he would have to wait for the squall to pass and hope she might at least give him a hint at the reason for her displeasure, but this time she was angry enough to tell him outright.

'You have been indiscreet, Will,' she said.

For a married woman's lover to lack discretion could lead to her ruin at court, but he was sure he was not guilty of the charge. It was hardly his fault that Robert Cecil had learned of their affair from one of his most cunning spies.

'I have not.'

'Really? What about that time you dragged me behind the arras to kiss me?'

'I did not drag you, I encouraged you.'

She raised her eyebrows at that description.

'I admit I was overcome with such passion for you that I could not help myself. I had to share a kiss with you to sustain me until our next meeting.'

'At the cost of my reputation?'

'No one saw.'

'Are you so sure? Because you stole a glance before pulling me to one side? I rather think your mind was on other things, don't you?'

'I admit it was folly and do repent it now, but I swear I saw nobody, so no one could have seen us.'

'You have been boasting about me in the tavern to your friends then? Telling them of your conquest of John Florio's wife?'

'Never!'

'Perhaps you did not take enough care to avoid being followed when we met?'

'I always take great care,' he assured her, and he did. Whenever they met somewhere between the court and his lodgings, he looked all about him, to ensure no one was watching his progress and often took a longer route, the better to shake watchers off. This was to avoid being named as an adulterer by John Florio, or even being attacked by friends of the wronged husband. It did not, however, mean he had the skills to outwit Poley. Robert Cecil's men were so seasoned in the art of following recusants, papists and traitors that Will was most likely unable to spot them, but he could hardly explain this to Avisa. If she knew Cecil was already aware of their affair, it might frighten her sufficiently to ensure she never saw Will again.

'Then how do you explain it?'

'Explain what? I wish *you* would explain it, whatever *it* is.'

'Things have changed,' she said softly, but as her anger cooled, it was replaced by something else he could only partially identify. A sadness perhaps, or a suppressed fear.

'How so?'

'Women stop talking when I walk by. They watch me as I pass and sometimes I hear them whisper.'

Was that all? 'What do they whisper?'

'Their words are too soft to be overheard.'

'Then they could be talking about anyone or anything,' he assured her.

'No.' She said it with conviction. 'Women know when they are the subject of gossip. Other ladies may mask their words, but they cannot disguise the glee in their eyes from knowing something about another woman and being permitted to judge her harshly for it with their friends. Some at court live for such a pleasure.'

'Then we should scorn them and swear not to care what they think or say,' he counselled.

'What they think doesn't matter,' she informed him, 'what they say can destroy me. If word reaches the queen, or John, I am undone. Even if it is heard by some jealous lord who failed to tup me, so I made a future enemy of him, that will be enough to see me disgraced, banished and ruined, and my husband along with me.'

'The whole court is filled with degenerates,' Will told her. 'I could name a dozen fornicators and sodomites.'

'You still don't understand the court, Will. There is only really one crime that matters.'

He questioned this with a look.

'Being caught.'

—

Will did eventually calm Avisa after reassuring her that he had not been boasting about their liaison in taverns, but she had not allowed him to enjoy her today. Avisa had given him no assurance that they would meet again soon and the thought of not seeing her threw Will into feelings close to despair.

There had been times lately when he felt that all he had, apart from his friends in the company and his writing, was Avisa. He knew this was entirely his fault, having neglected his family so that the last time he went home his daughters greeted him with an awkward politeness.

How had it come to this then? He had never told anyone about Avisa, but they had still been discovered. It was Cecil's way to inform Will that he knew about them but would not tell. This ensured another layer of loyalty to the man who already had such control over his life. But what would Cecil gain from letting their affair become gossip at court? Nothing. So, who would benefit from this and who else even knew about them?

Poley perhaps? He had been the one to inform Cecil about it. But why would Poley allow that secret out when it gave his master no advantage and they both needed Will to complete a task for them? Because he could. In wielding the limited power he possessed, Poley might feel satisfied simply from creating mischief for Will. Would that be its own reward? Will immediately disregarded that notion. Poley was too much of a loyal hound to his master, Cecil.

Who else then? William Wade, perhaps? Who else from Cecil's circle of followers knew about them, and how long before word of his affair with Avisa reached her husband or the queen? Then Will would be in a world of trouble.

Now, the women at court were giving Avisa sidelong glances, whispering as she passed and giggling about where she might be off to next. If it continued, he knew at the very least it would be the death knell of their affair, and he would lose her for good, a prospect he did not even wish to contemplate.

Chapter Thirty-Four

'But he that filches from me my good name
robs me of that which not enriches him
and makes me poor indeed.'

—Othello

In Ireland, men were dying in droves from sickness and wounds, yet all the court talked about for a week was the monstrous jealousy and tempestuous rage of their queen when she felt slighted in love, and her banishment of the Lady Miranda and her father. This got Will to thinking about the Lady Anne, who was known to be one of the fairest and most graceful girls in the palace and was around the same age as the newly banished Miranda. Anne had received a good deal of attention and admiration from the men at court. Would that have caused similar resentment in such a jealous queen, he wondered, who hated to be upstaged by anyone, especially a younger, fairer woman?

It was not that Will considered this in any way a possible cause of Anne's demise. Even Her Majesty did not make a habit of having her beautiful rivals slain. She had no need to, since she could simply send them away. But if she ever displayed that jealous nature openly, in regard to Anne, it might be useful to discover who prompted it? If Will could discover the identity of the offending gentleman, he might be able to narrow down the field from several suspected of meeting with her, to just one main admirer. He reasoned that man was more likely to have had something to do with her death than those who had never given the queen cause for jealousy where Anne was concerned.

But whom could he ask about such matters and who might know of them, without telling everyone else at court that Will Shakespeare had been enquiring about a dead girl and the queen's jealous temper? There was surely only one.

He found Beatrice alone, working on one of her embroidered collars. When she saw Will, she stopped what she was doing and put it to one side. 'Are you here to buy a partlet, Master Shakespeare? I thought you too old to play the part of a lady.'

He pretended to be offended by her teasing. 'Only by a year or two,' he mock-protested and she laughed, because his beard might have said otherwise.

'Then why are you here? To buy silk for your most favourite lady?'

'Why would I, when she already has so much of it?' He waved his arm to indicate the silks she had on display. Will was deliberately flirting with her, hoping she might like it and become more open with him as a result.

'Flatterer.' She pretended to be irritated by his attempt at charm, but he could tell she was secretly enjoying the game. Beatrice had a quick and sharp wit but spent not a little time on her own, working on her creations, and might be glad of a little attention from a man, even if she pretended not to be.

'What if I *was* here to talk of love? Would it fright you?' He made light of it, so she knew he was in jest, at least partially.

'What was that line from your play?' She recalled: '*I had rather hear my dog bark at a crow than a man swear he loves me.* You did not write that for me,' she conceded, 'but I swear you could have done.'

'Because you scorn love so?'

'I have no need of love,' she told him. 'And value it no higher than the woman in *Much Ado About Nothing*. Though I did notice she was called Beatrice.'

'Was she?' He feigned forgetfulness and she found that amusing too. 'I merely called her Beatrice because it means bringer of joy.'

'I'm not sure anyone has ever accused me of that crime,' she said. 'But I did like her. She was fierce and had a ready wit.'

'Beatrice is a lady like no other.' And their eyes locked then.

She broke the spell with: 'And yet still you ruined her. Making that poor girl fall in love with her chief tormentor, the vain and ridiculous Benedick.' She frowned her disappointment at this. 'What a waste of a woman.'

'The audience demanded it, and perhaps Beatrice enjoyed sparring with the man?'

'Perhaps she did, poor girl. Tell me, tormentor, why are you here again? Is it to pay me for using my name in your play?'

'Why no, 'tis to prise payment from you for making you famous at court and immortal.'

'Immortal?' She scoffed at the notion. 'Your play was good but will be forgot within a year.'

He shrugged. 'Perhaps two.'

'Then why are you really here?'

'To ask you something about Her Majesty.'

'Our jealous queen? Have you not heard, the court is in uproar over Miranda's fate. All of us ladies are keeping our heads low in case she decides to chop them from our shoulders.'

'Tell me, did Her Majesty ever have cause to be as jealous of the Lady Anne?'

'The Lady Anne again? And you had almost convinced me that you loved another?' She meant herself. 'Men were deceivers ever.'

'For someone who scorns me, you know a good number of lines from my play.'

'The plays are easier to enjoy than the man,' she teased him. 'But who said the queen was jealous of Anne?'

'No one, but she was young and most fair. The men of the court always notice that, and perhaps she could not help but offer them hope, even unwittingly. An innocent girl might not understand the game of courtly love and how it is played, but the queen, if she witnessed one of her favourites paying too much attention to Anne, might blame the girl and not the man.'

'You think the queen pushed Lady Anne down the stairs?'

He gave Beatrice a look that told her this was both preposterous and beneath her, and even she looked a little chastened then.

'She *can* be a jealous mistress,' she admitted. 'If Her Majesty notices one of her favourites wooing any of her ladies, she can fly into a rage or storm from the room, but never with the Lady Anne, who was spared her envy.'

'How can you be so sure?'

'Her Majesty does not bother to hide her feelings, as other ladies might, for who can shame or scold a queen?'

'So why was the Lady Anne spared the scorn she would have poured on others?'

'Anne was guileless. Not like those ladies at court who have more than one face. They seek to flatter the queen while taking the men she favours to bed behind her back. They do this out of sport, so they can tell themselves they have what the Virgin Queen cannot. Anne was different, though, and I sometimes wondered...' Her words trailed away as if she was pondering Anne now.

'What did you wonder?' Will probed.

'If the queen rather viewed her like a mother does, or perhaps it was because Anne reminded Her Majesty of her own younger self.'

'What made you think it so?'

'The queen held a masked ball to mark her ascension day,' she explained. 'There are always bonfires, feasting and jousts on the seventeenth of November, but 1598 was a special year.'

'The fortieth anniversary of the day she ascended the throne,' he agreed.

'The masked ball was part of a larger celebration than usual. All the ladies of the court were expected to dance with the lords and gentlemen, for the entertainment of the queen. Her Majesty used to love to dance a galliard or a volta in her youth but is past that time now. She still likes to watch the dancing, though. I think she lives through witnessing the actions of others doing what she once could, but when the gentlemen were all competing to dance with Anne, the queen was far from jealous. Instead, she encouraged them with clapping and cheering, urging her young men to lift the Lady Anne higher and higher during a volta. She liked that Anne was so small, light and graceful.'

'You said Anne was guileless, but she must surely have been aware that the men at court wanted her?'

'I think she was, but likely kept her virtue, for it was expected of her.'

'Who did she dance with most often at this ball?'

'The men were masked,' she reminded him.

'But you can usually tell who is behind those masks? From their height and shape, the way they move and dance, even the manner in which they dress, befitting of their station?'

'You can,' she conceded.

'So, who then?'

She seemed to be genuinely searching for that memory. 'I recall she danced with several men of the court and received attention from the finest of the land.'

'But who more than most?' he asked. 'Essex? Mountjoy?'

'Essex, yes,' she remembered then. 'He definitely danced with Anne, perhaps even from the beginning, as if she was the most desirable partner. Baron Mountjoy did also, I think, and Henry Wriothesley.'

'The Earl of Southampton was a rival for Anne's affections too?'

'Or perhaps the men were simply trying to outdo one another, in being the first to bed one of the queen's youngest ladies-in-waiting.'

'That is as likely,' Will agreed. 'What of Raleigh? Did he dance with her also?'

'I rather think he did not.' Then she added, 'Or was not permitted to.'

'Not permitted to by the Lady Anne or the queen?'

'Neither. He was not able to get near her because of the competing affections of the others and their closest friends, who took all her time on the dance floor.'

'You recall this so clearly?'

'I saw Raleigh watching Anne from the side of the room, while the others danced with her. I remember it because he had removed his mask before the ball was over and was scowling.' Then she said, 'Anne seemed so very full of life then but was dead within a week or two.'

'Thank you,' he told her.

'You think any of this has meaning?'

'It might.' Will now knew the Lady Anne was more sought after than any of those great men who danced with her had admitted following her death.

'Then you might like to learn about the favour too.' Beatrice should write a play, he thought, because she never gave you everything at first and always left you wanting to know what came next.

'A favour granted or received?'

'Received,' she said. 'By Anne.'

'Bestowed upon her by one of the gentlemen at the ball?' he asked and she nodded. 'Would she have accepted a favour lightly, or only if she looked kindly upon the man?'

'A lady does not accept a favour from just anyone,' she explained. 'It usually leads to an understanding.'

'Of a future meeting between them?' he pressed.

'Yes.'

'Innocent or carnal?'

'It could be either,' she said, 'or might start out as the former and end up as the latter, if he knows how to play that game of courtly love well enough.'

'What was this favour?'

'A handkerchief,' she said, 'and a fine one.'

'Did you see it closely?'

'Close enough to know it was a silk handkerchief with gold lace about the edges.'

'And the stitching on it?' Will knew a fine item like that bestowed as a gift would likely have a motto or livery on it.

'Alas, I was not near enough. Anne kept it about her person, though, and that was enough to cause gossip.'

'On who had given her that fine handkerchief?' he asked. 'And what she might be prepared to offer him in return?'

'Just so.'

He had a thought then. 'Would it be the custom to give a lady such a fine favour at the very end of the night?'

'It would.'

'Who danced with her last then?' *Please remember*, he urged her silently, for this might be the clue he needed to solve the mystery of Anne's assignation on the night she was killed.

'I think that perhaps it was' – she frowned as if recalling – 'the Earl of Essex.' And just when Will was experiencing a surge of elation, she corrected herself, 'Or was it Southampton?' And he realised she could not fully recall and that it could have been any of the men.

'And where is this handkerchief now?' Will knew the proof of that man's identity would likely be embroidered on the handkerchief.

'I assume it was returned to her family.'

'Her brother quit the court not long after her death,' Will recalled. 'So perhaps not.'

'Then it will likely be with her other possessions, stored somewhere in the palace.'

'I have to find it,' he said, for in finding it he might just catch the killer.

Beatrice took this to mean their business was concluded. 'Go then, if you must,' she told him airily. 'But return to me again if you wish to sharpen your wits.'

'Perhaps I will,' he told her.

'But know that I will never fall in love with a Benedick,' she warned him.

She truly was very like the Beatrice he had written, but was he really turning into a Benedick? Was his heart beginning to soften the more time he spent with a woman who professed no interest in him. Beatrice might not be quite as beautiful as Avisa but she was undoubtedly fair. Her mind increased that beauty somehow and it became more visible each time he duelled with her, so he told himself he would likely come back for more of this.

God, would he never learn?

Chapter Thirty-Five

'He lives in fame that died in virtue's cause.'

—*Titus Andronicus*

William Wade was the man to ask the whereabouts of the Lady Anne's possessions. Cecil once told him Wade had searched her belongings but found no letters, cyphers or forbidden books among them. But Wade had not been looking for a silk handkerchief and might easily have overlooked such an innocent item if it was among other clothes. Will went to see Wade and Cecil's man greeted the request with his usual suspicion.

'Her clothes and such like were in a wooden chest by her bed. I had it brought here.' He gestured to it. 'But first tell me why you need to examine the personal items of a dead girl?'

Will knew he had to give Wade an answer, but there was something quite menacing about the man who had risen to become Sir Robert Cecil's most powerful retainer. Cecil had more confidence in him than even the ruthless Poley, but Will could sense Wade was as pitiless as his master, so did not fully trust him with knowledge of the handkerchief's significance. He wanted to find it first, then consider his next move, which would be dependent upon the identity of its original owner.

'In truth, I do not have a reason, though I was hoping to find some clue in her belongings.' He hoped to sound vague. 'A letter, jewellery from an admirer, something written in code perhaps?'

Wade scoffed. 'You think I did not already search for just such an item?'

'Something else then?' Will offered, then he feigned helplessness. 'Apologies, but Sir Robert ordered me to revisit everything related to the Lady Anne. Now I cannot rest until I have completed that task for him.'

Wade did not bother to disguise his irritation, but the mention of Sir Robert was good enough. He retrieved the chest and brought it to the table, lifted the lid and showed Will its contents. 'See for yourself.' Wade seemed keen to prove he had not overlooked anything significant, and Will knew he would have to tread carefully here.

'I will, since I am here,' he offered and made a show of conducting a slightly perplexed examination of the chest's contents.

There were some fine gowns here, befitting of a lady-in-waiting to the queen, and some rigid skirts as well as kirtles, bodices and petticoats. It felt wrong to be delving into a chest full of a dead girl's clothes, but Will had to do it if he was going to find what he was looking for. But how to hide this from Wade? He was just contemplating that when a man appeared at Wade's door in some agitation.

'The Jesuit has been found, Master Wade.'

This was important enough news for Wade to turn his back on Will and go to the door. 'Where was he?' he demanded.

Will used his preoccupation with the latest captured priest to make his search swifter and more urgent, pushing dresses, hairbrushes and items of jewellery to one side as he probed deeper into the chest.

The man at Wade's door was offering a detailed explanation of the priest's whereabouts when he was found in a secret room on the property of some unfortunate recusant noble. Will was glad of this distraction, but he couldn't find a silk handkerchief with gold edging.

'Bring him to me,' ordered Wade. 'I will notify Sir Robert. He will be most pleased with our work this day.'

It sounded to Will as if their business was about to be concluded, so he decided to risk everything by speeding up his search, pulling out the remaining clothes, draping them across his forearm and enabling himself to see into the very bottom of the chest. Just as he was doing this, he spotted what he was looking for: a silk handkerchief folded so that only the outside of it could be seen, with no markings or lettering visible, but the gold edging gave it away.

'Go now and make haste,' Wade ordered the man, and Will knew he had to move fast but dare he? He reached for the handkerchief, grabbed it with his right hand and flipped the dresses from his other arm over it, while he pretended to stare into the chest, just as Wade turned back to him.

'Are you not done yet, Master Shakespeare?' He was clearly annoyed by Will's presence when he had more important things to consider, like the torturing of Jesuits.

'I am. You were right, there was nothing here.'

Wade looked at him as if he was wondering why Will was still holding the dresses. Will used that moment of slight confusion to scrunch the handkerchief tightly into his hand, then he gently returned the dresses to the chest. He turned as he did this and carefully slid the handkerchief into his hose on Wade's blind side, hoping he wouldn't spot that movement.

'I knew you were wasting your time.' Wade jerked his head towards the door to indicate Will should leave.

Will gave a slight bow and made for the door. He was almost through it when Wade called after him.

'Shakespeare?'

Will wondered if he should just keep going, while feigning that he hadn't heard the man, but the command was too loud for him to get away with it. He turned back to face Wade, fully expecting to be challenged about the theft of a valuable handkerchief. Instead, he told Will, 'You do know you must catch this killer for Sir Robert?' He said this as if Will had not already fully understood it and was somehow unaware of the jeopardy he was in. 'If you don't, this will not end well for you. Not end well at all.'

—

As soon as he was free from Wade, Will went to a quiet corridor of the palace and examined the silk handkerchief closely. He unfolded it to reveal the design at its centre. This depicted a lion rampant, standing on its hind legs against a blood-red background, between three *crosslets fitchee* – crosses with downward extensions upon each arm. It seemed familiar, but whose livery was this?

Was it the Earl of Southampton's? No, he had seen his patron's coat of arms often enough. That was a yellow cross dividing a blue background with four hawks as its escutcheons, one in each quarter. Henry Wriothesley did not give her this, nor did Raleigh, thought Will. His coat of arms was five white fusils, conjoined in *bend argent* on a red background. It wasn't Mountjoy's either. That was an elaborate, almost vulgar construction, featuring two wolves, a tower and some other designs.

Will had only really thought on the coat of arms of those other men to delay the inevitable. In truth, he had already recognised the arms depicted here and was merely hoping he was mistaken. It was often seen at court on banners or the livery of the man's servants. The rampant lion was such a fitting depiction for the Earl of Essex. This was his handkerchief. He had given it to the Lady Anne. Once she had accepted it, he had likely arranged an assignation with her on the night she had died, then quite possibly killed the girl or ordered her murder.

Why did it have to be Essex? Could it not have been a lowlier man than the queen's firmest favourite? Now Will would make an enemy of the most powerful lord in the country, who was already known to be unmerciful. He'd had the queen's own physician hanged, drawn and quartered for simply gossiping about him. What then would he do to Will if his evidence pointed to Essex as the murderer of one of the queen's ladies?

But how could he withhold that evidence from Sir Robert Cecil, when he had been ordered by the Secretary of State himself to find the killer? Wade had just reminded him what would happen if he failed to do that for Cecil, a man almost equal to Essex in power and influence over the queen. One day Cecil might even surpass the earl, if her favourite continued to fail in Ireland.

I am trapped between the two most powerful men in the kingdom and can see no way out of this. I can neither produce nor hide this evidence when either act will likely lead to my doom.

Will recognised the dilemma he faced and, as he held that silk handkerchief in his hand now, he knew it was finally time to decide. He would have to pick one of these men, then pray that whoever he chose proved to be the strongest.

Chapter Thirty-Six

'Art made tongue-tied by authority.'

—*'Sonnet 66'*

'What is this quarrel about?' Robert Cecil had broken away from the cluster of powerful men at court to interrupt the argument between Will and the Master of the Revels, who was refusing to accept Will's new work.

'Shakespeare here has written heresy.'

'I have not! I merely portray a king as a man, for he is a king and a man both.'

'And that is to question the divinity of kings and by implication her divine majesty. If a monarch is portrayed in the same way as any man or woman, then what majesty remains? I shall not allow this.'

'Then there is no play,' argued Will, 'for the entire purpose of *Henry V* is to show his true greatness by overcoming his manly doubts before Agincourt. Rid the play of this and you rob it of meaning.'

'Show me the offending passage,' Cecil ordered and the Master of the Revels drew his attention to it.

They fell silent for long enough to give Cecil the time to examine it.

'So, King Henry has doubts on the eve of a battle?' Sir Robert told the Master of the Revels. 'Who would not? I will allow it, and so shall you.'

The chastened Master of the Revels gave a brief bow to Sir Robert.

'It is sometimes a good thing for a monarch to be reminded they are mortal.' And with that Cecil strode away. Will noticed that he had deliberately used the word 'mortal', not 'human', which was surely a hint that the queen should be looking to the future and her successor. That had, of course, not been Will's intention, but he immediately began to worry that Her Majesty might take it to be so. Christ, what had he done?

—

'What happened with the Master of the Revels?' asked Richard, who had witnessed proceedings from a distance.

'He tried to silence me.'

'And?'

'Was overruled by Sir Robert.'

Richard frowned. 'Cecil permitted words the Master of the Revels sought to remove?'

'He did.'

'Oh,' said Richard, sounding troubled, for he too must have been wondering why Cecil would seek to do that.

'Exactly,' said Will and they shared their unease.

'Is that all?' asked Richard, who must have sensed his friend was worried about more than those few lines in dispute.

Will drew in his breath then and explained, 'I have watched our company go through the words of the play on stage and rehearse the tiny scuffles that represent the battle of Agincourt and I tell thee, I am shamed.'

'Why shamed?'

'Because we cannot confine such a vast and bloody battle to a mere wooden platform. We should have thousands of men, hundreds of horse, a sky full of arrows to blot out the sun, and yet what have we really got to put in front of a mighty and unforgiving queen? Nothing.'

'Not nothing,' Richard consoled him. 'Your words are poetry. For the rest, well, they will draw upon their imaginary forces, so they can see the battle in their mind's eye. You are right that we cannot place the Battle of Agincourt on a stage, but since everyone knows that, we do not have to apologise for it.'

Will stared at Richard then as if he had just said something shocking or outrageous.

'What?' demanded Richard.

'That's it!' Will declared.

'What's it?' Richard was clearly confused.

'What you just said. You are right… Actually you are wrong.'

'What say you? How can I be both? What are you talking about?'

'An apology. You said we don't have to apologise for it, but we do. That's what we *should* do! It's what I must do. Let us get the uncomfortable matter out there. Don't try to hide behind a curtain or pretend that one man can fill the form of a thousand. Admit that it cannot be done, so let us not even pretend.'

'Pretend is what we do, Will! What else is there?'

But Will was already heading back to his rooms so he could write more.

'I hope you know what you are doing, Will. Don't make us look foolish out there. I can't afford to look foolish!' But Richard was speaking to himself now, for Will was already gone.

—

Courtiers were starting to assemble and take up their seats in front of the stage, according to their rank and a hierarchy, which dictated where you were allowed to sit, but at this point, Will was still missing. Richard Burbage paced up and down a corridor to one side of the room in which they would be performing, while he fretted about his friend's lengthy absence and what he might have been using it for. An apology? Was he serious about that?

When Will finally appeared, Richard looked worried. 'Are you really going out there, Will? Before the play? To apologise for our limitations? Is that wise, do you think? Are we not supposed to excite an audience? Won't they all just quit the room for some other entertainment?'

'So many questions, Richard. I am going out there, but not before the play. This will be part of the play. I have written something that I think will help you today.'

'You have written me fine words already, illustrious enough to have fallen from Henry V's own mouth on the eve of Agincourt. Isn't that sufficient? Why diminish them now by apologising for the lack of horse or men on a stage?'

But Will was deep in his own thoughts. He only muttered, 'Trust in me, Richard,' just as a herald announced the arrival of the queen and her court.

Once they were all seated, Will stepped out, with no introduction or musical accompaniment. Alone on that bare stage, he waited for them to settle. When they were all silent, including the queen, he took in a deep breath and began.

'O, for a muse of fire that would ascend the brightest heaven of invention!' he pleaded. Then added, 'A kingdom for a stage, princes to act and monarchs to behold the swelling scene!'

That got their attention, for they knew that, aside from the actual monarch who was watching him now, his play would lack all of this.

Will continued the fantasy, as if they really did have all of that to offer the audience. 'Then should the warlike Harry, like himself, assume the port of Mars, and at his heels, leashed in like hounds, should famine, sword, and fire crouch for employment.'

Then came the apology Richard was fearing. Will addressed them directly, looking as many of them in the eye as possible as his gaze swept over them.

'But pardon, and gentles all, the flat unraised spirits that hath dared on this unworthy scaffold to bring forth so great an object.' He waved his arm towards the stage he stood upon. 'Can this cockpit hold the vasty fields of France? Or may we cram within this wooden O the very casques that did affright the air at Agincourt?' It was an absurd idea, and they all knew it, but better to confess it now than wait for their inevitable disappointment. 'O pardon, since a crooked figure may attest in little place a million, and let us, ciphers to this great account, on your imaginary forces work.' He was pleading for them to use their imagination while the play was on. 'Suppose within the girdle of these walls are now confined two mighty monarchies, whose high upreared and abutting fronts the perilous narrow ocean parts asunder.

'Piece out our imperfections with your thoughts. Into a thousand parts divide one man, and make imaginary puissance. Think, when we talk of horses, that you see them printing their proud hoofs in the receiving earth, for 'tis your thoughts that now must deck our kings. Carry them here and there, jumping o'er times, turning the accomplishment of many years into an hourglass. For the which supply, admit me chorus to this history, who, prologue-like, your humble patience pray, gently to hear, kindly to judge our play!'

And with that final roar, Will leapt from the stage. He was immediately replaced by actors from his company, who had just been rid of the responsibility of assuming the mantle of an entire nation at war with the French, only to be found wanting.

Will stood off to one side and watched his audience intently. No one had given up and left. They were relaxed in their postures but listening intently to the lines he had given his actors. He had them, he felt sure of it. There were no soldiers, horses or arrows to be loosed into the air, but each of them would hear the words he had conjured to describe the terror and thrill of England's finest battle, and their imaginations would do the rest. He almost dared not to think on it, but this might just work.

Chapter Thirty-Seven

'Oh God of battles steel my soldiers' hearts,
possess them not with fear,
not today, oh Lord, oh not today.'

—*Henry V*

'By God, Master Shakespeare, but that did stir my blood and rise me from my torpor!' the queen told him afterwards. 'I have not felt as inspired since I took horse in armour at Tilbury to rouse my own troops against the Armada. That was a good play! That was a damned good play!'

'Thank you, your most gracious Majesty.' Will was kneeling before her now, taking her congratulations in front of the courtiers who had proved such an appreciative audience for his *Henry V*.

'Agincourt on a stage?' She marvelled. 'Raleigh wagered you couldn't do it, didn't you, *Water*?'

Raleigh was dismissive to the point of impertinence. 'I simply said he *might* not be able to do it, 'twas all.'

'I think it was more than that.' But she was in a good mood and merely teasing Raleigh. Then she asked Will, 'And what were those lines you recited about my general?' She almost blushed to recall them and Will knew exactly what she wanted to hear.

He began to recite the lines he had carefully written just for her, performed by the chorus that he himself had played throughout the performance.

'As by a lower but by loving likelihood, were now the general of our gracious Empress, as in good time he may, from Ireland coming, bringing rebellion broached on his sword. How many would the peaceful city quit, to welcome him!'

The queen was thrilled anew by that prospect of her favourite, the Earl of Essex, returning from Ireland in triumph and all of London turning out to welcome him home. She applauded Will's words like an excited young maid. 'A fine sentiment,' she told him, but then a shadow seemed to fall on her face. 'There is one small but most important fault I must lay at your feet, though?'

'Your Majesty?' What inaccuracy had the queen noticed, what seditious word would he have to change at her behest?

'Why no Falstaff? Wither Sir John? Your actors told us of his death, but even this happened away from the stage.' She seemed quite appalled.

'That was my failing, Your Majesty.' He exchanged glances with Richard Burbage, who gave him a rueful look to remind Will he had predicted this reaction from the queen. 'I thought not to diminish King Henry's greatest triumph by accommodating that lewd and bawdy knight on the field at Agincourt.'

'Well, that was a great loss,' she told him. 'Forgivable perhaps, if it was done to respect the memory of King Henry, but I would wager a good number of wretched, lowly men were accommodated in his army that day.' She frowned at the memory of her favourite character. 'Bring him back to life, damn you. I'd like to see him in a comedy of his own. What if Falstaff were to fall in love? What mischief would ensue?'

'The devil's mischief, Your Majesty, but it is a most excellent idea and, like Lazarus, I shall indeed resurrect him.' The work would be a small price to pay to avoid the queen's displeasure.

'Splendid. Can you bring him back from the grave by the time I arrive at Windsor? The thought of it would make me most merry.'

Oh God, how many weeks did he have left before the drains were clogged here at Whitehall and the whole court would have to move to Windsor instead? And to think he had only just finished writing *Henry V*. It was never-ending.

'For Your Majesty, of course.'

The queen departed then and most of her courtiers went with her, but one of Essex's men, Sir Henry Cuffe, approached Will. 'The mention you made of his grace, my master, shall not go unnoticed, nor unrewarded. I will write and he shall hear of it.'

Will was assured and he gave a little bow in reply, though he was not sure he wanted to be rewarded by the Earl of Essex or even associated with him. The lines he had written were for the queen's satisfaction, not Essex.

'You are to be congratulated, Master Shakespeare. The queen was impressed by your play and the words you gave King Henry were most eloquent.'

'Thank you, good sir.'

'Or did you?' His tone was one of amused incredulity.

'What say you?' Will did not understand, but his instinct told him this was a challenge of some kind.

'I merely ask whether it was you who really gave King Henry his words.'

'None other.' Not this again.

'You are the son of a merchant, are you not?' There was some disbelief in his tone.

'I am.'

'Then how could a man such as you have written a play like that one?'

'A man such as I?' Will was telling himself not to rise to the insult, but it wasn't in his nature to allow it to pass without comment.

'Low-born, barely educated, untravelled, untested in battle and yet you lay claim to an understanding of matters that even a great lord like mine might struggle to master.' He leaned in as if confiding. 'So, tell me clear, who is masquerading behind you, sir? Who is the real poet Master Shakespeare pretends to be?' He almost winked at Will then, as if he alone had discovered the writer's secret.

'This again?'

'Is it Southampton?' the squire asked. 'Or the Earl of Oxford, perhaps? Who really wrote your plays? Francis Bacon? Now there is a wise man. Come, tell me, and it will go no further than myself and my master, who will be greatly amused to discover the truth of it.'

'I wrote them all, damn you,' he snapped.

'I refuse to believe it.'

'You might refuse to believe that the sun comes up in the morning, but it will still rise, whether you doubt it or no.'

'It is not possible for a man of your quality to have conjured up such a masterpiece.' He was getting angry now. 'So stop your pretence and tell me plainly, who wrote it, if not you?'

'No one wrote it, if not me, for I wrote it, and you sir will be struck if you continue to doubt me on the point.'

Will's fury took the steward by surprise, but he quickly recovered. 'Keep stating it if it amuses you to, but I know the truth of it and so does most of the court. Will Shakespeare did not write Will Shakespeare's plays.'

Before Will could strike him, deride him or contradict him further, Cuffe turned his back and was away.

—

Will should have been in a fine mood that evening, but the encounter with Cuffe had left its mark. Most of the court believed he did not write his plays? That was likely not true, but what if even some of them thought it? Truly, Will wondered how many idiots must there be at court, if a good number believed him a fraud?

'They used to say Marlowe wrote my plays,' he told Richard, who was in a far better mood, having been patted on the back by half the court for his most excellent portrayal of King Henry. 'As if he would have the time or the inclination, much less the lack of vanity needed, to put my name to his words, even if he wasn't dead. There are dullards in London who cannot conceive that I alone write what I alone write. Now this servant of Essex thinks them penned by Francis Bacon or the Earls of Oxford or Southampton.'

'Every actor and writer in London knows you write your plays, Will, and they are published in your name. If they were written by another, he would want his name on them instead. Why would he bother elsewise?'

'I'm even asked it in taverns,' Will continued glumly. '*Prove that you wrote your plays*, they say. I always reply in the same way: *Prove that someone else did* – but, of course, they never can.'

'Of course they cannot.'

'Then why do they believe it?'

'So that they can tell themselves they are so wise they know something their fellow man does not. You are not the only victim of these fools, Will. There are a good number of men in London who believe that the queen's strong and manly rule means she cannot have really been born a woman and is in fact a man. They cite her unmarried state as proof of it.'

'She has not married because she wishes to have no master. 'Tis all.'

'Not to those men. They say they will not be convinced until the queen stands naked before them. Even then, they would say she had her manhood snipped off as a child. If you have the proof, you can easily convince a wise man of something, but never a fool.'

Chapter Thirty-Eight

'Stiffen the sinews and summon up the blood.'

—Henry V

Will and the Burbages were granted but a little time to enjoy their triumphs or dream of the fruits that might come from them, before, once again, disaster struck.

'Giles Allen is suing us,' Cuthbert announced when they arrived at the Globe that morning. 'I knew he had taken this too quietly.'

'A curse on that bastard and his entire kin!' cried Richard.

Giles Allen had taken his time to devise a suitable plan for vengeance. They would have loved to have been there the moment Allen arrived after his Christmas festivities to find nothing but a bare patch of soil on the land that once housed a theatre. It almost did not matter that they failed to witness his reaction because so many others did, and the tale of it soon swept through their part of London. Giles Allen's rage that day became legendary and was much talked of. He railed, he swore, he sacked the men who were supposed to be guarding his property and kicked the clerk's arse all the way down the street before dispensing of his services. Then he returned to the empty site and began a loud rant against the Burbages, Will, the authorities and even God for deserting him. This was of such length it attracted a sizable audience. Men even left taverns to come and look at, then laugh at, the man whose pride had undone him, till he was left with naught for his troubles but the bare land he claimed to be of such value because he could build anything he liked upon it. Everyone knew the truth, though. He had been too greedy and hoped the Burbages would eventually surrender their theatre to him, so he would keep both the building and the land. Now he had nothing, and he had left that street roundly mocked by all and jeered on his way.

Now he was back and using the law to get his revenge.

'How much does he want to finally leave us be?' asked Richard.

'Eight hundred pounds.'

'*Eight hundred!* The man's mad! He'll never get it.'

'He will if a court decides he is right and we are wrong,' Cuthbert said flatly. 'I have read his deposition.' He waved a copy of it at them. 'He accuses us of riotous assembly and arming ourselves with unlawful and offensive weapons, daggers, bills, axes, and the like, before congregating at the Theatre in a riotous, outrageous, and forcible manner, contrary to the laws of the realm. He further states that when we attempted to pull down the Theatre, diverse of Her Majesty's subjects, going about their business in a peaceable manner, attempted to intervene to prevent this and were met with great violence, before the pulling, breaking and throwing down of that same theatre, to the great disturbance and terrifying of all Her Majesty's subjects who were near.'

'Did any of that happen?' asked Richard in disbelief. 'Any of it at all? I don't recall, and I was there!'

'That's quite an account from a man who wasn't,' acknowledged Will. 'He should write a play.'

'It matters not whether it happened or nay, only whether a magistrate believes it so,' Cuthbert told them.

'Then we'll need witnesses to disprove his account,' offered Richard.

'Do you really think Allen hasn't procured witnesses of his own, who will swear that his account is a fulsome and truthful telling of the events he has described?' Cuthbert pointed out.

'Our witnesses will contradict him,' said Will.

'And they will be disbelieved, for all of them will be members of our company.'

'Then what should we do, brother?' demanded Richard.

'There is, in truth, not much that we can do, except appear at court to answer his accusations and hope for a miracle.'

'What miracle is that?'

'That the word of a troupe of degenerate actors will be believed above that of a hand-picked band of well-bribed gentlemen, for if it is not, Giles Allen will be awarded his eight hundred pounds, our new theatre will fall into his hands, and we shall all be ruined.'

Chapter Thirty-Nine

'When valor preys on reason, it eats the sword it fights with.'

—Antony and Cleopatra

Will had finally come to a decision and he chose to side with the man who had ordered him to find Lady Anne's killer.

Robert Cecil stared at the coat of arms on the fine silk handkerchief. Will had just finished giving him his account of the masked ball, which Cecil himself had apparently not attended, presumably to avoid the public humiliation of being ignored by all of the fair ladies at court. Cecil had listened to Will's explanation of the popularity of Lady Anne and how she had danced with all of Cecil's enemies but only one had given her a favour, which she had accepted. He had then produced the handkerchief, explaining that he had found this among her belongings. Cecil had taken the handkerchief, unfolded it and examined the design at its heart.

'She took a favour from the Earl of Essex?' Will could not tell if he was surprised or disgusted by this unexpected turn of events.

'My understanding, Lord, is that men often give favours such as these to ladies they wish to see again privately.'

Cecil seemed to stiffen. 'I have heard this said,' he conceded.

'Since the Lady Anne was killed not long after this masked ball, most likely by someone she had arranged to meet...'

'You think Essex to be the most likely murderer?' He finished that thought for Will. 'It would not surprise me.' But Anne going so willingly to the assignation that led to her death seemingly did surprise him.

'What then should we do about it?' asked Will.

Cecil thought on this for a while, then said, 'There is naught we can do until Essex returns from Ireland. When he does, he can perhaps be confronted with the evidence of a liaison with Anne, possibly even her killing. Even when he doubtless denies this, it might be enough to damage him in the eyes of the queen.' Then Cecil admitted, 'But I am hoping for an even bigger crime to be levelled at his door.'

'What bigger crime, my lord?'

'Treason.'

'How so?'

'The situation in Ireland is very grave.' He sounded serious, but Cecil must surely have been gleeful, though he hid it well. 'Essex still ignores the will of the queen to take on the rebels in pitched battle. Instead, there have been skirmishes at great cost to us. The earl lost five hundred men in one of them alone, and hundreds more at an engagement by the River Slaney. He has marched his men from town to town, castle to castle, claiming small victories while never once engaging O'Neill's rebels in open battle. Many of his men have died of disease. He is running out of ammunition and victuals and there is scarce enough left on the land for his men to live off. Now the rains have turned every field into a bog, and he blames those conditions for his failure to subdue the rebels. He has been in Ireland three months and achieved nothing. No rebel leader has surrendered, nor any territory fallen to his control.'

This was evidently the latest news from the Privy Council meeting. Cecil must have felt compelled to share it with someone he could tut about it safely to, but he wasn't done yet.

'If that were not enough, we have just been sent word that he dispatched Sir Conyers Clifford to lift a siege at Collooney Castle. Clifford went through a pass in the Curlew Mountains with seventeen hundred men. There, they were ambushed by rebel forces and routed, with half their number killed, including Clifford. The Irish rebels cut off his head, then delivered it to the besieged castle to frighten its defenders. Irish casualties from this battle are said to be light.'

'It would be hard to imagine the Earl of Essex overseeing a bigger disaster had he planned his entire campaign in favour of the Irish. The whole court is in uproar at this wasteful loss of English life and the queen is most distressed. I said Ireland would be Essex's undoing and I have been proven right.'

Will wondered if Cecil had taken a moment to grieve the loss of those eight hundred or so Englishmen slaughtered in that ambush, or had he simply seen this not as a dreadful defeat for the realm, but a great personal victory for him over his enemy.

'I see no way back for him from here,' he told Will.

—

Will did not have to wait long for word about the Earl of Essex's final attempt to subdue Hugh O'Neill and his Irish rebels, nor did he need to hear it directly from Sir Robert Cecil, for within days, news of it was all around the court. In his eagerness to hunt down O'Neill and engage him in a major battle, Essex had taken four thousand of his men to Ardee. The opposing forces had quickly mustered to meet him on the opposite side of the river, with twice as many men as the weary English. Inferiority of numbers forced Essex into a four-day stalemate until O'Neill himself met with the earl to ask for the queen's mercy, but not without conditions favourable to the rebels. These included the right to hold onto every piece of territory they had seized so far. There was astonishment at court when the earl accepted these terms and agreed a treaty with England's bitterest enemy. There was general alarm when it was learned that his meeting with O'Neill had been a private one, and there were no other witnesses to the agreement they had made that day. The overriding question was: why? What had the two men agreed between them that was so secret it could not be shared with even their closest advisors? To some, this seemed like consorting with the queen's enemies, perhaps even to plan a rebellion, and it was not long before Robert Cecil's creatures started to spread rumours that treason had been committed.

The only thing that quelled the queen's fury at all was her sheer disbelief that this could have happened without her agreement. Surely the word from Ireland was mistaken. She had immediately written to Essex to demand his version of events, while forbidding him to give up his position in Ireland or to return to England. Even now, despite everything, he would still be given the chance to explain himself.

Chapter Forty

'Love is a smoke raised with the fume of sighs;
Being purged, a fire sparkling in lovers' eyes;
Being vexed, a sea nourished with loving tears.
What is it else? A madness most discreet.'

—*Romeo and Juliet*

Even Will had a premonition that Avisa was here to bring an end to their affair and though he was disappointed that she wanted to talk with him at the inn and not immediately retire to bed, it little surprised him. Avisa was cool, she was distant, above all she was adamant. John Florio was going abroad, to Italy, and she was leaving with him. Though she could probably have invented a pretext to stay at court by the queen's side and continue their affair, he could already see she had no appetite for that.

'You are going with your husband? Though you do not love him,' he observed, 'nor does he know how to love you.' This was hardly an insult, since she had confirmed as much to Will before now. He knew her husband lacked both passion and prowess.

'My husband, who you have mocked for his failings as a lover...' she considered this, then admitted, 'as have I, to my shame, may be wanting in one regard but is superior to you in all others.'

'How so?' Will was affronted now.

'He is a good husband – yes, it's true – and a good father also. Have you forgotten too that he is one of the cleverest men in the realm, writing books in Italian, working on his dictionary?'

'You think your husband a better man than me?'

'I know he is.' And when Will seemed about to chide her for this answer, 'My husband is surely a better man than you for he would never betray me, whereas you have betrayed your wife, Anne, with many women over time, have you not?'

'Don't say her name!' He was ashamed to hear it on his lover's lips.

'Why? Because I dishonour her or offend you somehow by the remembrance that you have a wife? Had you forgotten her or do you choose to?'

'You condemn me for committing the same acts with you that you commit with me? Does that not make you a hypocrite?'

'Yes,' she agreed. 'And I condemn myself along with you. At least I am honest enough to admit the sin. One day we will both face God. Then we will have to account for our deeds on this earth. I have already admitted mine and do not claim to be a good person. I have been wanton of late and much led by my appetites. There, you have it.' She meant her confession. 'Yet you, Will, seem loath to admit your own depravity. You are like those blushing, swooning girls at court, who claim virginity and feign virtue, then leave their rooms at night to meet men in dark corners of the palace. They won't admit their sins to themselves, much less to others, and so the pretence and the lying will continue, perhaps until the end of time. But you, Will, are not some callow lady-in-waiting. You should admit who you are, but you cannot, can you?' She was scathing and he did not like her tone. 'Why is that?'

'You make this sound like something it is not, as if we were beasts rutting in a field.'

'Well,' she smiled grimly, 'not in a field, but there was that time in the gardens at Greenwich.'

'I mean that it is more than just a tupping.'

'Was it?' She was already using the past tense.

'Yes!' At first he was outraged that she might think he considered it so, but then he looked at her face and finally realised the truth. *He considered this to be more than a tupping, but she did not.* 'Are you saying this was naught but lust?' he asked.

Seeing his distress, her tone softened then. 'I'm saying it was a game. You and I were a masque of love. We pretended it meant more, when neither of us could possibly leave the world we inhabit and run off with each other to a different one. I admit we both lived that foolish fantasy while in those moments together. But then we climbed from the bed and returned to the world we truly live in. Happier? Perhaps. Sated, satisfied, a hunger quelled, a longing fulfilled? Yes.' She nodded. 'But understand this, you were my lover, not my love.' She regarded him coldly then, dispassionately, and he knew even before she spoke further that it was definitely over between them, no matter what he said, and he was already missing how it had made him feel. 'You were a distraction, at best. For me, it was little more than the scratching of an itch.'

'Then I was deceived.' Avisa looked like she would react angrily then. 'Not by you,' he told her and she calmed herself. 'By myself. When I walked to meet you, I thought I was meeting my love. The dark lady I had written about so many times.'

'How could that be me, Will? When you have been writing about her for years. She is some other lady.'

'She was many ladies over time,' he admitted. 'Whenever I became enamoured of one, I would take a memory here, a fragment there, and I built that dark lady up in my imagination until she became the perfect model of my love. Though she did not in reality exist.' And he looked into her eyes. 'Then you came along. I thought my dream was made flesh for the first time and, from that day forth, I never did look to another. That need was gone and I was happy then. You were married of course, because God does like to mock me, so I never dared to think you could be mine, but you sought me out and chose to lay with me, and then I did dare to dream.'

'Of what, Will?'

'Some better future we might share.'

'How would we do that? By running away? Getting on a ship to somewhere? Pretending to be married to each other and not who we were truly tied to before God? How long before we were found out? Or did you believe your wife might die one day, my husband too, but not us, so we would be together then?' She scoffed at that notion.

'I don't know what I believed, but I had some small hope, and it felt better than this.'

'I am sorry, Will. I never thought of us at all beyond that bed or these walls.' She informed him coolly. 'We were just a happy dream but were always going to wake from it one day.'

'Then the dream is over?' he asked her and when she offered no words of comfort: 'Goodbye then, Avisa.' His voice cracked and he turned away from her because he did not want her to see the effect this parting would have on him.

She walked to the door then and when her voice reached him from it, its calmness cut into him like a dagger. 'Goodbye, Will.'

–

He remembered watching a game as a child, when several women had played a trick on a young man by teasing him with a blindfold. They spun him round until he was dizzy and urged him to catch one of them, while effortlessly skipping clear of his flailing hands, for they had the advantage of sight, and he had been rendered blind in their presence. Undaunted by how foolish he must have looked, the boy had kept vainly attempting to pursue them, spurred on by the sounds of their excitement and the possibility of catching and pulling them close to him. Oh, how they had shrieked and giggled, mocking his inability to trap one of them and make her his. He never did catch any of them but did injure himself more than once by bumping into tables. Will had watched the women and realised they wouldn't have done this to a man they actually wanted, someone they considered handsome or desirable. The entire point of the game was their enjoyment of how desperate the boy was to win one of them, and how equally sure they were that they could evade him. Their squeals of excitement came from the prospect of an unpleasant fate in his arms, and that provided the danger they needed to pass their time in the afternoon. Will had pitied him then.

He felt just like that boy now, as he left Avisa's company for the last time. He was a blind man, mocked and flailing at nothing, while she effortlessly evaded him.

Chapter Forty-One

'I know thee not, old man.'

—*Henry IV*

They were waiting for Cuthbert to join them at the tavern for food and ale. He was late, which was unusual for such a fastidious man. They filled the time with talk of the theatre and the latest news or gossip from the members of the main acting companies.

'Did you hear about Kempe?' asked Richard.

'I did,' Will replied.

'What about Kempe?' Cuthbert arrived then, just in time to hear Richard's news of their former comedic actor. 'Does he threaten to sue us too?' Since receiving Giles Allen's deposition, Cuthbert feared court cases more than bears, and he had always been frightened of the latter, even when they were chained. He knew the courts could bankrupt the company and worried that every letter he received was a summons.

'No. He is to undertake a jig,' said Richard.

'And why is this noteworthy? He has done many of those and each of them overlong.'

'This one will be even longer,' Richard replied, to Cuthbert's bemusement.

'He is to dance all the way from London to Norwich,' Will explained, 'setting off tomorrow.'

'But that's…?'

'More than a hundred miles,' Will confirmed.

'Has he lost his mind?' asked Cuthbert.

'He did not get the offers he was hoping for when he left the company,' Will explained. 'Henslowe won't have him at the Rose, nor Lanman at the Curtain. They both know what trouble he is, and the money we gave him for his share has almost gone.'

'I heard he tried to borrow money from Henslowe,' said Richard. 'And was refused.'

'So, he is to dance for a hundred miles?' Cuthbert was shocked.

'More like a hundred and ten,' his brother corrected him. 'Kempe aims to make it there in nine days.'

'His feet will be bloodied stumps before he reaches Norwich,' Cuthbert predicted.

'He hopes to make some coin in villages along the way,' said Will.

'He has fallen this low?' asked Cuthbert. 'Holding out his cap and begging for charity as he dances down the road like a madman. For shame.' He must have had a pang of conscience then. 'Did we do this to him?'

'No,' said Will firmly. 'He did it to himself.'

They were silent for a moment then while they contemplated the folly of Kempe's endeavour and how desperate he must have been to even attempt it.

'Well, he is still far from being the biggest fool in England,' Richard said, with the air of a man who has learned some new intelligence. 'Or should I say Ireland?'

'You talk of Essex?' asked Will.

'I was at court,' he said sheepishly and they both knew this must have been due to some liaison or other he had engineered in the aftermath of his impressive performance as Henry V. What lady had desired his presence there would remain a mystery and Will had the good sense not to ask.

'And what is the latest news of the queen's favourite?' asked Cuthbert. When Richard told them, they could scarcely believe it.

You had to wonder about the sheer folly of the Earl of Essex or was it his vanity that compelled him to go against the queen's wishes time and time again? Perhaps Cecil had been right all along. Ireland might indeed prove to be his undoing. He had been specifically ordered to remain there, but his first thought on receiving her letter had not been to obey his monarch. Instead, he must have worried that his absence from court might give others, namely Sir Robert Cecil, free rein to paint unflattering portraits, of himself and his conduct during the Irish campaign, to Her Majesty. He was right about that, of course, but still should never have considered abandoning his command. This he did, however, sailing to England and leaving his army behind.

Realising his best, or perhaps only, chance to regain favour with the queen was to see her in person, and fearing he might be prevented from doing so by Robert Cecil, Essex rode hard to Nonsuch Palace in Surrey, where she was enjoying a visit. Upon arriving there, he burst in on the queen in her bedchamber, to her general shock and alarm, since she wasn't even dressed. Was he perhaps there to take her prisoner and usurp the throne? She had no way of knowing at this point but remained calm and humoured Essex, hearing him out, until she could delicately ask him to leave her chambers so she could finish dressing and apply her wig and make-up.

Later that day, she met with the earl again and ensured she had guards with her. This time, the queen was far less forgiving of his follies in Ireland and accused him of making a dishonourable peace, with a devil whose word could not be trusted. She then called Essex an unruly beast and confined him to his rooms, while calling for the Privy Council to meet immediately and determine his fate.

Will later learned that Essex was interrogated by the council for five hours. To reach a judgement against him, however, took only fifteen minutes. They unanimously decided he had deserted his post in Ireland and concluded a treaty with the rebel O'Neill beforehand that was both unlawful and unpardonable. It was hard to imagine how even Essex could avoid his downfall now.

–

Will arrived at court expecting to find Cecil exultant. The Privy Council verdict must surely lead to the fall of the Earl of Essex. Was he now branded traitor, imprisoned in the tower, possibly being tortured by one of Cecil's inquisitors, while preparing himself for the block? All of this seemed likely.

Instead, Cecil informed Will that Essex was merely confined to his house. 'His house, mark you! Not the Tower, where I would have housed him, in chains. And do you think he will stay in this house? He will not! He was ordered to stay in Ireland but would not, and then he had a whole country to roam. Do you think he will stay in one building when he thinks all of London still loves him? Not when he can step out of his door expecting every man he sees to greet him as the saviour of England. All Her Majesty has done is take the monopoly on sweet wines away from him, so he has little income and large debts that cannot be cleared. I worry that could make him desperate. The most dangerous rat is a cornered one.' Will was shocked by the queen's leniency, even now.

'Essex will drum up a rebellion, but Her Majesty cannot see this. You cannot imprison a man in his own home if there are no guards and he alone holds the key. I'll have my men watch it, but he will do as he pleases, and I know the queen well; if I inform her he has quit the place to walk among the people, she will invent some excuse for it. She has already softened her view of the treaty he made with O'Neill, saying for all to hear that great good has come by it. What will it take for her to finally destroy the man? Will she wait until he has a knife at her throat, will she watch as he has me dragged to the block in front of her? When will she finally realise what a monster her endless indulgences has given birth to?' He banged his fist against the table then. 'Confine him to his home? There isn't a house in England large enough to accommodate that man's vanity!'

'What then will you do?'

'There is nothing I can do, for now,' Cecil concluded gloomily. 'Except wait for him to strike, and strike he will.'

Chapter Forty-Two

*'Ignorance is the curse of God,
Knowledge the wing wherewith we fly to heaven.'*

—Henry VI Part II

Cecil was proved right about one thing. There was no way that Essex would voluntarily stay under house arrest. Proof of his breaking the terms of his luxurious imprisonment at Essex House was obtained from the unlikely figure of Cuthbert Burbage, who met Will and his brother as they arrived for rehearsals and summoned them both to an audience with him in one of the Globe's galleries, while the rest of the company began their work upon the stage.

'Gentlemen, I have this very morning secured our futures,' Cuthbert told them, 'thanks to a visit from the Earl of Essex. Not from his man, mark you, nor his squire or his steward of matters domestical, but he, himself, the very same and none other.'

'He came alone?' asked Richard.

'Not alone. Obviously, members of his retinue were in attendance, but it was the earl who addressed me in person, and I concluded the matter with him.'

'The Earl of Essex came here?' Will enquired, astonished that he came at all, while under house arrest, but then immediately chiding himself for always underestimating the man's arrogance.

'He did.'

'And what is this business you concluded with him?' asked his brother.

'There is to be a performance of a play in front of an audience of privately invited gentlefolk, with no groundlings admitted. It will be gentles all.'

'When?' asked Richard, for he was eager to know how long he had to prepare for his role.

'Tonight, in fact.'

'Tonight?' Richard's voice went higher in alarm. 'Which play must I recall every damned word of from just a day's worth of rehearsals?'

Cuthbert waved away his objections. 'You have played the role before and will again, but this time for a sum that befits the performance, and it is only words.' He was dismissive. 'If you forget them, just make some up to fill in the gaps.' He turned to Will then. 'Apologies, Will, I know you think it's the words that count, but I know the groundlings mostly just want to hear my brother's voice whate'er he says.'

'For once, it is not the precise words I am worried about,' Will said.

'Nor me,' said Cuthbert brightly. 'For there will be no more worries for a while, when you learn the fee I have wrestled from the earl, using protestations of the need for more time to prepare, new costumes sewn in a hurry and other devices that must be bought to be used in tonight's stagecraft. I listed all and he did not blanch at the cost, the most part of which I did of course invent. He will pay us...' He looked expectantly at them both. 'How much do you think?'

'I know not,' said Will.

'Then guess.'

'I cannot.' Will's mind was occupied by more serious concerns than the fee, which would hardly matter if they never got to spend it. Cuthbert had just taken patronage from the most dangerous man in England.

Cuthbert turned to his brother. 'Then you guess, Richard. Pluck a number from the air, then think it too lowly, so double it, then remember this is a private performance like the ones you do before Her Majesty, then recall again that this is for the Earl of Essex, no man closer to her and one who carries a full purse that bulges at its seams. Now guess.'

'I know not either. Just tell us.'

'Guess!' he demanded. 'Guess, Richard, I beseech you, for I know you will never.'

'A hundred pounds then,' he snapped.

'No! Not a hundred. Good God, man, he didn't ask to buy the theatre! No, be reasonable. If I'd asked him for that, he'd have had me whipped. But I did ring forty shillings from him. *Forty!* For one performance. Oh, the lord is merciful to those who know how to help themselves.'

'Why would he give you so much?' asked Will.

'He is a generous lord.'

'Think you that is the only reason?'

'Why, yes?'

'And did you ask him why he wishes to put on this private performance, at such great cost and little warning?'

'I did not.' And when they both regarded him suspiciously: 'It was not my place to ask a great lord why he wished to stage a play.'

'I see,' said Will, through almost gritted teeth. 'Now tell me, Cuthbert, I beseech you. What play did he ask you to put on for him?'

'*Richard II.*'

'Oh, dear God.' Will turned to Richard. 'He's killed us all.'

'What?' demanded Cuthbert. 'Why do say you that? You wrote the damned play, Will. I thought you'd be happy.'

Richard regarded his brother as if he was a stranger then and one with little or no knowledge of the way the world worked. 'Will wrote that play when England was a different place, Cuthbert, and a much safer one. Now is a time of great tumult, with the queen fearing rebellion at every turn, and foreign invasion from the Spanish, should they be the slightest bit encouraged that she could fall at the hands of her own people.'

'And?' asked Cuthbert as if this was no cause for him to be concerned.

'And the Earl of Essex, who was once the queen's favourite, has been banished from court and placed under arrest in his own house, because he failed to do her will in Ireland.'

'I knew of that but assumed he was back in her favour. How else could he move freely around London?' Cuthbert looked bemused. 'Why else would he put on this play but to entertain her loyal followers and possibly even invite Her Majesty here?'

'The queen, here, in our theatre? When she can summon us to her court at will. Are you mad?'

'Not the queen then, but an audience of gentle folk, so what could cause us any ill?'

Will explained it to him. 'Richard II was deposed, man. He was brought down by an earl who took his crown and made himself monarch instead.'

'Henry IV,' recalled Cuthbert. 'And that reminds me, he wants a scene put back in.'

'The deposition scene?' guessed Will, with a heavy heart.

'The very same.' Cuthbert had clearly forgotten in the intervening years that this had been taken out for a reason.

'Did you not know of the queen's displeasure? We performed a scene that showed a monarch, however unfit, being removed by a subject, and she was not willing to countenance it. Her fury was eventually calmed, once she had accepted it was never Will's intention to hint that she should be deposed too.' He had agreed to remove the scene from all future performances. 'The play also shows King Richard was poorly advised by unwise counsellors and wicked favourites, who were banished or executed,' said Will.

'But that was long ago,' Cuthbert protested.

'The Earl of Essex has always said the queen is badly advised by corrupt men. If he shows this play to gentle folk, who take that lesson from the play, they might look to change the way the queen is counselled, by bringing down those men and placing others in their place.' Will did not understand why he was forced to explain this to Cuthbert. It should have been obvious.

'But that would be treason, surely.'

'Exactly!' said Richard. 'Now, do you see?'

'It *would* be treason,' agreed Will, 'and we would be blamed for inciting it by those same men who are close to the queen, chief among them, Sir Robert Cecil, a vengeful courtier who will thank none of us for planting that seed of rebellion in the hearts of those men.'

'I was wrong to take the earl's coin.' Cuthbert looked shaken. 'I see that now, but what can be done of it? Can we give it back?'

'Nothing can be done. Offend the earl or embarrass him and he will not forget. If he returns to favour, we would be doomed.'

'Will is right, Cuthbert. You took the earl's coin and we must stage his play, whatever it costs us.'

'And that could be everything,' said Will.

Chapter Forty-Three

'When devils will the blackest sins put on,
They do suggest at first with heavenly shows.'

—*Othello*

When the play was done, the Earl of Essex strode out onto the stage while the players were still taking their bows, to loud applause from the assembled gentles and a rowdy mob of groundlings, who had all been admitted despite Cuthbert's assurances to the contrary. Will wondered who these men were and how they had been invited here by the earl. Some seemed to be soldiers, perhaps back from Ireland or the Lowlands, who had probably been cashiered without pay and had fallen on harder times. Like Cassius in his Roman play, they all had a lean and hungry look about them.

'A fine play!' Essex roared to the crowd. 'Was it not?' and the applause increased at his urging. 'It tells of a time when tyranny could be overthrown, when evil counsellors could be cast down and the crown was something that had to be fought for.' Then he paused. 'But that was long ago. We live in a different age now, but there was a time when Englishmen could be proud,' he announced to general acclaim. 'We used to be the envy of Europe, but look at us now.'

Will knew his history and he wondered how long ago this might have been. As far as he could tell, England hadn't been the envy of Europe since Agincourt, possibly even before then, since the gains of that great battle had not lasted long, before everything England owned in France had been lost. Henry II perhaps? Now there was a king who could lay claim to large swathes of French land, including Normandy, Anjou and Aquitaine, but that had been more than four hundred years ago, so the Earl of Essex could hardly claim to remember it.

'We are less than we were,' he continued, 'cowed down, hiding in fear and startled by the glimpse of every ship on the horizon, lest it be the first sighting of a new Armada.' They laughed at that notion. 'But it is not too late to put right the wrongs of our time and take back our nation. We can make England great once more!

'The queen, our gracious and most noble majesty, is most poorly advised by rotten and corrupt counsellors. There is only one way to end this. We must strike now to remove them and save her from men who hate our country and wish only to destroy it. Tomorrow we will march on Whitehall, gathering men along the way, until we have so many in our midst that the queen cannot help but see how much in earnest we are. Then we shall tell her she must dismiss her base advisors – Robert Cecil chief among them – who daily fill their purses with the queen's gold. She has been badly served by them, and they will pay for it with their heads!'

There was loud approval of this idea.

'Go back to your homes now and prepare for the morning, when we will free our nation from tyranny. Tell your neighbours to quit their work tomorrow and join us on the march to Whitehall. As they rise, so shall thousands more and all will join with Essex and Southampton, until we sweep everything from our path and take the queen herself into our wise and loving care. Go now. Go!'

There were loud cheers, even as they all turned to leave the Globe and head home with news of the rebellion to share with their neighbours.

Will had never been more terrified than he was in that moment, and he was certain that Richard and Cuthbert Burbage shared his horror. Had he not just witnessed the Earl of Essex incite open revolt? Had the earl not just urged everyone in the audience to go to his neighbours and stir up rebellion in them too, until a vast army congregated in the morning to march suddenly on Whitehall? They would bring the government down and take the queen herself – as what? Their prisoner? Surely it had to be so, for she would never willingly surrender her closest advisors on the orders of an earl, no matter that he was once her favourite.

Worse, the earl had used Will's play to incite this rebellion. Essex had just rallied his own private army with a stirring speech delivered just feet from the players, and the writer who had penned the play he used to inspire them. Their presence on the stage must surely have made it look as if they were far from unwitting accomplices in this matter but instead trusted co-conspirators.

This could only end one way, with all of them arrested. Then they would be racked until their bodies were torn, and they would confess to anything, even treason, before being taken out to be hanged, drawn and quartered, on the orders of a furious queen. The whole company would die for this, their theatre would be torn to the ground and burned to ashes.

As the cheers and roars from the crowd continued, Will could not help himself. 'May God have mercy on our souls,' he said but the noise around him was too great for anyone else to hear.

The earl looked exultant then. Cecil had been right about him all along. Will made a decision there and then. As soon as he could, he would slip away from the theatre and warn Cecil of the revolt that was coming in the morning. It was the only way to prevent his own death, that of his friends, and the destruction of everything he held dear.

When the crowd had finally dispersed, the Earl of Essex's man paid them on the stage. Cuthbert received his forty shillings and, judging by the look on his face, it might as well have been thirty pieces of silver.

'Well performed, players,' Essex told them, still full of pride and bravado from his speech to the masses. He was walking up and down the stage now, drawn to his full height, with his hands placed on his hips, as if he had suddenly realised he too could be a player, if he were not already a great earl, and that the theatre suited him well.

Will could not have imagined this day becoming any more dangerous for them, until Essex said, 'Now, Richard Burbage and William Shakespeare, when we march on Whitehall tomorrow, I expect you both to be at the vanguard. You shall walk with me, one on either side. Your popularity with the masses shall help to bring even more men to my cause when they see how you side with me.' He must have expected them to respond with more enthusiasm and, when instead they merely stared back at him, horrified, he told them, 'Make sure you do. History will judge kindly everyone who is there, but it will also remember anyone who is not.' Then he added significantly, 'And so shall I.'

'My lord.' Richard gave a low bow and Will followed his example, though neither of them were foolish enough to agree to his ridiculous plan, nor stupid enough to specifically decline his invitation to rebel.

Perhaps sensing they were unlikely to present themselves in the morning, Essex pretended he had just had a finer idea. 'Come. You will stay at my house tonight, as my guests, along with the other most trusted men in my retinue.'

'Oh, really, Your Grace, it is so kind of you to offer your hospitality, but we could not possibly accept when it would be an obvious imposition,' Richard told him humbly.

Taking his cue from his friend, Will agreed. 'We are not worthy of such an honour and in such fine company.' As he said this, he automatically glanced at the assembled band of the earl's inner circle, which included great men like the Earl of Southampton but had room for some of those former soldiers who appeared to have little to their name. 'We can leave Your Grace now and return early next morning.'

Essex's smile had no warmth in it. He placed a hand firmly on Will's shoulder. 'But you don't understand, Master Shakespeare. I insist.'

Chapter Forty-Four

*'Beware the leader who bangs the drums of war
in order to whip the citizenry into a patriotic fervour.'*

—Julius Caesar

Once at the earl's house on the Strand, Will and the Burbage brothers stood in a quieter corner of a large room, filled with followers of Essex. While they earnestly discussed their options, they were forced to keep their voices low.

'What in God's name will we do, Will?' asked an increasingly agitated Richard. 'This is madness.'

'Nothing good can ever come from it, that is sure,' Will agreed.

'But we must go with him, mustn't we?' asked Cuthbert. 'A great lord commands it, so how can we refuse him?'

'Is he as great as the queen?' asked Richard.

'That we shall discover come the 'morrow,' Cuthbert reasoned. 'With Southampton, and all these others at his side, as well as everyone who attended the play, and thousands more who are likely to turn out for him along the way, won't he surely win the day? Robert Cecil is but one man and not even an earl. The queen will have to give him up. Who can stop Essex now? There is no one with the power, and if we are not there with him when he marches, he will likely prove to be a most vengeful lord indeed. Besides, how would we escape his house without being seen?'

Cuthbert made a good point. While many of the men were feasting and drinking, there were sober men on every door to ensure no one slipped away in the night to give away the earl's plans.

'But if we side with him and he falls, then we fall with him,' Will reminded them both, 'and will hang for it, or worse.' He didn't want to imagine what the actual punishment for treason was likely to feel like. It was almost impossible to think of a more terrible death.

'We have already sided with him, Will,' said Richard with not a little dread, 'and thousands did witness it. I say we are committed to this endeavour of his. If he succeeds, we rise with him, if he fails then…' He didn't need to explain further. They all knew the price they would pay if Essex's rebellion did not succeed. 'All we can do now is tie ourselves to the mast and wait for the squall to subside.'

—

The next morning, there were some two hundred men mustered in the inner courtyard of Essex House. All were armed and there was an air of excitement tinged with anticipation, and perhaps fear too, for to go against the queen was no small matter, but they all seemed sure of their cause, except for three of them.

'What are we doing, Will?' asked Cuthbert yet again.

'We are joining the muster.'

'And remind me why we are joining the muster?'

'We have been through this already.' And they had, repeatedly during the night, but Will got the impression Cuthbert needed to hear it again to harden his resolve. 'So as to be noticed joining it by the Earl of Essex,' Will recounted.

'And then?'

'And then, when his militia has almost reached the palace, we shall withdraw, hidden by the crowd that joins it along the way.'

'How will that help us?' Cuthbert asked.

'I wager that he will not notice us slip away from his vanguard,' said Will, more in hope than in earnest.

'Because he is too busy watching his other men being slaughtered by the queen's guard?' Richard asked with some resignation.

'Or he will be too engaged in storming the palace to realise when a couple of low-born actors slip from the ranks of his men,' offered Will.

'You think it might be so, when he specifically asked you to be by his side, as an example to those men?' asked Cuthbert, but neither man had an answer for that.

As they emerged from the house, Will half expected to see ranks of men facing them with raised muskets, for surely Cecil had spies in that audience at the Globe? He must have known that Essex was finally planning to do what Cecil always said he would. But no, they were entirely unopposed, and the men strode out of the house and came together in front of it in good order, before beginning their march with Essex on foot leading them on. Thankfully, he had not insisted that Will and Richard actually take their positions on either side of him, as he had stated, but he had glanced at them both before setting off, to make sure they were still with him. Instead, it was his dear friend, the Earl of Southampton, who ensured he was next to Essex as they began their historic march to bring down the queen's government.

As Essex moved his men further along the street, he shouted, 'For the queen! For the queen! The crown of England is sold to the Spaniard! A plot is laid for my life!' and he repeated this phrase over and over in a booming voice, like a market trader selling his wares, which alerted the neighbourhood to his grievances. Shutters, windows and the occasional door were thrown open, so those inside could see what all the noise was about. Essex urged them all to come out onto the streets and join him then, with more words and a wave of his arm, so they could save the queen from her wicked advisors by marching together on Whitehall.

Will watched those faces closely to see what they would do once Essex took the vanguard of his men beyond them. If they stepped out into the street as one, then the ranks of the rebels would instantly swell, and others would certainly follow. The momentum caused by this would soon lead to the rebel band becoming an army of the people, and didn't they all love Essex, while hating Cecil and despairing of the queen's judgement in letting herself be guided by him?

Will fully expected those first doors to yield a steady stream of people who would happily join Essex, but, to his surprise, that did not happen. Instead of the cheers he had heard when he had marched out of London, when all he was planning to subdue were Irish rebels, Essex received an eerily silent reception from the stunned onlookers, who had not expected this from him. Hardly anyone stepped out of their houses to join the earl. Perhaps some of them did not understand what was going on, but Will thought that many knew all too well what was afoot and were afeared of it. He could tell this from the look in their eyes.

As the columns of rebels marched further, the same scene was repeated, again and again, in street after street. Essex called out his rallying cries, of support for the queen and death to her advisors, while the grim-visaged and armed men by his side sent out a silent but all-too-clear message of their own. This was treason and Will could sense that the good folk of London understood and, so far, wanted no part of it.

Essex failed to rally anyone new to his cause, but perhaps he didn't need an army of citizens when he already had two hundred men under his command who all looked as if they had seen battle before. They marched further, until they drew closer and closer to their destination, yard by dreadful yard and, at first, they showed no signs of abating. Then, slowly but steadily, Will began to notice that, here and there, men were exchanging nervous glances with one another. They were looking around at the frightened faces who peered at them from upper windows, the better to distance themselves from a crowd that was starting to look like condemned men marching ever closer to the gallows.

Then Will heard the first shout of 'Traitor!'

Essex whirled round to note its origin, but Will had already realised it was coming from an adjacent street.

'Traitor!' a voice boomed again. 'The Earl of Essex is declared a traitor by the queen!'

'Silence that man!' ordered Essex and three men ran towards the sound, only for a second voice to repeat the accusation off to the other side of their column, perhaps a street or two away. Then a third could be heard up ahead of them. More voices were soon added as they marched, and each one denounced the Earl of Essex as a traitor to Her Majesty. This constant accompaniment was clearly an organised one and it was having a disconcerting effect on their group, whose members all knew they would be judged by the actions of their master.

Will and Richard exchanged worried glances then. If these heralds made the veteran soldiers in Essex's band more fearful, it had an even more damaging effect on the people he was trying to rouse from their homes. Instead of opened doors and windows filled with curious homeowners, the group started to be greeted by doors being firmly closed and windows bolted before they had reached them. The only sound coming from those homes now was from shutters banging and metal bolts being firmly drawn in place to keep the rebels out.

Essex glanced off to one side when he heard yet another accusation of 'Traitor! Robert Devereux is to be arrested as a traitor by order of the queen!' and Will could see that already some of the earl's confidence was starting to drain from him, because the people of London were abandoning him. The worried look on his face was enough to set some of the men around them to murmuring about the situation. Will started to pick up doubts, since the people of London were not rising up to join them as they had been assured they would. Would they have enough men to overcome the queen's guard? One man was even heard to say, '*He* might get a pardon from the queen' – meaning the earl – 'but we won't.'

Just then, one of the men Essex had sent on ahead to see if the way was clear came running back in a panic. Will was just close enough to hear his shouts as he ran to the earl. 'The way ahead is blocked! There's a barricade on Ludgate Hill by the city gate and armed men behind it with muskets!'

This set off a great murmur among the men behind Essex, as they had not expected their way to be blocked so early, before they had reached the palace. Someone had mobilised a force to intercept them along the way, and if they were unable to break that wall of armed men, then their rebellion was at an end. Will noticed no men with muskets among them, only swords, clubs, halberds, billhooks and daggers. They didn't even have any archers because no one had considered they might be so opposed.

'Keep moving!' ordered Essex, ignoring the man's warning about the barricade, and he waved his men forwards. That was when Will turned back and noticed the first man leaving from the rear of the columns. He watched as the fellow waved to a friend and they moved swiftly away down a side street. 'Onwards!' roared Essex and everyone else did move off, but they walked more slowly now and there was some jostling up at the front, presumably caused by an understandable reluctance to face musketry.

Essex must have noticed this. 'No true Englishman will ever fire upon another. Mark me when I say that no one will hear gunfire this day!' He seemed convinced of his reasoning and some of the men seemed to rally at this. They all moved on more quickly than before.

Will, Cuthbert and Richard tried to allow themselves to fall behind, so they could step out of the columns at some future point, as planned, but the men behind crowded in tightly around them and pushed and shoved them forwards. Will glanced back to the rear of the column in time to see another handful of men leaving it. *They have no heart for this fight*, he thought, *and we have not even reached the barricade*. All would depend on what happened there. Either Essex would be able to talk the men with muskets into coming to his side or there would be slaughter.

They marched on and Will, Cuthbert and Richard did manage to move back a little further from the front ranks but were still nowhere near the rear, where they might be able to slip away undetected. They were still trapped, and Will could see the arch at Ludgate Hill now. Though their ranks kept thinning, the men around them stayed. They were the most committed ones, buoyed by their leader's assurance that they would not be fired on.

'There's no way out,' Richard said as much to himself as to Will and Cuthbert. They were jostled forwards even further, the crowd picking up momentum now.

Someone shouted, 'Barricade!' The movement of the men slowed then as they advanced, but it showed no sign of stopping. Will could see it now and his eyes never left that barricade as the crowd pushed him towards it. He was desperate to break free from its ranks, but the mass of tightly packed men, still surely a hundred or more, made this impossible in the narrow street. It was all he could do to stay on his feet, and he had to use all his strength just to maintain his position in the ranks and not be pushed down and trampled on the ground.

All too soon, the men reached the barricade. Will saw an arm raised and realised this was the earl signalling for them to stop. No one spoke and an uneasy silence descended upon the scene. Will raised himself up to his full height and peered over the shoulders of the man in front of him. The sight that greeted him was daunting. Up ahead, a well-built and solid barricade, made of carts pulled into position and turned onto their sides, blocked the entire road. There was no way to outflank or go around it and the only way past would be to go over, but at what cost? Will was close enough to see the faces of those manning the barricade. They looked grim and determined. A good number of them were levelling muskets on the men in his group already and he hoped the earl was right. Would they really fire on fellow Englishmen? He prayed they would not.

'Hold your fire!' It was an order, not a request, and it came from the earl, who seemed to think he was the natural leader of the men behind the barricade, not the gentleman who stood off slightly to one side, surveying the rebels in front of him, who were packed in tightly in the narrow street. Essex must have spotted him too, for he addressed the man directly. 'Sir John Leveson. I see you behind that barricade. Tell your men to set down their weapons and move these carts, so I may continue my progress.'

'I shall not.' But his voice did waver a little. Was the man behind the barricades as scared as Will was?

'You know who I am,' Essex continued, 'all of London does, and the people love me. They understand I am here today to save the queen from her wretched advisors. You have no more love for Robert Cecil than I, and you know the realm is headed for calamity unless he is stopped.'

'That is for the queen to decide and command, not you.' Leveson was rallying now.

'Remember your place, man.' Essex sounded frustrated. 'You are a member of Parliament and I am an earl. You will do as I say.'

'You are an earl but not a king, nor ever shall be,' Leveson countered. 'What I do today is done in the queen's name.'

'Is this ordered by the queen, truly?' Essex drew his sword and pointed it at the offending barricade. 'Or by Robert Cecil?'

The earl was sure he knew the truth of it, but Leveson roared back, 'It is ordered by the queen!' and that seemed to surprise Essex, for he offered no immediate response. Worse for him, murmurs of dissent had started from within the ranks of the men. They were at best unsure of their course now, if the queen had indeed personally ordered them to be stopped by this militia? Essex must have assured them the queen would actually welcome his intervention to remove her crooked advisors, but now they began to see the truth of it. They were rebels and this was treason.

'Order your men to throw down their arms and turn them around,' Leveson commanded. 'Return to your house to await the queen's pleasure. End this madness.'

The murmuring rose in volume while the men debated among themselves what should be done. Will noticed that they were packed in less tightly now and he looked about him and began to understand the cause of this. Although the mass of men was still too tight for Will and the Burbages to escape it, he witnessed a good number at the back of their ranks leaving the main body and dispersing before they were given any new order by Essex. He was losing them, thought Will, but what would be his reaction? Any normal man would see he could not possibly win the day and would order a cessation of the rebellion then retreat. But Essex was not a normal man. Will waited for his response and realised he was holding his breath.

'Never!' shouted Essex. 'I would rather die than let the queen continue to suffer such unwise counsel from evil men!'

The word *die* caused even more dissent from within the ranks as they were far less enthusiastic to die than the earl was. Some cursed and others openly stated their intention to abandon his cause. Essex turned at the sound and watched as at least a quarter of his men abandoned their positions and began to walk away, some even ran. *A few more seconds*, thought Will, *and we will be able to push our way out of here and join them*. They would have to deal with the earl's wrath, but he would rather take his chances with Essex now than the queen, and he would be far from alone in abandoning the earl.

'Stand fast!' Essex called and his most loyal men did just that, though they had to number less than fifty by now.

Will, Cuthbert and Richard turned away then and tried to push their way out of the group but were unfortunate enough to be met by a line of large men who must have counted themselves as true loyalists, for they pushed back, preventing them from leaving. Will turned back to face the barricade once more, in time to see the earl give his next command.

'With me!' he roared. 'With me! Over the barricade, men, and onwards!' He waved his sword, and the men all roared in unison.

The men behind the barricade continued to aim their muskets into the ranks of the rebels at close range. Essex perhaps made a yard or two before his attack was answered by them.

'Fire!' roared Leveson and they did, without hesitation or any seeming reluctance to shoot down their fellow Englishmen. There was an enormous noise caused by perhaps twenty muskets being fired simultaneously and a terrifying burst of flame and smoke from their barrels. This was followed almost immediately by the sound of men roaring in terror or screaming in pain.

Will instinctively ducked and it was as well that he did, because a man close to him was struck by a musket ball and his arm shattered. The front rank took the brunt of the volley and they fell, but there was great confusion all around them now as men with fresh wounds turned away, desperate to escape a second volley.

Leveson's cry of 'Reload!' was enough to scatter them then and they ran, with no greater or more noble aim now than to save their own wretched lives. At last, the ranks broke and Will, Richard and Cuthbert were able to turn and run too. Will moved as fast as he was able, all the while expecting a second volley to hit them as they fled.

When they reached the end of the street, Will turned and looked back. Men were lying there before the barricade. One or two at least were motionless and likely dead. Others screamed in agony while trying to stand and flee but were hampered by all manner of wounds caused by that deadly volley of musket fire. Among their number was a tiny group of Essex loyalists who still remained, including the Earl of Southampton, but they were no longer intent on getting beyond the barricade. Instead, they were desperately trying to manhandle the earl away from the carnage he had created. Incredibly, though he had been at the very front of his men, he appeared to be unharmed, though he seemed bewildered, disbelieving and, for the first time since Will had known the man, he looked scared.

–

They fled back to Will's house and locked the door behind them. Cuthbert went out again that evening to see if he could learn what had happened to Essex and the rebels, leaving Richard and Will to go over the events of that day, again and again.

'Do you think we were seen, Will? Among the crowd? There were what? Two hundred of his followers or more there. Perhaps we passed unnoticed?' Richard asked hopefully.

Will looked at his friend in consternation. 'How many of those two hundred were actually Cecil's men, do you think? Five, ten, twenty? And is there a more recognisable face in London than yours, Richard?'

Richard looked sick then. 'Save for the queen's, I mean, and she wears more paint on her face than you do so could probably pass unnoticed through London without it. No, Richard, you were seen, and there is no point in denying that we were there.'

'You are right,' admitted Richard. 'My fame is a curse.'

'All we can do now when we are summoned, and summoned we shall be, is to explain that our presence there was forced, which it was, and hope this is believed.' He also had to hope that Cecil would not think that Will had turned against his master.

There was a loud bang on the door then and both men jumped, fearing arrest. Will went and tentatively opened it. Cuthbert burst into the room in a state of agitation.

'Thank God,' said Will. 'I thought you were the watch.'

'What news?' his brother demanded.

Cuthbert began a full report. 'Essex's page and two others were killed at the barricade. Many others were wounded. Essex has locked himself in his house and refuses to surrender, though the place is entirely surrounded by the Lord Admiral's men.' It seemed that the queen had sent an earl to deal with an earl, since the Lord Admiral was the Earl of Nottingham. 'He has sworn never to give himself up, so Nottingham has fetched cannon and placed them all around the house. Essex climbed up onto the roof and brandished his sword.' Cuthbert then recalled the words he had heard shouted between them from the street and the rooftop. '"*Surrender yourself, man. All is lost,*" said the Lord Admiral. "*I would sooner fly to heaven,*" quoth Essex. "*Very well then,*" said the Lord Admiral. "*If you will not leave your house, I shall blow it up!*"'

'He has given Essex another hour in which to surrender or he will fire the cannon at his home and blast it to rubble, with the earl still in it.'

—

They drew as close to Essex House as they dared. It was near enough to join the crowds watching the spectacle unfold, but not so close that they could be mistaken for supporters come to help the earl outwit the authorities. By the time they got there, it seemed that all efforts to bring him out of his house peacefully had failed. It was looking ever more likely that soon the night air would be filled with the sound of cannon, which had been lined up to face Essex House. They might actually witness the destruction of an entire building here in the middle of the most opulent part of London, where many of the nobility also had their homes. It was almost unthinkable to bring a level of destruction normally reserved for besieged castles in foreign wars to England's capital, but they lived in the strangest of times. How else would they prise Essex from his home, without entering into a pitched battle with his followers, who were locked inside behind its heavy doors?

With his customary feel for the dramatic, Essex waited the full hour before finally giving up. The doors opened and every soldier outside in the street stiffened in anticipation of the suicidal attack from him and his men that would likely follow.

In the end, despite his bravado, he went like a lamb. Advancing towards the Lord Admiral, he handed the Earl of Nottingham his sword in surrender. Essex was led away then, to join the more than eighty rebels who had been captured throughout the course of that day. Before long, the excited crowd that witnessed his arrest began to disperse, for there was little left here to amuse them, other than the withdrawal of the troops and cannon. The rebellion was finally over.

Chapter Forty-Five

*'Unthread the rude eye of rebellion
And welcome home again discarded faith.'*

—*King John*

It was all anyone in London talked about for a good while. Everybody wondered what would happen to the earl after the putting down of his rebellion, and men were strongly divided by their opinions on the matter. Many felt the queen must surely have exhausted any mercy left in her for this errant favourite she had given so much to. Her ungrateful servant had risen against her authority, in his treasonous march through the capital, while intending to turn Her Majesty into his puppet. No man, however exalted or once favoured, could surely commit such an act and get away with it. Others argued differently. The hero of Cadiz had done this out of loyalty to the queen, who had been ill served and undermined for years by her advisors, led by the unpopular Cecil, who often acted without her knowledge and had corrupted the state. Essex simply wanted to make England great once more. He was one man's patriot and another's traitor, depending on who you asked, and the capital seemed to be split down the middle on the matter.

Some predicted he would most definitely be hanged, drawn and quartered, along with all of his followers, even the lofty Earl of Southampton. If he was fortunate, the queen might show him enough mercy to demand a simple beheading, which was more than he deserved, by God. Others were just as convinced that she would soon see his motives were pure, if a little misguided, that he would receive a full pardon and would be elevated once more at court.

Every time Will heard these quarrels, which often became heated, he could not help but feel that each side had an equally convincing argument. He realised that, in truth, no one but the queen knew her own mind on this. Surely, by any normal measure, Essex was indeed a traitor, but if Her Majesty decided she wanted to forgive the man she seemed to love above all others, then wouldn't she always be able to find a reason? If she said he had acted rashly but with good intent, who then could contradict her? Not even Cecil. Essex's life now hung in the balance and all of London awaited the outcome.

—

'Whatever will we do, whatever will we do?' a terrified Cuthbert repeatedly asked his brother and Will, but for once neither could think of a solution.

Will was torn between staying away from court, hoping that being out of the queen's sight would prevent her from becoming enraged by his presence, and immediately attending it so he could beg for her mercy. He would then cite a misplaced loyalty to a great earl, as a reason for staging a most contentious play, on the eve of a rebellion he was then forced to go along with. In the end, he settled for drafting a message in his own hand to Sir Robert Cecil. In his letter, he explained the peculiar circumstances of being ordered by Essex to stage a play, then prevented from informing Cecil of the upcoming rebellion, being under guard at the earl's house. He did not at this stage confess his presence on the earl's doomed march to the barricade.

Will sweated for two days while he waited for an answer and when it came, Cecil's message in reply was deliberately opaque. 'Do not come between the dragon and its wrath,' he warned. Will thought he knew what Cecil meant. Some time ago now, he had explained to Will how the queen's mind worked when she was angered. 'There have been times when both my father and myself have been forced to quit the court awhile to escape the queen's fury. My father always used to say a fortnight away was enough.'

'A fortnight?'

'Fourteen days to let the queen's fury abate, for she rarely held on to a grievance or bitter thought longer than that.'

But what if the queen summoned him to her before that time had elapsed? The next two weeks would be an eternity of waiting, filled with sleepless nights and restless days for them all.

Essex, meanwhile, spent eleven days in confinement at the Tower, waiting to be placed on trial before his peers, along with the Earl of Southampton. The charge, as expected, was treason. The longer indictment claimed that Essex planned to depose then slay the queen, and that he and his men had wounded or killed many of the queen's subjects as they rampaged through London, inciting rebellion from all around them. Will did not recall a stated intention to kill the queen, nor had he witnessed any wounding or murdering on that march, but he realised the truth did not really matter anymore, only the example that would be made of the two treasonous earls – one of whom was his patron, which could prove to be another nail in Will's coffin.

It seemed that everyone, bar his fellow accused, had turned against Essex and the result was a foregone conclusion. It took scarcely an hour to convict them both. The verdict when it came was no great surprise. They were both found guilty and sentenced to a traitor's death. Despite facing this brutal and terrifying prospect, Essex refused to beg for the queen's mercy or even repent his crimes. Did he still cling to the possibility that, faced with the prospect of killing her beloved subject, she would weaken and have him set free?

The Earl of Southampton did plead for his own life, however, saying it had only been his love for Essex that had led him so far astray, but the court was unmoved. Both men were set to die. One of Will's earliest patrons would go to the block. Southampton's foolishness, in following Essex's lead by marching against the queen, had led to his undoing and, though his death was an almost inevitable outcome of this, Will found he was still shocked to learn of the sentence. The two men had known happier times, when the earl's love of theatre and verse had made up for his vanity and folly. He had been such a beautiful youth too, but soon he would be wiped from the world.

—

Between the guilty verdict and the scheduled day of execution, Will and the Burbages could only pray that their unwitting part in the rebellion had either passed unnoticed or, if it had been noted, was overlooked, since there were greater men than they to bring down.

Those hopes were entirely dashed when a messenger dressed in the queen's livery appeared at the Globe to formally demand their presence at court. 'Burbage and Burbage,' he told Richard and Cuthbert. 'You are summoned to appear before the queen to explain your conduct in putting on a seditious play, inciting treason in her realm.' Then he noticed Will and told him, 'You too, Shakespeare.'

Chapter Forty-Six

'What infinite heartsease must kings neglect that private men enjoy?'

—Henry V

There was one thing that almost all men could agree upon about the queen. She could be terrifying. Even those closest to her were afraid of her tempestuous rages, knowing that behind them lay an almost unchecked power. One word from her could consign you to banishment, arrest, torture or execution, once the machinations of a show trial had concluded, because she could always find a compliant jury of your peers to condemn you if she willed it. The power to confiscate men's goods and property, destroy their families and end their lives lay with her, and it made her fearsome.

Her Majesty's unforgiving demeanour had only worsened with age. There was something behind her tantrums that Will suspected may have been caused by a deep sadness, at the compromises she had been forced to make in her life to maintain her authority as queen. She had never married, for fear of gaining a master and losing her power, so she had never known a man. Or, if she had, was forced to do so in secret. As Will himself knew, the novelty of snatched or stolen kisses soon wore off. Deep down, he still longed to take Avisa from her husband then declare his admiration for her to all, even though he now knew his love for her was always one-sided, or so she maintained. He wished he could have lived openly with her and hadn't had to meet clandestinely and infrequently. Though he knew this of course to be folly, it hurt him dearly that he could never be fully with her. How then must the queen have felt after denying her own desires for a lifetime?

There was nothing for it but to beg Her Majesty for forgiveness, while trying to maintain some semblance of innocence in the whole affair. Cuthbert explained his naïve and unwitting part in allowing Essex to put on a play with a seditious scene restored to it. Richard swore he would never have uttered any of its words if he had known the true intentions of the earl, and Will described their imprisonment at the house on the Strand as the reason for not raising the alarm once the play was done.

Of course, none of this would really matter if the queen had already made up her mind. If she wanted to punish them, then their excuses were wholly inadequate. If, however, her vengeance was to be restricted to the leaders of the rebellion, then perhaps they might be pardoned for their treasonous behaviour.

They knelt before her for what seemed like an age, waiting to discover their fate. Finally, the queen spoke. 'You were mightily deceived by my Lord Essex,' she told them sternly. Then she sighed. 'As was I.' She surveyed the cowed offenders before her closely. 'Men shall die because of his rebellion.' Then she informed them, 'But not you three.'

Will realised that the exclamation of breath he let out at this news must have been audible. The queen seemed to find this almost amusing.

'We are Your Majesty's most loyal servants, to command as you desire,' Richard said immediately.

The queen knew this already, of course, and needed no prompting from them, but perhaps that promise, of doing whatever she desired, gave her a notion, for she demanded of Will, 'Where is my play? I want to see Falstaff again. He was missing from your *Henry V*.' Will had not forgotten the requirement to come up with a play about Falstaff for the queen, though the time he needed to complete it had been eroded somewhat by recent events. If finishing it was the price of their freedom, however, then he would ensure it was done in haste. 'I would like to see him in love,' the queen told him. 'And a wooing. That would amuse me, and Lord knows how much in need of some amusement I am in these very dark days. But tell me, did you write that same play for me as I commanded?'

'I did start to write it, Your Majesty.'

'And is it nearly done?'

'Almost.'

'Almost? How much longer do you need, by Heaven?'

In truth, he only needed a day or two more and wondered if that might be enough to fully abate the queen's fury. Then he recalled Sir Robert's words of caution.

'A fortnight.'

'Two weeks,' she challenged him, 'and it will be done?'

'It shall.'

'It had better be and I must be content with the finished work, if I am to forget my disappointment in you, Master Shakespeare.'

'You will be,' he blurted, unable to help himself.

'You presume to know my mind before I have seen your play? That shows an arrogance I would not have even expected from the Earl of Essex. Perhaps you have spent too long in his company of late?'

'Forgive me, Your Majesty. I meant only that I have toiled to make every word of this new play fit for a queen.'

'I will be the judge of that, Shakespeare,' she reproached him. 'But, come now, tell me the story of this play.' She waved him closer.

He rose and stepped forwards. In a low, confiding voice only she could hear, Will told her of Sir John Falstaff's scandalous plan to rescue himself from destitution by wooing two married women at once, in order to get at their money. For a second, he worried the story might be too saucy for a queen, but she let out a hearty laugh at the idea of the fat, errant knight wooing married ladies. 'Even his loyal servants, Pistol and Nym refuse to join him in this plot and he dispenses with them both, so they tell the women's husbands of his plan.' She snorted at that development. 'Meanwhile, both women separately learn of his deception and turn it back on Falstaff, by pretending to be beguiled by him. First, they force him to hide from their husbands in a basket of filthy washing, which is taken away and Falstaff tipped into a river.' She laughed at that image. 'Then they make Falstaff disguise himself as "the fat woman of Brentford" to deceive a returning husband who is fooled at first but strikes Falstaff for being a witch.' The queen was laughing heartily by then at the thought of her favourite comic character hiding as a woman then being beaten for it.

She raised a hand. 'Stop, cease, desist. If your actors be but half as persuasive as your words, then all will be well in Windsor Castle when it is performed. Lord knows how much we need laughter in these dark days. Tell me, what is this play called?'

'*The Merry Wives of Windsor*, with your permission, Majesty?'

'Granted.' Then she told Will, 'I'll spare you to write it.' It seemed she was offering him a pardon for a play. It struck Will then just how important it was to be capable of entertaining an unhappy queen, even for an hour or two. 'Master Shakespeare, you are a very wicked man, just like your creation, Falstaff. Bring this play, about that rogue and these merry wives, to me and you might not be overlong out of my favour – but only if I like it. And make sure you punish the rogue for his foul deeds, lest I punish the man who permits them. I have of late been too lenient to my subjects and they should be warned against committing their sins.'

'I will bring such a humiliation down upon the head of that abject and errant knight that he will ever regret his lust, greed and folly.'

'Make sure you do,' was her final word on the subject, 'or be damned.'

And with that, Will and the Burbages were dismissed.

–

'Saved!' said Cuthbert once they were gone from that room and walking briskly away from the palace.

'Aye,' agreed Richard, 'by a fat knight with a lust for coin and merry wives.'

'Who would ever have thought that Falstaff would be the hero to rescue us all from a traitor's death?' posed Will.

'I did always think she might be merciful,' said Cuthbert to the surprise of them both. 'She clearly lost the taste for blood once her favourite was condemned to the block.'

'I am glad you were so convinced we would walk away from here unpunished, Cuthbert,' said Will. 'For a moment, there I thought you were worried.'

'Not I. Not really.'

Will and Richard shared a look then and both men laughed at him in unison.

Chapter Forty-Seven

'He that is proud eats up himself.'

—*Troilus and Cressida*

Sir Robert Cecil must have decided it was safe to be seen again with Will, once he had been granted the queen's mercy. Will was summoned to meet the Secretary of State at the well-appointed rooms he used whenever he worked in the Tower of London. Will was forced to spend a good hour there explaining every moment of the company's interaction with the Earl of Essex, including the speech he had made from their stage and the state of things at Essex House on the night before the rebellion. If Cecil did know of Will's presence on the ill-fated march that was cut down at the barricade the next day, then he chose to pretend he did not, for he never mentioned it at all.

'The mother of the Earl of Southampton has been in with Her Majesty,' Cecil told Will then. 'I allowed her to plead clemency for your patron.'

'Which you will ask the queen to deny him?' Will naturally assumed.

'Why ever would I do that?'

'Because he is your enemy?' he asked uncertainly.

'He *was* my enemy and now he is brought very low. I am not a monster.' Then he added, 'Dead, he is of no use to me. Alive, he will know who keeps him in that state and may show his gratitude. Do you think I would allow a private quarrel to cloud my judgement on what is best for the realm?'

What is best for Robert Cecil, you mean, thought Will.

'I have urged the queen to be merciful and commute the death sentence to one of life imprisonment.'

A long and slow death for young Henry Wriothesley then, and he wondered if Cecil might not enjoy that rather more, while gaining control of the earl's lands and fortune, via the queen?

'And the others?'

'Danvers, Meyrick, Cuffe and Sir Christopher Blount will hang,' he said resolutely. Presumably because they were of no use to him to be kept alive. Blount was the Earl of Essex's stepfather and no relation to Charles Blount, Baron Mountjoy, who had stayed loyal during the rebellion and was already made commander of the queen's forces in Ireland, now that Essex was gone from there. 'The remainder will be fined or imprisoned.'

Will recalled Gelly Meyrick now. The arrogant steward had once bumped into him in a corridor and threatened Will with the words: 'Men will hang.' Now it seemed he would be one of them. Then there was Sir Henry Cuffe, who had doubted Will to be the author of his plays, and had apparently been responsible for some of the worst advice the Earl of Essex ever heeded, which contributed to both their downfalls.

'What of the earl?' asked Will.

'The queen has already told the French ambassador that she would willingly pardon Essex, but knows she cannot. She blames herself for his behaviour for indulging him so long. There is truth in that, of course, but you cannot spare the dog you feed when it keeps on biting you. We questioned his closest men, of course.' By questioned, he meant tortured. 'And they confirmed what I had already suspected. While Essex was locked up in his home, he burned letters from King James. Doubtless the Scottish king welcomed his overtures to come and take the English throne, perhaps even before Her Majesty's rule was ended.'

'Treason then?' offered Will.

'Treason.' Cecil seemed satisfied by that. Then he told Will, 'I want you to see something.' And he gestured for Will to follow him.

They walked for some time until they reached a much bleaker and colder part of the tower, where prisoners were housed. Cecil escorted Will along several dark corridors to a cell at the end of one that was guarded by an armed man.

Cecil motioned for Will to look through the barred window and there he saw a broken man. The Earl of Essex was sitting on a bare wooden stool with none of his usual luxuries or refinements around him. Not even a desk or books had he been allowed. Presumably this was to prevent him from writing to the queen to ask for clemency. Essex did not look up, so Will assumed they could see him from their vantage point, but he was unaware of their presence.

'Not such a great man now, is he?' whispered Cecil. 'Wait here while I speak with him.'

Cecil indicated the guard should open the cell door and he went inside. The door was pulled closed and Will, while still hidden from Essex's view, remained close enough to hear what was said between them. By standing back slightly from the door, he could still see Essex without being seen himself in the gloom. The earl looked up at Cecil then and Will could see that his face was dirty and his eyes red, perhaps from weeping.

'Have you come to gloat?' the earl asked.

'Would you be surprised to hear that I have not?'

'I most certainly would, Sir Robert.'

'I find that the defeat of an enemy and the bringing of him so low, no matter how dangerous or illustrious he once was, is never as satisfactory as one imagines,' Cecil observed.

Essex seemed surprised, but then he thought on this and appeared to concede the point. 'You are quite right, of course. Winning is never as joyous as the all-consuming fear of the prospect of losing, but then there was very little in this life that proved as satisfactory to me as I imagined it would beforehand.'

'And yet you had so much. Land, money, the queen's favour.'

'Yet still…' Essex waved a hand as if that were little.

'You wanted more?' asked Cecil.

'Is ambition a crime?'

'No,' Cecil conceded, 'but treason is.'

'Treason? An interesting word. I thought you a traitor who used his position to ill advise Her Majesty. I still do. Had my rebellion been successful, you would have been the one accused of treachery and would be sitting here now, awaiting your own execution.'

'I did know of your intentions, Devereux. I have always known of them. Which is why I ensured you went to Ireland. I knew that would be your undoing.'

Essex scoffed at this notion. 'No one fought harder to keep me out of Ireland than you did, Cecil.'

'Publicly, I backed you to be Lord Lieutenant there, repeatedly.'

'And yet privately, behind my back, you told the queen I was not up to the command and she must on no account choose me or there would be disastrous consequences for the realm.'

Cecil smiled at him then. 'Not so.'

'Did you think I would not hear of it? My spies informed me it was true.'

'And they were misled,' Cecil assured him, 'by my spies. It was a trap I set for you, Robert, and I knew you would fall into it. Your vanity ensured you would fight even harder for the chance to go to Ireland, if you believed I was opposed to the idea. You didn't even want it, man. Deep down, you knew you would fail, but you cast your sensible doubts to one side and begged Her Majesty to send you there at the head of her army, just so you could say you bested me.'

The earl opened his mouth as if to protest but closed it again without a word. Perhaps it was the assured look on Cecil's face that prevented him from arguing the point further, because he seemed to suddenly realise that he had been thoroughly outmanoeuvred by the queen's 'pygmy', and it was indeed his own vanity that had brought the Earl of Essex to ruin.

'So, a war has cost me my life, but I regret nothing. Better to live as a lion than a cowed dog. I have many times said peace to be dishonourable.'

'Do you remember what my father told you in the council chamber when you said it there?' Cecil asked.

'That I breathed forth nothing but war, slaughter and blood.' Essex snorted as if he was quite proud of that description.

'He did say that,' Cecil nodded, 'but he also said, "Bloodthirsty and deceitful men shall not live out half their days", and he was right about that, wasn't he?'

'Then he could have been talking about either of us. Do you really think you will live to see old age, Sir Robert? I very much doubt that.'

'But you will never know.'

As if to banish that grim thought, he snapped, 'Ireland is an impossible place. No one can tame it.'

'Yet they say Mountjoy does sterling work there already and he has the rebel O'Neill on the run.'

'Mountjoy? How?' he asked in disbelief.

'By building forts and establishing garrisons, then burning the rebels' corn to cause them famine. Once they are weakened and desperate, he aims to drive them out into the open and defeat them in battle.'

'Not possible.'

'For you it was not. Apparently, for Mountjoy, it is.'

'It is of no matter to me. Nothing is any more, except the queen's love, which I aim to reclaim, no matter what. What are you even doing here, Cecil? If you have come to torment me, go ahead.'

'I bring you good news, Devereux. The queen is happy to show mercy to you, and will commute your sentence.'

'Praise be to God.' Essex almost collapsed in relief. 'Has she forgiven me? Am I to be released?'

'You misunderstand me, sir. You were sentenced to be hanged, drawn and quartered, a traitor's death, but the queen in her infinite mercy has commuted that sentence to one of death by beheading, to spare you the greater part of your suffering.'

Essex realised that he had once again been confounded by Cecil, who had given him false hopes of a reprieve only to dash it. It was generally accepted that hanging, drawing and quartering was only reserved for the very worst kinds of traitors and would not be a punishment suitable for a high-born man, when the axe was surely enough. 'I never did believe my beloved queen would see me murdered in such a barbaric manner, though I know you wished it so.'

'I never did.'

'But you did wish me dead. Don't deny it.'

'I did and I do,' Cecil admitted. 'I won't deny that. You are too dangerous to live more, Devereux, or ever be trusted again. As for blaming me, you must surely see that you brought this all upon yourself. No one else did this to you, only your pride.' He waited for a response then and when he received none, he told Essex, 'The Earl of Southampton has also had his sentence reduced.' Essex must have assumed he meant Southampton had received the same level of mercy from the queen. 'He will be spared death and instead shall be imprisoned for life.'

Essex snorted his derision at this. 'Because he is a lesser criminal or a lesser man? Did she think him incapable of treason, being such a fop? I tell you that he marched in my footsteps as if he was wearing my borrowed boots.'

He meant that Southampton was as guilty as he was, but Cecil explained, 'The queen believes that in following you he caused his own doom because you misled him as to the justness of your cause.'

'That must have ruined your plans to kill us both.'

'On the contrary, I argued for Southampton so his life could be spared.'

'But not for me.' His resentment was obvious.

'No, not for you.'

'My son lives on, Cecil,' he said, as if all was not yet lost. 'And will inherit my title. He knows all about you and will avenge me one day. He achieves his majority in eight years and will come for you, with, I trust, greater success than I ever achieved. I might not have brought you down, but he shall. This I swear.'

'Didn't you know?' Cecil was a study of calm. 'Your son is disinherited. Because of your rebellion, he is to be punished too, in case the apple proves as rotten as the tree. The title is lost to your family and shall not pass to him.'

'Damn you, Cecil! This is your work!' Then his fury was replaced by grief at this loss. 'Not my son.'

'Why not, when by your own admission he is already sworn to destroy me? You would see him grow to make the same mistakes as his father, which shows you have learned nothing and will go to your death no wiser for it.'

Essex tried to rally then. 'You think to have me executed, but I doubt that. I was once the queen's favourite, and she did love me well. Even now, I know she will blanch at the thought of placing my head upon a spike,' he assured Cecil. 'Not mine. Anyone's but mine.'

'You are right,' Cecil told him. 'You were once the queen's favourite, and there was a time when I did envy you that position. Now I would not be you for all the tobacco in the Americas. Her love for you has led Her Majesty to consider you worse than a traitor, precisely because of your abuse of it. She did hold you so dear in her heart and now, being scorned by you, she tells the court how deceived she once was to see any good in you at all. She *will* pass your sentence.'

'It took her three months to sign the warrant against the Duke of Norfolk and he was only her cousin. The Queen of Scots was in her custody for twenty-one years and plotting all that time before Elizabeth agreed to be rid of her. Even after she signed the death warrant, she tried to avoid the sentence being carried out. Your father had to do it behind her back and was almost brought down for it,' he reminded Cecil defiantly.

'My father knew his duty and so do I.'

'Even so, I am no Scottish queen or errant cousin. I am the love of Her Majesty's life. Do you honestly believe she could ever kill me?'

'I do,' Cecil replied, but Will could hear the hesitation in his voice and knew that he too was beginning to doubt this, just as Will was.

There was a moment of silence between them then, until the earl felt compelled to fill it with more bravado. 'Urge her to sign my death warrant then and be done with it,' he told Cecil, 'then lead me to the block and see what happens.'

'You shall lose your head. That is what shall happen. What else is there?'

'Rebellion,' promised the earl. 'Thousands of my followers shall flock to hear me speak and it is my right to be heard. When they listen to my words of defiance, they shall rouse themselves and their neighbours. If they see me die that day, they will seek vengeance, for I shall be sure to say that it is Cecil who has urged the queen to kill me. Do it then and say a prayer, for you shall be next.'

'It is done already,' he said simply and Cecil produced the document he had held upon his person all along. The earl stared at the death warrant and in particular the writing at the foot of it, which was in the hand of the queen. 'She has already signed it.'

His voice wavered then when he said, 'Damn you to hell then, Cecil, and remember I did warn thee. I'll bring down such wrath upon thy head from a great multitude after I speak to them.'

'I doubt that men in London will flock to avenge you in death, Robert, when they failed to join your rebellion while you lived. But perhaps you are right. I did warn the queen it might be possible, and she agreed with me that there should be no multitude allowed to hear your final words, bar her most loyal followers from court, all of whom will be there to see you die and ensure the realm is rid of you for good. You will be executed on Tower Green, within the walls of the Tower, and no man who is not entirely true to Her Majesty shall be admitted. You can make your grand speech, Robert, but your words will be wasted there and soon forgot.'

Chapter Forty-Eight

'I wasted time and now doth time waste me.'

—*Richard II*

It was a complete victory for Sir Robert. Will could see that and so too could the former Earl of Essex. There was no formal farewell between the two men. Cecil merely left Robert Devereux to think on all that he had said and feel the full magnitude of his downfall.

Once he had quit the cell, Cecil took Will to one side and told him, 'Stay here for half an hour, then speak to him.'

'What about?'

'What this has always been about, since I enlisted you, the death of Lady Anne.'

'You still think she may have died by his hand?'

'I have always thought it likely, or that another controlled by him may have done it. That is usually how it proceeds in these situations.' And Cecil ought to know about that, thought Will, for he himself was a master of *these situations*. 'Go to him on a pretext and extract the truth from the man. You remembered to bring the handkerchief?'

'I did.' Will had of course remembered, since Cecil's message had expressly asked him to.

'Then show it to Devereux and get him to confess.'

Will could think of no suitable pretext to gain access to the earl, nor, once inside his cell, of how to compel him to confess to either the murder of Lady Anne, or the ordering of it. 'Have you ever spoken to him on the matter?' he asked Cecil.

'I have not. I do not wish Robert Devereux to know of my interest in it, even now.' He looked awkward then, almost embarrassed in fact. There was something about the gentle Lady Anne that had brought on uncharacteristic feelings of, if not love, then deep and abiding affection in the usually iron-hearted Sir Robert. It had undone him, and he knew it. He did not want his enemy to realise it too, even one that was about to go to the block. 'But we learned he was in communication with the Scottish king. If the Lady Anne had proof of this, then he would have silenced her. I am sure of it.'

'I am not sure how I can expect to be granted an audience?' Will protested.

'Appeal to his vanity. That always works with him.' And when Will was no further enlightened by this, Cecil sighed. 'I would have thought it was obvious, Shakespeare. Tell him you want to write a play about him. Give Essex the chance to explain his version of his life to you and tell him he will be immortalised. Tantalise the prospect of Richard Burbage playing him on the stage. He won't be able to resist that.'

—

Cecil was right, as he usually was about these things. He could always read a man and he'd had plenty of opportunity to observe Essex over the years. The former earl was instantly taken by the idea of a play about him, even though he would not live to see it. He even went so far as to state that it would likely rehabilitate his reputation, with not just the queen but the whole of London. Will was forced to play along with this charade by enthusiastically agreeing with him.

'I always liked you, Shakespeare,' Essex said. 'I know you likely didn't believe that, but I admired your command of words. Your fellow players too, particularly Burbage. Is he not the finest actor of his age?'

'I believe he is.' It was good to be able to say at least one thing to the condemned man that wasn't a lie.

Will had to sit through more than an hour of Robert Devereux recounting the main events of his life, while he dutifully listened. At one point, the man stopped speaking, looked closely at Will and asked, 'Will you not write any of this down?'

'No need,' Will told him firmly. 'It is all up here.' And he tapped the side of his own head to show he was committing every word to his prodigious memory. He *would* remember almost all of it, he was sure about that, but had no need to. No one would ever want him to write a play depicting the relatively short, disgraceful life of the queen's former favourite and, even if they did, she would never allow it to be performed. He was surprised Essex did not realise this for himself, but perhaps Cecil was right. The man's vanity would always overpower good sense.

Will passed another half-hour asking him questions that gently and inextricably led him back to the events at court before his departure for Ireland, which happened to loosely coincide with the shock at court following the death of Lady Anne.

'Oh Anne,' he recalled, as if her memory was something of a distant one, or perhaps it was because he had not given her another thought since her death. 'That was a most unfortunate event.'

Will noticed how he called it an unfortunate event and not an accident and wondered if this was a partial admission of guilt.

'There are some at court who say she died for a reason,' Will said, but he got no reaction from Essex. 'Because she was caught up in an intrigue to perhaps set the Scottish King James up as the heir to Her Majesty.'

'Really?' He sounded surprised to learn of this, but was it genuine?

'I heard he sent a man to our court to convey messages to his daughter, who was in daily close contact with our queen.'

'She was.' But this was the only part of Will's account that he confirmed. Essex seemed quite unperturbed by it.

'It is thought that her father managed to come by some secret correspondence, perhaps written in code, between a great man close to Her Majesty and the Scottish king. A letter was then brought down to London by this trusted courier and given to the Lady Anne.'

'With what intent?' he asked.

'In the right hands, it could have brought a great man down.'

'You think that is why she died perhaps? To prevent this?' Devereux asked. If he did know something, he was hiding it well.

'I do.'

'And you have spoken to this courier?'

'I have.'

'Will he testify on this matter if summoned to the council?'

'He would have, most likely, if he had not been stabbed to death in Clink prison.'

'I see.' Was that interest or relief in his eyes, Will wondered as he watched the former earl, who appeared to be thinking this through.

Will waited patiently for Robert Devereux to speak again because it looked as if he might be about to say something of significance about the Lady Anne.

'I could have had her,' Essex told Will then. Christ, was that all he had to say about the matter of her death? That he could have tupped her if he had wanted to? 'I could have had them all.'

'Would not Her Majesty have forbidden it?' asked Will. 'Of you?' Then he added, 'And of them?'

'She did,' he confirmed, 'and there's nothing sweeter or riper than forbidden fruit. I thought a playmaker would understand that. Those ladies are under her command from the moment they rise in the morning until they retire at night. How tempting it is for them to break free of the Virgin Queen's control and find love in her favourite's arms? To enjoy what even Her Majesty never can. Had I not been so fair, they would have still wanted me.'

'So, you admit it then?'

'I admit some but not all. Not every woman there appealed to me, and I tell you now, though I have confessed to everything else, that I did not take the Lady Anne, though I may have got around to it eventually.'

'You gave her a favour,' Will reminded him.

'Did I?'

'You gave her this.' Will produced the fine silk handkerchief then and handed it to the earl, who did not deny it. 'Would you have given something so fine to a lady you were not planning to have, and have soon?'

'You think it very fine?' asked the earl. 'But I confess I must have given one of these to half the ladies at court. Some I have had and some I did not. Anne was a little young and not yet ripe for the plucking, but I enjoyed the sport with her.'

'You thought it a game?'

'Courtly love *is* a game, and I flatter myself that I play it well.'

'But you did kill her?' asked Will. 'Or had her killed?'

He frowned at Will, then shook his head. 'Why would I?'

'Because she was dangerous. She knew.'

'Knew what?'

'About your letters to the Scottish king, inviting him to take the throne of England.'

'How could she?' He seemed genuinely confused.

'She had a family link to the Scottish court, through marriage.'

'That's impossible.'

'Because you thought yourself too clever? Too discreet? Anyone from King James' court could have betrayed you at any time. As it turned out, it was the father of a young girl at court who discovered your treason, and he would have used her to expose it.'

'I tell you this, Shakespeare, since it will make no difference to my fate at all, and to prevent you from slandering my name further with a crime I did not commit. I did not kill that young maid, nor order her death and had no reason to. I swear that on my son's soul. I did write to King James. I admit that. It was a kind of treason, because we all know the queen will not hear any talk of an heir, much less name one, which places her entire realm in peril by her neglect of duty. King James did honour me with his replies, and I made sure to burn his letters on the night they came to arrest me, before I surrendered myself to the queen's mercy, all of them.'

'Well then.'

'But I did not write to King James until I could see no other course set fair before me, and that was not until I was in Ireland.' Essex gave Will a meaningful look. 'The Lady Anne was already dead by then and long before I sent a letter to King James.'

'Is this true?'

Essex looked exasperated then. 'Why would I lie about this when I have admitted all else and will soon be killed for my supposed sins?'

Will could think of no good reason. 'But if they were not your letters, then whose?'

'Whose indeed?' But it seemed the earl was no better informed about this subject than Will.

—

When they were done, Will summoned the gaoler and he opened the prison door, while never taking his eyes from Essex, who sat placidly by the window, making no move to rush him or try to escape. Just as Will was about to leave, the former earl spoke.

'Will?'

He was surprised to be addressed by his first name as if they were almost equals, but then the former earl was only Robert Devereux now.

Will turned back to the condemned man, who said, 'There won't be a play, will there?' And there was a look of such sad resignation in his eyes, as if he had only belatedly realised that Will had tricked him.

It would have been far easier to lie then, but for some reason Will couldn't bring himself to do that. Perhaps because the former earl only had a short time left to live.

'No.'

Robert Devereux nodded slowly as if he understood the situation completely. The look on his face told Will he realised he had been fooled again, most likely by Cecil, and had come to terms with this, along with everything else.

'The man who makes you do his bidding is the devil,' he told Will quietly. 'All shall fall because of him. I am just the first.' *Not the first*, thought Will, but then Essex had barely noticed when other men fell because of Cecil. 'May God go with you, Master Shakespeare. For you will need him.'

—

It was the threat of a final reckoning with that same God and the promise of eternal damnation that finally did for Robert Devereux and his pride. Though he would still not beg for mercy from the queen, nor acknowledge any guilt for his actions up till now, it took a lowly chaplain to remind him of what he faced, following his appointment with the executioner. This, along with the realisation that he might not actually receive his expected stay of execution from the queen, was what finally broke him, and he agreed to confess all.

The council members were summoned to witness Essex admit that 'I am the greatest, the most vilest and most unthankful traitor that has ever been in the land.' He then went on, at some length, to admit virtually every crime he had been accused of and had previously denied, betraying almost all of his followers in the process and calmy condemning them too. Shockingly, he even denounced his own sister, Lady Rich, mistress of his close friend Mountjoy, the new commander of Her Majesty's forces in Ireland, accusing her of being a traitor as well. The queen deliberately and tactfully turned a blind eye to this. Perhaps denouncing all those close to him was part of the bargain he hoped to make to save his immortal soul from damnation, but it was just one more in a series of his betrayals.

The only crime Essex would not admit to at the end was the murder of Lady Anne. He never mentioned it in fact, so perhaps he was telling Will the truth after all. But if Essex did not kill the girl, then who did?

Chapter Forty-Nine

'He that dies pays all debts.'

—*The Tempest*

On the morning scheduled to be his last, Essex took a moment to apologise to his guards at the Tower for no longer having any means to reward them for their service. He had nothing now, except perhaps his dignity, which he still clung to, along with the diminishing hope that the queen might grant him mercy by sparing his life at the last, though her advisors had all told her he was far too dangerous to live beyond this day, in case he attempted another rebellion.

Will was surprised, and not exactly delighted, to be invited to witness the execution by the Secretary of State. Cecil commanded it, in fact, so what choice did Will have? The queen's spymaster still assumed Devereux was guilty of both treason and the murder of Lady Anne, so perhaps he thought Will might enjoy seeing him publicly put to death at the end of what had been a difficult investigation for Will. He could only hope that Cecil would be content to see his nemesis die and not interrogate Will further about the crime. Should he pretend that Devereux had confessed to it privately, or that he had at least not denied it, so Will could finally put an end to this investigation and escape from Cecil, at least for the time being? Not when the man had felt strongly enough to swear his innocence on the soul of his son.

Walter Raleigh had no choice but to attend the execution; in his capacity as Captain of the Gentlemen Pensioners it was expected of him, but the crowd thought otherwise. They assumed he was there to gloat over the death of his great rival, and there was much muttering when he appeared, seemingly without a care, to witness a man's head cut from his shoulders. The first loud boo caught him quite unawares and the second gave him pause. He looked about him and realised that somehow the doomed man, who had plotted rebellion against the queen, was still more popular at court than he was. Will could see in his face that this, and the misguided notion that he was here to glory in the execution of a defeated rival, hurt him deeply. He quietly walked away from the throng and went inside the White Tower but soon took up another less noticeable vantage point by a window, where he could see all that followed. Perhaps he would never believe Essex was truly dead unless he witnessed it for himself.

Cecil had already decided not to show his face. Unlike Raleigh, he had read the mood of the crowd, and he also watched proceedings unseen from a window with Will, so he could witness what he had orchestrated, with no one even knowing he was there. It was the perfect illustration of the man's power. Cecil had watched Raleigh's retreat ruefully, then sneered at the crowd, which was supposed to be filled with nobles and loyal courtiers but was already sowing the seeds of dissent, thanks to Raleigh's ill-advised public appearance, as if that was somehow in bad taste.

By a strange twist of fate worthy of one of Will's plays, Robert Devereux already knew his executioner. The former earl had once spared his life in fact, which now meant the man was able to take his. Thomas Derrick had been brought before him years earlier, having been found guilty of rape, and should have been hanged, but Essex struck a deal with him instead. He was offered the choice of death or a pardon, on the condition he accepted the position of executioner. This he duly did. Neither man could have suspected then that they would eventually meet again at the block, with their roles reversed. Essex no longer had the power of life or death over Derrick. Now it was the other way around.

Devereux was attended by three priests, sixteen guards and the lieutenant of the Tower. The walk to the scaffold was a short one and he took each step as slowly as he could without being pushed forwards by his guards, who treated him lightly. As he walked, he looked around him, presumably to see if the queen was there to witness his final downfall. Even now, he must have still clung onto the tiniest possibility that she did not have it in her heart to see him killed. Would she appear at the very last moment, just before the executioner's axe fell, to grant him clemency and spare his life? With each step closer to the block, that hope receded.

The silent crowd regarded him respectfully as he reached the scaffold. He had ceased his watchfulness for the queen by now and instead gazed at the block, perhaps in disbelief that his life had finally come to this end. In the entire history of England, had a man ever risen so high, yet fallen so low? He seemingly had everything, then lost it all. Even he might concede by now that he had nobody else to blame for that but himself.

He turned to face the crowd, straightened and began to address them. Will noticed new resolve in him then. Perhaps he was encouraged by the good number that had turned out to hear his last words. *He looks like a player on the stage*, thought Will. He wondered if Devereux would talk of rebellion, claim he had acted to save the queen and possibly even urge retribution on Cecil, as he had promised to. Instead, the scaffold became his confessional, as Essex spoke in a loud, clear voice that did not falter.

'My sins are more in number than the hairs on my head. I have bestowed my youth in wantonness, lust and uncleanness; I have been puffed up with pride, vanity and love of this wicked world's pleasures. For all which I humbly beseech my Saviour Christ to be a mediator to the eternal Majesty for my pardon, especially for this my last sin, this great, this bloody, this crying, this infectious sin, whereby so many for love of me have been drawn to offend God, to offend their sovereign, to offend the world. I beseech God to forgive it me, most wretched of all.'

He was determined to take all the blame now and leave this world a penitent man before God and a crowd of witnesses. At least he had finally found his humility and would die with dignity.

When he was done, Essex knelt before the block and the chaplain encouraged him to say a prayer. 'Lord be merciful to Thy prostrate servant,' he called. 'Lord, into Thy hands I commend my spirit.' Then he bent lower and placed his neck upon the wooden block, while the chaplain helped him recite psalm 51.

'Have mercy upon me, O God, according to Thy loving kindness: according unto the multitude of Thy tender mercies blot out my transgressions.' It was easier to hear the chaplain's voice from this distance, but the condemned man's was clearly wavering now that his head was actually on the block. 'Wash me thoroughly from mine iniquity, and cleanse me from my sin.'

There was a terrible restlessness in the crowd now because no one knew how much more of this there would be, least of all the executioner, who stood nervously to one side, waiting for permission to kill the great man before him but not daring to intervene. This was Devereux's final scene, and he would be the one to say when it was over, but would they go through every verse of the psalm?

Just when Will was beginning to think they might, the condemned man's voice trembled as he recited, 'For I acknowledge my transgressions: and my sin is ever before me.' Fear must have taken hold of him then and he abruptly ceased his prayer, held out his arms and shouted, 'Executioner, strike home!'

Derrick must have expected it would take longer for the psalm to be completed, for the command seemed to take him by surprise. The executioner quickly lifted his axe, took two steps closer to the block and brought it crashing down on Devereux, but he had been too hasty with his aim. Panicked by the order from the great man who had once spared his life, his first blow failed to find its right mark. The axe came down hard upon his victim, but the head stayed firmly in place afterwards, causing great gasps and terrible groans from the onlookers. No one could tell if the blow had been fatal or not, but Derrick soon saw that he had not completed the job and the din from the crowd seemed to panic him further. He staggered back, surveyed the incomplete damage he had wrought, then hastily lifted his axe once more. He stepped forwards again and brought it down hard on the prostrate figure before him. Again, it was a mighty blow but not a true one. The head stayed firmly on its shoulders and the crowd was in uproar now. Whatever anyone might have thought of Devereux before, surely all were united in hoping the first strike had been the death blow and he was not condemned to further suffering.

Even from a distance, Will could see the look of disbelief on Derrick's face. He was used to hanging men, but an executioner did not get much practice in the art of decapitating nobles with an axe, and this was going very badly.

For the third strike, Derrick took more time. He stepped closer to his victim, steadied himself, took a moment to raise the axe and paused while aiming at his mark, then with a great cry of frustration and determination, he brought it crashing down upon what was left of the neck. Finally, on the third blow, the head came off, causing more groans and mingled cries of both relief and disgust from the onlookers.

Derrick picked up the head by its hair and held it aloft for all to see, while shouting, 'God save the queen!'

Some of the shocked onlookers did manage to say this back to him in response, but many simply stared at the macabre sight of Robert Devereux's head being held aloft dripping with blood.

'What a wretched way to die,' said Cecil and when Will turned towards him, he could see that the look of shock on Cecil's face was genuine. The man was not gloating. His moment of triumph had been diminished by the gory and ungraceful way in which his old enemy had been hacked to death. 'Like watching a butcher.'

Chapter Fifty

'My dull brain was wrought with things forgotten.'

—*Macbeth*

Once the execution was over, they went back to Cecil's rooms. They had not yet discussed Will's interrogation of Essex, and he assumed that would be the first thing on Cecil's mind, but it appeared his concern for the queen was uppermost.

'The effect of this affair on Her Majesty has been devastating. Being forced to kill her favourite, though it was a necessary act, has not gone well with her,' Cecil explained, as if he himself had not been one of those urging that killing upon her. 'She stays in her rooms, her ladies tell me she has no appetite for food, nor does she wish them to wig or dress her in the usual finery.' Then he said something truly shocking. 'I fear she may not be long for this world.'

Had the execution she had ordered, of the man she had loved more than any other, finally done what all the Catholic plots against the queen's life had failed to do? Was she now dying of a broken heart? Cecil seemed to think so.

'What of the succession then?' Will asked.

'That is in God's hands,' Cecil told him.

And yours, thought Will, but the Secretary of State moved quickly onto other matters.

'What did Devereux tell you of the Lady Anne before he died?'

Will did not hesitate. 'Essex swears on his son's soul that he had naught to do with her death.'

'And you believe him?' Cecil sounded sceptical.

'I do, my lord. He confessed to worse crimes and knew he would die anyway. All he had left was his disinherited son. To swear on his soul is no small thing.'

Cecil nodded slowly in agreement. Then he suddenly slammed his fist down hard upon his desk, causing Will to flinch. 'Damn it all! I thought we were close to the truth, but you are no nearer now to solving this than on the day I first summoned you to me.' Though this seemed harsh, Will knew better than to argue the point with an enraged Cecil. 'Get out! Go back into the court and find the man who did this. Do not rest until you have succeeded. Bring me the name of the killer or never prosper through me again!'

Will bowed quickly and quit the room. As he walked briskly away, it struck him that he'd had barely any respite since his enlistment by Cecil to look into the death of Lady Anne. There was the gargantuan effort of tearing down and rebuilding their theatre, his writing and staging of *Henry V* at court, then being dragged, albeit unwittingly, into the Essex rebellion. Now he was being plunged back into a world in which his fate still rested in the hands of those greater than himself, and it seemed as if it always would. Once more, he was at their mercy, but this time he would have to earn Cecil's pardon by delivering something that was currently not within his power: the name of Lady Anne's killer.

What had he just said about never prospering from him again? When had Will ever prospered at the hands of Robert Cecil? The man took but never gave, threatened much but promised little in return. No wonder so many people wanted Cecil dead when this was the reward he gave for service.

–

Will did not immediately quit the place, knowing that leaving it wouldn't help him to solve the crime at the heart of Lady Anne's death. Instead, he walked the corridors of Whitehall and thought the whole thing through again, while trying not to agree with Cecil's accusation that he was no closer to identifying her killer now than he had been on the day Cecil first enlisted his services. He was as certain as he could be that an otherwise entirely repentant Essex was innocent of the crime, so who was the real guilty party and how could he prove it? Maddeningly, he seemed incapable of using that supposedly sharp mind of his to solve this mystery. The man who understands everything? Pah! If recent events had proven anything, it was that Will understood little.

As he walked, he asked himself what he really knew about the Lady Anne, her life and death, and was any of it in any way more significant than he had at first realised? Surely there was something here that he had overlooked.

Anne was of noble birth but the daughter of a minor northern lord. She had been such a gracious beauty that even Sir Robert Cecil, a man not known for romantic attachments, had been a little in love with her, albeit from afar. Others wanted her too, including the usual rakes: Essex, Southampton, Mountjoy and Raleigh, but her dearest friend had said how virtuous Anne had been. There was no hint of a scandal involving her or any of the men at court, save for the presence of a silk handkerchief in Essex's colours among her possessions, and that had turned out to mean little. Will had wasted precious time pursuing the notion that she had been undone by an affair with one of those powerful men, only to realise it was actually the Lady Imogen who had fallen.

Will walked deeper into the palace and tried not to think more on the drowning of poor Imogen. His thoughts immediately turned to that other unfortunate victim of Will's investigation, the poor wretch Edward Seagrave. Will had visited the family steward in the Clink and he had admitted delivering letters to Anne and her brother, from their father, implicating her in intrigue. Seagrave was likely imprisoned to prevent anyone looking into the death of Lady Anne, but Cecil had found him and sent Will to question the man. Not long after, he was killed in a quarrel with another prisoner, which could have been coincidence, but Will doubted it. More likely that powerful men at court had a hand in this, to silence the man for good.

What else could he be sure about? Will had seen how Anne's prayer book had been altered so it could hide secret letters. According to Seagrave, one of these contained a cypher, but he did not know who had written it. Following that discovery, he had made scant progress. Other than this, what did he really know about Anne's death? But little.

Will stopped suddenly then and realised where he was. It was the presence of that particular tapestry on the wall that gave him pause. Without even consciously realising it, he had walked to the exact staircase that had been the scene of Anne's death. Here were the stone steps that led downwards and curved at the bottom, at the point where Anne was found. Wouldn't an accidental fall from the top have ended with a body striking that barrier, before it rolled round a corner to the floor beneath it?

To Will's right was the balustrade that seemed to him the most likely point at which Anne met her death. Either she fell, threw herself or was thrown from it, onto the ground below. Surely you would not seek to commit self-slaughter in such a manner, and the balustrade was high enough to prevent even the clumsiest of souls from falling over it. She was pushed then, but by whom? No one knew because nobody saw it happen, and that was likely to be the end of the matter.

Will glanced back at the tapestry then and took it in. It was an impressive work, with a hunting scene at its heart, surrounded by allegorical representations of Jesus, the queen, maternal love and evil, depicted by a unicorn, a lion, a pelican and a monstrous devil.

It was the image of the devil that made him think of her then. That serving girl? What was her name, damn it? She had been a witness of sorts, not to the crime but someone fleeing from the scene not long after she had heard Anne's scream. Her account had been dismissed on the seemingly reasonable grounds that she claimed to have seen the devil. Or had she?

Will recalled now that the young girl had been examined by William Wade, a man he instinctively did not trust. Wade's dismissive account of the servant's testimony had convinced Cecil to ignore the girl on the grounds of her youth, sex and low social standing, but what if she was telling the truth? Perhaps she had seen something, and Wade had lied about it being the devil, or she thought she had seen him but was mistaken? Could he possibly get her to describe the scene anew and make some sense of it? Should he even attempt to talk to her of Satanic things, even if that might help him discover the truth? Will felt his situation was desperate and he had no choice. He stared at the tapestry with renewed determination then and told himself he was not afraid to look the devil directly in the eye.

—

Will never did recall her name, but he did remember the man of the watch who had found Lady Anne's body and stolen her prayer book. Vaux looked alarmed to see Will coming towards him, but was quickly assured that all he wanted was information on the one witness who claimed to have seen someone fleeing the scene that night.

'She claimed to see the devil,' scoffed Vaux. 'And I never have seen him this past year, though I be here on watch most nights.' He seemed almost aggrieved to have missed the opportunity to witness Beelzebub in all his might – a prospect which would not have appealed to Will.

'What was her name? This servant who saw Lucifer?'

'Agnes.' Vaux must have been keen to aid Will, so that his previous sins were more likely to be forgiven, for he offered to take him to her then.

—

Will had timed his visit well. He knew she would not be far from here, if her quarters were on the same corridor. They found the girl at the end of her working day, as he had hoped, and Will was allowed to take her with him, since it involved business for Robert Cecil's office. He was past caring about discretion now.

Agnes was a small, meek girl with a pale face, and he guessed she was not long past fourteen. He dismissed Vaux and went back with her to the tiny, windowless room in which she slept. It was little more than a closet and he would have been frightened by the prospect of being closed up in it at night. Perhaps she was too, if she had been able to see the corridor from her bed.

'You were asleep on a cot that overlooked the corridor?'

'No, sir,' said Agnes.

'You were not?'

'I was not asleep, sir.'

'You were *awake* then, on a cot that overlooked the corridor?'

'Yes, sir.'

'And why was your door not closed?'

'The daylight, sir. I needs it to wake me up in the morning and there is no window in my room, so I must keep the door half open all through the night.'

'And why were you not sleeping, after a long day tending to the needs of your masters?'

'I was afeared, sir.'

'What about?'

'Not waking in time to start my duties. I worried I might sleep too late and be punished or put out of the palace, then I would have nothing and nowhere to go.'

'Had this happened before – sleeping late, I mean?'

'No, sir.'

'And yet, you still worried?'

'I did, sir.'

He realised Agnes was a timid creature, worrying about things that had never come to pass, and would likely not happen in future. She might also have been frightened of him, or all manner of men who were higher in status than she was, because she hardly offered more than a *yes sir* or *no sir* in answer to his questions.

'So, you were already awake when you heard a scream?'

'I was.'

'And from which direction did it come?'

She pointed. 'From the end of the corridor. I reckoned from where they found that poor young girl, God rest her soul.'

'You are sure it was a scream, and it definitely came from that direction?'

'It sounded like a woman's scream and my ears told me that was where it come from.'

'Did it make you sit up in alarm, leave your bed, call for the watch?'

She shook her head.

'Why not?'

'I don't know, I...' She hesitated, as if she didn't understand the reason for this herself or had never given it much thought. 'I s'pose I questioned whether it really was a scream or, if it was, maybe it was just someone crying out in their sleep?'

'But it wasn't only the scream that alarmed you, Agnes?' When she failed to answer but looked down instead, he added, 'You saw something that night too, did you not?'

'Devil,' she answered and it was almost a whisper.

'You saw *a* devil or *the* devil?'

She looked up then and stared straight back at him. '*The* devil,' Agnes assured him.

'And what did the devil look like?'

'He was big.'

'How big? The size of a man? Smaller? Larger, perhaps?'

'Like a man, a tall man.' She recalled nervously.

'So, big, but not so very big? What form did he take? Did this also resemble a man?'

'He took the shape of a man but was different from a man.'

'In what way?'

'He had wings?'

'Wings?'

'They flapped behind him as he went.'

Will remained sceptical, though he did not seriously doubt that the devil existed. He believed in God after all, and the role of the devil in God's story was well established in scripture. But, as for whether the devil would interrupt his work, to attend the scene of a young girl's fall from a balustrade, or even to push her over it, as this girl seemed to believe? Well, he did doubt that. Surely the devil was too busy with higher things than to throw a girl to her death.

'What did they look like? These wings?'

'Black and long and they billowed.'

'It would have been quite black in the corridor,' he reminded her. 'Not much light will have reached him as he marched along it.'

'There was some candlelight,' she insisted. 'I saw his face.'

'You did. What did he look like?'

'Hard.'

'He had a hard face?'

She nodded. 'Looked like he had killed before.'

'Soldiers can look like that,' he told her. 'Some of them have killed before and often. They can take on a visage that looks like it is forged from rock.'

'But the wings?' she reminded him.

'Yes, the wings.' He had been pondering this. 'If a man kills someone in the night, he would wish to escape afterwards. He would move more swiftly than normal and might even run. I imagine he would favour a disguise, something to mask him from the glance of any guard or observer. A cloak perhaps? A black cloak with a hood would be perfect,' he suggested. 'And if he was pulling it about him as he ran, then might it not billow?'

He watched her face as she thought about this, and he could tell it was giving her pause. Her eyes told him that she realised she might not have actually seen the devil himself after all, but a man in a hurry wearing a cloak, but when she spoke it was only to reaffirm, 'He *was* the devil.'

'But the devil in human form? I think we can agree on that at least, and if he is still here at court, making mischief, tempting sinners from the true path of righteousness, then it might be possible for you to recognise him, if you saw him once more?'

'Oh, I would never forget that face, so hard,' she said.

'As hard as stone?' He was encouraging her to recall it.

'And those eyes,' she remembered.

'What about the eyes?'

'As black as coals they were.'

Chapter Fifty-One

*'The evil that men do lives after them,
the good is oft interred with their bones.'*

—*Julius Caesar*

He would rather not have done so, but Will could think of no better plan than to bring the girl to the attention of Robert Cecil. He would need the Secretary of State's help if they were ever to bring Will's plan to fruition.

Cecil took some persuading, but the presence of the girl in his rooms alongside Will helped to convince Cecil she was in earnest and might be of help. It greatly aided Will when he got the girl to concede, in front of Cecil, that she might have seen a man fleeing the scene and not the devil. Cecil could then see the possibility of her possibly identifying the killer.

'Then we are agreed,' Cecil said, once Will had explained everything in some detail 'We are to set a trap. We put this girl before the court and she waits and watches all who come by, until she is confronted with this devil she saw and can point him out.' When the girl looked very alarmed at this prospect, he spoke directly to her. 'For it is certain he was not the devil in human form but merely a man, who had been doing the devil's work that night. The men of the watch are all accounted for, and were dressed in the queen's livery, so this man, seen coming back from the staircase so soon after Lady Anne screamed and went to her death, must surely be the one who caused it.'

'But, my lord—' Will began.

'But my lord what?' Cecil interrupted. 'You think my plan foolish?' He did not take kindly to that notion. 'You have a better one?'

'No, my lord. It is a fine idea to set her up where she can see all the lords and ladies of the court passing by, but how do we explain this?'

'Explain what?'

'A servant's presence in the same position at court, seemingly idle, for perhaps hours, until all have gone before her, so she can identify one of them as the man who did this foul deed?'

It was clear Cecil had not thought of this, though he seemed reluctant to admit the flaw in his plan. 'I suppose someone might order her to move away and attend to some task or other,' he admitted. 'So, what is the remedy for it?'

Will had not expected to be tasked with filling the hole in Cecil's plan, but an idea struck him then. 'What if we were to dress her in some finery, pass her off as a new lady arrived at court – not an earl's daughter, mark you, but the niece of a newly knighted man, say, or a country squire come to present her at court?'

'Who? Whose daughter could she be?'

'It scarcely matters, my lord. We could even invent the man. People come and go all the time, and one lady from a family of lesser nobility looks very like another.'

'But wouldn't someone recognise her as the servant she is?'

'I doubt anyone at court could tell one servant from another, even without finery. No one looks at them.' Cecil did not argue that point. 'If she is bathed and dressed according to her new station, then all might be well.'

'Until someone speaks to her?' Cecil reminded him.

'New arrivals at court are so common they are barely noticed, much less acknowledged. My noble lord, you are used to an audience with the queen and have perhaps forgot how many men and women vie daily for her attention.'

'My lord and good sir.' The girl's voice was almost a squeak, so nervous was she to speak up at this point, but she was determined to have her say, addressing them both. 'What if a serving girl is discovered wearing clothes above her station? The queen has laws about such things, does she not?'

The girl was right. Under the queen's sumptuary laws, wearing clothes you were not entitled to was a serious offence. The law was brought in to ensure that, at a glance, you could tell a duchess from her housekeeper and never confuse an earl with a squire. Everyone believed that everybody had their rightful place, and if you could not tell who someone was from the fabric used to make the garments they wore, then the hierarchy they lived in was torn down.

'I might be whipped,' the girl concluded anxiously.

Will expected Cecil would have a swift counterargument. Could he grant the girl a special exemption perhaps? But, as usual, he did not wish to be directly associated with one of his own intrigues. To Sir Robert, the ability to deny their existence was everything.

'There are dispensations,' Will told her instead. 'Actors receive them, else they would never be able to play a duke or a king in a play. Perhaps you shall have one too, since we are asking you to perform like an actor in a scene of our own devising.' He did not mention that the actor's dispensation only covered them while they were actually upon the stage. They could be prosecuted if they stayed in costume away from it.

The girl seemed content with that, and they returned to the detail of where best she could be positioned to see all who entered and exited the court, without arousing suspicion.

Poley came into the room then, carrying a small strongbox, which looked like it might have been used to carry jewels or other precious items. 'Letters, my lord,' he told Cecil. 'From our men in the Lowlands.' It seemed this was a regular enough occurrence for the matter to pass between them without any further comment. Will had heard Cecil kept men everywhere, in France, Spain, Germany, the Papal states and, of course, the Lowlands, so often an area of conflict between Catholic and Protestant nations, and a place of exile for those opposed to Queen Elizabeth, where they could plot to overthrow her.

'Set it down over there,' Cecil ordered without taking his eyes from the serving girl. He clearly cared more for the identity of Lady Anne's killer right now than reports on exiled papists from his spies.

Poley did what he was told and the girl's eyes nervously followed him. None of them spoke for a time while Poley moved to the desk, carefully used one hand to move other letters to one side, then set down the small chest with its precious contents. He straightened then and looked directly at Cecil, as if noticing Will and the girl for the first time. Was it his natural curiosity that caused him to outstay his welcome? Always the spy, Poley took his time before edging away from the desk and standing before Cecil.

'Is there anything more I can do to be of service to my lord?' Poley asked him then.

'Not presently.'

But Poley did not move. He merely stood there, as if he expected to be included in Cecil's latest intrigue, until Sir Robert told him, 'Be gone, Poley.'

Poley accepted this but seemed frustrated not to be brought into his master's confidence, particularly when Will so clearly had been. He gave a curt bow and left the room.

Cecil turned back to the girl then. 'You should be situated by the door of the small hall,' Cecil decided. 'The better to see all who enter or leave. Master Shakespeare is to stand with you, off to one side, in case any gentleman or lady should stop to speak with you. He can then invent a reason why you are here and prevent you from giving yourself away with your common manners and rough tongue.'

But the girl wasn't listening and, to Will's surprise, he realised she wasn't even looking at the queen's spymaster, who was likely to react with fury to her careless disregard for his words. Will noticed it before Cecil. The girl appeared confused perhaps, or was it something else? Shock even. No, Will understood it now and he got there ahead of his master. This was fear. She was scared, and not just because she was in the presence of a great man at court. Just then, it hit Will. Suddenly, he understood almost everything.

Cecil noticed her tardiness too then, but he was baffled. 'What say you?' He demanded an explanation from Agnes, but all she could do was open her mouth and let it gape. 'Speak, girl, what is it?'

'It was him.' Will addressed the girl firmly in the hope of coaxing it out of her. 'He was here, just now, the man you saw fleeing from the scene?'

'What?' Cecil turned to ensure that Beelzebub himself had not just appeared in front of the young girl in his own study. Of course, there was no one there and he turned back to the terrified servant.

'Tell my lord the truth,' Will urged her while praying she would find the courage.

'It *was* him,' she said, her voice sounding far away now. 'He was here, before me. The devil who killed Lady Anne. Did you not see him?'

'I saw no one?' protested Cecil.

'It was him!' she insisted and Will realised there would be no need now for the girl to take up her position by the small hall to watch the court.

'It was Poley,' he told Cecil.

'The man carrying your letters,' she said. 'He is the one I saw from my cot. He killed Lady Anne. It was him!'

—

Cecil did not let the young girl leave for some time. He wanted to be sure she was not mistaken, but Will could see that the more he pressed her, the more he became convinced the girl was not lying to him. He threatened her with severe punishment if she was, but this only made her more resolute. She offered to swear on a bible that the man she had just seen – Robert Poley, Cecil's most obedient, long-standing and trusted servant – was also the man who had taken Lady Anne's life that night. Whatever other reason could there have possibly been for him to be prowling the corridors of the palace at that hour? Cecil knew, as much as Will did, that there could be none.

In the end, he did make her swear on a bible, promising the girl her soul would be condemned to eternal damnation if she was lying to him, or even mistaken about who she had seen that night. She might have been young and unworldly, and easily cowed by men like Cecil, but this time she did not flinch. Instead, she offered oaths and prayers and swore that Robert Poley was a servant of the devil himself, for she had seen him march by her just seconds after she had heard the screams of Lady Anne.

Cecil withdrew his threats then. Instead, he made her swear a new oath, that she would reveal this information to no one and would promise not to flee the palace, in case she would be needed by him again. He even gave her coin in reward and made her vow never to reveal it came from him. Satisfied, but still clearly in fear of this great lord, she left them both.

Will watched her go, then he turned back to Cecil to learn what he had to say on the matter and what would happen now. To his surprise, the queen's spymaster, who had been involved in complex plots and cold-hearted intrigues across the realm and beyond it, was sitting bent forwards at his desk and he had his head in his hands. They sat in silence for a considerable time and Will dared not utter a word even to break the tension between them.

Finally, Cecil spoke. 'Leave us, Shakespeare.' And that appeared to be all he was able to say. Cecil had placed his palms against his face and kneaded his closed eyes with the tips of his fingers, as if he was suddenly incredibly weary after the longest of days. Most probably, it was guilt, coming from the knowledge that Lady Anne's death had likely been caused by a man who worked for him. In some twisted manner, Poley might even have committed this terrible act in the name of his lord and master.

Was it the realisation too that this might be enough to bring them all down – Poley, Cecil, even Will – if the queen or Sir Robert's enemies should learn of it? Would Cecil seek to arrest Poley on some invented charge and see him executed, or would he just have him murdered in an alleyway or tavern perhaps, like Kit Marlowe, another dangerous man Cecil had once employed as a spy, until Poley and two others had murdered him? There'd be some irony in that.

But if Poley was obeying orders and would never act without them, what was he doing when he killed the Lady Anne? This was an act that had devastated Cecil, leading him to place Will in his employ to investigate who might be responsible. He would hardly have done that if he had known about it already and, if this latest show of shock, grief and despair was put on, then Cecil could have a future teaching Richard Burbage how to act, so convincing was it to Will's eyes.

Will may have felt some sympathy for Cecil then, but knew he was a ruthless master. If Cecil might be prepared to have Poley killed, which seemed possible, then it was likely he would wish to be rid of anyone who could speak the truth of what had happened on the night Lady Anne was killed. That meant the serving girl was in danger as well, and Will too of course. As he left Robert Cecil's study, Will had to wonder if his life was already forfeit.

Chapter Fifty-Two

'Vengeance is in my heart, death in my hand,
Blood and revenge are hammering in my head.'

—*Titus Andronicus*

It was three days before Will was summoned back before Robert Cecil again. During that time, he had done his best to put his affairs in order. He had taken his firmest friend, Richard Burbage, to one side and, while telling him as little as possible about his current situation, for Richard's own safety, he allowed him to know enough to understand that it was perilous.

In case Will did not return from his next visit to court, Richard was trusted to administer his share of the company and the theatre, for the benefit of Will's wife and daughters. He also gave Richard the manuscript for *The Merry Wives of Windsor* – the new comedy for the queen he had managed to finish somehow, despite his thoughts rarely straying from contemplation of his own fate. Will wrote down all of his wishes and instructions for Richard, then waited for the summons to Cecil's side. When it arrived, he bade his friend farewell and went to meet his destiny, knowing he might never return.

Cecil's room seemed too small for the big men he had assembled there. Four of them stood off to one side with their backs to a wall and each looked capable of easily crushing Will on his own. Cecil sat at his desk and looked up on Will's arrival, only to bid him wait there in silence for a time, while he dealt with his correspondence. Will stood awkwardly next to those rough men, not knowing what he was waiting for and privately praying it was not his doom.

Robert Poley arrived then and, as he entered the room, he seemed as perplexed as Will was by the presence of these others. He may have known some or all of them, but they looked like the kind of men Cecil would have normally employed well beyond the palace's walls and were probably more comfortable working in the shadows.

Sir Robert eyed the man he had used as his creature for ten years or more. As he did this, two of the men moved so that they took up new positions directly behind Poley. They would easily be able to block the door to prevent his exit.

'Poley, you know I tasked Shakespeare here with finding out the reason for the death of Lady Anne?' Cecil began.

'I did, my lord.' It was clear from the look on his face that Poley was trying to understand the reason for this questioning.

'And that I told you he was not to be harmed, nor impeded in any way while he did this?'

'You did.'

'I employed you to watch over him, in fact to make sure of it.' His voice was hard.

Poley nodded his recollection of this.

'Then tell me why you disobeyed me?'

'I never did, my lord.'

'You should take credit for your work. When I sent him to the Clink, he was attacked and slashed with a dagger on leaving the prison. Only William Wade and yourself knew that Seagrave was in that jail. It was Wade that found him there. If *he* had wanted the man dead, he would never have alerted me to his presence. That leaves you as the only one who could possibly have arranged his killing. Seagrave barely lasted a day before he was murdered by another prisoner. That's too big a coincidence.

'Tell me, how did you convince a man to take his life like that? Did you promise him coin and a pardon? He was a fool to trust you then, since he was hanged the next morning. Did you let him swing because he failed to murder Seagrave before Master Shakespeare could question him? That's the trouble with employing villains,' Cecil sneered, 'they seldom do exactly as they are told.'

Poley managed a weak shake of his head in protest at these accusations, but it lacked conviction.

'You even spread gossip at court about Will and Avisa Florio, and that was a mistake, since only you and I knew of their dalliance. I told you it was none of our concern where he was dipping his quill, but you thought to distract him. Come now, was not all of this your work?'

' 'Twas not I.' But he was jittery. 'When have I ever disobeyed an order from my lord?'

'Perhaps when knowing that order could place thine own self in grave peril?'

'How so place me in peril?' He nodded at Will. 'What am I to him or he to me?'

'Why, didn't you know? Master Shakespeare is the harbinger of your doom, Poley.'

Poley opened his mouth to speak but was unable to form the words. He glanced either side of him and saw that Robert Cecil's men were watching him intently, with a steely determination, lest he try to attack his master or flee the room.

'He found the one witness who saw you leave the scene of Lady Anne's murder and encouraged her to discount the idea that she had seen a devil that night, though I am inclined to believe that she did. For who but a devil would murder such an innocent young girl? You didn't recognise her, did you, though she was in this room? One servant in her bed looks very like another when you are rushing past her, or perhaps you didn't see her at all that night – but she saw you and did not forget your face. She saw it just moments after she heard Anne scream.' Then his voice hardened. 'You killed her, Poley. You murdered that sweet maid, Lady Anne, and for what?'

There was a moment when Will could tell Poley was carefully weighing up what he should give by way of an answer. Would he deny everything then and continue to do so, knowing that his master had already made up his mind, and probably had all the proof he needed? Perhaps he would throw himself on his knees and beg for mercy? But that was not Poley's manner. Would he choose defiance instead and admit that he did this terrible crime but say hang the consequences and dare Cecil to punish him?

'To protect you, my lord,' he blurted instead and Will felt a surge of relief that Poley had decided to admit the crime, while citing mitigation. He was playing the loyal servant now, who had acted independently from his master but only out of the finest of motives.

Cecil stared back at him, a pot slowly coming to the boil.

Poley did slump to his knees then, in an act of supplication. 'Grant me mercy, Sir Robert, for I acted only to protect your position.'

Cecil seemed unmoved. 'And your own.'

'I am your most obedient servant,' Poley reminded Cecil, 'and ever shall be.'

'Tell me what led you to commit this foul act then and we shall see if mercy is due, but I warn you, Poley, omit nothing.'

'I had heard the Lady Anne was secretly enamoured of your enemy, Robert Devereux, and likely to do whate'er she could to be noticed by him,' he began. 'The Lady Anne's half-sister, Mary, is wed to a Scottish noble and attends the king's court. Her husband told her of a plan to place his king on the throne of England. He claimed its origin came from letters written by someone close to the queen. Treason, then,' he affirmed. 'Though the letters were in code, King James boasted that a great man wanted him to succeed Her Majesty on the throne. The Lady Anne heard that the name being spoken about so openly was…' He glanced at the men next to him then to see if he was being indiscreet, but Cecil urged him.

'Go on.'

Poley took a breath then and said, 'Sir Robert Cecil.' Even as Poley spoke the words, Will could tell he must have wondered if they would seal his doom.

Cecil smiled. 'And she believed this monstrous notion?'

'She did.'

'And you did too, I suppose?'

Poley looked confused then, presumably because he was evidently privy to the secret that Cecil had actually written to King James to offer him the throne. Perhaps he had even been the one trusted to deliver those very letters.

Will was astonished at the brazen manner of it all. Hadn't Sir Robert told him that writing to another monarch to offer him the throne before the queen's death was a vile treason, punishable by death? Had he really been playing the same game as the others he despised – Essex, Southampton and Mountjoy – all along?

'I did fear for you, my lord, if any of this came out,' Poley went on. 'If the queen heard of it and was convinced it was the truth, then she might not easily believe it to be false.'

'But where was the proof of such a slander?' Either Cecil was calm, despite these damning allegations against him, or he was trying to look as if he was.

'One of the letters found its way back to London,' Poley told him, 'to the Lady Anne.'

'How?' he demanded.

'Baron Percy had managed to come by the letter, procured from her sister's husband.'

'He stole it for his father-in-law,' Cecil observed. 'And Anne's father sent it to her, via his courier Seagrave. For what purpose?'

'He knew there are men here and in Scotland who are prepared to act treacherously. Some in the Scottish court would welcome the queen's spymaster as an ally. Others preferred that puffed-up peacock, Essex, or the sodomite, Southampton. They know them both to be your enemy.'

'Then why not send this supposed letter straight to them, so they could see me condemned for it?'

'Because the queen would likely dismiss the accusation of an enemy and think the letter a forgery, but she listens to her ladies. If one of them, who was known to be an innocent and honest maid, was to bring the letter to her, explaining it came from a sister in Scotland, might Her Majesty not then take the matter more seriously?'

'She might,' agreed Cecil. 'But that young maid hesitated.' He seemed newly proud of her for that.

Poley said nothing, confirming Cecil's theory.

'She held something of import but, being such a young girl, knew not how best to wield such a weapon and dare not take it straight to Her Majesty, even if her father urged her to, in case she caused a tempest that blew away the court and her with it.'

'Very like,' said Poley.

'Instead, she sought someone out who knew of such things?' he suggested. 'Someone who could guide a girl in how best to make the letter public. Should she go direct to the queen or through another powerful man?'

Poley nodded.

'Let's see then. Who would she choose? Not you, Poley. You are too lowly and known to be my man. Who was she enamoured of though? Robert Devereux, but how could the queen's maid approach the Earl of Essex directly without being noticed? She could not and she knew it. They might call her his whore for one thing. No,' he ruminated, 'she would go to someone close to him. His page or steward perhaps?' And when Poley did not contradict him: 'Both men love money and never have enough, so perhaps whoever she selected thought about what he was being offered. Then he chose not to use the letter to destroy the earl's enemy but to prosper from it personally. We have long heard how the Earl of Essex berates the queen because she does not allow him to reward his favourites richly enough to keep them happy. It has been his most common complaint in fact. He knew that loyalty has to be purchased, and one of his followers must have grown tired of waiting for their reward.

'However, that person would not want to risk coming to me directly. Instead, they chose one who is known to be in my service. Who was it that approached you, Poley? Cuffe or Meyrick?'

Poley almost smiled at Cecil's powers of deduction. Will could tell he was impressed. A mind like a trap, they said about Cecil and they were right. 'Meyrick,' he admitted.

'And you did not think to bring this intelligence to me?'

'She still had the letter about her person. I thought to retrieve it first, for you would surely have bid me to do so if I had come to you without it.'

'I *might* have ordered that,' Cecil conceded, 'but I would also have told you not to harm the girl.'

'Oh,' said Poley, 'would you?' He sounded doubtful. 'When the risk of another letter landing in her sweet lap a month later was so high?'

'What did you do?'

'I told Meyrick he would be richly rewarded if he arranged to meet the girl at night to receive the letter from her.'

'And this he did,' suggested Cecil, 'but you took his place. Then you killed her.'

Poley's silence told them the truth of that.

'Did Meyrick know what you were about?'

'He thought I would fright her into giving up the letter and staying silent about it.'

'What happened when he learned the truth?'

'He was much aggrieved.'

'I'll wager he was.'

'But what could he do?' countered Poley. 'Report his own treason? Confess to a role in the girl's murder, admit he betrayed his own master and the queen for money? No. I told him he would fall if he did. Besides, he knows I have proof that he likes boys.'

So, it was a combination of bribery and blackmail that made Meyrick into Poley's creature.

'Did you even pay the man?' asked Cecil.

Poley shrugged at that. Meyrick must have been too terrified to insist on the reward for his treachery. Either that or he was so ashamed of his part in Lady Anne's brutal killing that he did not pursue it.

'And you did all this for me?' Cecil asked with mock esteem. 'Broke a pure, innocent maid's neck?'

'She was no innocent,' Poley retorted and Cecil shot him a look of hatred. 'I was not talking of her maidenhead. She knew what she was about. She set herself up as her father's spy, then became Robert Devereux's agent, as soon as she agreed to bring that letter to Meyrick.'

'You are saying that a young maid would know how her life was in danger, from passing on a letter?'

'I am. It was her choice. She didn't have to spy.'

Poley looked as if he understood that his fate, whatever that may be, was already sealed, that Cecil would have made up his mind before he even sent for the man he had always relied upon to do his worst deeds. He would have to endure the approbation first though.

'I can see the guilt in you but find it hard to believe you could have committed such a heinous act.'

'I have done worse,' Poley said pointedly, as if reminding his master of just who had ordered those more dreadful acts.

'I don't believe it so.' Cecil shook his head, and Will was struck by the anger in his face then. He really had cared for the Lady Anne. *Here was a gentle lady, with a kind and goodly heart who feigned to join the other ladies-in-waiting, when they called me a crookback and a toad, nor did she think me unworthy of a smile.* Was a smile from a lady such a very rare thing for Cecil, possibly now the most powerful man in the kingdom? Would he give all that up to be fair, wondered Will, to be smiled at, to be loved?

'I am your man, take me for all in all,' Poley told him and he even gave a little bow. Then he added pointedly, 'And everyone here knows it.'

Just then, a face appeared at the doorway. It was William Wade, and he had an urgent look about him, but Cecil made him wait.

'You *are* my man,' agreed Cecil. 'And all this was done for me.' But following that admission, he said, 'Yet you did not bring me the letter?'

Poley looked nervous then. 'I chose to keep it for a while,' he admitted.

'For a long while,' Cecil reminded him. 'You held onto it for your own protection, in case you were discovered to be the one behind the killing of Lady Anne. Then you would need the help of a more powerful man.' Cecil did not say which powerful man he was thinking of, but he surely meant himself. 'Did you find it?' Cecil asked the man by his door and received a nod in reply.

Wade fished inside his doublet, pulled something out and handed it to Cecil. 'It was in his rooms,' he nodded at Poley, 'just as you said it would be.'

Cecil glanced at the letter, evidently recognised it and tucked it inside his own doublet to keep it about his person. Poley looked even more worried then, having just lost the one thing he had left to bargain with, barring an appeal to Cecil's loyalty to his henchman.

'Don't worry, Poley. You won't stand trial. That would not be to my advantage.' And Will was struck by how easily Cecil sought to shrug off the matter of justice for the Lady Anne, once he realised it would place his own person in peril. 'The queen shall hear that Anne's death turned out to be an act of self-slaughter. She secretly carried a child in her belly, placed there by the Earl of Essex, who bedded Anne to spite Her Majesty for not giving him enough rewards. Being dead, Devereux can hardly contradict this account.'

Poley smiled at this, but Will felt sick at the desecration of Lady Anne's memory and wondered why Cecil might be so happy to play along with the despoiling of her. Cecil had invented a liaison that most likely never happened, as well as an unborn, bastard child that would ruin her reputation in death, as it most surely would have done in life.

'Once the queen believes it, the court will too, and I will ensure they all hear of this. You, in the meantime, must be gone, for your presence here could be damaging. You are a fox that might be set upon by hounds at any moment. If Master Shakespeare learned of your guilt, others can too. You shall leave tonight on a ship for the Lowlands, where you will deliver a letter to a contact of mine.' He reached for that letter now and passed it to Poley. He also took some money from a small strongbox that already lay open on the table. 'You will stay there awhile, until I deem it safe to call you home again. Here is ten pounds to live on.'

Poley's face betrayed his relief. He had clearly expected a worse punishment for murdering a young girl than a comfortable exile abroad. Not only would there be no justice for the Lady Anne, her good name would die along with her, but Poley, her killer, would be set free. What had been the point of any of this, thought Will, who felt betrayed by Cecil's leniency in the name of self-preservation? His investigation into Lady Anne's murder had been all for naught. How long before Sir Robert brought Poley back to court and re-enlisted him into his service once more? Then all of this would be forgot.

'My lord.' Poley accepted his exile without further comment.

'Take him from here and make sure he boards the ship,' Cecil instructed his other agents.

One of them clamped an enormous hand on Poley's arm and steered him from there. Will had to step to one side to allow them to pass and Poley stopped momentarily as he did this.

'Master Shakespeare,' he muttered as he locked eyes with the man who had uncovered his terrible crime. 'I bid you good day.' Was there hatred in that look, a promise of vengeance perhaps or a realisation that this would be quite impossible for a time, at least while he was banished to the Lowlands? Perhaps it was all three. Will watched him go, while dreading the thought of his eventual return.

Soon, Will was alone again with Cecil and perhaps he failed to mask the disappointment on his face because Sir Robert asked him, 'What would you have me do?' It was clear he felt he had no choice but to exile Poley, and perhaps he didn't, but that was not the reason for Will's disenchantment.

'You once said that writing to the King of Scotland was treason, my Lord.'

'It is,' agreed Cecil, 'when it is done solely for the advantage of the person writing to him. If it is for the benefit of the realm, then that is an entirely different matter.' And he failed to look entirely convinced by his own argument. He must have detected scepticism in Will's face for he continued. 'No one is even allowed to mention the prospect of the queen's death, much less consider aloud who her successor might be. Do you understand the peril that places us all in? With no fixed succession, we are open to plots from the Spanish, the French and even our own disloyal courtiers; Essex and Southampton are but two of them. There are more, be of no doubt. I am merely planning for a day when, instead of chaos and anarchy, I can bring peace and order to this realm and that can only be achieved with a legitimate heir to the throne, who must, of course, be a Protestant. Only I can be trusted to deliver this favourable outcome for us all. Believe me when I say that I do none of this for my own personal benefit.'

'You would look to continue in the service of a new king?'

'Who else can be trusted with such power?' Cecil asked. 'You think any of these other men can?' and he waved an arm to indicate everyone about them at court. He rallied then. 'Why am I even bothering to explain myself to you?' he chided himself. 'You will never understand. Now, get you gone, before I begin to fear I should worry about you too, on top of everything else.'

'My lord, you have nothing to fear from me. Do you really believe I would want anyone to know I had any part in this?'

And the look on Cecil's face told him two things. First, that the queen's spymaster believed Will was quite genuine in his desire for complete secrecy in the matter, and secondly that, like Will, only more so, Sir Robert Cecil felt genuine shame for his actions and where they had led him.

With Poley gone, no one could force a confession of murder from him, much less implicate his master in the writing of a coded letter to King James; one that had prompted Lady Anne to try to meet with a member of the Earl of Essex's household in the night, to expose Robert Cecil's treason. Could Cecil forgive her for that? Judging by the besmirching of her memory, with talk of her carrying the Earl of Essex's bastard child in her belly until she killed herself, he could not.

How quickly love can turn to hate when we consider ourselves scorned, thought Will.

He doubted the rough men who led Poley to that ship would be able to understand what had passed between them all that night, much less explain it, even if they could be found and questioned. They were little more than muscle, hired to bend men to their master's will. It struck Will then that he was the only one left at court who knew the complete truth about Lady Anne's murder and the reasons behind it. The treasonous correspondence between Sir Robert Cecil and the Scottish king would have to remain secret, at least until Her Majesty's death, and quite possibly forever. From now on, Will knew he would have to find ways to make himself far more valuable to Cecil alive than dead. He realised with a sense of increasing dread that he might be bound to the queen's spymaster forever.

'You have done me good service, Shakespeare,' said Cecil. 'Most importantly, you have kept that service a secret, so none can say you are my creature. I wanted subtlety and you gave me that, for the most part.'

'My lord.'

'And discretion,' he reminded Will. 'I value that highly. You have been discreet.' Then he looked at Will meaningfully. 'Can I assume you will continue to be so? Do I have your word on the matter, in fact?' Then he added, 'For the sake of you and your family?' An oath was always considered more meaningful by Cecil if it could be extracted with a threat.

What else could Will say but, 'You do, my Lord. I swear it.' He had neither the strength nor the desire to try to bring Robert Cecil down. Not for the first time, Will was grateful that he was considered such an ordinary man, with no interest in court politics and only a tiny amount of wealth or status, which meant we would never be seen as an adversary to Cecil. That might just keep him alive.

In that moment, Will resolved to do one more thing. If Cecil allowed him to leave the palace alive, as soon as he could, he would leave London to visit Anne and his girls. Despite, or perhaps because of, everything he had been through of late, he had finally realised that his family meant more to him than anything else; more than money, or fame as a writer, more than being a courtier, a company player or the lover of another man's wife. Death would find Will eventually, as it did all men sooner or later, but how foolish to die a virtual stranger to your family, which is what he had allowed himself to become, because of the loss of his son. In that instant, Will knew he could bury his grief for Hamnet, in order to see and embrace his daughters once more, but would Cecil grant him that opportunity, or was it too late?

'Word reaches me you are being sued in court,' Cecil told him. 'By one Giles Allen, for eight hundred pounds.' This seemed an unusual thing to say at this point, unless Cecil was hinting that he might be of help in the matter, to make up for the service Will had done him. 'He says you stole his theatre?' Cecil's tone was hard to decipher. Was he shocked or impressed by Will's nerve?

'It was our theatre, on his land. The man was greedy for too much rent, so we tore it down and took it away.'

'His demands must have been very high, if you went to all that trouble?'

'They were.' Will decided to try to benefit from his service to Cecil. 'My lord, you said I have served you well? If this case goes before a court and we lose, I will be ruined and left with nothing. If there was a way for a man as powerful as you to influence that court—'

He was not allowed to finish. 'Influence the court?' Cecil was indignant. 'I think you are much mistaken, Shakespeare. I do not interfere with English justice.' This claim seemed outrageous to Will, but Cecil was perfectly serious, and even appalled by the suggestion that he might do such a thing. He regarded Will sternly but possibly then remembered that he did in fact owe him something for his service. 'I could perhaps slow the progress of the case through the court,' he offered then, 'delaying it, perhaps for a year or two?'

'Thank you, lord.' Will would take whatever he was given at this point. If the case was delayed for so long, then perhaps Giles Allen would eventually give up, or his grievance might never see the inside of a courtroom.

'But only because such frivolous matters should always be decided outside the courts,' Cecil explained, 'without wasting the time of other more learned men, who stand in judgement. In the meantime, seek out Allen and offer him something. Come to an agreement,' he urged.

'I will, my lord.' Though Will had no intention of ever doing so. You could not reason with Giles Allen, but nor could you deny Sir Robert Cecil. Better to agree to do his bidding and hope he never asked about the matter again.

'Now, if there is nothing else.' Cecil was preparing to dismiss him.

'There is one more matter, my lord.' And quite a delicate one in its way. Will retrieved the miniature portrait of the Lady Anne from about his person and held it out to his master. Cecil seemed taken aback to be confronted with the image of the woman he had so recently and cruelly besmirched. Will expected he would tell him he had no use for the lady's portrait now that the mystery of her death had been solved, but he recovered himself.

'Leave it.' He avoided Will's eyes then. 'I will see to it that the likeness is returned to her family.' But there was something about the look on his face that told Will he was lying, and that the portrait of Lady Anne was unlikely ever to find its way home. It would instead be kept by the queen's spymaster, but what as? A macabre souvenir of an intrigue, of which she was an unwitting victim, or a genuine keepsake to remind him that he once gazed upon that young woman with something more than affection? Will had spent some considerable time with Robert Cecil, especially of late, but even he felt he would never know the man well enough to guess the answer to that one.

Chapter Fifty-Three

'And thus the whirligig of time brings in his revenges.'

—*Twelfth Night*

Will did not realise it at the time, but no one would ever see or hear of Robert Poley again. The men who led Poley away kept a close eye and a tight grip on him, to ensure he walked onto that ship. They even joined Poley on board, to accompany him to the Lowlands. Perhaps they told him they had business of their own there.

His ultimate fate would remain something of a mystery, but when that ship returned from Antwerp, crew members spoke of how a man on their outward journey had mysteriously fallen overboard one night and was lost to the sea. Because it was dark, no one had seen him go into the water, not even the watch, who could have been paid to look the other way.

Will could see it now: a sleeping Poley, grabbed by the firm hands of the men Cecil had sent with him. They would have stuffed something into his mouth so he couldn't cry out, but there would have been no need to bind his hands when their strength so easily exceeded his, and there were too many of them even for Poley to fight off. They would have dragged him out to the side of the ship, and he could easily picture Poley's terror as he realised what was about to happen to him. They would have hoisted him into the air, then thrown him overboard into the icy water. Poley wouldn't have lasted long before succumbing to that cold and watery grave, but there would perhaps have been enough time for him to repent his folly, for ever becoming involved in Robert Cecil's secret world.

Of course, no one would ever know for sure what happened that night, nor ever be able to prove it. Poley was simply a man overboard and that was that. He was gone, drowned on the crossing, and would meddle no more in plots and intrigues involving his master. The man who had once helped to bring down a queen was dead.

By his own admission, he had been responsible for the murder of Edward Seagrave and the slaying of Lady Anne Percy. They were just two of Poley's many victims. He had played a large part in Christopher Marlowe's murder too, and Will had never forgiven him for that. In short, Poley finally got what he deserved and wasn't that always what an audience demanded of a villain?

Afterword

'If we shadows have offended,
Think but this, and all is mended:
That you have but slumbered here,
While these visions did appear.'

—*A Midsummer Night's Dream*

The real events described here occurred between 1598 and 1601. For the purposes of this story, I had to compress them into a tighter timeframe. Like Will in his *Henry V*, I am guilty of 'Turning the accomplishment of many years into an hour-glass'. I'm sure he would have approved. They include the tearing down of the Theatre and its rebuilding across the Thames in Southwark as the Globe, the first stagings of *Julius Caesar* and *Henry V*, and William Kempe's quitting of the Lord Chamberlain's Men after a quarrel. In 1599, Kempe did indeed Morris-dance to Norwich from London, passing through Essex and Suffolk along the way – a distance of 125 miles. He was met by a great crowd in the marketplace. Kempe wrote a book about his stunt, called *Nine Daes Wonder*, though it actually took him a little over three weeks. After this, he seems to have largely disappeared from public life and he died in 1603.

The Earl of Essex's doomed campaign to subdue O'Neill's rebels led to him fleeing Ireland in a panic, and he really did burst in on Her Majesty's bedchamber. Queen Elizabeth never recovered from the trauma of having to execute her favourite, who was quite possibly the man she loved above all others, judging by the way she continually indulged him. She died just two years later.

Baron Mountjoy achieved much greater success campaigning in Ireland than his former friend Essex. He subdued the rebels and signed a peace treaty with them. Hugh O'Neill eventually left Ireland altogether in 1607, during the Flight of the Earls, never to return.

The Earl of Essex, Baron Mountjoy and Sir Robert Cecil all kept up separate secret, arguably treasonous correspondences with King James VI of Scotland, at the same time. Cecil ensured he was the man to smooth the way for the king to march south and peacefully take the throne on the queen's passing. His reward was to be made first a baron, then a viscount and finally an earl. The new king then worked Cecil to death. He passed in 1612, aged forty-eight.

Though the Earl of Southampton had been sentenced to life in prison, he was released by King James, having served just two years of his imprisonment.

The king was more ruthless with Walter Raleigh, who was implicated in the Main Plot in 1603, to depose James and put Lady Arbella Stuart on the throne instead of him. Raleigh was imprisoned in the Tower of London for thirteen years. He spent much of this time there working on his book, *The History of the World*. Five years after his release, he was tried again, for attacking Spanish territory in defiance of a peace treaty. Under pressure from Spain, James condemned him to death. He was executed in 1618, aged sixty-five.

The 9th Earl of Northumberland, Henry Percy, proved to be just as treacherous as the 6th, 7th and 8th earls, who were all either executed or died suspiciously in the Tower of London. Suspected of being complicit in the Gunpowder Plot of 1605, he was imprisoned in the Tower for sixteen years.

Essex's disinherited son, also called Robert Devereux, had his peerage restored to him by King James in 1604 – three years after it was taken from his father by Queen Elizabeth. Almost forty years later, he would rebel against James' son and heir, King Charles I, commanding the Parliamentary army during the English Civil War – a somewhat more successful rebellion than his father's.

Giles Allen sued the Burbages for the unlawful removal of the Theatre from its original spot, claiming £800 in damages for the destruction of the building and a further forty shillings for trespass onto his land. The case dragged on in the courts for four years without resolution, before he finally gave up.

By 1601, Queen Elizabeth was seen as an aged, isolated and unloved monarch, until she made a speech before parliament in November of that year. Her 'Golden Speech' specifically referenced that 'To be a king and wear a crown is a thing more glorious to them that see it than it is pleasant to them that bear it,' and her assertion that 'I do not so much rejoice that God hath made me to be a queen, as to be a queen over so thankful a people. And though you have had, and may have, many princes more mighty and wise sitting in this seat, yet you never had nor shall have, any that will be more careful and loving.' It was a speech and performance of which Shakespeare himself would have been proud and it restored her popularity.

William Shakespeare prospered under King James. His company became the King's Men and wore his livery. He wrote *Macbeth* for the new king and his plays were regularly performed at court.

The Globe Theatre was a huge success. People flocked to it for fourteen years, until a fire, caused by a cannon used as a prop during a play, burned the entire building to the ground in 1613. By June of the following year, the Globe had been entirely rebuilt on the same site. It stayed open for a further twenty-eight years, before finally closing at the onset of the Civil War. Will did not stay in London to witness its rise from the ashes. He left London and returned home to Stratford-upon-Avon, to live out his final years in retirement with his family. He died in 1616, aged 52.

Avisa Florio is one of several possible candidates for the subject of Will's sonnets. No one knows for sure who that Dark Lady really was, and we probably never will.

Howard Linskey, May 2025

Acknowledgements

I would like to thank everyone at Canelo for publishing Muse of Fire. Thanks to Kate Shepherd, Kim Yudelowitz and Chere Tricot, and to Clare Stacey of Head Design, who created the cover. A big thank you goes to my fantastic editor, Craig Lye, for all his help with this one.

I'm lucky enough to have the best literary agent in the UK and I've been with Phil Patterson at Marjacq since book one. Thanks for all your hard work over the years, Phil, and for keeping me going.

I owe thanks to all of the following for being so supportive of my writing over the years; Adam Pope, Andy Davis, Nikki Selden, Gareth Chennells, Andrew Local, Stuart Britton, David Shapiro, Peter Day, Tony Frobisher, Katie Charlton, Gemma Sealey, Susan Jackson, Ion Mills, Annette Crossland, Peter Hammans, Emad Akhtar, Kit Nevile and Keshini Naidoo.

A big thank you to my wonderful wife, Alison, for all her support and for not minding too much that she has a slightly eccentric writer in the house.

Finally, huge thanks to my amazing daughter, Erin. I love you more than life.

Howard Linskey
September 2025, Hertfordshire